Praise for the Dove Pond Series

THE SECRET RECIPE OF ELLA DOVE

"A homecoming story that hits the sweet spot. . . . A must-read for fans of Sarah Addison Allen and all who love an immersing book, preferably read while sitting on a front porch and eating a piece of hummingbird cake (the recipe is helpfully tucked into the back of the book)."

—Karen White, *New York Times* bestselling author of *The House on Prytania*

"A charming, whimsical, magical ride. Readers will long to be a part of this spellbinding story and fans of Alice Hoffman will be overjoyed to add this writer to their shelf of favorite authors. It's a heart throb!"

—Robyn Carr, #1 *New York Times* bestselling author of *A Family Affair* and the Virgin River series

"Enchanting . . . filled with emotion and magic. . . . An enthralling story of losing, loving, and finding your way home again."

—*Woman's World*

A CUP OF SILVER LININGS

"Like tea, a new Karen Hawkins book is always a good idea. A visit to Dove Pond, where the real magic lies in forgiveness and acceptance, is balm to my readerly soul. Write the next book quickly, please!"

—KJ Dell'Antonia, *New York Times* bestselling author of Reese's Book Club pick *The Chicken Sisters*

"With an eccentric cast of characters, Hawkins has written a charming mix of romance, light fantastical elements, and small-town fun. . . . Recommended for readers looking for a cozy, bighearted read."

—*Booklist*

"Full of heart, *A Cup of Silver Linings* offers up the perfect blend of family, forgiveness, and healing. With quirky, lovable characters and abundant small-town Southern charm, I enjoyed every minute spent in Dove Pond, where life is truly magical."

—Heather Webber, *USA Today* bestselling author of *Midnight at the Blackbird Café*

"A novel of loss, love, and letting go that holds magic for the residents of Dove Pond and for readers who believe that sometimes miracles really do happen."

—Nancy Thayer, *New York Times* bestselling author of *Family Reunion*

"The beauty of Hawkins's writing is that even when it moves into the magical—and rest assured that it does—the emotions of the characters are authentic. Every scene is rooted in kindness and friendship, the belief we can all be better, and the hope that starting over is possible. The perfect way to spend an afternoon, teacup in hand, dreaming about what could be."

—*Manhattan Book Review*

"The literary equivalent of warm custard or fuzzy socks. . . . For readers who enjoy the warmth and Southern authenticity of Fannie Flagg novels mixed with a dollop of Sarah Addison Allen–style magical realism."

—*The Augusta Chronicle*

THE BOOK CHARMER

A LIBRARYREADS PICK

A SIBA OKRA PICK

A *WOMAN'S WORLD* BOOK CLUB PICK

"Entrancing! Fans of *Practical Magic* and *Garden Spells* will love this book."

—*New York Times* bestselling author Susan Andersen

"Hawkins has created a delightfully quirky town. . . . Reminiscent of Sarah Addison Allen, Abbi Waxman, and Fannie Flagg, this is a great summer read for those who love small Southern towns filled with magic."

—*Booklist*

"This heartwarming story by Hawkins will delight fans of cozy romantic fiction with its quirky characters and charming small town."

—*Library Journal*

"I didn't ever want it to end!"

—Maddie Dawson, bestselling author of *Matchmaking for Beginners*

"A tale of friendship and family and love in all its forms, of taking chances and starting over, of opening your heart and finding who you were always meant to be. Toss in a touch of magic, and prepare to be enchanted."

—*New York Times* and *USA Today* bestselling author Mariah Stewart

"Brimming with enchanting charm. . . . A heartwarming and mesmerizing testament to the power of a good book."

—*Woman's World*

Also available from
Karen Hawkins and Gallery Books

The Secret Recipe of Ella Dove

A Cup of Silver Linings

The Book Charmer

THE BOOKSHOP OF HIDDEN DREAMS

KAREN HAWKINS

G

Gallery Books

New York London Toronto Sydney New Delhi

G

Gallery Books
An Imprint of Simon & Schuster, LLC
1230 Avenue of the Americas
New York, NY 10020

This book is a work of fiction. Any references to historical events, real people, or real places are used fictitiously. Other names, characters, places, and events are products of the author's imagination, and any resemblance to actual events or places or persons, living or dead, is entirely coincidental.

First Gallery Books trade paperback edition August 2024

Simon & Schuster: Celebrating 100 Years of Publishing in 2024

For information about special discounts for bulk purchases, please contact Simon & Schuster Special Sales at 1-866-506-1949 or business@simonandschuster.com.

The Simon & Schuster Speakers Bureau can bring authors to your live event. For more information or to book an event, contact the Simon & Schuster Speakers Bureau at 1-866-248-3049 or visit our website at www.simonspeakers.com.

Interior design by Erika R. Genova

Manufactured in the United States of America

10 9 8 7 6 5 4 3 2 1

Library of Congress Cataloging-in-Publication Data

Names: Hawkins, Karen, author.
Title: The bookshop of hidden dreams / Karen Hawkins.
Description: First Gallery Books trade paperback edition. | New York, NY : Gallery Books, 2024. | Series: Dove Pond Series ; vol 4.
Identifiers: LCCN 2024005241 (print) | LCCN 2024005242 (ebook) | ISBN 9781982195960 (trade paperback) | ISBN 9781982195991 (ebook)
Subjects: LCSH: Historians—Fiction. | Family secrets—Fiction. | LCGFT: Domestic fiction. | Novels.
Classification: LCC PS3558.A8231647 B68 2024 (print) | LCC PS3558.A8231647 (ebook) | DDC 813/.6—dc23/eng/20240206
LC record available at https://lccn.loc.gov/2024005241
LC ebook record available at https://lccn.loc.gov/2024005242

ISBN 978-1-9821-9596-0
ISBN 978-1-9821-9599-1 (ebook)

To my beloved and always-reading parents, Evelyn and Bernard,
who never sat unless they had a book in hand.
Thank you for sharing with me your love of reading.
You made my life richer in so many ways.
Love you!

THE BOOKSHOP OF HIDDEN DREAMS

CHAPTER 1

TAY

Tay Dove returned to Dove Pond early one frosty February evening. She didn't go straight home, though. Instead, she headed for her special place: Rose's Bookstore.

Whenever Tay felt sad or upset or lonely, she always went to a bookstore. Some people enjoyed online book shopping, with its slick, algorithm-driven ease, but she preferred to touch the books as she shopped, to smell the vanilla-and-ink scent of new pages, and even read a chapter or two when possible. She especially loved older bookstores, those with worn and raspy floors and overcrowded shelves packed with rows of gems. They calmed her, soothed her, pacified her, and even healed her.

Of all the bookstores in the world, none was better than Rose's Bookstore, which sat on Peach Tree Lane in Tay's hometown of Dove Pond. The old bookshop was on the bottom floor of an old stone building with large wrought-iron windows and a huge green door—the very one, in fact, that Tay was standing in front of right now.

She stepped inside and was welcomed by the delightfully familiar jingle of the bell that announced her arrival. In Tay's opinion, Rose's should have been declared a national treasure. Inside, the old wooden floors creaked with each step and gleamed as the setting sun spilled through wavy windows. All around, the scent of pine oil and books rose from large oak bookshelves. It was a truly lovely place with amazing ambience, but the best thing about Rose's was the thousands of books that waited for new homes, all carefully selected by the meticulous curator.

Try as she might, Tay couldn't think of a single time she'd left the store without at least one book, and usually more, tucked under her arm. But as excellent as Rose's taste in books might be, it was obvious she wasn't a fan of organization. Books were on shelves sometimes two rows deep, sitting in random corners, and even stacked in numerous too-tall piles left on tables and windowsills. To an ordinary person, such chaos might mean it would be hard to find a specific book. But somehow Rose always knew where each and every book waited.

Normally, Tay would have found such disarray annoying. But over the years, she'd grown to love the older woman's unconventional methods, especially when—in an effort to keep customers from bothering her when she herself was reading at the front counter—she labeled stacks with bright pink Post-its scrawled with things like "Hallmark Channel Cocaine," "Not-Creepy-Heroine-Obsessed Heroes," or "Scary. DO NOT READ BEFORE BED."

The whole place was glorious and chaotic, and Tay always felt that she was on a treasure hunt as she browsed. Growing up, whenever her sisters were at the library, she would sneak out the back door and make her way here, where she'd wander up and down the aisles, looking for that one special book that would take her away for an adventure or—when times were tough—offer a refuge from life.

Which was why Tay was in Rose's Bookstore when she should have been on her way to see her three younger sisters, who were waiting for her at their family home, ready to bombard her with a thousand-and-one questions, none of which she wanted to answer right now.

Up until five months ago, if someone had asked, Tay would have said she had a wonderful life. She had a PhD in history with a focus in literature, loved her job teaching at a prestigious university in Boston, had had numerous papers published in a number of accredited journals, and had just finished a book she'd coauthored. And, added to all of that, unbeknownst to her colleagues and almost all her sisters alike, she'd been in what she'd thought was a serious romantic relationship.

Sadly, she now knew that she'd been the only one to think her relationship was either serious or romantic. That alone was as embarrassing as it was heartbreaking. "I should have known," she muttered, the words annoyingly loud in the nearly empty bookstore.

It was just an hour to closing time, so it was quiet. Other than the creaky floor under Tay's feet, the distant hum of a furnace, and the sound of Rose Day, the eighty-two-year-old owner, turning the pages of her ever-present book as she sat at the checkout counter, it was deliciously peaceful. Rose had nodded to Tay when she'd come in but hadn't offered anything more, knowing that a book search was a solitary and personal quest, not a group effort. Oh sure, if Rose saw a reader hesitating, she would ask if they needed something, but for the most part, she allowed her customers the comfort of wandering uninterrupted.

Yet another sign that Rose's Bookstore was a special, perfect place. And right now, the bookshop was balm to Tay's ragged soul. For the next half hour, she walked up and down the aisles, soaking in the feeling of the place, although she wasn't having the best of luck in finding a book to read. Normally, she'd find something within minutes of arriving. But this time, she found herself randomly picking up books just to put them back on the shelf unread, her thoughts as listless as her bruised spirit.

"So?" a sharp voice said from behind her. "Is anything calling to you?"

Tay turned, and there, at the end of the aisle, stood Rose, looking like a silver-haired, bright-blue-eyed, rather sarcastic elf. Tay slid her reading glasses back to the top of her head. "I've looked at a few, but they haven't held my attention. I keep getting lost in my thoughts."

Although Rose's tongue had sharpened over the years, her eyes still held the same warm sparkle. "Lost in your thoughts, eh? That's dangerous. If you wander around inside your head like that, you might not be able to get back out."

"Don't worry. I have a map." Tay forced a smile. "How are you doing? I haven't seen you since the last time I was in town. It's been a while."

"I'm doing better than you, it seems." Rose came down the aisle, the rubber tip of her cane thumping on the creaky floor. "I'm not the one lost in a fog. I said hello twice."

"It's just jet lag. I came here straight from the airport."

"Ah. You were in England, weren't you?"

"I was doing research for a book I coauthored with my—" *Boyfriend.* The word hung on her tongue. He wasn't her boyfriend. Not anymore. In truth, he hadn't ever been that. Not really.

She realized Rose was still waiting on her to finish her sentence, so she said instead, "My department chair. That's who I coauthored the book with."

"I see." Rose placed both hands on her cane and leaned on it, her bright gaze never leaving Tay. "Have you been teaching a lot of classes?"

"No, I've been on research leave since August. That's what I was doing in England. I'm not scheduled for any classes until the fall term."

"Then you'll be staying here for a while?"

"A month, at least. The book is finished, so I'm hoping to start a new project." She could have gone home to her apartment in Boston and taken a break there, but then she'd have no excuse to avoid campus. The last thing she wanted right now was to see Richard with his new girlfriend.

Rose nodded her approval. "I'm glad you're here. I saw Ella this morning. She stopped in to pick up a Suzanne Enoch book, *Every Duke Has His Day*. Such a fun one."

Tay agreed. "Ella's been on an historical romance kick this year. I love those, too."

"She stops by often, but it's been almost a week since I've seen either Sarah or Ava."

Tay's youngest three sisters all lived in Dove Pond, while her three older sisters lived elsewhere. She was glad she didn't have to face all six of them right now. Three would be enough. Too much, in fact. "Ella says Sarah and Ava are crazy busy right now. Ava's tearoom is booming, and Sarah's reorganizing the library's historical section."

Rose snorted in disbelief. "It's not just work keeping them busy. All three of your sisters have boyfriends now. I'm waiting for the wedding invitations to start arriving. I hope they need Crock-Pots, because I bought six from that huge sale at the Costco in Asheville in November, so that's the only wedding gift I give out nowadays."

Rose was right about Tay's younger sisters. Despite the fact that their hometown was ever-so-small, they'd all somehow found love. Meanwhile, over the past year, Tay'd traveled to visit archive collections in three different, wonderful countries and had been surrounded by fascinating men, only to be conned and dumped by the last person she should have been dating.

She realized Rose was studying her, so she grabbed a random book off the shelf and pretended to examine it. Rose was sharp, and Tay didn't want anyone digging around for the real reason she was back in Dove Pond. "I haven't been home yet, so I'm not sure what they're up to. I came here first to get something to read in case I can't fall asleep tonight. Different bed and all." It had been months since she'd slept well—five, in fact. And no book would help her change that. However, they did help pass the time during the darkest, loneliest hours.

"That's not the book for you, then." Rose tapped the one in Tay's hands. "Lisa Gardner writes thrillers. It'll get the adrenaline running. But sleep? I wouldn't count on it."

"It'll be fine. To be honest, I always *plan* on sleeping. I just never seem to do it." Not since— *No, don't think about it. Not right now.*

A flicker of concern crossed Rose's face, and she shifted from one foot to the other. "Are you okay? You're thinner than you were the last time you came to town. A lot thinner, in fact."

No. Everything was not "okay." Tay's heart had been broken, and—worse—it was her own darn fault. She kept returning to the same painful question: How had she been so foolish? The signs that the relationship was one-sided at best, and toxic at worst, had been glaringly evident, but she'd ignored every one. *I'm not an idiot, so why didn't I pick up on the clues?*

"Oh dear. There's no need to cry." Rose awkwardly patted Tay's shoulder.

Tay realized a tear had indeed slipped out and was even now dripping down her cheek. *Darn it!* Her face heated, and she reached into her purse for a tissue. "I'm sorry. I'm fine. It's nothing, really. I was—"

The words stopped on her tongue, refusing to come out. *Why am I hiding it? It's been over for months now. And yet I still can't bring myself to say it out loud.*

Maybe that was to be expected. During the seven months of her relationship, whenever anyone asked her if she was seeing anyone, she'd lied and said no, for no other reason than because Richard had asked her to. He'd said he was worried that if their colleagues knew they were a couple, they might think he was favoring her when, as department chair, he set schedules, approved requests for leave, and divvied up prime research opportunities. He'd even suggested that other people in the department might question her recent promotion from assistant to associate professor, which had happened a few months before they'd started seeing each other and had very little to do with Richard, as it had been decided by a committee. But she'd been so swept up in and so enthralled by him that she'd agreed without hesitation.

It had even been fun at first. They'd shared covert glances, hidden notes, and top secret dates. When she'd headed to Oxford six months ago to finish the research for the book they were cowriting, they'd gone to great lengths to hide from their friends and colleagues his two brief visits during her first month there. But she'd soon realized that he'd had other reasons for keeping their relationship in the shadows.

"You need a pick-me-up," Rose announced. She moved down the aisle, her purple tennis shoes scuffing across the wood floor as she began examining the shelves.

"I could use a happy book," Tay admitted. "It's been a rough year."

Rose glanced back and raised an eyebrow, waiting for Tay to continue.

Tay supposed she'd better get used to saying it out loud, so she took a steadying breath and added, "I was dating someone, but it ended badly." There. That was a start. *Cara would be so proud of me.*

Of her six sisters, Cara was the only one Tay had confided in, as the two of them were closest. They'd shared a room growing up and, as teenagers, had looked so much alike that people who didn't know them often assumed they were twins. They didn't look alike now, thanks to the fact that, after moving to New York City to start her elite matchmaking business, Cara had become a fashionista in order to impress her wealthy clients, while Tay had gradually slipped into a style that Ella mockingly referred to as "Comfy Professor."

Still, Tay and Cara remained close and called each other often. When Tay's world had crumbled after she'd discovered Richard was cheating on her, it had been Cara who'd gotten the sobbing, middle-of-the-night phone call.

"Men can be idiots." Rose bent down to eye a row of books at knee level. "I didn't know you'd been dating someone. Ella never mentioned it when I saw her, and she usually shares all the family gossip."

"She doesn't know about it. Neither do Sarah or Ava." Nor did her friends. Or, true to Richard's request, anyone in her department at work, either. "I didn't tell many people about the relationship."

Rose had picked up a book, but at that, she turned back, frowning. "Wasn't married, was he?"

"No! Nothing like that. Richard was a colleague. Is a colleague, I should say." Tay tentatively took a measure of her feelings and was disappointed to discover that not one drop of her hurt and sadness had melted with that admission. She sighed and rubbed the back of her neck, where a slow ache was beginning to appear. "Not many people know we dated, since he's also my boss."

"Ah. Dating your boss can be complicated. That'll take a heck of a good read to get over. Probably more than one." Rose slid the book she held back onto the shelf and then stepped away, scrutinizing the titles in front of her like a general evaluating the strength of her troops. "I don't suppose he cheated, did he? Seems like a good setup for it, what with you needing to keep things on the down-low."

Tay couldn't keep from wincing. Five months ago, the department had held their annual birthday party for the division secretary, a sweetheart of a woman who kept them all caught up on the rather tangled paperwork required by human resources for annual leave, insurance, and other irritating issues. At the time, Tay had still been in Oxford working on the book, but she'd seen the pictures her colleagues posted. In those random shots, Richard was hovering over Dr. Abigail Metcalf, the division's new Asian history professor, as if staking a claim.

Tay wasn't the suspicious type, but it had bothered her, especially as Richard had been calling her less and less. So the next day she'd found an excuse to call one of her closest colleagues in the history department, Dr. May Freeman, and casually ask about the new professor. It hadn't taken long before Tay's worst fears were realized. According to May, Richard and Abby had hit it off from the first day. "She's only been here a month, but it's obvious he's crazy for her," May had said with what seemed like gushing enthusiasm. "They're so cute together, always holding hands and making eyes at each other."

Sick to her stomach, Tay had quickly gotten off the phone, her mind spinning. It was as if someone had ripped a blindfold from her eyes. Richard had begun a new relationship without ending theirs. As if that wasn't insult enough, he was obviously more than comfortable letting the world know how he felt about Abby while his entire relationship with Tay had been kept in the dark.

How had she not seen this coming? On some unspoken level, she'd known things weren't good. He hadn't been calling as often, and the very few times he had visited, he'd spent a significant amount of time on his phone. But for reasons she couldn't yet fathom, she'd pretended not to notice. *How did I get to be so foolish? So many signs and I just ignored them all, one after the other.* That was the part that struck fear in her soul. She was an educated, capable woman—or had thought she was, anyway. How had she ended up in such a stupid predicament?

"Men can be such nuisances." Rose pulled a book from the shelf and scanned the back cover. "Dating a boss only works in Hallmark movies, and not always there, either. To get over that, you need a cheerful book. Something not too romantic, but still hopeful."

As if such a book existed. Tay glanced at her watch. "I should get going soon. I'm sure my sisters are already wondering what's keeping me."

"This is the one." Rose handed the book to Tay. "*The Sugar Queen* by Sarah Addison Allen. Chicken soup for the reader's soul." She tapped the book with one finger. "This will make you smile and restore your belief in humanity."

As if anything could right now. "And if it doesn't?"

"I'll refund your money." Rose limped toward the checkout counter, her cane thumping with each step. "We'd better get you home before your sisters come looking for you."

Tay followed. She guessed there was no real benefit in putting off her return any longer. She placed the book on the counter. "I didn't tell them I was stopping by here, but I bet they've figured it out."

"They figure out a lot of stuff, those sisters of yours." Rose scanned the book and then frowned at the wand. "It didn't beep." She glared at the mechanism and shook it. "Darn Luke and his newfangled crap. What was wrong with the old way of doing things?"

The "old way" consisted of Rose handwriting each title and price in a carbon-copy notebook of receipts and then using a calculator to figure out the tax and total, so Tay could think of a few reasons why the "old way" might have needed an update. "Who is Luke, and why is he putting newfangled crap in your bookshop?"

"He's my grandson. He moved back to Dove Pond three months

ago. He was born here, but his parents relocated to Atlanta when he was six. That's where his sister, Caitlyn, was born. I doubt you remember either of them, as they only visited on holidays. But now Luke's moved here permanently with Caitlyn's daughter, Lulu."

But not Caitlyn? Catching the flicker of worry across Rose's narrow face, Tay decided not to ask any more questions. "I bet it's nice having a child around."

Rose's expression softened. "Lulu is a card. She makes me laugh a dozen times a day, mainly because she's realized that her uncle Luke is a nerd." Rose nodded to the copy of the *New York Times* that sat beside the register, folded open to the half-finished crossword. "If it has to do with computers or puzzles, he's there for it."

"I'm glad you have some help."

"It's been nice. Luke did tech stuff for some companies in Atlanta, so he keeps trying to 'update' things here." Rose squinted at the computer screen and then poked it. "Let me try that wand again. I think that fixed it." She rescanned the book and this time was greeted with a satisfying beep. "Ha! Beat you at your own game, you stupid computer." She sent Tay a sheepish look. "I'm not saying I'm not grateful for Luke's help. The last few years have been tough for the shop. Luke says that if we don't improve things . . ." She clamped her mouth closed over the rest of her sentence. "Sorry. You don't need to know all that."

Tay suddenly wished she'd bought more than the one book sitting on the counter. "I'm sure things will get better. I love this place. Remember when I was a kid and you bought that beanbag chair because you didn't like me sitting under the table in the children's reading corner?"

Rose chuckled. "No one else could use the reading table when you were under there because you'd accuse them of kicking you. This place was much busier back then. Now . . ." She cast a wistful glance around the empty store. "People still come, but a lot of them just decide what book they want and then go home and order it from an online retailer. Which would be fine if it paid enough to keep the lights on."

Tay glanced around the bookshop and noticed a few things she hadn't before. The wood floor urgently needed refinishing in some spots, while two of the light fixtures weren't even working. The color on the walls, which had once been a warm pumpkin shade, had faded over the years into a mild peach, and one corner of the ceiling looked a little damp, as if a slow leak was just beginning to show. When had things gotten so worn-out looking?

She always came to this bookshop, but it was as if she were seeing it for the first time. Apparently, she had blinders on when it came to both the places and people that she liked. *I guess it's easier to see what you want to see, rather than what's really there.* How many times would she be guilty of that? The reassuring smile that had been on her face started to quiver, and she hurried to fix it more firmly in place. "I promise to buy a lot of books while I'm in town."

"I know you will." Rose leaned her cane against the counter and then slipped back onto her stool. "Things are different now, aren't they? There's e-books and online shopping and something Luke calls 'streaming.' He says we could compete against one of those things but not all three, not unless we start doing things differently." Rose sighed and tucked the receipt into Tay's book before sliding it across the counter. "Oh well, what can you do?"

"Rose, are things that bad? Are you—"

"Pah! I'm fine, and so is my bookshop. There's no need to worry." Rose waved an impatient hand. "Luke's overstating the situation because he doesn't know this business the way I do. Things will get better. They always do. That said"—Rose nodded toward the clock that hung over the door—"it's getting late, so you'd better head home. Heaven knows, I don't want your sisters descending on us like a plague of locusts. Especially seeing how excited they are about the tin box they found. Ella said they're all dying to know what you think of it."

Oh yes. The box Ava had found behind a loose fireplace tile in the dining room. Right now, that discovery was the one bright spot in Tay's life and, as Cara had so wisely pointed out, had been a terrific excuse to visit Dove Pond instead of returning to the office. Tay would stay here, at home, until she found a way to get over Richard.

Rose leaned forward, her eyes bright with interest. "What was in that box, anyway?"

"Ava said there are some love letters, a few Valentine's Day cards, and some other things. It's not clear who wrote the letters or cards, but they were addressed to Sarafina."

"Sarafina Dove," Rose said in a thoughtful tone. "I'd say she's the most famous person to come from this town."

Tay agreed. Way back in the late 1890s, Sarafina Dove had become one of the first female reporters to win acclaim when she wrote for a New York City newspaper about the horrid conditions of children who worked in the many wool mills lining the banks of the Hudson River. The scathing, well-documented series of articles she'd written had caused a huge public outcry and later led to the passage of important child labor laws, many of which were the basis of those still in existence today. That had been only the first of Sarafina's many contributions to the world, each one making it a better, safer place.

"She was a pioneer." Rose crossed her arms and leaned against the counter. "She put Dove Pond on the map. Didn't the Smithsonian run an exhibit on her life?"

"I saw it. They had a lot of information on her reporting, as well as some details about her personal life after she arrived in New York, but Dove Pond was barely mentioned, as not much is known about her life before she went to the city."

"That tin could be a big find, then." Rose tilted her head to one side, reminding Tay of a curious wren. "Can you use your Dove family gift and figure out who wrote those letters?"

"I'm going to try." For centuries, the people of their little town had known that whenever the Dove family had seven daughters, each of the daughters would be gifted with special talents, which they would discover at various times in their lives. Her sisters all had amazing abilities. Her oldest sister, Madison, could tell how someone felt with a simple touch, while Alexandra could commune with animals, and Cara knew just by looking at two people if they should be together. Ella's delicious baked goods stirred up precious memories, and Ava knew which plants and flowers could heal people and used that knowledge to make the most amazing teas. To the delight of the town, their youngest sister, Sarah, could talk to books and knew which book needed to be read by whom—the perfect gift for the town librarian.

While Tay deeply respected her sisters' gifts, she was disappointed by her own. Instead of being able to do something helpful like curing illnesses, or something interesting like flying through the air like Supergirl, whenever Tay touched someone's handwriting, she got a flash of the world through the author's eyes at the exact moment their pen or pencil crossed the page. Included with that flash was an unvarnished glimpse of their location, feelings, and thoughts.

But that was it. Try as she would, she'd never found a genuinely useful day-to-day application for her special talent, using it only to facilitate her research on various historical figures. That was as far as she'd been able to take it. As special abilities went, Tay's was both useless and, most of the time, boring.

Rose reached across the counter and patted Tay's hand. "Let me know what you find out from Sarafina's letters. One's ancestry is important. I'm the Day family archivist and keep all our family records back there." She inclined her head toward the office at the back of the bookshop. "Luke says they should all be scanned in, but I like being able to touch the old papers and certificates and whatnot. It's a form of living history, isn't it?"

While the Days needed an entire office space for their records, Tay's family, who had founded this town, had only a few small boxes of scrapbooks, photos, and assorted birth, wedding, and death certificates stored in their attic. "We should have a family archivist."

"Family records teach us where we came from." Rose's bright blue gaze returned to Tay. "Sarafina was a real hero in her time. Our town could use more of those."

Tay couldn't argue with that. "I'll let you know what I find out." She collected her book from the counter. "I'd better get going. It was nice seeing you, Rose."

"You too. Come again."

"I will." With a wave, Tay headed out to her car. At least she was here in Dove Pond and away from her empty apartment and the complications of being in her office right now. She supposed she wasn't the first person to run back home after a big upset. She definitely wouldn't be the last, either.

And at this moment, she had a wonderful new book to read, and—hopefully—an exciting new research project to distract her from her tangled, painful thoughts, which had refused to dissipate, no matter how many days marched past.

For now, that would have to do.

CHAPTER 2

TAY

Tay had her fifth-grade teacher, Mrs. Wrexham, to thank for setting into motion the events that had allowed her to discover her Dove family talent.

One bright spring day, Mrs. Wrexham had requested that every student bring a photo of one of their ancestors and share that person's life with the class during show-and-tell. Naturally, Momma had suggested that Tay talk about Sarafina Dove.

Tay had been excited to learn she was related to a famous reporter. When show-and-tell day came, Momma had helped Tay write a few salient facts on a piece of notebook paper and had put it in an old manila envelope together with the one and only photograph they had of Sarafina. With the envelope tucked safely in her backpack, Tay had headed for school.

When it was finally her turn to stand up and talk about Sarafina's colorful life as a journalist in the Victorian era, Tay had dutifully read what she and Momma had written on the notebook paper, and then reached into the envelope for the photograph.

As Tay pulled it out, her fingers brushed the blotted name written across the back. For the first time in her life, her Dove ability kicked in. For a startlingly clear and crazy second, she was there in 1897 as Sarafina Dove sat at an elaborate desk, her fountain pen in hand. Beside her, a fire crackled in a heavy iron grate while, outside, a restless wind rattled against the windows. As Tay watched, the pen flew across the back of the very photograph she now held, spelling out Sarafina's name. As hard as it was to understand, Tay realized that she wasn't just a faded presence in Sarafina's world. For that long second, Tay was *really* there and knew exactly what Sarafina felt, saw, heard, and thought.

Tay knew the clock on the mantel in the room was ticking so loudly that it was annoying Sarafina. Tay also knew Sarafina was hungry because, instead of using her half-hour break to eat her lunch, she'd instead stopped by the newspaper office to pick up the photograph she held. The room smelled of woodsmoke and iron-scented ink, and Sarafina was upset her aunts had insisted she spend her evening writing a letter to her father, which she knew would be a waste of time since he rarely wrote back.

The second Sarafina's pen lifted from the back of the photograph, Tay was instantly back at school, standing in front of the class, blankly staring into space.

"Taylor?" Mrs. Wrexham's voice had broken into the moment.

Tay, disoriented and still trying to process what she'd just experienced, could only blink. She was so pale and trembly that her teacher had halted show-and-tell and escorted her to the school nurse, who'd taken one look at her and then promptly called Momma. Fortunately for Tay, her mother had realized what had happened, that Tay's special Dove gift had finally arrived.

The gift was part of the reason she'd gone into academia. Now, as a thirty-seven-year-old professor, she was on her way to becoming one of the country's foremost historical researchers. She specifically focused on important figures known to be ardent letter writers, which meant they'd left behind large troves of resources she could access. Using her gift on their letters and written works helped her gain additional, and sometimes novel, insights that often directed her research into fresh and exciting paths.

The book she'd just finished writing with Richard was about Mary, Queen of Scots, and the notorious Casket Letters that had led to her beheading. It was a popular topic, and the book was set to be published next spring by a large university press. Tay was happy she had that going for her. The book would be popular with academics and would be a huge asset on her résumé. Before she'd left England, she'd emailed the final chapter to Richard and had gotten a chilly, impersonal response, which had hurt even though it was what she'd expected. She wished he'd been at least a little emotionally torn over their breakup. But no. Other than being upset she'd been the one to break up with him, he'd discarded her as easily as if she'd been a used paper cup. Meanwhile, here she was, unable to stop thinking, wondering, and asking herself useless what-ifs.

"Stupid man," she muttered under her breath as she removed her two crazy-heavy suitcases and her backpack from the trunk of her rental car.

She didn't love easily, and never had. Before Richard . . . well, there hadn't been anyone before Richard. She'd been told by both her sisters and various friends over the years that no one—absolutely *no one*—friend-zoned men as quickly as she did. Because she'd been so busy teaching classes and doing research, she'd had neither the time nor the inclination to commit to a relationship.

Somehow, Richard had been different. She hadn't friend-zoned him. Instead, she'd foolishly allowed herself to be swept away. And now, here she was, heartbroken and alone and stuck in the past. "I should have friend-zoned that jerk the first time I met him," she told herself as she headed for the porch with her luggage.

As if to mock her words, her larger suitcase slipped off the walk and one wheel sank into the damp grass, jerking her to a halt and causing her backpack to fall off her shoulder and bang into her knee.

She grimaced and then dropped her backpack to the walkway, released the handle of the other suitcase, and grabbed the stuck one with both hands. It took all her efforts to wrangle it back onto the walkway. "Stupid suitcase and stupid men," she said through gritted teeth. "I hate them both!"

Once she had her luggage back under control, she paused to rub her sore knee and looked up at the familiar two-story, nine-bedroom, Queen Anne–style house that rose before her. Dove House was her childhood home, and she knew and loved every creaky inch of it.

Her favorite spot was the primary bedroom, which her sister Ava now occupied. It was a huge room with a fireplace and a circular sitting area formed by the upper floor of the fairy-tale-like turret that sat to the right of the porch. She loved that turret. When she was a child, she and her sisters used to tie together bedsheets and play Rapunzel out that very window. At one point, Alex—the biggest tomboy among them—had even tried to climb down their bedsheet rope, but Momma had caught them in the act and had declared her bedroom off-limits after that.

Tay adjusted her backpack so that it was more firmly on her shoulder and then, taking a big breath, lugged her suitcases the rest of the way down the walkway, up the wide wooden porch steps, and to the front door. She stopped there, pausing to catch her breath. Inside, she could hear her sisters laughing and talking, obviously excited about her return home.

A pang of guilt hit her. She loved her sisters. She really did. It was just that, right now, all three of Tay's younger sisters had turned into wildly interfering matchmakers.

She mentally steeled herself and reached for the brass doorknob. Just as her fingers closed over it, one of her suitcases suddenly rolled across the uneven porch floor and fell, slamming into her knee. She toppled forward and, propelled by the weight of her backpack, hit the door with her shoulder. "*Ow!*"

Inside the house, the excited talking ceased and a second later, the door flew open.

Sarah rushed outside. Tay just got a glimpse of her sister's librarian-style T-shirt, which read BOOKS DO IT FOR ME, before she was enveloped in a huge hug.

"Tay!" Ava appeared in the doorway behind Sarah, wearing her usual bright-colored coveralls and grinning from ear to ear, her long blond hair hanging in a braid over one shoulder. "We've been waiting forever!"

"Where have you been?" Sarah demanded as she released Tay and stepped back. "Your plane landed hours ago."

"I stopped by Rose's. I haven't been sleeping well, so I needed something to read."

Ava nodded, as if she'd already figured out where Tay had gone. "Jet lag can really mess up a sleep schedule."

"Let's get your luggage inside." Sarah took the largest of Tay's suitcases and began hauling it over the threshold.

Ava grabbed Tay's other suitcase and followed Sarah. "Ella's finishing up the dishes. Are there more suitcases?"

"No, this is it." Tay rubbed her sore shoulder and followed them into the foyer, the door closing behind her. "I mailed everything else."

"Your boxes came last week." Ava rolled the suitcase to the bottom of the stairs where Sarah had placed the larger one. "You must be exhausted."

"Tay!" Ella appeared, an apron tied around her plump waist. She gave Tay a quick hug that smelled of cinnamon and cake. "It's so nice to have you back home!"

"It's overdue," Tay admitted.

"And then some. Are you hungry? Or thirsty? We have tea or—"

"No, no. I'm fine."

Ella looked her up and down. "Right. I'll fix a pot of decaf. You look like you could use something warm to drink." With that pronouncement, she disappeared back into the kitchen.

Tay watched her go. Their aunt Jo, who knew their family better than anyone else, had said on more than one occasion that she could tell a member of the Dove family with one glance. As she liked to point out, they were all short and blond and had startling gray-green eyes. But they had their differences, too. Ella was plumper and curvier than her other sisters. Ava's hair was a shade darker, while Sarah's smile was bigger than anyone else's. Madison and Alex were the tallest, compared to the rest of them.

Tay supposed the main difference between herself and her sisters was that she was a smidge shorter and kept her hair at shoulder length so it wouldn't swing forward into her face when she was bent over a computer.

"Sheesh." Sarah rubbed her lower back and then nudged the largest suitcase with her foot. "What's in this thing? Bricks?"

Tay raised her eyebrows.

Sarah sighed. "I don't know why I asked. Why do you travel with your own reference library? I could get you any book you want."

"Tay doesn't like to borrow books. She likes to own them." Ava held out her hand for Tay's coat. After getting it, she hung it on the coatrack. "Still, I bet there's not a single fiction book in this entire suitcase."

Tay grinned. "Care to make a little wager on that?" After leaving Rose's, she'd slipped the new book into the outer pocket of her suitcase. "We can bet cash. Or dishwashing duties. Name your poison."

Sarah leaned close to Ava. "I wouldn't bet if I were you. She was just at Rose's."

Ava cut Sarah a hard look. "I'm not stupid." She turned back to Tay. "What delectable delight did Rose recommend?"

Tay pulled out the book and handed it to Ava. "Where did you all put my boxes?"

Sarah inclined her head toward the sitting room. "Beside Momma's desk. We thought you'd like to work from there."

Ava glanced up from where she'd been reading the back book cover. "You got some mail, too. It's there on the table behind you."

"I asked the university to forward my mail here until I notify them otherwise."

"So they're not expecting you back right away!" Sarah clasped her hands together and gave a happy hop, as if her biggest wish had just come true.

Tay shrugged. "I wanted to see what's up with that tin box you found in the fireplace surround. The timing was perfect, as I need a new project, and I'm on a break." She picked up her mail, which consisted of some official-looking manila envelopes and one small flat-rate package. She absently patted her pocket. *Where are my glasses?*

Sarah pointed to Tay's head.

Of course that was where they were. That was where they always were, and yet she still "lost" them at least twice a day. "Thanks," she muttered, sliding her sneaky glasses back to her nose. *I hate that I can remember things I don't need to, like the assumed date of Shakespeare's death and how Richard's eyes were such a beautiful brown, but I can't find my glasses when I need them.*

Her expression must have showed her frustration because Ava cut her a sympathetic look. "You're exhausted. That was a long flight followed by a long drive."

"The drive wasn't bad, but the flight? Ten hours from London to Atlanta. And no one hates flying more than me." Tay hated planes. For that matter, she wasn't overly fond of cars either, having managed to do without one by living first in New York, then Boston, and then—for the past six months—Oxford. *Oh, Oxford. How I loved your library. The Bodleian was a magical place, and it gave me shivers every time I stepped inside.*

She missed it, which wasn't surprising. Like bookstores, every library had its own personality and flavor, and she loved them all. She'd have to be careful not to admit that to her sister Sarah, though. Sarah ran the Dove Pond Library better than anyone else could, but it didn't hold the sort of research materials Tay typically required for her work.

Ava patted the book Tay had just bought. "I like the looks of this. May I read it when you're done?"

"Sure. You can have it tomorrow."

Sarah eyed Tay with approval. "You don't read. You devour."

"If it's a good book, how can I help it?" Tay flipped through the small stack of mail. Most of it was the usual English department nonsense, but then she saw her name scribbled across the small package in an all-too-familiar scrawl.

Time screeched to a halt.

She curled her fingers into her palms as she stared at Richard's name, which was stamped in the upper corner, her heart thudding sickly. She simultaneously didn't want to open the package and yet was burning with curiosity to do so. This was how it always went. Whenever something had to do with Richard, even something as ridiculous as this little package, her heart ached as if she'd broken up with him only minutes ago, and not months. It was stupid and she knew it, and yet she had no control. *I should be furious with him. Why am I so . . . frozen?*

It didn't make sense. She had more pride than that. Didn't she?

With fingers that trembled, she ripped the package open. Inside was her apartment key and a note with one sentence dashed across it. *Thought you might need this. Hope you're well.*

That was it. Nothing more. She turned a little so her sisters couldn't see her face and rested her fingertips on the handwriting. Her ears rang, and for one brief second she slipped into Richard's mind as he wrote. She could hear the click of his dog's toenails across a wooden floor somewhere behind her, could feel the ribbed pen in his hand, could smell and taste the lingering flavor of the nearby cup of coffee that sat at his elbow.

But more than that, she could feel Richard's every emotion as his pen flew over the paper. There was mild irritation at having to take the time to mail her back her spare key, a hint of urgency to get it done quickly because he was late for a meeting, and—threaded through it all—a strong flash of self-satisfaction and pity.

Pity? Her throat tightened painfully, and Tay yanked her hand off the note. Careful not to touch the handwriting again, she crumpled it up and dropped it into the trash can beside the table.

Slightly sick to her stomach, Tay slid the key into her pocket, opened one of the manila envelopes, and—to give herself time to recuperate—pretended to be interested in some sort of worthless interdepartmental memo about leave time.

"Anything important?" Ava asked.

"No." Tay forced a smile before she turned back around. "Just junk mail. That's all." To her relief, her voice sounded normal. But then, she was getting a lot of practice at that.

"I just heard the coffeepot beep," Sarah said. "Let's go to the dining room. We have a nice fire going there."

Ava put her arm around Tay's shoulders and directed her toward the dining room, Sarah following. "We want to hear what's happening in your life. Surely there's a man somewhere who is going to miss—"

"Tell me about this tin you guys found," Tay interrupted. "Ella sent me a picture, but it was hard to tell how big it was."

Ava guided Tay into the dining room. "Dylan was looking at a loose tile at Christmas, and it just fell into his hands."

"And there was the vault," Sarah added.

Tay went directly to the huge fireplace that dominated one end of the room. It was original to the house and had a heavy oak mantel, peacock blue and green tiles decorating the ornate surround. On one side, a missing tile revealed a small iron door. *Oh wow.* Tay slipped a finger through the small iron ring and opened the door, wincing as it creaked loudly. She peered inside and saw where the bricks had been chipped away to make room for the cubbyhole.

Ava now stood beside her. "That's where we found the old tin box."

Tay turned to her. "Where is it?"

Sarah had already opened the elaborate corner cupboard that held what Momma used to call their "fancy ware" and pulled out a rusted tin box.

Yes! Tay eagerly held out her hands.

Sarah tucked the box behind her. "Not so fast. You can't have this until you promise to eat dinner with us at least five times a week."

Sheesh! "Five? I can't promise that."

"Then you can't have it." Sarah backed away.

Ava sat in a chair at the long dining room table. "Sorry, but once you start a project, you disappear. If we don't make you promise to spend some time with us now, all we'll see of you is the top of your head while you're staring at some dusty papers or typing on your laptop."

Tay scowled at her sisters. "I came all the way from Oxford to see what's in that box. You know how important it could be. If there's something I can use to define Sarafina's life here in Dove Pond while she was growing up, I might be able to finally write her biography."

Ava sniffed. "We know you've been collecting reference materials on her for years now. We figured that was what was in all of those boxes you sent."

"Then let me see that tin!"

"Not until you promise to spend some time with us."

Tay had to fight the urge to say something sharp. Of all the subjects she'd researched, few had proven as elusive as the childhood details of her own famous ancestor. Everyone knew about Sarafina's life after she turned nineteen and left their small town for the bright lights of New York City. There was more than enough primary source information to write a credible biography from that point on, beginning with her first legitimate writing job at the *New York World* newspaper. According to the story, Sarafina had gotten that job after pestering a burned-out editor so much that he finally caved and gave her a supposedly impossible assignment: to report on the conditions of the female garment workers who, as a whole, refused to speak to the press under threat of retaliation.

Sarafina had taken that impossible assignment, had infiltrated a garment plant as a worker, and—after weeks of backbreaking work—had written about it with sympathy and grace. The series of articles she'd produced had garnered a lot of notice, and it was claimed that she was following in the footsteps of her contemporary, the intrepid female reporter Nellie Bly.

Sarafina's clear and crisp writing style, aided by her willingness to go undercover even in dangerous situations, quickly made her one of the most popular reporters of the day, and a celebrity of her age. The society papers and personal journals of the time also chronicled her personal life, especially her brilliant marriage to the wealthy businessman who'd purchased the *New York World*. According to eyewitness accounts, David Tau had met Sarafina in the newsroom and had fallen in love with her on the spot. No one was surprised when the two married a scant six months later. They were inseparable until their deaths.

It would be an amazing biography filled with real-life adventure and romance, but Tay had already gone through most of the Dove Pond town records and had found precious little about Sarafina's early life. There was little more than a birth certificate, a few mentions of the family in the local newspaper, and a small bit of information about the two spinster aunts who'd raised her. Which was why this box was so important. It just might hold the key to explaining the how and why of Sarafina Dove.

Tay eyed the box now, where Sarah held it just out of reach. "I need to see what's in there. Ava said there are photos and even letters."

"Oh, there's more than that in this old cigar box." Sarah held up the box and gently shook it, causing an intriguing rattle. "There are keepsakes and Valentine's cards, and—oh, all sorts of things. All you have to do is promise you'll eat with us often." When Tay just glared at her, Sarah sighed. "Okay, okay. Three times a week, then."

Ava added, "We don't want you to be a hermit."

This was *so* irritating. Still, Tay supposed her sisters had a point. She did tend to become a hermit when deep in her research. She sighed and impatiently tucked a strand of hair behind her ear. "Fine, fine. I'll eat with you all . . . once a week. How's that?"

Sarah raised her eyebrows while Ava sent her an annoyed frown.

"Two days, then," Tay offered. "Now can I *please* see the box?"

"I suppose that'll have to do," Ava said grudgingly.

Grinning, Sarah placed the box on the table and pushed it in Tay's direction before turning to Ava. "I'll go help Ella. Be right back."

Tay didn't wait for the door to close before she sank into a chair across from Ava and pulled the box close. "Finally."

Ava rested her elbows on the table and leaned forward, watching.

Tay ran her fingers over the old tin, the surface rough and yet cool to the touch. The faded mustard-and-red print on the lid featured a man in a yellow slicker fishing in a stream, his line taut as if he was just about to reel in his catch. Just up the stream from him was a large tree, a little girl in a red dress hiding behind it as she watched him fish.

Whatever the box once held, it was now a treasure chest. Tay ran her hands over it and whispered softly, "Oh, Sarafina, who were you?"

Ava rubbed her arms. "That gave me the shivers."

Tay ignored her sister and opened the box. Inside sat a packet of letters tied with faded, frayed blue ribbons, two old Valentine's Day cards, and several old tintype photos. Beneath the photos, she caught a glimmer of something and pulled out a long silver chain that held a small key.

Tay held the brass key up to the light, admiring the engraved scrolling. "It's so fancy," she murmured. "I wonder what this goes to?" Enamored with the possibilities, she carefully replaced the key in the box and then pulled out the photos.

Ella came out of the kitchen carrying a tray, Sarah following. "It's a great find, isn't it?" Ella set the tray on the table and put a mug of decaf coffee and a small plate near Tay's elbow.

The rich smell of hot coffee, toasted walnut, and cinnamon rose up to meet Tay.

"It's Ella's cinnamon bread," Sarah announced as she positioned a pitcher of cream and a sugar bowl in the center of the table before sitting. "Try it."

Tay placed the photos on the table in front of her and pulled her plate closer. She was dying to look at the letters, but it would be better if she took her time. Besides, she was starting to feel the effects of missing her dinner. "I've been dreaming of your baking."

"As you should." Ella sat beside Ava and leaned forward so she could see the photos. "That's Sarafina, isn't it?"

The picture showed Sarafina as a young woman. She was wearing a big apron over her long dress, her hair loosely pinned atop her head. She stood outside beside a large pot that hung over a fire and was stirring the contents with a huge wooden paddle, grinning at the camera.

Ella picked up the photograph. "I love that hairstyle."

Tay liked it, too. "She was a Gibson girl before Gibson girls had a name."

"Gibson girl?"

"An advertising model that came about in the 1890s. They were the It girls of their era."

"It girls today are all makeup and Photoshop, which isn't near as fun." Ella handed the photo to Tay. "How old is Sarafina here? There are no dates on any of these photographs."

"At least sixteen, as her hair is up. That was the mark of a girl entering womanhood." Tay examined Sarafina's expression, remembering how she'd looked the first time Tay had seen her during show-and-tell so long ago. "You can't tell from these black-and-white photos, but she has the Dove gray-green eye color like we do, although her hair was dark."

Ella sent Tay a curious look. "You've seen her before? Through your gift?"

"A few times, but not many." Tay placed the photo back on the table and broke a corner off her cinnamon bread. "There's not much of her handwriting to be found, which is a pity. She never kept a diary, and although she wrote plenty of letters, she typed almost all of them."

"That's too bad."

"Tell me about it." Tay started to pop the bite of bread into her mouth, but her gaze was caught by the photograph once more. "Judging by the sheets hanging over the clotheslines in the background, it appears that it's laundry day. That must be what's in that big iron pot."

"She had to do laundry like that? I thought our family was wealthy back then."

"Her father was wealthy, but not her aunts. He was the only son, so he inherited a large sum of money and this house from his parents. He could have done anything he wanted with the place—live in it, rent it out, or even sell it—but instead he let his sisters live there and raise his daughter after his wife died when Sarafina was born."

"If he inherited the house, what did his sisters get?"

"A hundred dollars each. That was it."

Ella looked horrified. "That doesn't seem right."

"I expect her aunts felt the same way. According to the traditions of that era, their parents probably just expected their brother to take care of them—which he did, in his way."

"By making them raise his daughter?"

"From what Sarafina wrote, her aunts loved her as if she was their own, which was good because once her father handed her over to them, he moved away and established a new life in Charlotte. He remarried when Sarafina was just two years old."

"Did he visit her often?"

"Very little is known about her early life, so I can't answer that question." Tay suspected the answer was no. Sarafina's determination to become someone important had to have stemmed from something, and a neglectful parent would have been just the spark to light that flame. *Which is the type of confirmed information I need for a book.*

Ella sniffed, obviously outraged. "I, for one, am glad I didn't live during that time."

"It must have been challenging." Tay ate some of the cinnamon bread, the rich flavor raising a sharp, vivid memory she'd been trying to forget. Two months after her big breakup with Richard, she'd stopped by the café near her assigned apartment after a long day researching in the stacks. She'd gotten a coffee and a walnut rugelach and had sat down with her laptop, trying to focus on her latest finds about the Casket Letters. Her and Richard's theory was that the letters were fake, fabricated by Lord Walsingham to implicate Mary, Queen of Scots, in an act of treason.

Of course, by then Tay knew he had fabricated the letters because she'd touched the handwriting and had seen the author—Walsingham himself. But as with all the glimpses she discovered with her Dove family gift, she then had to prove those events actually happened using existing primary source evidence available in dusty libraries and document collections. More importantly, she had to do it thoroughly enough to meet the critical eye cast by her academic peers.

That was where her real skills came in. No one was better than she at delving into the dusty and musty contents of various libraries, archival collections, and personal records. There, she worked tirelessly to find the sort of refined source material that would prove what her brief peeks into history had already showed her.

And so there she'd been, trying to lose herself while editing a chapter, when her phone rang. The second she saw the number, her heart had leapt and she'd instantly been swamped with the hope that—contrary to all evidence otherwise—he'd finally regretted his choices. So hopeful a fool was she that she'd eagerly reached for the phone. But instead of saying he missed her, he'd said—

"*No.*" Tay dropped the final bite of the cinnamon bread back onto the plate as if it had burned her. *Darn Ella and her memory-inducing desserts. That is the problem with having a sister whose baking skills are not only excellent but have the tendency to pull memories—even ones I don't want—out of the hidden corners of my mind.*

Ella's eyebrows rose. "Are you okay?" Her gaze moved to the abandoned bite of cinnamon bread and then back to Tay. "What did you remember?"

Tay shook her head. "It doesn't matter. We were talking about Sarafina, not me."

Ava's gaze narrowed on her. "You are rarely upset, but right now you look as if—"

"It's nothing. I just—I made a mistake, that's all. One I won't repeat again." *Ever.*

Ava leaned back in her chair, her gaze dark with concern while Sarah and Ella exchanged worried glances.

Before they could say anything, Tay said, "Look, I'm just jet-lagged to the max and—" She realized from her sisters' expressions that they didn't believe a word she said. "Fine. Something happened. But I'm not ready to talk about it yet. Do you mind?"

Ella's frown let Tay know she did mind.

"Tay—" Sarah started.

"Hey!" Ava interrupted. "Let's give her some space. She just got here."

Tay sent Ava a grateful glance. Ava flashed a quick smile and then asked Ella if she'd finished up the video she'd been working on. It was an obvious ploy to direct attention away from Tay, and she couldn't help but be thankful.

She listened as Ella answered, even sharing some of the social media events her team was planning for her channels. Everyone in the family thought Ella had the easiest job in the world. She was a chef without the responsibilities of a kitchen, and an online influencer with a production company–level group of assistants who kept her life well sponsored and well funded.

While they talked, Tay picked up the closest photograph where Sarafina was sitting on a bicycle. She was dressed in a long skirt and ruffled shirtwaist as she shyly looked at the camera, her hair pinned on her head. Standing behind her, almost in the background, was a thin young man with limp blond hair wearing a pair of threadbare pants and dirty boots, his shirt too large for his thin frame. He had a narrow face and a weak chin and looked far from happy. "I wonder who this man might be. He looks older than Sarafina."

Ella leaned over to see. "He seems sort of sullen, doesn't he? There's nothing written on the backs of these photos, so I guess there's no real way to find out."

"It would be difficult to figure out with just this one photograph, but not impossible."

"If you're wondering what he looked like grown-up, he's in this other photograph, too." Sarah placed a new picture in front of Tay.

The thin young man was older now, although he was still reed thin and seemed even paler. He wore a rather threadbare suit as he sat on a bench, a hat loosely held between his hands, a thin chain draped from his right watch pocket to a button on his vest. Sarafina stood nearby, holding a fishing rod. She looked older and wore a ruffled dress with a wide band at the waist, her long dark hair piled on top of her head, a pert straw hat pinned on top. This time, she smiled directly at the camera, her eyes bright, as if she'd been caught mid-laugh.

Ava pushed her coffee cup to one side and leaned across the table to get a better look at the picture. "She looks happy, but he's obviously miserable."

"Opposites." Ella finished her bread and then nodded toward the Valentine's Day cards that sat in front of Tay. "These were a bit of a disappointment, to be honest. There's not much written on them, but they're all signed 'W.' That's it. Just 'W.'"

"The letters are much more romantic," Sarah said. "Haunting, even. And they're all signed with that same 'W.'"

"They're beautifully written." Ava added some cream to her coffee.

"We've been trying to figure out who Sarafina's beau might be, but we've had no luck, so we decided to wait until you got here."

Tay untied the ribbon on the packet of letters, removed the top one, and spread it open, careful not to touch the writing so she could approach this first read as objectively as possible. She took her time as she read. Sentence after sentence floated before her. *I'm without you, and it's as if my soul has lost its way. . . . I think of you and all the darkness disappears, because you are my brightness, my light. . . .* She sighed. "Wow."

Sarah clasped her hands together. "I know, right? *So* romantic, but sad, too. Whoever wrote these was obviously deeply in love with Sarafina, but their circumstances were dire."

It was too early to get excited, but Tay couldn't keep a wave of hope at bay. She'd always wondered if Sarafina had left anyone behind when she'd gone to New York, and here sat the answer. "How many letters are here?"

"Seven," Ella answered promptly, taking a sip of her coffee. "They're all very sad. He knew her dream was to go to New York City and 'be someone,' and he tells her to go without him because he won't be able to join her now."

"Now?"

"He doesn't say what's happened that changed things. He must have known she'd understand what he was talking about, because he didn't bother to explain it."

Tay nodded. "That happens often. If both the letter writer and the letter receiver know someone had an accident and are already familiar with the details, then they might never reference or even describe the accident at all, but just say things like, 'I hope Reggie is feeling better now.' Or 'I hate what happened to Reggie.' That sort of thing."

"Ugh. That's inconvenient." Ava sent her a curious look. "What do you do when that happens?"

"You would cross-reference all available information from a variety of sources—the more the better. Sometimes it works and you can find out exactly what they're referring to, but sometimes you're just left wondering."

"What an unsatisfactory career you've chosen." Ella slid the letter closer to Tay. "Touch it. We need answers, and we've been waiting for over a month now to see what you can figure out from these."

This was it, then.

Taking a deep breath, Tay placed her hand flat on the closest letter and closed her eyes. Instantly, she was in a dark room, lit only by a dim glow from a tiny window that was so high up she couldn't reach it. She was sitting on a hard, packed-dirt floor and was cold. So cold that her body and hands ached with it. She could tell little about the room other than that it held a narrow cot with one thin blanket on it.

Tay looked down and could dimly see the man's left hand as he wrote. It was a beautiful hand, graceful and long, but dirty, the nails tattered and torn. He held the stub of a pencil that had been rudely sharpened, and he was using a book as a lap desk. Somewhere in the distance, she could hear the deep mutter of voices, none of them clear enough for her to make out any words. Once in a while she heard a startled shout followed by a loud clang of metal. A horrible stench lingered in the damp, fetid air.

She could feel what this man felt—fear, deep loneliness, endless pain, and heartbreaking uncertainty. And yet, as he wrote, his emotions calmed. Quieted. Just writing to Sarafina was lifting his spirits.

Tay soaked in the feeling coming from the author as his broken pencil scratched its way across the precious paper. *He loves her so much. Every ounce of him yearns for her. Every thought is focused on her. Every hope is for her.*

And yet mingled with the love was an unmistakable sense of

despair. As Tay watched the pencil move, a single, salty tear fell onto the paper. *He's crying.* Her heart ached with his, and— A shout echoed in the dark, so close it made the man gasp and drop his pencil.

She blinked. She was back in the dining room, all three of her sisters staring at her.

Ella spoke first. "Are you okay?"

"She's shivering," Ava said. "Would you like more coffee?"

"No, thank you." Tay pushed the letter away, her fingers still icy cold. "Whoever he was, he was in a very dark place." She tucked her hands under her arms, trying to warm them. "It was freezing there. And damp, too."

"A cellar, maybe?"

"Maybe. I'm not sure." She thought about it, trying to separate the many feelings that had slipped through him as he wrote. "He was afraid."

Sarah leaned forward. "Of what?"

Tay hesitated. Finally, she admitted, "I'm not sure. But he hated that place, wherever it was." And who would blame him? It had been deeply uncomfortable there. *Why didn't he just leave? Was he trapped there?*

"Who was he?" Ella asked. "Could you tell?"

"No." Tay rubbed her hands together, trying to get the blood flowing again. "He wasn't thinking about himself, but about her. He loved her a lot." *I wonder what it's like to be loved like that?* To be honest, she'd never loved anyone like that, either.

She couldn't help but compare the deep feelings in the anguished writer's letter to the shallow irritation in Richard's note. It was a stark, rather bleak comparison.

Aware of her sisters' gazes on her, she collected herself. "I should check the other letters." She pulled them closer and, bracing herself, touched them one at a time. Every time, she got the exact same feelings of love, desperation, and hopelessness.

But as she touched the last letter, just as the author signed his name, a metal ringing sound jerked his gaze to one side, and she caught sight of an iron-barred door.

The sound of an iron key being thrust into a rusty lock rang loudly in the small room as the door swung open and a raspy, masculine voice uttered a name. The writer replied, "Yes?" and lifted his pencil from the paper.

Just like that, Tay was back in the dining room. Shivering, she looked down and pulled her hand from the letter.

Sarah grasped Tay's arm. "What did you see?"

"He was in jail." Tay carefully rested her fingers on the edge of the letter, away from the writing, and pushed it away. "It was William Day. He wrote these letters."

Ava's eyes widened. "William Day, the train robber?"

Tay nodded. Everyone in Dove Pond knew the story about how, back in the late 1890s, William Day and two other men had robbed a train carrying an army payroll's worth of gold. Unbeknownst to the three robbers, the train company had been alerted about the possibility of the theft, so they'd hired Pinkerton agents to protect the shipment. A gunfight had ensued, and one of the robbers had been injured. They'd all managed to escape but were quickly arrested, tried, and sentenced to prison for their crimes.

Ella, who'd just reached for her coffee mug, suddenly stopped. "Does this mean Sarafina was in love with a *criminal*?"

"Maybe not," Tay said. "We know he loved her; these letters prove that. But who knows if his feelings were reciprocated. Sarafina repeatedly told her daughter and others, too, that she'd only loved one man in her life—David Tau."

Ava frowned. "He was Lucy's father, right?"

"Yes. Sarafina met him in New York City." Tay eyed her empty plate and wondered if she should get another slice of Ella's cinnamon bread. "His marriage to Sarafina was considered scandalous. He took

New York society by storm when he arrived as he was fabulously wealthy, handsome, and charming. Meanwhile, she was just a newspaper reporter from an unknown family."

"She must have been an exciting woman," Ella declared. "She had two interesting men crazy for her—a millionaire *and* a famous train robber. I'm a little jealous."

Tay was, too. "I was hoping there might be a letter from Sarafina in this box. She left so few examples of her handwriting—which, by the way, was atrocious. Even her editor couldn't read it, so she used a typewriter for almost all her correspondence." That was just one of the many things Tay found fascinating about her ancestor. "She had a strong personality but was passionate about only a few things: her family, her work, good whiskey, and secret codes."

Ella blinked. "Secret codes?"

"After her daughter, Lucy, married and moved to France, she and Sarafina wrote often to each other, and their letters were filled with secret codes. Most of them were just little messages like 'Can't wait to see you!' but they were super creative in how they created those codes. Sarafina used them at work, too. When she went undercover, she sent her reports in code in case someone intercepted them. She disguised them as letters to her aunt."

"Have you seen them?"

"Only two survived. They were on display at the Smithsonian." Tay had spent a long time with the collection and had even gotten permission from the curator to see the items that hadn't been put on display. "Sarafina's editor hated her use of codes. He wrote in a letter to his sister that Sarafina's secret codes drove him crazy. He could never figure them out without help."

Ava raised her hand. "That would be me. I'm stumped by Wordle most days."

"Oh, there's more," Tay said, warming to her subject. "If you think secret codes are exciting, upon Sarafina's death, Lucy was given a poem that, if she followed the clues, would reveal a family secret. Lucy never bothered to do it, though, so it's a mystery to this day. People have tried to figure out the clues in that poem, but no one has succeeded."

Sarah's eyes couldn't get any wider. "Lucy didn't even try?"

Ella frowned. "Maybe the secret wasn't something positive. It's possible Lucy was smart in not chasing it down."

"Maybe," Sarah said, although she didn't look as if she believed it.

Tay smiled. "I have a copy of that poem in one of the boxes I sent here. I'll make copies for you. Who knows? Maybe one of you can figure it out."

"What fun!" Ella rubbed her hands together. "Ava may suck at puzzles and riddles, but I excel at them."

Sarah bounced in her seat. "I love this! A train robber admirer, a millionaire husband, a dashing career, covert codes, and a family secret. Tay, if you don't write this book, someone else will."

Tay couldn't argue with that. "And now I know to research William Day. There was a connection there of some sort."

"Come to the library," Sarah said. "The town archives are still there. You'll need access to the Day family archives, too, which are stored at Rose's Bookstore. The library uses those documents for various exhibits. And, Tay, if you need help, let me know. I might be able to find some time now that the town has given us the funds to hire an assistant librarian."

"I can help, too," Ava offered. "If you need me."

Ella raised her hand. "Me too! I'm going to take lots of pictures. My social media followers will eat this stuff up with a spoon. It's so intriguing!"

Tay knew that her sisters had neither the time nor the necessary mindset to spend hours and hours reading old documents, but she appreciated their enthusiasm. "Thank you," she said with a polite smile. "I'll keep that in mind." She watched as Sarah placed William Day's letters into a neat stack.

She really shouldn't have been surprised that Sarafina and William knew each other. After all, Dove Pond was a small town and had been even smaller back then, but the connection had never dawned on her. *I wonder how they first met. I hope I get a few clues to that, at least.*

Tomorrow, she'd dive into this new research lead. She leaned back in her chair, suddenly exhausted from her travels. But sitting here with her sisters, the fire crackling nearby, William Day's letters in front of her promising a fresh look into Sarafina Dove's intriguing life, Tay felt, if not happy, at least hopeful.

Thank you, Sarafina. It's a start.

CHAPTER 3

SARAFINA

APRIL 10, 1894

There are times in life when seemingly small moments aren't small at all. Like the sudden flash of lightning that announces a coming storm, these moments mark the beginning of something larger. Something powerful but not yet seen, hovering just out of sight. The first time you spoke to me was one of these moments, and neither of us could have predicted how fierce the storm that followed would be. . . .

—letter from William Day to Sarafina Dove

In all her sixteen years, Sarafina Dove had found only one thing she hated: Miss LaFont's School of Comportment for Young Ladies. According to Miss LaFont, that tightly laced-up and strict epitome of supposed female virtues, "true ladies" never discussed real-life issues, laughed aloud, read interesting books, or had even a hint of an original thought in their purposefully-kept-empty, well-coifed heads. Each day there, spent embroidering ridiculous homilies about "quiet patience" and "womanly virtues" on endless handkerchiefs, or sipping tepid cups of weak tea while discussing absolutely nothing of interest, made Sarafina feel as if her soul might expire.

Which was why, after a particularly boring day of trying to stay awake in Miss LaFont's too-warm front parlor, instead of going home, Sarafina headed to her favorite fishing hole. As she left the road for the pathway through the woods, she checked to make sure the piece of Aunt Emily Anne's famous cornbread, which she'd wrapped in waxed paper that morning and tucked into her coat pocket, was still there. Happy to find her snack in place, she set off for an adventure.

Society at large—even her unconventional aunts—would have given a collective, horrified gasp if they'd seen how, as soon as she was safely away from the main road, she'd quickly and expertly tucked her skirts into her waistband. Then, humming to herself, she ran—yes, *ran*—down the wooded path, leaping across puddles left by the spring rains and ignoring the tug of branches as they caught at her coat sleeves. It was a beautiful day, the first in a week of gray skies and unending rain, and she couldn't keep from skipping a little whenever the path permitted it.

Smiling, she rounded a corner and found herself facing Sweet Creek. She'd never seen the water as high as it was today, but—unwilling to waste even a second of her free time—she went straight to the large rock that stuck a third of the way over the creek and prepared to leap.

Crossing the creek was always an adventure in itself, since it required a rather daring hop, but today it looked especially challenging, as the chilly water had risen until it lapped over the edges of the rock. Sarafina made sure her skirts were still safely tucked into her waistband, then straightened her shoulders, stepped out on the rock, and—with a huge breath—jumped.

That's when she discovered that the grass on the other side was sopping wet, and the dirt under it an oozing, muddy mess. She landed with a thick splash, and her feet instantly shot out from under her, her arms waving wildly as she tipped back toward the raging creek.

She clenched her eyes closed and, heart racing, waited for an icy dunking. But instead, at the last possible moment, someone caught her and set her firmly back on her feet, their hard hands now holding her upright.

Shocked, she slowly let out her breath and opened her eyes. William Day stood in front of her, his black hair tousled, his blue eyes far too close to hers, his hands still firmly wrapped around her upper arms.

Although they'd never spoken to each other, Sarafina Dove had known William Day for most of her life. Or at least had known *of* him. They were of a similar age—he was only two years older—and they'd grown up in the same small town, too. Sadly, their tiny town seemed obsessed with the salacious bits of gossip that chronicled his family's misfortunes.

Everyone in Dove Pond knew the story of how, twenty-odd years ago, the Day family had been sundered in two. It began when brothers Edward and Charles Day had a violent falling-out over the inheritance left them upon their father's death. After a long and very public fight, the two had settled their disagreement, but they had never spoken again.

Over the next few years, older brother Edward had invested his portion of the inheritance wisely in numerous businesses and was now a pillar of their small town. He had built an impressive house on the hill overlooking Dove Pond and was now the sole owner and editor of the town's newspaper, the *Dove Pond Register*. Meanwhile, younger brother Charles went in the opposite direction. He wasted his inheritance on gambling, drinking, and other unsavory pursuits. As time went on, he slid down the social ladder, taking his long-suffering wife and children with him, until the family ended up at the edge of town in a tiny clapboard house so close to the railroad tracks that it shook every time a train went by.

Charles Day never forgave his brother for being successful and, fueled by his growing anger, eventually added "town drunk" to his list of non-accomplishments. Years later, to no one's surprise, Charles's battered wife left him, as did his three oldest sons, who silently disappeared one after the other as they got old enough to fend for themselves. Eventually, only Charles and his youngest son, William, were left in the shambles of their family home.

Most people expected that William would eventually leave just as his brothers had, but before that could happen, his father—staggering home drunk and alone on a bitterly cold winter night—had slipped and fallen into an icy pond and drowned. His funeral was held two days later, with fifteen-year-old William his only mourner.

The town gossips surmised that William, who looked more like his father than any of his brothers, would naturally follow his father's path of debauchery. True to their expectations, William quit school and was often seen loitering around town. Personally, Sarafina thought that was a harsh way to describe what William was actually doing, which was lingering in front of various businesses, waiting to do all the odd jobs no one else wanted to do. Occasionally, he chatted with a few of the town's other less fortunate young men, who often worked the jobs with him. Over the years, she had seen him loading bags of feed into the backs of wagons at the general store, cleaning stalls in the town stables, and sweeping the sidewalk in front of the mercantile, just to name a few of the tasks he'd shouldered.

Which was why, while she was surprised that William Day had helped her, it wasn't because she thought him rude or unwilling. It was simply because she'd never seen him on this particular path, one she'd taken hundreds of times before. She'd never seen him this close, either. He was taller than she'd realized, and much stronger, too. But the most astonishing difference was how his bright blue eyes—a Day family tell—were flecked with gold.

She noticed all of this because, although he'd released her soon after he'd set her back on her feet, he was still standing much too close.

He must have realized it, too, because his face grew slightly red. Without a word, he abruptly left and headed for the exact path she'd been planning to take, the one that led to the pond.

She should go somewhere else now. That would be the prudent thing to do. But instead, as if the words had been pent up inside her, she blurted out, "Wait!"

He stopped and glanced back at her, his brows knit, distrust in those blue, blue eyes.

Her face warmed even more. Still, she managed to choke out, "I'm going that way, too. We should walk together."

A flash of surprise flickered across his expressive face.

He didn't expect me to offer to walk with him. She supposed there were some people in town who would have eschewed his company, but she wasn't one of them.

To be honest, she was curious about him and had been for a long time now. She'd seen him on Main Street numerous times, sometimes sitting on a bale of hay outside the livery stables, reading a tattered book as he waited to help someone with their horses. She'd overheard the stable owner's wife, Mrs. Marks, saying that William Day might be "wilder than a wet cat" and didn't know good literature, as he "loved those dime novels," but he was good with the horses, even the less tamed ones.

Unbeknownst to many people, especially Miss LaFont and her overgrown sense of outrage, Sarafina loved the same colorful, rag-paper books she'd seen William read. The novels sold for a dime each at the general store and were filled with exciting stories. Her personal favorites contained a female detective named Lucille Freemont, who lived an unforgettable life solving various mysteries and even the occasional murder. While sitting in the boring confines of Miss LaFont's, Sarafina often imagined herself being like the intrepid Lucy Freemont, and one day moving to a big city to become a detective herself.

In fact, Sarafina kept a box under her bed filled with these dime novels, and she read them over and over into the wee hours of the night. She loved them so much that she'd even started writing her own, and often entertained Aunt Jane and Aunt Emily Anne by reading aloud her latest episodes by the fireside in the evenings.

"You took a big chance with that jump." William tilted his head to one side, his gaze locked on hers. "I've never seen a girl do something like that."

His voice was deeper than she'd expected, and far more refined. *Another surprise.* "Maybe you don't know enough girls."

His eyes twinkled, and a lazy half smile touched his mouth. "Apparently not." His gaze moved across her face and then up to her hair. "You've started wearing your hair up."

Taken aback, she put a hand to her hair. When she'd turned sixteen a few months ago, she'd started pinning her hair up. Aunt Jane said it was an unofficial announcement that Sarafina was no longer a child. It was startling to realize that he'd noticed, as she'd never seen him spare her so much as a glance. Sarafina suddenly realized that William was still standing in front of her, a question in his eyes, and she dropped her hand from her hair and tried to calm her nervous heart. "I'm surprised you noticed."

His smile, which had never left, now widened. "I couldn't miss it."

She didn't know how she was supposed to take that, but if her face got any hotter, it would burst into flames. She shifted awkwardly from one foot to the other, and his gaze moved to her muddy boots.

She glanced down and realized her skirts were still tucked into her waistband, her petticoats on full display. *Oh no!* Frantic, she freed her skirts and dropped them back into place. "That was—I didn't realize—I shouldn't have—" The words froze in her throat, and she couldn't think of another thing to say.

His lips quirked as he fought a smile. "I should leave you now. I'm sure you have places to go." He turned away as if to head back down the path.

She hurried to his side. When he looked at her, obviously startled, she said, "You were taking the path to the pond. I'm headed that way, too. We can walk together."

William's smile had disappeared. "I'm not going to the pond. I'm only walking this way until the path turns."

"We can walk that far together, then."

"No," he said shortly. "We can't."

"Why not?" Sarafina was sure her aunts could think of a hundred reasons why she shouldn't walk with William Day, but she'd had enough "rules" for one day.

"People might talk. You know that."

"They're already talking, so—" She shrugged.

"Not in the way they'll talk if they see you with me." He sent her a cold, hard look. "Go home. I have things to do that don't concern you."

Who did he think he was? She lifted her chin in the air and crossed her arms over her chest. "I'll go home once I'm done fishing. I've been waiting for this all day."

He grimaced and said in a rather surly tone, "Do what you want, but walk there by yourself." With that, he walked past her and headed down the path in long strides.

She almost had to run to keep up with him. As she walked behind him, she noticed his long, ragged-edged coat as it swirled around his legs. His clothes were clean but roughly mended, the poor stitching on the patches far more in keeping with what one might see on a saddle blanket than a pair of pants.

He cast an impatient glance over his shoulder and, seeing her scrambling to keep pace with him, lengthened his stride yet more.

Soon, she was almost breathless, and yet determined more than ever to stay with him. Panting, she managed to call out, "A polite person would at least *pretend* we were walking together."

He stopped so suddenly she almost ran into him. He turned and scowled down at her. "Surely you've been warned about me."

She studied his face as she caught her breath. Some people said William was just like his father, but she'd never discerned even a hint of alcohol in either his clear gaze or his steady hands. Now that Sarafina thought about it, she couldn't recall a single negative comment from the town gossips that was based on his actual actions other than that he appeared to know some of the town's other rejects. *Who else can he be friends with, since no one will acknowledge him?* She lifted her chin and said in what she hoped was a superior manner, "I never listen to gossip."

"Everyone listens to gossip." His gaze moved over her face. "They talk about you, too, you know."

She knew. People talked about her absent father: why he left, why he'd never come back, why he'd abandoned his daughter so soon after his wife's death. They also talked about her two aunts. People said that when there were seven sisters born in the Dove family, the women inherited magical gifts, and Sarafina's aunts were no different. Although their five younger sisters had all moved away years ago, the remaining two still lived in town and had raised her.

Sarafina dearly loved Aunt Jane and Aunt Emily Anne and was rather envious of their unusual talents. Aunt Jane was a diviner who could find lost things, while Aunt Emily Anne could speak to birds. Aunt Jane's ability made her quite popular with the locals, who never failed to call whenever the family cow went wandering or someone was missing a ring or other piece of precious jewelry. But Aunt Emily Anne's family gift was far less welcome, especially by Sarafina, who knew that it was highly likely that some of the birds singing in the trees overhead were spying on her.

She sighed and wished for the thousandth time that she had a special Dove gift, too. Her aunts both swore that the stories she wrote for them displayed an unusual amount of talent, but while Sarafina appreciated their enthusiasm, she knew talent wasn't real magic. Not like theirs.

Still, she loved to write stories for her aunts, magic or not. That was her life now—reading, writing, avoiding her father's scant attention, and attending Miss LaFont's after her father decided during one of his rare visits that she was sadly lacking in social graces.

Aware that William's gaze still rested on her, she sniffed. "I know people talk. What did you hear?"

"That your father never visits, and that your aunts . . ." He hesitated.

Of course. "My aunt Jane is a finder of the lost, and my aunt Em talks to birds. That's just the way things are."

Disbelief flickered in his blue eyes. "Can they really do those things?"

She nodded. "I've seen them."

"That's ridiculous."

"It's the truth. I swear it."

His gaze narrowed, but after a moment he said, "What about your father? Can he do stuff like that, too?"

That almost made her laugh. "No. Aunt Em thinks that's why Papa's always so grouchy. He's a bit resentful. I suppose it's a good thing he visits only once a year."

William shot her a curious look. "Doesn't that bother you?"

She liked that he'd asked that. Whenever she mentioned her father, most people tended to look uncomfortable and then say something condescending, like "He's an important man, so I'm sure he's busy."

But not William. She liked his comment better than the others'. "It used to bother me, but not anymore." In some way, she'd developed a hard casing in the spot of her heart where her father resided.

A soft breeze sent a loose leaf tumbling across the toe of her boot, and she reached down and picked it up. "I see Papa every Easter, and that's enough. To be honest, it would be nice if he'd skip an Easter or two."

If she'd said that to anyone else—even her aunts, who had no love for their haughty and judgmental brother—she'd have been castigated for being rude.

William nodded. "My father wasn't the best, either."

From what she'd heard, that was an understatement. That his father's drinking had ignited an unstable temper was a well-known topic of conversation in every house in town. "Aunt Jane says your dad was a jackass."

A flash of surprise followed quickly by one of amusement crossed William's face. "You're an unusual girl, Sarafina Dove."

She flushed, regretting her impulsive speech. "I shouldn't have said that, should I?"

One corner of William's mouth curled into a half smile. "You're honest. I like that."

There was something unsettling about that half smile. It made her far too aware of him, and in ways she wasn't sure about. Suddenly eager to change the direction of their conversation, she said, "I haven't thanked you for keeping me from falling."

He shrugged. "It wasn't a big deal."

She reached into her pocket and dug out the cornbread she'd been saving and held it out. "Here. Take this as my thanks."

He stared down at the cornbread, and his mouth thinned. "No, thank you. I don't take handouts."

"It's not a handout. It's a thank-you gift."

His jaw tightened. "Keep it."

"There's a whole pan of it waiting for me when I get home." She shook it impatiently. "It's delicious. My aunt Emily Anne made it."

"I said no." His voice was almost harsh.

Goodness, but he had an uncomfortable amount of pride. She sighed, grabbed his hand, and placed the cornbread in it, noticing how rough his fingers felt against hers. "Eat it or feed it to the fish, the choice is yours. Just don't throw it away. If Aunt Em finds out someone has disrespected her baking, we'll both regret it."

He scowled. "You're not giving me much choice, are you?" He muttered something under his breath and then stuffed the cornbread into his coat pocket.

She hid her smile behind a prim sniff. "You're making a big deal out of this. I just wanted to thank you for saving me from getting a dunking, that's all."

"I didn't do that much. But—" After a tight pause, he grimaced. "Thank you."

To hide her smile, she dropped her gaze, noticing his tired-looking boots. They were scuffed and scratched, the heels low and worn down. She wished she had more to share with him than just cornbread.

He nodded toward the path. "Let's go."

Surprised, her gaze flew to meet his.

"I'll walk slower this time." He walked down the path, his stride noticeably shorter than before.

She smiled and took off, hurrying to catch up to him. As she fell into step with him, he moved over slightly so they could walk side by side.

This was nice. Sarafina clasped her hands behind her back and cast him a short side-glance. "Where are you going?"

"I'm meeting a friend."

"Ah." They walked on, and she noticed what a pretty day it was now, the sunlight filtering through the branches, dried leaves crunching under their feet.

"Who taught you to fish?"

"My aunt Jane. She used to fish with her father when she was little. She doesn't fish anymore, though." Aunt Jane had become far too aware of what she called "life's proprieties" to do something so fun, which was a great pity, in Sarafina's opinion.

"How often do you go fishing?"

"My aunts are at their church meeting every Tuesday. I try to come other days, too, but sometimes I can't get away." A crow called from a branch above. Sarafina glanced up into the tree where the bird sat. It stared at her, tilted its head, and gave another caw.

"Stupid tattletale," Sarafina muttered as she came to a stop.

William stood beside her and eyed the bird curiously. "Tattletale?"

Sarafina reached into her skirt pocket and pulled out a small bag. "If that bird tells Aunt Em I'm here, I'll be in trouble." She poured some breadcrumbs from the pouch into the palm of her hand.

"Hold on. You think your aunt sent that bird to spy on you."

"She doesn't send him; she just rewards him whenever he tells her where I am, so he's permanently on patrol. She calls him 'Blackwing,' which is a dramatic name for 'nosy snitch.'" Sarafina held her cupped hand in front of her and waited.

It took only a few seconds before the crow flew down and landed on her wrist.

William took a startled step back and watched with wide eyes as the bird pecked away at the breadcrumbs.

"There," Sarafina told the bird when he finished. "Stay until I'm ready to leave. Then you can tell Aunt Em where I am. By that time, I'll be headed home."

The bird cawed as if it agreed and, the last breadcrumb gone, flew back to its perch in the branches overhead. Sarafina carefully tightened the drawstring on the little bag and tucked it away.

"That's the strangest thing I've ever seen." He stared up at the trees overhead. "Do they all take bribes like that?"

"The smart ones do." She continued down the path, William falling into step beside her.

She could feel his gaze resting on her from time to time, but she didn't bother speaking and just enjoyed his quiet company. It was nice to have someone to walk with, which was a new feeling, as she didn't have a lot of friends. Most of the girls in town were the sort to find Miss LaFont's detestable school enjoyable, and the few who didn't, the ones she might have been able to strike up a friendship with, weren't comfortable with her aunts and their abilities. Which meant that when she wasn't at Miss LaFont's, Sarafina was usually alone.

Until now, that is.

They reached a fork in the pathway, and William slowed to a stop. "This is where we part. I'm headed this way." He tilted his head toward the other path.

That was too bad. It was odd, but she didn't want their walk to end. "I guess you have a lot to do this afternoon."

"I'm expected back at the stables today. There's a shipment of feed arriving at five."

"I see." She should just say goodbye and leave. And yet she stayed where she was.

So did he. He watched her, his eyebrows lowered. "You should head on to the lake."

She should. She really, really should. And yet she couldn't seem to make her feet move. "I . . . I don't suppose you'd like to meet me here next Tuesday?" She could tell she'd surprised him, so she hurried to add, "I'll show you how to fish, if you'd like. I know a lot of tricks that could make you really good at it."

His mouth quirked into that half smile she was beginning to like way too much. "I already know how to fish."

Oh. She wished he'd already told her that. "Are you any good at it?"

"I'm not bad."

"Then come next week and we'll fish together." She found herself holding her breath as she waited for his answer, which was ridiculous, because he was going to refuse to do it. He'd already made it obvious he didn't think—

"Tuesday, then. I'll see you at the lake."

She gave an excited hop before she could stop herself. "Tuesday, then!"

His mouth curved into a smile. Before she could say another word, he left, his boots crunching on the fallen leaves that filled the path.

She watched until she couldn't see him anymore, and then, certain she was alone, she gave a happy twirl, going so fast that it left her feeling dizzy. The day now seemed even brighter than before.

CHAPTER 4

ROSE

Rose Day had a problem, and he was currently leaning against the counter in her bookstore, working on the *New York Times* crossword puzzle with, of all things, an ink pen. *Show-off.*

To be honest, she didn't mind that her grandson Luke was doing the puzzle. It was a slow day, and she often read while sitting right where he was. But unlike her, whenever Luke focused on something, he became completely oblivious to his surroundings, including their one and only customer at that moment—Kat Carter—who'd brought a stack of books to the register and had been trying to get his attention for the last minute and a half.

Standing an imposing six foot two, his dark hair a tangle of black curls and his thickly lashed eyes as blue as the ocean, Luke was once again proving that he was the world's worst counter help. Rose was growing surer by the day that even those people who tried to be bad at customer service couldn't—and wouldn't—find more ways to ignore customers than Luke. In fact, poor Kat had already said hello twice now, and he'd yet to respond.

Disgusted, Rose dropped her pen onto her desk and scowled out of the window of her office. "Sheesh. Pay attention, will you?" It was a pity he was so lost in his puzzle because Kat, besides being a very pretty girl with long dark hair and the type of figure that men back in Rose's day would have called a "classy chassis," was one of the bookshop's best customers.

Just as Rose reached for her cane so she could get up and get Kat checked out, Luke dropped the pen onto his newspaper, lifted his head, and said, "I'm glad you're here." He placed both hands on the counter and leaned forward, his face now even with Kat's.

She turned a bright pink, interest sparkling in her eyes. "Yes?" Her voice was warm and husky.

Luke smiled, a dimple appearing in one cheek.

Rose stifled a groan. Poor Kat. She had no idea how thick and unwilling of a wall she was about to run into. It was ironic God had gifted this man, a complete and utter computer nerd, with such a face and smile. Rose cast a sour glance at the ceiling. *You do have a sense of humor, don't you?*

Luke pushed his newspaper across the counter. "What's a seven-letter word for 'compete in a hybrid water sport' that ends in 'i'?"

Kat's smile froze and then faded. "Oh. I don't know."

"Darn it." He grabbed the newspaper and turned away. He was soon once again lost in his puzzle.

Kat's bewildered gaze moved from him down to her stack of books and then back.

That's it. Rose picked up her cane and got up from her creaky 1920s office chair, a relic from when her grandfather and then her father had worked in this very office. She took a step forward and winced as she put her weight on her left leg. *Darn arthritis, darn chilly springs, and darn my grandson for not listening to a darn thing I say.*

She made her way out of her office and into the shop, the delightful smell of books welcoming her. "Hello, Kat." Rose went behind the counter and pushed Luke out of the way. "Next time, just whack him on the side of the head with one of your books. That'll get his attention."

Luke blinked. "What? Oh! I was going to ring her up. I was just—" He slapped his hand on the counter. "I know it!"

Rose frowned. "You know what? That you're horrible counter help?"

"It's para-ski." He filled in the word.

"Fool!" Rose took Kat's books, making small talk even as she wondered what she was going to do with this handsome, guileless, rudderless grandson of hers. From the time he'd first charmed the world with his dimples and curls to now, Luke had managed to be the star of his own life, the darling of everyone he met, the apple of his parents' eyes, and the unaware crush of numerous women, all without actually doing anything or—worse yet—accomplishing a thing.

She'd been worried about the kid his whole life. To the average onlooker, it probably seemed as if he'd always had the world at his feet. As a teenager, despite spending thousands of hours playing video games, he'd somehow managed to graduate high school as valedictorian and had gotten a full-ride scholarship to Georgia Tech. Although no one had ever seen him study or even touch a textbook in college, he'd graduated summa cum laude in three and a half years with a degree in computer something-or-another. Life came far too easily to this young man.

It hadn't stopped there, either. For a normal college graduate, a tech degree would have been enough to set their feet on the path to success. But instead of getting a steady job at a well-established company like a smart person would do, Luke had scoffed at what he called "nine-to-five slavery" and had instead decided to do something called "consulting," which—from what Rose could see—meant he flitted between assignments at will; traveled for weeks at a time to uncomfortable places like China and South Korea; and then, when he was home, spent a lot of time fiddling on his laptop. She was certain he was making a mere fraction of what he could have been had he taken a traditional job. It was maddening, seeing so much potential just evaporating away a drop at a time.

Ignoring him now, Rose asked Kat, "How's your mother?"

Kat smiled. "She's doing great. She's in Atlanta this weekend shopping with friends."

"That sounds like fun." The Carter women were known for their frivolous and sensual natures. It was said they lured wealthy men to them like sirens and then trapped them in a matrimonial web. Of course, it was one thing to lure a wealthy man, another to keep him. The Carter women couldn't seem to do that, and they had a long record of divorces. *Kat's mother has been married—what is it now? Four times? Or is it five? I can't even remember.*

So far Kat had avoided the Carter women's traditionally rocky and always brief marriage trend. She'd had only one serious boyfriend, if one could call him that, as he seemed to drift in and out of her life like a windblown leaf. Rumor had it that, although he'd proposed more than once, Kat had turned him down each and every time.

One might think that meant she was a woman of sense, and yet here she was, looking at Luke as if she were about ten seconds away from hopping across the counter and throwing herself at him. It was a good thing Luke was protected by both his low bank account and his own lack of awareness of the world around him, or he might have unwittingly become a notch on the infamous Carter bedpost.

Rose picked up the scanner and started ringing up Kat's books. "Did you find everything you were looking for?"

"I did. Mom wanted the latest Robyn Carr book, so I got that, and then I bought three others, too." Kat made a face. "I can't come in here for just one book. I always end up getting more."

"That's what we're here for." Rose glanced at the clock over the door and said over her shoulder, "Luke, it's almost three."

"Already?" He dropped his pen onto the folded newspaper. "I'd better go."

Rose reached into her cardigan pocket and pulled out a set of keys. "Check the post office while you're out. I'm expecting a package from my accountant."

"I can't." Luke slanted Rose a slow smile. It was one of his most annoying habits, flashing that "I know you're mad, but it won't last" sort of look used by mischievous and charming men the world over. "Grandma, I have to pick up Lulu in twenty minutes."

"So?"

"So it'll take me at least that long to get into that nightmare of a pickup line, scoop up Lulu, and navigate out of the parking lot, which will be filled with precious little things trying to find their mother's minivans in a sea of other minivans. Then I'll have to drive all the way back to town, and—because of the time—will most likely get stuck behind a school bus, which will stop at every home between here and there. Which means that by the time I get to the post office, it'll be closed."

Damn it. She hated it when he used common sense to argue. She muttered "Ungrateful brat" under her breath and returned the keys to her cardigan pocket.

"I'd better run. Kat, it was nice seeing you." He grabbed his coat from under the counter and put it on as he headed for the door. "Back soon." The soft jangle of the bells above the door announced his departure.

"He's fond of his niece." Kat's eyes were now on the door, her gaze concentrated, as if she were attempting to use brute mental will to force Luke to come back.

"Yup. By the way, the new Carr book is excellent. Read it just last week and loved it." Rose returned the scanner wand to its holder. "Your mom never misses a Carr release. She must be one of her biggest fans."

Kat dragged her gaze from the closed door and smiled at Rose. "You have no idea. Last year, Ms. Carr held a book signing, and Mom and four of her friends drove three hundred and thirty-two miles just to get signed books. They're crazy fans." Kat pulled out her credit card and tapped it on the pad Rose had just pointed to. "I was telling Mom that you've made a lot of improvements here. The scanner is a lot faster, isn't it?"

"Faster isn't always better," Rose said sourly. It was nice having Luke here at the bookstore, as she never had to eat lunch alone anymore, which she appreciated. But his desire to change everything was a bit off-putting. Whenever he wasn't absorbed in a crossword or playing some sort of weird game on his laptop or doing his own "work," he walked around the bookstore, making suggestions she wished he'd keep to himself.

She supposed she was partially at fault. After the family had realized how dire Caitlyn's situation was and that the chances were high of her going to jail for ten years if not more, Rose had invited Luke and Lulu to live with her. Somehow, he'd gotten the mistaken idea that meant he'd also been invited to modernize every aspect of her beloved bookshop.

Rose should have put a stop to that line of thinking then and there, but she'd soon discovered that her seemingly aimless grandson was amazingly persistent once he got an idea in his head. So persistent that he'd eventually worn her down and she'd reluctantly allowed him to implement a few of his less intrusive and more reasonable ideas. Thus, over the past few months, she'd gotten that infernal scanning wand and a newfangled register that at times seemed to have a mind of its own.

But it hadn't stopped there. He'd also reorganized the filing system, which made tracking sales "easier," and had completely changed the website. Now people could order books directly from the store. Every morning, after Luke opened the bookstore and restocked the shelves, he would print up the orders that had come in overnight and get them packaged and ready to ship.

While she found most of his upgrades ridiculous, she had to admit she rather liked the online shopping they now offered. It had given her a nice surprise when she'd looked at their total sales at the end of the month, adding hundreds of dollars of net profits to their bottom line.

Rose slid Kat's books into a bag. "Here you go."

Kat took the bag but stayed at the counter. "I was sad to hear about your granddaughter going to prison. Mom said Caitlyn got involved with the wrong crowd."

Rose had nothing to say about that. Caitlyn was a discontented soul who, when she couldn't find trouble, made it for herself, running full steam into every pitfall available. In middle school, she'd been expelled for fighting; she'd then been expelled from high school after dozens of absences and several brash scenes.

After that, she'd been homeschooled, finally graduating, much to her family's relief. Caitlyn had reluctantly agreed to go to college, only to drop out in her first semester and never return. She'd run even wilder after that, drinking far too much and dating a whole line of horrible men and following them into a ton of new mistakes and reproaches. That was Caitlyn for you. Over the years, she'd caused her family untold agony, which had made her parents idolize Luke even more, despite Rose's warnings.

Rose worried just as much about Luke as she did about Caitlyn. When life came too easily to a person, they never learned how to recover, how to get back on their feet when they were knocked down by fate's cruel hand. Luke didn't yet know how unfair life could be, even to the kind. Just take her beloved bookstore, for example.

She sighed. The past few years had been hard on her business and, even with Luke's improvements, it seemed to be growing weaker by the month. She and the bookshop had endured a lot together: financial crises, Covid, crazy interest rates, supply chain issues, the rising cost of books—the list was endless. The downward slide that had begun years ago had become ingrained in some way, and she couldn't seem to stop it. If things kept going the way they were, she'd have to close the bookshop for good. Her heart ached at the thought.

"Rose?"

She realized Kat was watching her, a worried expression on her face.

Rose forced a smile. "Sorry. I was just thinking about something. I—" The computer beeped and flashed a message. "What's wrong with this thing now? I wasn't even ringing anything up."

"Is it giving you problems?"

"It's always giving me problems. I don't know why I let Luke talk me into getting rid of my old method of sales. Why fix something that isn't broken? The old register worked just fine."

"Maybe he thought it would be easier to track your stock."

"Easier?" Rose scoffed. "Easier for the IRS to audit me, perhaps. And who would want to help them?" As if she cared about them. Let them just try to decipher her spidery handwriting in her huge, blotted ledgers, and let them wade through the wads upon wads of receipts that she kept stuffed in old shoeboxes stacked in the back of her office. *Ha! If they come for me, they'll face months if not years of work, and they'll deserve it, too.*

Kat watched as Rose punched random buttons until the computer stopped flashing the error message. "How's Lulu doing? Mom and I saw Luke in the park with her last week. They were having such a good time."

"Lulu's doing great." Better, probably, than the rest of them. "It's nice having her and Luke here. We'd originally hoped that my son and his wife—Luke and Caitlyn's parents—would take care of Lulu, but my son has health issues, so Luke stepped in."

"Health issues? I hope he's okay."

"He fell and needs a hip replacement. He'll be fine in a few months, but his wife has back problems, so neither of them are in any shape to chase around a kindergartner. Luke's young, so it's not too much work for him."

"I can tell he's fond of her. Mom said that Luke's a computer genius." Kat waited, an expectant look on her face.

Rose wondered why Kat was asking so many questions. As much as Rose liked the younger woman, Kat was still a Carter and not to be trusted, especially with a guy as softhearted as Luke. *I should put an end to this.* "It might not be a lot of work for Luke to watch after Lulu now . . ." Rose paused for effect. "But it will be."

Kat's smiled faltered. "Will be?"

"Lulu's only six right now. Things will change once she's in her preteens, which will be here before you know it. Luke's only got four years or so before the moods, the fights, and the yelling arrive."

"Wow. I didn't think about that. But . . . won't Lulu be back with her mother by then?"

"Lord, no. Lulu's mom made a long series of reckless decisions, so she'll be in jail for at least ten years."

"Ten years? Goodness. What did she do?"

"Stupid things." Using a falsified résumé written by her then boyfriend, who was a real loser with a criminal history longer than he was tall, Caitlyn had gotten a job working in the accounting office of a used-car lot in Asheville. For almost a year, with her boyfriend's encouragement, she'd filed hundreds of fake invoices that had funneled almost a million dollars into their bank account. Rose was so embarrassed by her granddaughter's inexcusable actions that she refused to talk about it outside of the family. "Luke has made a huge commitment in taking on Lulu and her future bad moods."

"It was nice of him to do it."

"Very. It cost him dearly, too, although he'd never admit that to anyone. He had to quit his job once he got custody of Lulu, as he could no longer travel. From what I can tell, he's just working part-time now. He must be pretty much broke, too." And seemed perfectly okay with that, which annoyed Rose to death. She'd tried to bring up his money situation numerous times now, but Luke just smiled and said he was "fine." *Fine, indeed. Fine with being broke. What's wrong with that boy?*

Kat eyed Rose uneasily. "Maybe he's doing better than you think. It's a gig economy, so it's possible that—"

"He's as broke as a rotten board. Sold his sports car just a month ago. Some sort of BMW convertible. Gave up his pricey condo in Atlanta, too, after he and Lulu moved in with me. Fortunately, I have plenty of room in that huge old house of mine for the both of them."

She loved her old house, too. Some people looked down on older structures, with their uneven floors and less than perfectly sealed windows. But she knew that old homes were better made than new ones. The wood they used was the lovely, stretchy kind, which bounced as one walked and yet never split or gave way like newer, modern wood. *They always go for the cheaper products nowadays. Everything is faster and worse.*

She needed to become more like the old wood when it came to

her own life and stretch a bit when she dealt with Luke. It would take some work, but she supposed she could manage it over time.

"Poor Luke." Kat slowly backed away from the counter.

Rose hid a smile. "Yeah, he has it rough. I help him when I can, but it's brutal, raising a kid alone. He gets up at six a.m. every morning to get her ready for school. He has to pack up her lunch, get her dressed and fed—which can be a fight—and then he takes her to school. Every afternoon, he either picks her up or waits for her at her bus stop and walks her here, and then there's homework and dinner and a bath. Whew!" Rose grabbed a brochure for Ava's teashop from the pile by the register and fanned herself. "I made myself tired, and I haven't even finished describing a whole day yet."

"Poor guy was really thrown into the deep end, wasn't he?" Kat glanced at her wristwatch. "I should go. I—"

"Honestly, I wish Luke would just find himself a nice woman, settle down, and get married."

Kat blinked. "Married?"

"For Lulu's sake. He needs someone smart and has a good job so it won't matter if he works or not, and— Wait one minute." Rose looked Kat up and down. "Maybe you—"

"Whoops! Look at the time!" Kat was almost at the door. "I'd better get back to work. Tell Luke good luck for me. Bye!" The bell on the door jangled as it closed behind her.

Well. That hadn't taken anywhere near as long as Rose had thought it would. *Good.* Now that she'd gotten rid of Luke's potential distraction, she'd get out the last carton of books and have them ready for him to shelve when he got back here with Lulu.

Rose checked to make sure the unfinished crossword puzzle was well hidden under a stack of flyers, and then left her cane behind the counter and reached for one of the carts. As she wheeled it down the aisle toward the storage room, a thought struck her.

Maybe what she'd said to Kat hadn't been far off the mark.

Perhaps marriage *was* the answer to Luke's problems. It would be lovely for both her and Lulu if Luke found a nice girl, someone who would accept his lackluster approach to life.

Not Kat Carter, whose mother had had so many divorces that it almost took two hands to count them out. But someone nice, someone kind, someone from a good family, and someone who loved children, too. And yes, someone with a promising career who could support the whole family.

But who? Rose wasn't sure who in Dove Pond could meet those criteria, but as she started opening cartons in the storage room, she began to make a mental list.

Luke might not be interested in bettering his life, but she was, and she wouldn't stop until she'd done it.

CHAPTER 5

LUKE

"No," Lulu said for the umpteenth time since Luke had picked her up from school.

"Yes." He bent down so that his face was even with hers. "Homework first. Snack after."

Lulu crossed her arms and stared at the ceiling, rebellion in every line of her little body.

He stifled a sigh and said, "Tell you what. Once you finish your homework, we'll walk over to Ava's tearoom together and you can pick out your snack by yourself."

Lulu's blue eyes met his. "I can have anything?"

"Well . . . not a whole cake, no. But a cupcake? A donut? A scone? One of those? Yes."

She pursed her lips, her blue gaze considering. After a moment, she gave a deep, deep sigh and said in a morose tone, "Okay. Homework first."

She sounded so sad that he had to hide his laugh behind a cough. She was so funny, this little bundle of outrage, charm, curiosity, and—on occasion—fury. In her red flannel shirt, blue jeans, and dirty tennis shoes, her dark and curly hair contrasting with her blue, blue eyes, she was just about the cutest thing he'd ever seen.

He got Lulu situated at the small table in the children's reading area, and then dropped her book bag on the counter beside Grandma Rose. He caught sight of a filled book cart off to one side. "I told you I'd unpack the boxes of new stock. You'll hurt your back."

Grandma Rose got busy adding bookmarks to the small plastic stand beside the register. "If you want to help, stock the shelves."

"I already did that this morning."

"Then do it again."

He had to fight the urge to blurt out "No!" the way Lulu had just done. But he figured that stocking already overstocked shelves would be better than just standing around. The truth was, as much as he loved his grandmother and Lulu, he was bored. And not just a little bored, but deeply, wildly, painfully so. He missed the high-intensity pace of his old job, which he'd had to leave to take up residence here. Life in Dove Pond was charming but slow, and while it was good for Lulu, he chafed at the lack of challenge. Lately, the most exciting thing in his life was his quest to finish the *New York Times* crossword puzzle in thirty minutes or less, which was sad, to say the least.

Grandma Rose pointed to the cart. "The more stock on the shelves, the more people will buy."

That summed up his grandmother's entire business plan. Stack, stash, and stuff more books on every shelf and surface to make more money. Sadly, when he'd arrived, her accounts—handwritten in indecipherable handwriting in ancient-looking ledgers—had been proof of how ineffective a strategy that was.

Luke had been shocked when he'd realized how badly her business was actually doing. It was why he'd agreed to work in her bookstore a few hours every day. Not only did he want to give her a break now and then, but—unbeknownst to her—he was also trying to figure out how to get her much-loved business back in the black.

He shot her a curious look. "By the way, what did you say to Kat? She passed us on the sidewalk and was almost running. She looked like a bear was chasing her."

"She had some sort of meeting. Something to do with her real estate office and—I don't remember now. I—" Rose bent down, and Luke realized that Lulu was now standing up on her tiptoes so she could see over the edge of the counter.

Rose smiled. "How was your day, sweetheart?"

Lulu's rosebud mouth pressed into a full pout. "I didn't get to go on the playground."

"Why not?"

Lulu's pout deepened.

Luke slanted a frown down at Lulu. "Tell Grandma Rose what happened."

Rose raised her eyebrows. "Something happened?"

Lulu crossed her arms over her chest, her chin in the air. "No."

Rose frowned. "Lulu?"

The little girl didn't answer, instead slowly sinking back behind the counter until she was out of her great-grandmother's sight.

Luke bent down, picked up Lulu, and set her on the counter. "Tell Grandma Rose why you were in time-out when I came to pick you up."

The little girl sniffed. "I'm too tired to talk right now."

"Secrets are burdens, Lulu." Grandma Rose reached over to smooth the little girl's messy curls. "Even small ones can grow if you don't air them out."

Lulu sighed and her little shoulders drooped. "I had to spend time in time-out today because I told Macie Lewis she was a . . ." Lulu's gaze flickered up to Luke and then away.

Rose leaned closer. "She was a what?"

Lulu's cheeks pinkened, and she heaved a huge sigh before saying in a sharp tone, "A horse's butt!"

Rose immediately turned away, choking on her own laughter. After a moment, she managed to say, "Why did you call poor Macie Lewis such a thing?"

That was a good question, one Luke hadn't been able to get his niece to answer. He eyed her now.

She picked up a nearby stack of bookmarks and pretended to straighten them, sending a good half of them tumbling to the ground.

Grandma Rose picked them up. "Well?"

Lulu fisted her hands in her lap, her bottom lip poked way out. "Fine. I'll tell you. She stole my boyfriend."

"Your *what*?" Luke didn't know whether to laugh or cry.

Grandma Rose snorted at his shocked expression. "You didn't know it started this early, did you?"

He blinked slowly, trying to grasp this new, horrifying revelation. "Lulu, I— You have a boyfriend in *kindergarten*?"

Lulu nodded, her curls bouncing. "He gave me his lunch box and everything."

"He gave you— Why would he do that?"

Lulu sent him an impatient look. "When you have a girlfriend, you have to give them nice things. So Grant gave me his lunch box."

Grandma Rose's gaze sharpened. "Lulu, when Grant gave you his lunch box, did you give him something?"

Lulu nodded.

"What did you give him?" Luke asked.

"The house key."

Luke almost choked. "*What?* You gave our house key to a kid we don't even know?"

"Yes," Lulu said proudly, but then her smile disappeared and her eyebrows lowered. "But then Macie made him give it back."

"Do you have it now?"

Lulu reached into her pocket and fished out a key on a pink-and-silver pompom key chain.

"Thank goodness." Luke took it from her. "I'll hang on to that for now." Maybe forever, if this was an indication of how things were going to be.

Grandma Rose's mouth quivered. "Good to know our key is no longer in the pocket of some stranger, even one too short to reach the lock."

Lulu scowled. "He's not a stranger. He's my boyfriend." She caught herself and winced. "*Was* my boyfriend."

"Oh Lord." Luke rubbed his eyes, oddly exhausted by the implications of the whole thing. He thought he had a good eight years or more before he had to deal with stuff like this. "Lulu, we gave you that house key for emergencies. You can't give it to anyone else, not even a boyfriend. Do you understand?"

Lulu crossed her arms and turned her shoulder to him, her mouth in a mulish line. "I don't want to talk about this anymore. I need to do my homework." Muttering about how unfair everyone was, Lulu slid off the counter to the floor and then stomped back to her table. She dropped into her seat and started digging out some papers and a pencil from her backpack.

Grandma Rose gave Luke a sympathetic pat on the shoulder. "You've been dismissed."

Luke said in a morose tone, "I just realized that the term 'happy hour' was created by parents as a way to make it between 'after school' and 'bedtime.'"

"Most likely." Grandma Rose glanced over at Lulu, whose bottom lip couldn't have poked out any farther. "Young lady, you'd better hope no bird flies by and sees that perch!"

Lulu gave a huge, noisy sigh before, with an air similar to that of someone who'd been sentenced to life breaking rocks, starting her homework.

Luke watched her, still stunned. "I don't know what to do with her sometimes."

"Just love her. The rest will come out in the wash."

"I wish it was that easy. She's driving me batty." He rubbed his stiff neck. "I guess I'll finish putting out the new stock." He sent his grandmother a sharp look. "In the future, leave the boxes to me."

Grandma Rose snorted. "I'm not a weakling, you know. But if it'll make you feel better, I'll refrain from picking up the bigger ones."

But he knew better. His grandmother was a strong, wonderful, and uniquely stubborn woman. She'd been alone since the death of her husband almost twenty years ago and had made it seem as if she didn't need help, but he knew otherwise. In fact, he was worried—

The bell rang as the door opened and a blond woman walked into the store, a leather satchel hanging from one shoulder. She wore brown ankle boots, and a heavy calf-length cardigan covered her springlike dress, which made sense as it was unusually warm today. She had a young air about her, like a college student even, but upon looking closer, Luke realized she was older than she appeared at first glance.

She paused and stood just inside the bookshop, her sharp gaze moving here and there, flickering over him, and then moving on as if he were nothing more than another bookshelf.

That stung for some reason.

"Good afternoon, Dr. Dove!" Grandma Rose called.

Doctor? Interesting. He leaned closer to Grandma Rose and asked in a low tone, "'Doctor' as in 'How's your heart?' or 'doctor' as in 'Please write your name on your essay before you turn it in'?"

"Essay," Grandma Rose answered shortly.

Luke rolled the cart to a nearby aisle and started shelving books. He knew a little about the Dove family, as did everyone who'd ever lived, or had relatives, in their town. His grandmother, bless her heart, even believed the local lore that the Dove sisters all had special "abilities" that would have labeled them "witches" in any other town. *Ha. As if.*

Still, whoever this woman was, she didn't look like any witch or college professor he'd ever seen. She was tiny, for one thing—the top of her head would barely reach his shoulder. *She's a little witch if she's a witch at all.* She was also far prettier than any witch or professor had a right to be.

She sent him a flat look as if she'd heard his thoughts, and neatly tucked a strand of her shoulder-length hair behind her ear as she went to the counter. "Good afternoon, Rose."

"Good to see you again, Tay." Grandma Rose settled on her stool. "How was the Sarah Addison Allen book?"

Ah. Her name is Tay. She's short and snappy, too. It suits her.

Tay smiled now. "I read it last night. I was hoping you could show me her backlist. I even brought you a bribe." She set a small bag on the counter.

"Oho," Grandma Rose said. "What do we have here?"

"Orange scones from my sister Ava's bakery. Ella made them."

Grandma Rose opened the bag, a lovely orange scent lifting through the air. "I'll enjoy these. Mighty nice of you to bring them."

It was nice. Luke pushed the cart closer to the counter. "You're Tay Dove, aren't you? Hi. I'm Luke Day."

Tay cast him a brief glance and flashed a quick, I'm-really-busy-here smile. "Nice to meet you."

"You, too. What brings you here today?" He waved at the books still stacked on the cart. "If you're looking for something to read, I can make some recommendations."

"Thanks, but I came to see your grandmother." Tay's smile flattened from "polite" to "goodbye," and she turned so that her shoulder tilted toward him in a way that reminded him instantly of Lulu.

He'd been dismissed. That was twice today. Oddly enough, it stung just as bad when done by a stranger.

Tay smiled at Grandma Rose. "I opened that tin my sisters found hidden in the old fireplace surround."

Grandma Rose's face brightened. "What was in it?"

Interested despite himself, Luke moved a little closer, leaving the cart behind.

"There were a number of items, including love letters written by William Day to Sarafina Dove."

"*What?*" Grandma Rose's eyes widened. "Are you sure?"

Luke knew all about William Day, although not from Grandma Rose. She never spoke about the infamous train robbery, saying there were more worthy members of their family who deserved attention. But Luke's parents, who'd grown up here in Dove Pond, had shared the tale whenever they were talking about the town's colorful history.

"I'm positive. I—" Tay glanced toward Luke and—finding his gaze on her—turned her back even more in his direction as she bent closer to Grandma Rose. "I *saw* him."

Luke frowned and moved a little closer, the cart now forgotten.

Grandma Rose's eyes had widened. "You saw him with your—you know."

Tay nodded.

What in the heck is a "you know"? He wanted to ask, but it was already annoyingly obvious he wasn't allowed to be a part of this discussion.

Grandma Rose said, "I see. Where are these letters?"

"At the house. I'll make copies and bring you the originals for your archives."

"Thank you. Are you certain they were written by William Day?" At Tay's nod, Grandma Rose sighed. "I guess you think you've found quite a treasure, then."

"I know, right?" Tay's voice had softened, excitement warming it. "No one knew William was in love with Sarafina, yet these letters prove it. That's why I'm here today. Ms. Rose, may I have access to the Day family archives? It's obvious their story had a tragic end, as William died in prison right after Sarafina moved to New York. Plus we know she eventually married someone else, but maybe something in the archives will let us know just how close they were."

Grandma Rose frowned. "I don't like bringing attention to William Day. He was a scoundrel, and I'd rather not have people discussing him any more than necessary."

"But he loved Sarafina. That's new information, and it needs further research. We don't know how they met, or when they fell in love, or—" Tay waved her hands. "So many things."

"You'd be wasting your time looking through the archives. I'm familiar with every piece of paper back there, and I don't recall seeing a single item that indicated the two of them even knew each other." Grandma Rose's face had folded into a deep scowl. "There are better members of the Day family to write about than William. There's Lilah Day, who was a nurse in World War II and lived a life of excitement and drama. Or Mander Jonah Day, who ran a ship against the British blockade during the Revolutionary War. There was Tallulah Day, too, who traveled all through Egypt and found not one but three hidden tombs. She kept great records, that one."

"I'm sure she did, but I'm researching Sarafina Dove, and there was a connection between her and William. That's the only reason I'm looking into him."

Grandma Rose's mouth thinned. "You're opening a can of worms. Some of the gold from that robbery was never found. People tore this town apart looking for it, too. We don't need a bunch of gold-seekers here now, either."

"No, but I—"

"They would do it; you know they would. You can't trust people."

A flicker of frustration crossed Tay's face. But she seemed to mentally shake herself, and—after an obvious struggle—she managed an awkward laugh. "I don't want this town deluged by fools looking for gold any more than you do. Fortunately, there's no need to make any decisions now, so just think about it. I can promise you this, though—I have no intention of portraying William Day in a negative light. In fact . . . Rose, why don't you read the letters before you decide? They may change your mind."

"Why?"

"They're beautiful letters. He was so eloquent that you can feel how real his emotions were. If people read them, they wouldn't think of him as just a train robber."

Grandma Rose looked slightly mollified, although not completely convinced. "I'll read them, but I'm not promising you anything."

Tay's smile was instant. "Perfect. There's one more thing I wanted to ask. I'd like to see the old copies of the *Dove Pond Register.* Your grandfather and father were both editors, and Sarah mentioned that you have copies of every issue they dealt with. Would you mind if I looked through them? The ones stored in the library basement are in horrible shape and most are unreadable. Sarah says yours are much better preserved."

Luke found himself nodding. It was a grand compliment when the town librarian admitted your family-kept copies were better than the town's official ones.

Grandma Rose's expression had softened, too. "There's almost a hundred years' worth of *Dove Pond Registers* in the back room. My husband insisted we keep the room humidity and temperature controlled to protect our stock, which was good for the newspaper archives, too."

Luke spoke up. "We should scan those, just in case."

Grandma Rose cast him an exasperated look. "Why bother? We've kept them in that storage room for years and years, and they're well preserved."

"It wouldn't hurt to have a digital copy. You never know what could happen. You could have a roof leak or a fire or a—"

"Stop being so negative. They'll be just fine where they are."

He had to fight the urge to argue with her. Grandma Rose had refused to consider getting a specially sized scanner to accommodate the newspapers, saying it would be too expensive. Luke hadn't yet told her that he'd already ordered one, as he planned on pretending he was borrowing it from a friend.

Grandma Rose was odd when it came to talking about her financial situation, getting riled up over the slightest mention, so he'd learned to avoid such conversations. Whenever he saw that she or the bookshop needed something, he would just buy it and explain it away with "I already had one" or "I borrowed it." Either of those worked.

"You're welcome to look through the *Registers*," Grandma Rose told Tay. "I keep them with the family archives in the storage office.

You can't take anything from the premises, of course, but there's an old desk back there that you can use while you're here."

"That would be great. I won't need access right away, as I'm going through the town archives first. That'll take a week or two, at least."

"Come by whenever you're ready." Grandma Rose climbed off her stool and picked up her cane. "I'll show you where the *Registers* are kept and how they're organized."

Luke pushed the cart out of the way. "I'll do it."

"Nonsense," Grandma Rose said. "Ms. Tay here is on a deadline. She rarely stays in Dove Pond long, anyway, so I might as well be the one to take on the task."

She rarely stays in Dove Pond? What does that have to do with anything? He started to ask, when Lulu called for him to sharpen her pencil.

He stifled a sigh. He normally enjoyed helping Lulu, but today bigger things beckoned, like a coolly intriguing college professor and a real-life mystery featuring one of his own ancestors. It had been months since he'd heard anything so interesting. Three, in fact.

He watched as Grandma Rose and Tay went into the storage room. Hmm. Maybe Tay could use some help with her research. He got the impression she was the prickly and proud type, somewhat like his grandmother. Fortunately, he had some experience in dealing with just such women. *If I prove myself useful in some way, she just may let me join in her search.*

It was worth a shot. Besides, what else did he have to do?

Smiling once again, he went to sharpen Lulu's pencil.

CHAPTER 6

TAY

Tay closed the folder, pushed her glasses back on her head, and pressed her hands over her tired, hot eyes. The Dove Pond Library was a lovely place, filled to the brim with rows and rows of well-organized but dusty, vanilla-scented books. What made the library so valuable to Tay wasn't the books that sat on the shelves, but rather what was stored in the climate-controlled basement. It was there, in boxes, large file cabinets, and several old display cases, that the historical records for their town sat.

For the past week and a half, she'd made the library conference room her research center. Once she was through using the town archives, she'd wrap things up here and head over to Rose's Bookstore and start going through the old *Registers*. Rose hadn't exactly agreed to give Tay access to the Day family archives, but Tay was hopeful it would happen when the time came.

For now, she had other things to do. She sighed and pulled her notebook closer. Over the past few days, she'd touched William Day's love letters again and again, hoping to find more clues. It was heartbreaking work. Whatever his situation was, it was frighteningly dismal. The darkness of his jail cell, and the sense of hopelessness that dripped from his dirty stub of a pencil, shook her to her core.

And yet, she'd found no answers to her many questions. "None," Tay muttered. She propped her elbows on either side of her notebook and dropped her head into her hands, staring down at her scribbled notes. *What am I missing?*

"More coffee?"

Tay looked up to find Sarah standing in the doorway, a pot of coffee in her hand. Tay forced a smile and slid her mug closer to the edge of the table. "I can always use more coffee." Sadly, the coffee Sarah made in the library break room was more like hot water with a faint hint of coffee flavor than actual coffee. *Ava warned me to get some from her tearoom or to stop by the Moonlight for a to-go cup. I should have listened.*

Sarah refilled Tay's mug and then disappeared for a brief moment to replace the pot in the break room before returning with her own mug. She sat down beside Tay and looked at the papers, folders, and notebooks spread over the table. The tin—and its contents—occupied the center. "Find anything interesting today?"

"No. I should look through the town's expense records during this time and make a list of—"

Sarah stifled a yawn. At Tay's amused look, she flushed. "Sorry. I love hearing about your research, but I didn't get to sleep until late because I was reading. You were up then, too. I saw your light shining under your bedroom door when I got up for a glass of water."

Tay shrugged. "I haven't been sleeping well lately."

Sarah's gaze moved over Tay's face, a hint of worry in her eyes.

"Is everything okay? You've been really quiet since you got home. Unusually so."

"I'm just busy with this stuff. It's absorbing." *Thank goodness for that.* Focusing on Sarafina had been a welcome relief. "You should get more sleep. Remember when you used to sleep in class because you'd stayed up too late reading the night before?"

"You'd think I'd be over that, wouldn't you? But you know how I am once I get started on a book." Sarah's gaze flickered over Tay's face. "What's keeping you up? Did you get another book from Rose's?"

"Not yet. I'm sure it's just jet lag."

"Still?"

Tay didn't like that Sarah looked worried. *The last thing I need right now is a bunch of questions.*

"Hey, when's your book about the Casket Letters coming out? You worked on that project for a long time."

That was a good question. As Richard had signed the contract with the publisher before she joined, she'd left him in charge of the details. But Sarah was right, and the publication date should have been decided. "I'll have to ask about that."

Her gaze cut to the small but expensive fountain pen that rested on a stack of papers. She should get rid of that thing even if it *was* the only present he'd given her.

Sarah raised her eyebrows. "You finished the book, though, right?"

Tay nodded. "Yup. My colleague should have edited it by now." Come to think of it, she should have heard from Richard about the edits, too. She'd spent long months collecting the research for that book, assembling it into chapters, and writing it one careful line at a time. After that, she'd sent the finished chapters to Richard for his input, which had mainly been tiny, inconsequential line edits.

Their original agreement had been quite different. They were supposed to research and write the book together, authoring alter-nate chapters, but Richard kept prevaricating and missing deadlines. He'd blamed it on his responsibilities as department chair until she'd finally stepped in and completed his portion of the book as well as her own.

I shouldn't have done that. It almost physically hurt to think about it. She was now one of the millions of wronged women in the world, those who had trusted someone based on nothing more than how they'd made a person feel special. *I hate that. I hate that that's all it took.*

"Tay?"

Tay looked up to find Sarah eyeing her with a concerned look. Determined to turn her sister's attention elsewhere, Tay pushed her notebook to one side. "Want to see what I've figured out so far about the mysterious man in the photos?"

Sarah perked up. "Yes, please!"

Tay dug through some of the papers on her desk and handed one to her sister. "I'm fairly certain he is one of the men on this list."

"Why do you think that?"

"The man wasn't wearing a ring, so most likely he was a bachelor. Second, we know Sarafina moved away when she nineteen, but her hair was up in the photographs, so the photos were taken between the years of 1894 and 1897. I checked the census records, and there were a total of twenty-one single men in Dove Pond around that time."

Sarah's eyebrows rose. "Census records? I never thought of those."

"They're online and are pretty easy to find. They're very useful."

"How handy!" Sarah looked at the list. "What will you do with this?"

"I'm going to Rose's tomorrow to start looking through the old *Registers* for mentions of these guys. I'll also check the church records to see if their families went to the same church as Sarafina's. That sort of thing."

Sarah handed the list back to Tay. "I'm impressed."

Tay smiled. "Thanks."

"I hate that you have to go to Rose's to access the old *Registers*. We should have had a complete set of those newspapers in the town archives here. But back in the day, they stored them in the town hall basement in open boxes right beside the heating system, which caused a huge humidity problem, so they got moldy."

"That almost hurts to hear about."

"Records like that are precious. Thank goodness for the Day archives." Sarah eyed the stack of letters from William. "I saw you touching these earlier. Did you find out anything new?"

"No," Tay admitted. "His emotions are stealing every bit of emotional bandwidth I have." And she didn't have a lot left.

Sarah sighed. "You can see from his letters that he loved her and was a truly caring man. How did he become a train robber?"

"I don't know, but I'm determined to find out."

"You will," Sarah said firmly. "No one does research as well as you."

"Yay, me!" Tay said with her fist in the air.

Sarah laughed and then glanced at her watch. "Oh! I need to go." She stood. "I wish I could stay and help, but I've got to get everything ready for our Silent Book Club."

"*Silent* Book Club?"

"People bring their books, or check out a new one, and then they sit and read together."

"That sounds sorta fun. In a way."

"I love it! The membership has been growing every month, too." Sarah eyed the stacks of materials that filled the conference table and grimaced. "We were hoping you could do your work at Momma's old desk, but it's way too small. You need more space than I realized."

"This place is fine."

"Not really. Tay, I'm sorry to even mention this, but there are meetings scheduled for this conference room."

Great. Just great. "Starting when?"

"It's getting close to budget season, so soon. I think the first meeting is in two days."

Tay hid a wince. "I'll find someplace else to work. No problem." Which was a lie. To be honest, it wasn't the small size of Momma's desk that had made Tay move here. Every time one of her sisters walked through the house, they'd invite themselves in and start asking questions, as Sarah had just done.

Tay wasn't used to that. She worked alone. Sometimes, when she was in Boston, days would go by when she wouldn't speak to anyone except the occasional food delivery driver, and that was usually by text.

She liked being alone. Or she thought she had until, unexpectedly, she hadn't. When she looked back on the time of her Greatest Mistake, she couldn't help but wonder if her own self-imposed loneliness hadn't made her an obvious, and willing, target.

Her chest tightened, and she forced herself to shove away her unpleasant thoughts. She should be good at doing that, but somehow, it seemed that each time she tried, her thoughts got heavier. She suddenly realized that Sarah was still staring at her with that same concerned gaze.

"Tay, are you—"

"Hello, you two!" Ava appeared, carrying two bags marked MOONLIGHT CAFÉ. She placed them on the table. "Making progress?"

Sarah pulled her gaze from Tay and sent Ava a smile. "Tay's already got a lead on that guy in the photographs."

"Maybe." Tay started replacing papers into their folders. "We'll see if it checks out."

"Give yourself some time," Ava said. "You've been in town less than two weeks."

Sarah added, "Tay made a list of all the bachelors from that time period."

"Can you do that for the present time? But just the bachelors with rizz. Kat and Zoe would love that." Ava slid one of the bags to Tay. "I brought you lunch. Sarah said you didn't eat at all yesterday."

Sarah eyed the other bag. "Is that for me?"

"No."

Sarah's shoulders fell. "Well, darn."

Ava grinned and sat down. She opened the other bag and pulled out a plastic container and a fork. "I saw Blake at the Moonlight. He ordered the meatloaf platter for you and said you should come as soon as possible, or it'll get cold. He looked pretty cute in his sheriff uniform."

Tay reached for her food. "I've always had a soft spot for a man in uniform."

"So does Sarah."

Sarah sniffed and said stiffly, "I don't need to stay here and be teased."

Tay opened her box. "Mm. Turkey, avocado, and bacon. Ava, I owe you a lunch."

"Yes, you do." Ava waved Sarah toward the door. "Begone! I saw your assistant librarian on my way in. She said she'd already had her lunch, so she can cover the desk while you're out."

Sarah picked up her coffee. "I guess I'm not of much use here." She headed for the door. "Tay, call me if you need anything else from the town archives."

"Will do."

As the door closed behind Sarah, Ava turned to Tay. "It's funny, but I was thinking that the man in the photos was William. Don't you think so?"

Tay shook her head. "According to the newspaper articles I've read about the train robbery, William had dark hair. Plus, he was left-handed. I saw that when I touched his letters. The man in the photos is right-handed."

"How can you tell?"

"His pocket watch. It's in his right pocket." She reached for the open tin and pulled out the photo. "See the chain?"

"Oh wow. I didn't even notice that." Ava looked back at Tay. "How did you get the names of the town bachelors?"

"From the 1900 census. They did a census every ten years, but the one from 1890—which was the one I needed—was destroyed in a fire in Washington, DC, in 1921. So I got copies of the later one and correlated it with the birth records from both the Baptist and Methodist churches here in town."

Ava's gaze moved over the neat stacks of folders that sat on the table. "You're really, *really* good at this. I didn't know they did censuses that far back."

"The first one was done in 1790, which is why researchers love them. Of course, they're not always accurate, but they can give you a good start." Tay picked up her sandwich. "Sadly, there were a lot more bachelors in Dove Pond back in the day than I expected—twenty-one, in fact. I was hoping there would only be a dozen or so, but a lot of people had huge families back then."

"Farmers."

"Yup. Someone had to plow those fields." Tay took a bite of her sandwich.

"Did you find anything else?"

"Not yet." Tay wiped some mayonnaise off her fingers with her napkin. "To be honest, since Sarafina loved codes, I was hoping there might be one in William Day's letters, but I couldn't find any indication that's true."

"Secret codes." Ava shook her head. "That's some Batgirl stuff right there. And to think that Sarafina used to live here, near Bat Cave, North Carolina, too. Coincidence? I think not."

Tay grinned. Bat Cave was a little town not far from them that had been named after a deep cave where a large number of bats lived. They were easily disturbed, though, and thus a bit of a nuisance to the surrounding area. "Remember when Dad used to tell us that was the original Bat Cave, created by Bruce Wayne and staffed by Alfred?"

Ava scowled. "I got in a fight at school with one of the Coopers over that story. I should never have believed Dad."

"He told a lot of stories. His version of things was always more fun than the original, too."

Ava picked up one of her potato chips. "I loved his stories. I think that's why all of us are such big readers." She frowned. "I wonder why Sarafina loved puzzles so much?"

"That's a good question. I have no idea, really." Tay took another bite of her sandwich and eyed her special red folder, which held a copy of every letter Sarafina had sent that had a secret code or puzzle of some sort in it. "I'm hoping to figure that out as we uncover her history. We know so little about her formative years, and yet who we are as adults is set in place during that time."

Tay knew this was true for herself. Her three older sisters had always been super outgoing, and the center of their high school social scene. Tay had always been included in their invitations out and such, so she'd never had to develop her own network of friends. That had all changed when she'd left for college on her own. For the first time, she'd been without the support of her more outgoing sisters, and socializing suddenly hadn't been so easy.

At first, she'd been agonizingly lonely, but once she'd dived into her studies, she'd found that she didn't have time for friends. Or that's what she told herself, anyway.

Still, in some ways, being alone had been a positive experience. Having faked being an extrovert for so long before going to college, she'd rediscovered the pure pleasure of a silent and sometimes nearly empty library. The peacefulness of eating without having to make conversation. The tranquility of sinking into her research efforts without having to apologize or make time for someone else.

She hadn't been a complete hermit, of course. She'd been friendly to her fellow professors and had stayed in close touch with her sisters. But forming deeper relationships beyond the acquaintance level had held no appeal and always seemed to cause complications she didn't want to deal with. *Like with Richard.*

Tay's sandwich suddenly lost all taste.

"Tay? Are you okay? You look upset."

"I'm fine." Tay forced a smile, shut the food container, and returned it to its bag. "I was just thinking about the *Dove Pond Register.* That's a treasure trove of information and could tell me all sorts of things about the guys on this list. Those old papers mention every birth, death, town meeting, social event—they're amazing."

Ava wiped her hands on her napkin and tossed it into her empty sandwich box. "I'm surprised our mayor hasn't gotten those records scanned yet. Grace is a huge fan of modernization. You should see how she's updated the accounting system."

Grace Parker was the town mayor and was married to one of Sarah's oldest friends, Trav, who had always lived next door to the Doves. "It's a huge and complex job to archive historical documents. Every piece of paper has to be individually analyzed, categorized, and then preserved before you can even begin the scanning process. It's very labor-intensive and thus expensive."

"If it's expensive, then that explains why Grace hasn't had it done." Ava picked up the closest folder and flipped through it. "Who's Lucy? She wrote a lot of letters to Sarafina."

"That's her daughter. Lucy was a character in her own right. She was in France when World War II started, and she refused to leave despite the danger. She was married to a French doctor, and she stayed with him in Paris even after the line collapsed. They were trapped there for months. They made good use of their time, though, and helped a lot of people escape."

"It sounds as if Lucy was a brave soul. That makes me wonder why she didn't follow the clues in that poem Sarafina left her that would have exposed that family secret."

"Whenever people asked her about it, Lucy said she didn't want to know anything about her parents' past. She loved her mother and father as they were."

"You were going to make copies of that poem for us." Ava looked at the piles of folders. "Where is it?"

"Sorry, I forgot about that. I'll do it today." Tay got up and went to one of the stacks at the far end of the conference table. She'd just pulled a folder from the pile when a *tap-tap-tap* in the hallway heralded the arrival of a round Black woman dressed in a bright blue suit and hat, holding a cane in one hand.

Tay immediately dropped the folder and went to hug the woman. "Aunt Jo!"

"Don't look surprised. You had to know I'd come." Aunt Jo held Tay at arm's length and scowled. "You've been home for a while now and haven't come to see me once."

"Sorry. I had a rental car, but I had to turn it in, so I've had to get rides from my sisters." To be honest, Tay had thought about visiting Aunt Jo but had decided against it, as the woman had a way of seeing right through a person. She'd been their mother's best friend since forever, so Tay and her sisters were close to her, and her hugs always made Tay think of Christmas and cake.

"I shouldn't look at you, much less hug you, but you know how considerate and sweet I am." Aunt Jo patted Tay's cheek and then sank into a nearby seat and hung her cane on the edge of the table.

"How did you know I'd be here?"

"Oh, a little bird told me."

"Ella?" Ava asked.

"Might have been. Ran into her at the hardware store this morning. She was picking up some flowerpots. Said she was going to make some flower cupcakes for TikTok and thought it would be fun to set them in a real flowerpot like actual flowers." Aunt Jo shook her head. "I swear but I can't believe that girl gets paid to do things like that."

"Me neither," Ava admitted.

Tay agreed. "She makes a lot of money doing it, too, judging by that new car she just bought."

"BMWs are expensive," Aunt Jo said. "Personally, I'd rather have a convertible coupe than a boring sedan, but no one asked me, so—" She sniffed her disapproval.

Tay handed the folder to Ava and then sat back down. "What brings you to town?"

"You. And I needed some dog food for Moon Pie, too."

"Where is Moon Pie?"

"He fell asleep on a dog bed when I was at the Mayhew's pet store buying him an antler chew. Ed said I should just leave him and pick him up when I headed home." Aunt Jo patted the closest stack of folders. "What's in all of these? Anything interesting?"

"This is all research I've done on Sarafina Dove."

"It's pretty cool stuff." Ava pointed to the folder that was now open in front of her. "This is a poem Sarafina wrote to her daughter, Lucy, that holds a key to a family secret. It's written in some sort of code."

"Code?" Aunt Jo leaned forward, her bright gaze scanning the paper. "Be still, my heart!"

Tay had to smile. Everyone loved secret codes. No wonder they'd been used by marketers through the ages, who'd printed them on everything from Popsicle sticks to cereal boxes. "Historians have tried for years to figure out what Sarafina's last coded poem to her daughter could mean, but no one's done it yet."

"Historians are too busy thinking about facts." Aunt Jo scooted her chair closer, the legs scraping on the tile floor. "What sort of family secret is this poem supposed to reveal?"

"No one knows," Tay said.

Aunt Jo looked unimpressed. "If I did all the hard work it takes to write a decent secret code, or riddle, or whatever you call it, then I'd make darn sure there was a treasure of some sort at the end of it as a reward."

"Sarafina told her daughter it hid a family secret, not a family treasure."

"Humph. I'm going to pretend it leads to a real treasure. I bet I can solve it, too. I do the *New York Times* crossword every day, and I only have to look up one, maybe two, answers at best."

Ava snorted. "I've seen you do those at my tearoom, Aunt Jo. You look up more than two answers. It's more like a dozen or mor—"

"Give me that poem!" Aunt Jo snatched it out of Ava's hand. "I'll read it out loud. Let's see what we can come up with." She cleared her throat. "*A truth, a name, a number. Told to all yet soon mentioned by none. So he carved it in stone where peace meets up in oaken silence.*"

Aunt Jo placed the poem back on the table, pursed her lips, and stared at the ceiling, immediately lost in thought.

"Hmm." Ava settled deeper into her chair, crossed her arms, and tilted her head to one side.

Tay repeated the poem to herself, her lips moving silently. She knew it by heart and hadn't been able to make heads nor tails of the thing even after hundreds of attempts. Still, it didn't hurt to try again, so she pulled her notebook closer and picked up a pen just in case inspiration struck.

The silence lengthened and time ticked by while Aunt Jo frowned at the ceiling and Ava, her arm now propped on the table, rested her chin in her palm, her eyebrows lowered.

Tay realized she wasn't thinking about the poem at all but was instead doodling a circle over and over and over. She sighed and set down her pen. "I still can't figure it out."

"Me neither." Aunt Jo handed the poem back to Ava. "It's too hard for me."

"I got nothing," Ava agreed, dropping it back into the folder and sliding it toward Tay. "We apparently aren't very good at puzzles, any of us."

Tay had to laugh as she put the folder back on the stack. "I told you it was unsolvable. At least for now."

"What a pity," Aunt Jo said, looking disappointed. "Maybe it's just a poem and not a riddle at all."

"There's something there, I'm sure of it," Tay said. "That's how Sarafina did things. One time, she and her husband sent out invitations to their annual Christmas party with a poem like this. Their parties were swanky and attended by all the best people, too. But the poem didn't give a time or date or even a place. Everyone had to figure it out or they wouldn't know where or when to show up. It was the talk of the season."

"That's a fun idea," Ava said. "Did a lot of people show up?"

"About half of them, although there's evidence there was a lot of information-sharing going on. Her codes and riddles were never easy."

Aunt Jo rubbed her hands together. "Between that hidden tin box Dylan found in your house and this poem-puzzle-code, I feel like I'm in a real-life Agatha Christie novel."

Ava chuckled. "It's a pity Sarafina typed her poem, or Tay could touch it and get an idea of what she meant."

"Wait a minute," Aunt Jo said. "They had typewriters back then?"

Tay nodded. "The first one was patented in the 1860s. I saw one of the early models, and it had treadles on it, like an old sewing machine."

"No way!" Ava shook her head. "I can't imagine that. But I guess it's a good thing it was invented."

"They opened new career opportunities for women, once the business world began to utilize them."

Aunt Jo cut a curious glance at Tay. "I take it you've already touched the letters from the tin. Your sisters shared them with me, and I have to say, they just about broke my heart."

"Oh!" Ava said brightly. "You don't know. Tay says the author was William Day."

"What? The train robber?"

"None other," Tay said. "And he was deeply in love with Sarafina."

"I'd say so, judging by those letters." Aunt Jo picked up the photograph of Sarafina and the mysterious boy. "This is from the tin, too. I've seen it. Is this Sarafina?"

"Yes, but I'm not sure who the man is yet."

Aunt Jo tapped the photograph with one red-painted nail. "If you ask me, I'd say that man's a McCleary."

Ava and Tay exchanged a look.

Tay moved a little closer to Aunt Jo. "Why do you think he's a McCleary?"

"Just look at him. Tall, with thin blond hair, a weak chin, and narrow eyes. Slightly handsome blond weasels, the lot of them. Although they look less handsome and more weaselly as they age."

Ava reached over and picked up Tay's list of bachelors. "There's a McCleary on here."

Aunt Jo handed the photograph to Tay. "The last of the McClearys died when you were little, so the line is gone, but once you've seen that kind of face, you don't forget it."

Tay looked at the photo. That was the funny thing about history. No matter the number of written records, oral histories sometimes preserved the more important details. "If you're sure this man is a McCleary, then it must be Marcus McCleary. He was on my list of bachelors."

"He was one of the train robbers, too," Aunt Jo added.

"What?" Ava's eyes couldn't have gotten any bigger.

"Oh my gosh, Aunt Jo, you're right!" Tay put the photograph down and leaned over to find a purple folder. "I saw his name in the articles about the trial. Several of them said that, at the time of the robbery, he and William were as close as brothers."

Tay pulled out an article and showed it to Ava. "Aunt Jo, I'm so glad you came by!"

Aunt Jo beamed at them both. "I'm glad I could help. I have to say, though, I wonder why McCleary and Sarafina are in those photographs together?"

Ava put down the article she'd been reading. "Maybe it was a classic love triangle. Maybe both McCleary and William Day had a thing for Sarafina."

"Nonsense." Aunt Jo reclaimed the photograph Tay had set down and then dug the others out of the tin. "Look at their body language. You can tell they're not fond of each other."

Tay took the photograph from Aunt Jo and looked at it. "But she looks so happy in this one photograph."

"Yes, but she's not looking at McCleary, is she? She's looking directly at the camera. No one looks at a camera like she wants to kiss it."

Tay dropped back in her chair. "She's looking at the photographer."

"Exactly. And if she and William Day were an item, then he must be the one taking that photograph."

Ava looked at Tay. "Was William Day a photographer?"

"I don't know." Tay's mind raced through the intriguing possibilities. "Cameras were around then, but they weren't common. That's one more thing for me to research." It was a new lead, and an exciting one. Even though she was sitting down, she gave an excited shimmy. "Aunt Jo, you've given me a lot to think about."

"Of course I have." Aunt Jo picked up her cane and stood. "Now that I've saved the day yet again, I'm going to leave you two alone here to do whatever it is you were doing before I arrived, and head on down to Ava's Pink Magnolia Tearoom. I've earned myself a cupcake for all the hard work I've done here."

"Do you need a ride home?" Ava asked. Aunt Jo had given up driving when her eyesight grew weak, and the people in town took turns taking her wherever she needed to go.

"No, thank you. Nate Stevens from the hardware store has already promised to drive me and Moon Pie home. I'm to call him whenever we're ready."

Tay got up and gave Aunt Jo a fond hug. "You're the best. Thanks for helping out."

"My pleasure." Aunt Jo smiled warmly. "It's nice to be useful now and then."

"Let me walk you outside."

"I wouldn't say no to that." Aunt Jo waved goodbye to Ava and then took Tay's arm. They walked quietly through the library, but the second they stepped outside into the brisk wind, Aunt Jo pulled her coat closer and faced Tay. "So? What happened to send you racing home? And don't tell me 'nothing,' because I can see in your eyes that it was something."

Tay tried to hold her smile and failed. Trust Aunt Jo to be able to see through her. She always did. "I've had some trouble."

"I knew it." Aunt Jo slipped her hand into the crook of Tay's arm and led her to the bench in front of the park. "Sit."

"But I—"

Aunt Jo pushed Tay onto the bench and then sat beside her. "Out with it."

This was the very reason Tay had avoided visiting Aunt Jo. "It's been a difficult few months. Things—something—hit me harder than I expected, and I'm trying to get over it."

"'Something,' huh? I don't suppose that 'something' has two legs and needs a good wallop up the side of his head?"

Tay had to laugh. "That would describe him exactly. I dated this guy and he cheated on me and—I hate to admit this, but I can't seem to let it go. I try not to think about it, but I do. It's worse at night. If I don't distract myself, I end up lying there awake, thinking and thinking and—"

"Whoa! Easy, child. You're spinning up. I can see it."

"Sorry. I should be over this, as it's been months. He was a complete and total jerk, too. I should be furious, but I can't seem to find the energy for it. I'm—" *Lost.* Emotion clogged her throat, and she swiped a tear from her cheek.

Aunt Jo folded her into a swift hug, wrapping her in a momentary cocoon of warmth and love.

Tay soaked it in and then gently untangled herself. "I needed that hug."

"Let me know if you need another. I have extras and carry them with me." Aunt Jo took Tay's hand between her own. "Meanwhile, stop being so hard on yourself. You haven't had much practice with this sort of thing, so of course you're not good at it. Want to know who probably is? Your sister Ella. Before she met Gray, she went through men the way most women go through breath mints."

"She used to date a lot." A crazy lot, in fact.

"But not you." Aunt Jo squeezed her hand and then let her go. "You're like me. You've always been careful who you got tangled up with. Maybe a little too much."

"I wasn't careful this time. There were so many signs he wasn't being honest with me, and I ignored them all."

"So you were too trusting. Now you know that. Next time, you won't be."

Tay sighed. Maybe that was true. "I don't think there will be a next time."

"Oh, I don't know about that." Aunt Jo patted Tay's knee. "Wait before you swear off men altogether. You never know what will happen."

Tay didn't think she'd ever trust again. *Not for a long, long time, anyway.* Still, she managed a smile. "Thanks for listening."

"That's what I'm here for. I promised your momma when she got sick that I'd be here for you girls. Call me if you need to talk some more. Don't make me chase you down like a stray cat. If you do, I'll send Moon Pie after you, and you know how bilious he gets when he's been forced outside in the cold."

"Your bulldog has a legendary temper," Tay said, although, to be honest, Moon Pie was most famous for his chunkiness and his loud snoring. Still, if it made Aunt Jo happy to think he was a protective sort of dog rather than a napmeister, Tay wasn't about to argue. "I'll call. I promise."

"Good. That's what I want to hear. I'll be waiting." She gave Tay another big smile, and they both stood. "Are you sure you don't want a nice cup of tea before you go back to your work?"

"I'll take you up on that another day."

"Fine then. I'd best be off. Take care, sweetheart." She waved and then headed in the direction of Ava's tearoom.

Tay waited until she saw Aunt Jo go inside; then she went back to the conference room.

Ava was already collecting her things. She shot Tay a regretful look. "I wish I had more time to help, but I've got a lot going on today."

"Heading to the tearoom?"

"No. I've got that covered, but we're expecting a truckload of mulch at the warehouse for my landscaping company, and I need to be there to unlock the door."

"Of course. Sarah needs this room for some meetings, so I'm going to go ahead and get everything boxed back up. Tomorrow, I'm going to Rose's Bookstore to start going through the old *Registers*."

"I'm glad you have some new leads. That's something."

"It's a start. There's so much I want to know about Sarafina and William, things we might never figure out. How they met, how long they were in love, how the train robbery occurred, and—oh, so many things." She probably wouldn't figure out the answer to every last question she had, of course. Research was funny like that. A good researcher might find assorted bits of information about important historical persons or events, but without a direct eyewitness account, those finds often ignited a firestorm of new questions rather than offering up answers.

As Ava pulled on her coat, her gaze moved over the stacks of folders and papers that surrounded Tay. "It's going to take you a long time to pack this up. I'll stop by later if I can."

"Thanks, but I've got it. You'd better get going." Tay waved goodbye to Ava and then set to work.

She had a lot more research to do, but she was starting to feel hopeful. Now she had a new name to research, too, that of Marcus McCleary. *One more name, one more clue.*

Still, from what she'd seen so far, she felt that William Day was the key to unlocking the secret of how a young girl from their tiny town became such a fierce and intrepid reporter. All Tay had to do was follow the clues, wherever they led.

Come on, good luck. You owe me this much, at least.

CHAPTER 7

SARAFINA

APRIL 16, 1895

From the moment you first smiled at me, I liked you because of your generous heart and strong spirit. But you rapidly became more than a friend, and I grew to love you in spite of the fact that I knew from the very beginning we could never be more than that, no matter how much I wished it otherwise. . . .

—letter from William Day to Sarafina Dove

Sarafina's favorite place in the whole world was the pond. It was really a lake, but it had been called Dove Pond since the day it had been discovered by one of her ancestors almost two hundred years ago. They'd loved the little lake so well that they'd even named the town after it.

For her, the pond was a beautiful, magical place. The water was deep and blue and so clear that, near the shoreline, she could see the rocks that lined the bottom. One side of the pond abutted a steep cliff that was carved out of a mountain. The other side was delightfully level and rimmed with weeping willows. Her special fishing spot was tucked inside a little cove lined with those trees, and she loved how they trailed their leaves across the glassy water, leaving delicate swirls in the mirrorlike surface. When one added in the convenient fallen log that sat along the pond's bank, right where the water was the deepest, it wasn't just a perfect place to fish, but it was also a perfect place to write or spend time with a friend.

On this particular Tuesday afternoon, after paying out the necessary breadcrumbs to the birds Aunt Emily Anne had sent to spy, Sarafina took her fishing pole from where she kept it tucked behind the log, dug an earthworm out of the soft dirt under a tree, and baited her hook. Then she set her line and rested the pole against the fallen log. Satisfied, she settled down with her notebook and a pencil to work on the latest chapter of her new story.

She was writing a series for her aunts called "Pauline Xavier, Egyptian Explorer Extraordinaire." Her aunts were currently obsessed with all things Egyptian and scoured the national newspapers for stories about newly discovered tombs and artifacts, so they especially loved the new story.

As Sarafina wrote, an early spring breeze rose, stirring up the damp forest scent and ruffling the edges of her skirts. She tried to stay focused on her writing, but she couldn't help but stop every few seconds and glance back at the path.

Over the past year, every Tuesday afternoon, no matter the weather, she and William Day had met here by the pond. They'd even managed a few Friday afternoons when her aunts had extra meetings with their sewing circle because of various holidays.

Sarafina found him fascinating. He was surprisingly funny for such an intense person. But over their visits, she'd found that he was also one of the most polite, cautious, and thoughtful people she'd ever met, which was both delightful and frustrating. It was delightful, as it proved that he was a far better person than the horrid gossips in their town would admit. But it was frustrating because that same caution and politeness kept him from overstepping the boundaries of their friendship, something she was increasingly hoping he'd do.

To be honest, she wished he were a bit more of a masher, as Aunt Jane called men who flirted. Aunt Jane didn't care for mashers, while it seemed that Aunt Em had a soft spot for them.

Sarafina sighed and tilted her face up to where the sun flickered through the branches overhead. She wasn't sure when it started, but lately just seeing William made her heart flutter. She supposed she shouldn't be surprised that she didn't know the exact date her feelings of admiration and friendship had started changing to something more. It wasn't as if the first signs of spring showed up all at once, either. You sort of noticed those changes little by little until, suddenly, there it was.

She was pretty sure she liked him far more than he liked her. Enough that—unbeknownst to her aunts—she had used her allowance to purchase a tin of Dr. Campbell's Lilly White Wafers. According to the ad Sarafina had read in the back of *The Ladies' World*, the wafers would give her a dazzling, glowing complexion that would draw admiring gazes from men everywhere. She didn't care about men everywhere, just William. But so far, he didn't seem to notice her suddenly bright complexion.

A rustling noise from the pathway announced his arrival. Sarafina's heart gave an excited jump, and she had to force herself to lock her gaze on her notebook.

"Hi." William sat on the patch of grass beside her feet and leaned against the log next to her, his shoulder just inches from her knee. He reached into his pocket and pulled out his ever-present book, this time a dime novel called *The Ranch*. He glanced at her notebook. "I see you're still writing that Egyptian adventure for your aunts. Let me read it when you're done."

"Of course," she said, hoping her hot cheeks weren't as pink as they felt. *This isn't the glow I was hoping for.* Suddenly awkward, she dropped her gaze to his book and noticed a folded slip of newsprint tucked between the pages. "What's that?"

He pulled it out and handed it to her. "A news article from the *Daily Tribune* about the new advances in photography. My uncle wants me to start helping out in the photography studio that's over the *Register* office."

William's uncle was the owner and editor of the *Dove Pond Register*. A bluff, hearty man with a broad, kind smile, he was quite influential in town, sponsoring many events and sitting on a number of town committees. After the death of William's father, Edward had tried to assist his nephew when he could, getting him odd jobs here and there.

According to William, although his uncle owned many businesses—the *Register*, the photography studio, and the local grist mill among them—he was generous to a fault, giving away money he'd have been better off keeping, and often hiring people with no qualifications who ended up costing him far more than they earned him. Which was why he wasn't nearly as wealthy as people thought him to be.

William slid the article back into his book. "Uncle Edward wants me to start taking photographs of local people who—" A rustle from the pathway drew William's attention, and he turned and stared for a moment before turning back around and resuming his reclined post against the log. "Must have been the breeze. I thought it might be Marcus."

Of the few friends William had, he was closest to Marcus McCleary. Sarafina didn't like the man. He drank frequently, had a sad tendency to gamble, and got into so many fistfights that it was painfully obvious to her, at least, that he was most likely the cause of the majority of them. Worse than all of that, though, was that he always expected William to bail him out of whatever trouble he had gotten into, which was far too frequently for Sarafina's peace of mind. Twice, in fact, just in the last three months, William had shown up with black eyes and bruises from rescuing his friend from men he owed money to. It was heartbreaking for her to see.

She shot William a curious look. "Why did you invite him here?"

"He's avoiding town right now."

Sarafina's suspicions were confirmed by that answer. "He's in trouble again."

"Probably." William rested his open book on his knee, his gaze moving to the rippling water beneath the trees.

Sarafina so wanted to ask him why he stayed friends with such a troublemaker, but she felt she'd be encroaching too much into his personal life. Her gaze followed his to the pond. "You should take a photograph of this."

He slanted a look up at her. "Maybe I could take some of you. Just for practice."

All he had to do was ask. She pretended not to be excited. "Just let me know when and where."

"Thank you." He smiled and then settled down to read his book.

She pulled her notebook closer and readied her pencil, but her gaze kept drifting back to him. She wanted to ask him so many things. Why did he keep meeting her here? Did he enjoy their afternoons together as much as she did? Did he, perhaps, like her? He never missed a single Tuesday, so that was something.

Wasn't it?

She sighed. There was nothing for it, she supposed, except to wait until he was ready to tell her all the things she was dying to know.

If there was one thing she was good at other than writing stories to amuse her aunts, it was waiting. When she thought about it, she was waiting for a lot of things. She was waiting to figure out what life had in store for her. Waiting to find her place. Waiting to figure out what would make her happy, and what didn't. And now, she was waiting for William Day to move forward with their friendship.

William lowered his book and nodded toward her fishing pole. "Have you caught anything today?"

"Not yet, but I only got here a short time ago."

"You will." He said it so easily that she had to hide a smile. "You're very good at fishing."

Why did people find that so unusual? Even her own aunts, who'd raised her since she was a baby, called her ability to fish "an unfortunate gift."

She eyed the cork bobber on her line and made sure it was still undisturbed, and then turned her face to the sun, letting the late-afternoon warmth wash over her. The quiet, the peacefulness of the water, the feel of the sun-warmed ground beneath her feet, William's gratifying presence—there was no better place to be.

William had picked up his book once more, and she saw that the cover featured a cowboy shooting a rifle from the back of a wildly galloping horse. "Do you like that story?"

"It's very good. A lot of people might think Westerns are just about shoot-outs, but there's more to them. In this one, there's a rancher who's about to lose his property to the bank. He's married and has two children, so he's willing to fight hard to keep his land. There's a curse, too, made by an old crone who lives down by the railroad who's—" He caught himself and sent her a self-conscious look. "It sounds ridiculous when I describe it, but it doesn't seem that way when I read it."

"It doesn't sound ridiculous at all. I like books with curses or mysteries or hidden treasures. Things like that. Maybe I can borrow it when you're done?"

"I'll bring it back next week. You can take it home then."

"Thank you." The breeze fluttered the edge of her notebook paper, and she laid her hand on it. "My aunt Jane says that books are fresh air for the stale soul."

"That's a good way to put it." He leaned against the log, his broad shoulder once again just inches from her skirts.

They were quiet after that. She wrote a little here and there and waited for a fish to bite while he read. It was cozy and natural, and she couldn't help but sigh happily. Twice she got a nibble on her line, but nothing more than that. In the quiet, she could hear the hum of bees, the occasional splash of a fish, and the rustle of the pages of William's book.

She took the opportunity to steal a few glances at him. She'd never before thought to use the word *beautiful* to describe a man, but in this instance, it was accurate. He had thick black hair that curled over his collar and made her think of a swashbuckling pirate, and ridiculously long lashes that framed his astonishingly blue eyes. Added to that, he was powerfully built, as if he could carry her without straining a bit or—

"Stop staring." He didn't look up as he turned the page, as if her actions weren't worth his attention.

She flushed and returned her gaze to her fishing line. "Sorry. I was just wondering about something."

"What?" he prompted when she didn't add more.

"Why are you friends with Marcus McCleary?" Despite her earlier determination to stay away from such a sensitive topic, the words bubbled out.

His blue gaze darkened. "Why shouldn't I be friends with him?"

The stiffness in his voice made her pause, but only for a moment.

She'd said the words aloud and was committed now. "Being seen with Marcus . . . doesn't that make people talk more? He's always in trouble, and he always drags you into it, too."

William's gaze dropped back to his book and he absently traced the line of the horse on the cover. "Marcus was good to me when most people wouldn't even say hello when I walked down the street. He's never had much, either, but he's always shared it with me. He's my friend because he's never treated me as if I was a nobody."

She couldn't ignore the bitterness in William's voice. "You're somebody. Don't let anyone tell you otherwise. Just as I don't let people tell me girls can't fish."

He cut her a sharp glance, and recognizing her sincerity, some of the stiffness left his expression. "You're the first girl I've ever seen fish."

"Mrs. Barton does it."

A smile flashed across his face. "Does she?"

"And so do Mrs. Boone, Miss Felton, *and* Mrs. Wheaton." To be truthful, both Mrs. Wheaton and Mrs. Boone just accompanied their husbands while they fished, sitting nearby and reading, much as William was doing. But now and again, if their husbands baited their hooks for them, they would cast a line.

"You're a strange girl, Sarafina Dove."

She was oddly pleased at the seriousness of his words. "Strange is better than boring. According to the drivel I'm being taught at Miss LaFont's, women aren't supposed to be interesting in any way. They aren't supposed to have opinions or thoughts. They're supposed to act the same, do the same, think the same, *be* the same. Heavens to Betsy but I hate that school, and Miss LaFont, too, and I—" She made a face. "You know how I feel about it. I've complained about it a lot."

"You've mentioned it a time or two," he admitted with an amused look. "You said your father decided you should go because he didn't like the way your aunts have been raising you."

"My father is good at one thing: telling everyone what they're doing wrong. I hate it when he blames my aunts for my shortcomings, saying I'm ill-mannered and too outspoken."

"Those aren't your shortcomings, Sarafina. They're his."

Sarafina's face warmed. "I wish I could tell him that. I'd—" Her line jiggled, yanking her attention back to it. *A fish!* She grabbed the rod and twitched it up, setting the hook into the fish's mouth.

She jumped up and hurried to the pond's edge, grabbed the line, and pulled the fish to the bank. "There!" She grinned down at the big, beautiful bass now flopping at her feet on a flat rock.

William came to watch. "That's a big fish."

"I'm lucky the line held." Usually, when she caught a fish, she'd unhook it and release it back into the water. But today, she held it up. "Want to take this home? It would make a fine dinner."

He started to say no, so she added, "Please. I can't take it with me, as I can't tell my aunts where I've been."

William's gaze moved to the fish, a slow grin crossing his face. "Thank you."

"I'll run a stringer line here in the shallows to hold it until you're ready to leave." She put her foot over the fishing line so the flopping fish couldn't escape back into the pond and then reached behind the tree where she stored her rod. She removed a small leather pouch and opened it. Inside sat two more hooks, a bobbin of braided thread, and a rusty knife. She cut a length of the braid, picked up the fish, and removed the hook. Then she slipped the braid through the fish's mouth and gills, tied it off, and attached the free end to a limb near the water's edge. She carefully released the fish back into the water. It immediately tried to swim away but was held there in the shallows by the line.

She rinsed her hands in the pond and then dried them on some moss before putting everything back into the pouch and returning it to its hiding place.

William was now sitting on the log, watching her, his elbows resting on his knees. "That'll taste good with the potatoes I got today for carrying feed at the stables."

She knew then that before she'd caught this fish, he would have had only potatoes for dinner. She thought about the beef stew Aunt Em had waiting and a pang of guilt hit her. She sometimes forgot how different their lives were. She had her aunts, and although he wasn't often present, her father still contributed to her welfare. But William lived on his own and had since he'd been a troubled teen.

She'd be sure to bring him some cookies next week, or maybe some jelly biscuits the next time Aunt Emily Anne made them. Sarafina glanced up at the sky and realized the sun was sinking fast. "I should get going." She put away her fishing rod, careful to wedge the tip of the hook into the wood so it wouldn't get rusty.

"Be careful getting home."

"You too," she said. "I hope McCleary comes soon. It'll get dark before long."

"He'll come." And yet a flicker of worry crossed William's face.

She realized he felt responsible for his friend. "Maybe he's just late."

William didn't look convinced. "Maybe. He's impulsive and sometimes makes stupid decisions. I—" He seemed to think he'd said too much, because his mouth thinned and he shook his head.

Overhead, the crow cawed, and she glanced up at it, scowling.

"You'd better go. He doesn't seem to want more breadcrumbs."

That was true. She stuck her tongue out at the crow and then turned back to William. "I'll see you next week."

He flashed that half smile that made her feel a little dizzy. "I'll bring some breadcrumbs, too. Just in case."

"That would be handy. Until Tuesday, then."

She waved and then made her way to the path. As she stepped onto it, she glanced back. He wasn't reading as she'd expected, but was once again staring out over the pond, his book still open on his lap, the sun glinting blue off his dark hair.

Next week, he'd return, and when he did, she'd be here waiting. With an extra little lift to her step, she turned back toward the path and headed home.

CHAPTER 8

LUKE

Luke pushed open the door to Ava Dove's new Pink Magnolia Tearoom, glad to get out of the chilly morning breeze, and glanced at the big clock hanging on the back wall. He had fifteen minutes before he was due at the bookstore for his morning shift. Fifteen minutes to find an answer to the question that had been clanging around in his head since he'd listened in on Tay Dove's discussion with his grandmother in the bookshop almost two weeks ago.

It was a pity he didn't know Tay well enough to ask her directly, but there was more than one way to skin a cat. Which was why he was here, looking for Tay's sister Ava.

He'd spent a considerable amount of time between that conversation and now quietly quizzing those people in town who were close with the Doves. While he hadn't found the answer to his question, he had discovered several useful facts about the intriguing Taylor Dove. First of all, he'd learned from Marian, the waitress at the Moonlight Café, that Tay was tight with her sister Cara, who lived in New York and ran some sort of elite matchmaking service. He'd also discovered from Zoe Bell, the vice president of the local bank, that Tay was deeply respected in her field and was on the cusp of having a book published about something called the "Casket Letters," whatever those were. And Kat Carter had offered a tantalizing tidbit, sharing that Tay was not only deeply private, but was known to be very stubborn. Kat had gone so far as to say that it would "take dynamite" to get Tay to budge once she'd made up her mind about something.

Which meant he couldn't fool around if he wanted to kill his boredom by joining Tay's intriguing research project. *I'll have one shot at it, and if I blow it, that could be it.*

He sighed and looked around the tearoom, a little surprised at how busy it already was. Ava was taking orders at the register, and she waved on seeing him. He waved back and then looked for a seat, realizing that the only ones open were at the counter. He headed that way and noticed that Dylan Fraser sat there. He was a tall and lanky man with auburn hair and beard who was dressed in his usual contractor wear of jeans and flannel. Dylan seemed to be a quasi-permanent fixture here at Ava's, which wasn't surprising, as he was dating her.

On his other side sat Blake McIntyre, the town sheriff and Sarah's boyfriend, his name neatly inscribed on the brass name tag of his uniform. Blake was a fit individual and had a no-nonsense attitude that probably made him very good at his job.

Luke slipped onto the stool beside Dylan. "Good morning."

"G'morning," Dylan said.

"Hi, Luke." Blake pulled his breakfast sandwich a little closer. "Your grandma let you out of the bookshop?"

"For a while." Luke waved at Ava to let her know he was ready to order whenever she had a minute.

Dylan grinned over his coffee at Blake. "Come on. Luke's running that bookshop. His grandma just doesn't know it yet."

Luke snorted. "As if she'd let such a thing happen." As sleepy and boring as this little town was, it was an amazingly friendly place. The high-rise in Atlanta where he used to live had over five hundred people within its walls, and he'd known the names of only three people—one of the security guards, the afternoon porter who delivered packages, and one of his neighbors who kept accidentally putting his condo number on her UPS orders.

That hadn't really bothered him, though. His biggest problem wasn't a lack of friends, but boredom. It was funny, but he couldn't remember a moment of his life when he didn't feel at least a little bored. From his first memories to now, the world around him had seemed as if it were a play being performed on a stage in front of him, while he was the sole member of a very uninterested audience.

School had been easy for him, even college. He'd majored in computer security, hoping for a challenge, but then he'd sailed through his classes without expending much effort. After college, he'd been swamped with job offers, but none of them had caught his interest, and, unwilling to sign up permanently for a job he didn't love, he'd ended up doing contract work at a friend's tech security firm just to help the guy out. It had worked out well, and Luke had made a mint and been able to travel to the four corners of the globe, too, which had been fun and had kept him too busy to get bored.

Now, though, because of Lulu, he'd changed his consulting business model from full-time to part-time. He worked whenever, however, and in whatever way he wanted. That also gave him—and now Lulu—a steady, although reduced, income stream. For a lot of people, that would have been the ultimate freedom, but although he loved Lulu to death, Luke couldn't help but feel as if he was caught in his own version of *Groundhog Day*.

Which was why Tay's research seemed so intriguing. He enjoyed figuring things out, whether it was something small like solving the weekly crossword or something big like successfully programming a hacker-proof firewall. Solving a real-life mystery would be the ultimate mind challenge.

"How's your grandmother?" Blake asked. "She looked spry when I saw her marching around town yesterday afternoon."

Luke had to grin. "She does march, doesn't she? Even with her cane."

"She's must have been a general in a past life." Dylan took a sip of his coffee. "Blake, I hate to mention this, but our man Luke here is a loser. He thinks he's too good to join a premier softball team like the Dove Ponders."

"Sheesh," Luke muttered. "Not that again." For the past two weeks, Dylan had been after Luke to join the local softball team for the Town-to-Town Softball Jamboree.

Blake eyed Luke now. "Too good, are you?"

Luke shrugged. "I'm still thinking about it." That wasn't exactly a lie. He did think about it, but only because he was glad he wasn't going to do it. Softball was about as interesting as watching mud dry, and he wanted no part of it.

"Sign up," Blake ordered. "We only have five positions left."

Which meant they were desperate, as they'd had six positions open two weeks ago. "I'd like to, but right now, I'm overwhelmed with work and Lulu's schedule."

"You'll be sorry if you miss out." Blake took a tentative sip of the coffee steaming on the counter in front him and grimaced. "Whew, that's hot."

"Stop drinking it black, then," Dylan said with a look of disgust. "Order a flat white instead." He picked up his cup and took a loud sip. "It's perfection."

Blake pulled his cup closer. "I'd rather get gored by a wild boar than order a—what did you call it? A fat bite?"

"Flat. White." Dylan turned his attention to his avocado toast.

Luke needed a cup of coffee right now and—the real reason he'd stopped by—a chance to talk with Ava about Tay. He glanced down the bar and eyed the clean, sparkling mugs lined up near the coffee maker, but Ava was busy at the register, ringing up other customers.

Dylan must have realized that Luke was trying to get Ava's attention to place an order, because he held up his cup. "Best flat white in Dove Pond—you should give it a try."

"Probably the best in the South," Luke corrected. "I have one every day, although I usually have mine around three in the afternoon."

Blake nodded wisely. "The three p.m. caffeine bump works wonders."

"Everyone needs one." Dylan leaned across the counter and called to the teenager with pink-streaked hair who'd just come in from the kitchen with a tray of clean cups. "Kristen, when you have the time, could you please bring Luke here a flat white?"

"Sure." She went right to work on it.

Dylan watched as Kristen fixed Luke's coffee, a gleam of pride in his eyes. "My daughter's a great barista, but she'll be an even better doctor once she graduates from high school."

"Medicine is a terrific field," Blake agreed. "She'll make crazy money."

Luke nodded. "She'll be able to support you in your old age."

Dylan slapped the counter and beamed. "That's my retirement

plan in a nutshell. Everyone should have at least one wealthy, able-to-diagnose-kidney-failure kid."

Luke wondered if Lulu would make a good doctor, but then remembered how she usually tore the arms off her dolls while saying coldly, "They had it coming." Maybe medicine wasn't in the cards for her. "It's good your daughter already knows what she wants to do."

"Oh, don't let Dylan fool you." Blake blew into his mug, the steam rising. "Kristen doesn't know about the whole be-a-doctor thing yet. Does she, Dylan?"

Dylan sighed. "Not yet. I just thought of it on my way home from work yesterday. I still need to convince her of it."

Luke laughed, and Blake sent Dylan an amused look. "You love shrimp. I'm surprised you didn't decide she should become a shrimp boat captain."

"She gets seasick, or I would," Dylan admitted. "Which is why, instead of captaining a shrimp boat, my daughter is now destined for medical school. She's a straight-A student already. All I have to do is explain how the profession desperately needs new prospects filled with questionable fashion sense and loads of sarcasm."

"You make it sound so easy," Luke said. "It's all I can do to keep Lulu from wearing her tutu when we visit her momma at the prison."

Blake finished the last bite of his breakfast sandwich and wiped his hands on his napkin. "How does Lulu handle those visits?"

"Better than we expected. Grandma Rose and I visit Caitlyn once a week, but we only take Lulu once a month. It was tough for her the first time or two, but honestly, Caitlyn looks better and better, so I think Lulu knows her mother is in a safer place now."

"How long is she in for?" Blake asked.

"She was sentenced to twelve years, although we expect her to get out early for good behavior, so hopefully no more than ten."

"Ten years is still a long time."

Luke had to agree. "Fortunately, although Lulu is small in size, she's big in determination and personality, so she seems to be handling it okay. My only complaint is that she delights in being contrary. I never win any arguments, even the easy ones, which sucks. Just this morning she decided I'm too tall."

Dylan shot him a surprised look. "Too tall? Really?"

"She said it hurt her neck to look up at me so I shouldn't walk standing up straight." Luke nodded a thank-you to Kristen as she set his coffee in front of him. "I can change a lot of things, but not my height, so she'll just have to get used to it."

Kristen crossed her arms and leaned against the counter. "Anything else for you guys?"

Dylan and Blake shook their heads while Luke ordered a breakfast sandwich to go and then absently watched as Kristen left to put in his order. "I can't wait for Lulu to be that age."

Dylan snorted. "Really? I have to worry about school, homework, sulking, does she work too much or not enough, boyfriends— Lord, don't get me started. It's a long list."

"I worry about all of that now. Lulu is six and she's already dating."

Blake looked stunned. "Don't you think it's a little early?"

"She didn't ask for permission." And probably never would. "I wish Lulu was a little older. Then she'd be easier to argue with. Right now, she wins every argument by throwing up her hands and saying, 'I can't deal with this right now.' And then she saunters off like she's a forty-year-old in desperate need of a fresh vodka spritzer."

Dylan laughed. "I stand corrected. Kindergartners are just as difficult as teenagers."

Blake announced, "This conversation is making me rethink the idea of having children at all. Plants are just as good, right? They freshen the air and none of them talk back."

Dylan eyed Blake up and down. "You think Sarah won't mind having plants instead of children? Can I be there when you tell her that? I'll record it and release it on the net."

"That'll trend." Grinning, Luke glanced at his watch and realized his fifteen minutes had come and gone. He looked down the countertop to where Ava was ringing up her last customer. The second she glanced his way, he waved. She stopped to pick up his breakfast sandwich where it sat waiting in the kitchen pass-through.

She placed the small white bag in front of him and then looked from him to Dylan and Blake. "What sort of trouble is going on here?"

Luke smiled and, more to irk Dylan than anything else, said, "Why, Miss Ava, you're looking as pretty as a peach this morning."

Dylan's smile disappeared, and he narrowed his eyes at Luke.

Ava laughed as she leaned against the counter. She looked a lot like Tay, but was shorter and had much longer hair, which was neatly braided. She sent him a curious look. "What's got you out and about this early? You don't normally visit until Lulu comes home from school."

"I wanted to see you. I have a question about your sister."

Dylan straightened in his seat, while Blake turned to look at him.

"Ohhh!" Ava leaned forward, her eyes bright. "Which one?"

"Taylor. I don't know her well, but I need to ask her for a favor, and I thought you might know the best way to approach her."

Dylan elbowed Blake. "This is getting interesting."

"Very," Blake agreed.

Ava patted Luke's arm. "Ignore them or they'll take it as encouragement and talk more. What favor do you want from Tay?"

"I'd like to help her with her research."

Ava's smile dimmed. "That's a tough one. My sisters and I always promise to help her, but to be honest, we're just being polite. We have no idea how to do any of the stuff she does, and the few times we did try to help, you could tell she didn't think we did it right, anyway. She hates being interrupted when she's working, too, so . . . Honestly, I don't know what to tell you. When it comes to research, Tay would rather be left alone."

That wasn't at all what he wanted to hear. "I'm really good with online searches. And I know she wants to see the Day family records, so she's going to need help getting past my grandmother."

"Getting past her?"

"Grandma Rose believes William Day is a stain on the family history and hates even hearing his name. Heck, I'm a part of the family, and I wouldn't have even known about the train robbery he took part in except for my parents. Grandma Rose won't give Tay access to the family archives if she thinks Tay's shining too bright of a light on William."

Ava looked concerned. "Can you help Tay get access to those records?"

"I can try. Grandma Rose is a bit paranoid when it comes to William. She's even worried that Tay's research could attract treasure hunters who will tear the town apart."

Blake had just dropped his napkin on his empty place, but he looked up at that. "As town sheriff, I have to agree with your grandma about the treasure hunters. What with social media and the like, things could get ugly fast."

Dylan eyed Luke over his cup of coffee. "You're quite the gentleman, offering to help Tay. Maybe later you can carry her books home from the library, too."

Ava cut him a hard look. "If you keep that up, I'll put you on our blacklist."

Dylan's smile disappeared. "You have a blacklist?"

"Yes. You can still come here, but your coffee will be lukewarm from that day on."

Dylan gripped his cup protectively. "Don't joke about my coffee."

"Who's joking?" She took a dishrag from its hook and wiped down the counter. "Luke, I hope your grandmother doesn't give Tay a hard time about those family archives."

"So do I. I'm intrigued by the whole story—the train robbery, the unknown link between our ancestors, the lost gold—all of it. It's fascinating and, to be honest, things are kind of slow for me lately."

"So it's not really Tay you're interested in." Ava seemed disappointed to discover that.

Luke hated to let her down, but the truth was the truth. "I'd like to help her with her research if I can. In return, I'll do my best to make sure she gets access to everything she needs."

"That seems like a fair bargain." A flicker of concern crossed Ava's face. "She takes her work seriously. I don't think she slept at all last night. Her light was still on this morning."

Blake frowned. "She'll wear herself out doing that."

Yet more evidence that Tay needs my help. "Ava, what's the best way to approach your sister about this? Any hints?"

"Explain to her why you want to help and what you'll do in exchange. I can't promise that'll work, but she's a pretty direct person."

"I'll try that, then." He hadn't gotten as much help as he'd hoped for, but it was a start. He glanced at the clock and then pulled out his credit card. "I should head out. Grandma Rose will have a cow if I'm late."

"Sure." Ava took his card and left.

Blake shot a curious look at Luke. "Are you so bored that research sounds like fun?"

"Secret codes sound like fun. Even Grandma Rose was intrigued when Tay mentioned them."

"Really?" Dylan asked. "I mean, Wordle is great, and a sudoku is okay if you're stuck in the dentist's office, but where's the fun in an unsolvable secret code?"

"No puzzle is unsolvable," Luke said.

"If Tay and the rest of the world's overly enthusiastic historical researchers can't figure it out, neither will you."

"Doomed to fail," Blake agreed, finishing his coffee.

Luke looked around. Where was a glass of tossable water when you needed one?

Ava returned. "Leave Luke alone, you two." She slid his credit card, the receipt, and a pen across the counter to him. "I hope you can convince Tay to let you join in. Even if you can't solve any of Sarafina's codes, Tay could use some help."

Dylan smacked Luke on the shoulder. "Awesome! You just have to expend some effort, not get results."

Blake pushed his empty coffee cup away. "Sounds too good to be true." He stood. "If you all will excuse me, I've got to get back to work. Ava, it's good to see you." He waved and headed for the door.

Ava reached over and poked Dylan in the chest. "Don't you have work to do, too?"

He sighed. "I'm being dismissed." He stood and collected his coat. "Luke, I'll see you around. Don't forget the Dove Ponders, will you? We need you on the team."

"Look for someone else, and soon."

"Nope, just keep thinking about it. Bye, y'all." He winked at Ava and left.

Luke picked up the bag holding his breakfast sandwich. "Thanks for this." He started to leave, but then stopped and turned back to Ava. "Where is Tay today?"

"In Asheville. She said she'll be going there for the next few days, as she's searching the court archives for trial transcripts. *But*, this coming Friday"—Ava stacked the empty plates and mugs—"she's meeting some friends for lunch at the Moonlight Café. I heard her making plans on the phone this morning."

"If I don't see her beforehand, I'll catch her then."

"Don't let her turn you down. She seems a little lost since she got back. Just be persistent."

"I like having you in my corner. It's nice."

Ava grinned and carried the dirty dishes to a nearby tub. "You're doing us all a favor. Tay's always been happier hidden off in a corner somewhere. That was fine when we were kids because there were so many of us that even then she was still in the middle of our madness. But now she's alone way too often, sometimes for days. Who does that?"

He sometimes did. Or used to, before he'd gotten Lulu. Programming work was like that, and apparently so was academic research. "Thanks for your help, Ava."

"Good luck. I— Oh, there's a customer. See you around." She headed to the register.

Luke left, tugging his coat closer as he stepped out into the cool morning air. It was up to him now. Somehow he had to convince Tay to let him in on the most exciting treasure hunt this town had ever seen, one with a real-life secret code to solve and the possibility of an age-old lost treasure, too. Better yet, the whole thing would happen under the supervision of a very pretty, somewhat mysterious, rumored-to-be-magic college professor. *It's like Agatha Christie meets Harry Potter.*

Grinning to himself, he headed for the bookshop, the cool and crisp air invigorating. The first thing he had to do was convince his grandmother to give Tay the key to the Day family archives, which was a difficult, if not impossible, task.

Well, he'd wanted life to get more interesting, hadn't he? Straightening his shoulders, he headed for the bookstore, ready for battle.

CHAPTER 9

ROSE

Rose crossed her arms over her chest and scowled at her grandson. "Baloney!"

"It's not baloney." Luke sat with an open box of hardbacks in front of him, a roll of stickers resting on his knee. "It's common courtesy. We should extend Tay the courtesy of—"

"Pah! I don't owe Tay Dove anything."

"It's not about *owing* her. It's about *allowing* her." He slapped a 20% OFF! on a book cover and placed it on the waiting cart. "She's a researcher. If you want fair and honest representation of William Day, then she's the best one to—"

"Fair to whom?" Rose tried to keep from raising her voice, but it was difficult. "William Day was a train robber. He's not going to get fair treatment from anyone, even a 'researcher.' "

"A train robber who wrote some beautiful letters," Luke pointed out.

Darn it, he must have watched as she read the copies of the letters Tay had sent over. Rose had hoped he hadn't seen her wipe away that tear she'd shed. "He's got more depth than I previously thought," she admitted reluctantly. "But *still*."

Luke's jaw tightened in a stubborn look. "No matter what you do, at some point, someone is going to look into that train robbery. It might not be today, but it'll happen and you know it, especially as there are still rumors that there's gold hidden somewhere in this town."

"People don't remember that anymore."

"Don't they? Whenever I mention William Day, the first thing people mention is that gold."

Rose pretended to be busy straightening the bookmarks beside the register. She'd had the same experience.

"Grandma, it's only a matter of time before some streaming service crime show runs out of modern-day material and starts digging into the past. William Day's story has it all—drama, romance, a missing treasure—it doesn't get much better than that."

"So?" she replied grumpily, although she could see his point. "What do you want me to do? Tell Tay to go ahead and yell William's name from the rooftops?"

"Better her than some cheap television producer. Don't you think Tay's a fair sort of person? Do you think she would lie? Or exaggerate William's part in the robbery?"

"No. Maybe. Oh, I don't know!" She scowled at him and considered tossing a book at his rock-hard head in the hopes of knocking some sense into it, but decided she wasn't going to waste her good stock on such a hopeless case. "What's gotten into you? You've been after me about this for more than a week now and have been especially annoying since yesterday. Let it go, will you?"

"I can't. Eventually someone is going to research the train robbery whether you let them into the archives or not. At least with Tay, you know she'll be honest. Plus, if you're nice, she might even share what she finds out."

Rose grabbed her cane from where it sat in the corner, got off the stool, and made her way to where Luke was working. "She's supposed to be writing a book about Sarafina Dove, not William Day."

"She has those love letters now. How can she write that book and not mention their relationship?" Luke fixed a cool gaze on her. "Let her see the family archives. *All* of them."

Why does he have to be so dratted specific? Rose supposed she didn't really have a choice. He was right—it was only a matter of time before the world decided to refocus on William Day's foolishness. "I'll let her see some of the archives. What's necessary, but no more." Rose showed her teeth in a not-nice smile. "Happy now?"

"No. Everyone in the family knows you edit those archives and don't share information about anything you think might hurt the Day family image."

"Do they? Then why hasn't anyone complained? I've never missed a family reunion, either, so it's not as if they haven't had the chance."

He sighed and leaned back in his chair. "No one says anything to you because they don't want you to quit and leave them with the job."

She sniffed. "They don't criticize my methods because they know I'm doing a good job."

"Right." He finished putting the SALE sticker on the last book and placed it on the cart, then he stood and picked up the empty box. "I saw you clip a ton of articles from the newspaper about Caitlyn's trial. I'll bet I can't find any of them back there." He jerked his thumb toward the archives.

Rose's face heated. "They're there," she lied.

He turned as if to go look.

She cracked her cane onto the floor in front of him, stopping him in his tracks. "As if you'd want that sort of thing lying around where just anyone could see it. It could hurt Lulu's feelings."

"Ignoring something won't make it disappear. Lulu will know what happened to her mother whether you hide those news articles or not. Heck, if I typed Caitlyn's name into a search engine right this second, everything that happened will pop right up."

That was true, Rose supposed glumly. Which, in her opinion, was why the downfall of society was imminent. People used to be able to keep their secrets, but now they posted every last darn thing they thought, did, or ate online. Rose suddenly felt tired. "I've kept every single document on the Days I've come across. I just don't keep them all in the same place."

Luke broke down the box and dropped it onto the cart. "You know I love you. And for the most part, you've done a fine job with the family records. But you can't keep hiding the stuff you don't like. It's not right."

"If people read about William Day's life of crime, they might start seeing our family as a bunch of useless, shiftless, no-good thieves. Do you want that? Plus, if Tay even mentions the missing gold, crazy people will come swarming to this town, ready to rip it apart again."

"I know that scares you." Luke frowned. "To be honest, Blake said the same thing."

"He's the town sheriff. Listen to him if you won't listen to me. If he's afraid—"

"He wasn't afraid. He just mentioned it in passing. To be honest, he was more upset I wasn't going to join the town softball team." Luke pushed the book cart out of the way and, arms crossed, leaned against the nearest bookshelf. "I don't want to cause a ruckus, but what could it hurt if you shared the archives with Tay? She's a trained researcher. And who knows? Maybe she'll discover a clue that will lead to that lost stash of gold. Then you'd find it first."

Rose had to fight not to roll her eyes. "People almost razed this town to the ground looking for that gold after the trials. If it was ever here, which I doubt, it's long gone now."

"Yes, but what if it was hidden so well that it was overlooked? What if the key to it all is right here, in the very records you won't let anyone see?"

Rose eyed her grandson carefully. Luke was livelier today than—well, ever, really. His face was flushed, while his gaze was laser-locked on her as if he expected her to sprout wings and horns. *What's going on with him? He's been here for more than three months now, and not once has he argued with this much energy about anything. The boy must have gold fever.*

She supposed it could happen to anyone. It was a pity he wasn't focused on a more realistic goal. Like a woman.

For over a week now, Rose had been mentally making a list of eligible females here in town who might make a good partner for both Luke and Lulu. Of course, not just any woman would do. It would have to be an exceptional sort if she was going to spur Luke back to life *and* help raise the precocious Lulu. But Rose was finding that Dove Pond was sadly lacking in that very thing—the type of woman who might gain the interest of her persnickety, lazy, sort-of-employed, rather unambitious grandson, someone sharp enough to whip him into shape while also helping stubborn little Lulu navigate life.

Rose caught herself wondering . . . was Tay Dove the answer?

The thought surprised Rose. *Could it be? She has potential, but from what I've heard, she's not planning on staying in town for long.* Still . . . what if Rose could convince Tay to stay here? *If I can do that, then she's as close to perfect as I'm likely to find.*

Rose thought about it some more. Tay was pretty in a sort of nerdy, glasses-wearing way, seemed kind, and was obviously smart enough to keep Luke busy for years to come. And if Lulu took a liking to Tay, *and* Rose could convince her to stay in town . . . well, that would settle matters.

Maybe, just maybe, this whole William Day situation could be parlayed into a bigger, better plan. Rose would allow—no, *encourage*—Tay Dove to use the archives and spend as much time as possible here in the bookshop. Then Rose could see for herself how both Luke and Lulu were with Tay, and how Tay dealt with them as well.

It would be a test of sorts.

Plus, it would allow Rose to keep an eye on the direction Tay's research was taking. If it looked as if her poking into William Day's life was headed in a bad direction, then Rose would just slam the lid closed on the whole thing. *This might be for the best, then.*

Aware Luke was watching her, Rose pretended to sigh and then said in a deliberately grouchy tone, "I guess I can see your point about letting Tay use the archives."

He straightened up. "You do?"

"I'll tell you what." Rose rested both hands on the top of her cane and leaned against it. "I'll give all the William Day documents to Tay. Well . . . not give, but she can look at them here at the bookshop. But *only* here at the bookshop."

"*All* the documents?"

She scowled at him. "Yes, blast you! Every last one."

"Where are they now?"

"In a secret, don't-ask location," she said bluntly. "I'll bring them back in the morning."

Relief flickered across his face. "Really?"

"Yes, but in return, I expect *you*"—she poked him in the chest—"to be present when she's looking at the archives. Every time, too. And nothing, not one scrap of paper, is to leave this place. You got that?"

He nodded, his grin instant and wide. "That's not necessary, but I'll do it."

Huh. He didn't put up much of a fuss, did he? Was that a good sign? She decided to take it as one. *One step at a time. I'll get them to spend some time together and throw Lulu into the mix and see what's what. After that . . .* Well, that was for later.

Luke flashed another grin. "Thank you. Why don't you go sit while I put these books on the New Releases table?"

She nodded. "Do that. And while you're helping Tay, if it looks as if the gold really is here in Dove Pond, find it for me. I could use it for a lot of things here in the bookstore."

It made her giddy to think about all the improvements she could make with money like that. She'd get more shelves, have the floor refinished, and paint the whole place a warm, happy yellow. She'd have the old windows reglazed so they didn't let in the cold, and— Goodness, there were a dozen things she wanted and needed.

Luke couldn't have looked more pleased as he pushed the cart past her. "I'll do my best, Grandma. That's all I can promise."

For now, that would be enough.

CHAPTER 10

TAY

"Ketchup?"

Tay took the bottle from Sarah and poured a healthy amount onto her fries. She loved fries like these, crispy on the outside and soft in the center. The Moonlight Café always did things right.

She looked around the café, with its charming red checkerboard tablecloths, mason jar water glasses, and old diner-style china. The owner, Jules Stewart, had made improvements over the years, but the café still had the same southern charm it had always had.

Sarah reached across the table and helped herself to one of Tay's fries. "By the way, did you know that Aunt Jo makes most of the baked goods here?"

"No, but I'll get some on my way out." Tay ate another fry. There was comfort in returning to a familiar place, and she needed it today. Last night had been rough, and she'd gotten less than two hours' sleep, her mind racing. Maybe it was because, after collecting the last batch of court records, she'd headed for the University of North Carolina library to look at property records. Being on a college campus had reminded her of Richard far too much.

Her imagination was out of control lately. Combined with her conversation with Aunt Jo, she was a bit shaken. She had to admit the truth—she'd lost herself in her relationship with Richard, something she'd never thought she'd do.

"Tay?"

She looked up and found Sarah regarding her with a worried look. Tay's face heated. "Sorry. I was just thinking about how to organize the trial notes I got yesterday."

Sarah put down her glass with a thump. "Stop it."

"Stop what?"

"Stop pretending." Sarah's gaze flickered over Tay's face. "Ella and Ava think I should just let you alone, but I can't, not when it's obvious you're upset. You're not sleeping, you're not really talking to anyone, and every time someone tries to—"

"Hello, everyone!" Zoe Bell appeared at their booth and slid onto the seat beside Sarah.

Relieved to be spared Sarah's questioning, Tay welcomed Zoe with a bright smile. She'd always liked Zoe, who was the vice president of First People's Bank. Black, slim, and elegant, she always looked as if she belonged on a yacht or at a swanky hotel in Paris rather than in their little town.

Zoe tossed her sunglasses onto the table, the corners of her hazel eyes crinkling as she smiled. "Good to see you two! Where are Ella and Ava? Aren't they coming?"

Sarah shot Tay a firm we-will-talk-later look before turning to Zoe. "Ava has to meet her fertilizer supplier for her greenhouses, but Ella flat-out bailed. Some cookware company contacted her social media assistant about a sponsorship, and they needed to 'talk.'"

Zoe nodded. "I'd be mad about that if I didn't know how much she's making. Who knew you could make that much cash just from posting a video."

Sarah sighed. "I guess so. Did you order?"

"I stopped by the counter before I joined you all." Zoe put her elbows on the table, clasped her hands together, and leaned forward. "So, Tay. How's the research going? Sarah says you've already uncovered some new information about Sarafina Dove."

"Lots. The letters in that tin Ava and Dylan found in the dining room prove that William Day was in love with Sarafina. I've been researching his life. I spent the past few days getting copies of the trial records."

Sarah picked up her chicken and avocado panini. "Tay's been at it since she got here. It's nice she took the time out of her research schedule to meet up with us."

"Even professors have to eat." Tay took a bite of her egg salad sandwich. "Mmm. This bread is amazing."

Sarah wiped her fingers on her napkin. "That's Aunt Jo's sourdough."

The waitress, Marian, stopped by the table. A tall, angular woman in her seventies with hair dyed bright red, she'd been a waitress at the Moonlight for as long as Tay could remember. She placed an iced tea and a large salad in front of Zoe. "Here you go." The waitress swept an experienced eye over their half-empty glasses. "I'll bring more tea. Anything else?"

"I think that'll do for now," Tay said.

"I'll be right back, then." Marian left.

Zoe picked up her fork. "From what I've heard Sarafina and William were Dove Pond's own Romeo and Juliet."

Tay agreed. "They were from different social levels. Her aunts couldn't have been happy about that relationship, even before the train robbery."

Sarah added, "I shouldn't be surprised they knew each other, as they were in this town at about the same time period. I just never thought about it."

"I didn't either," Tay admitted. "Sarafina left Dove Pond for New York in 1897 just weeks after William Day went to jail for the robbery. So far, I haven't found a direct connection as to how they met or fell in love—nothing. We may never really know, either."

"Is Sarafina mentioned in the trial records?" Sarah asked.

Tay shook her head.

"Too bad," Zoe said. "What's your next step?"

"I'm going to do another deep dive into the town records and the *Dove Pond Register*, too, and look for everything about the Day family, including William. The newspaper offers a pretty active look at the events in town—who attended what, and all that. I'll make a chart to see if there's any crossover. To be honest, I don't expect that to yield much. From what little I've seen so far, Sarafina's aunts are mentioned often, as they did a lot of charity work, but there's very little about Sarafina and almost nothing about William Day until the robbery. At least not in the few copies of the *Register* I've seen so far."

"Tay's going to look at the copies of the *Register* that Rose Day's keeping," Sarah told Zoe. "Our archives are missing quite a few copies from that time, and the issues we do have are in poor shape. I've done what I could, but the last librarian didn't understand the importance of humidity control. At least Rose does."

"Rose can be a little thorny, if you'll pardon my pun." Zoe tilted her head to one side. "What did you see when you touched William's letters?"

"He was in prison and was deeply in love with Sarafina. He seemed . . . to have given up hope. He kept telling her to go to New York without him."

"I don't suppose he mentioned the missing gold in any way."

"Not a word." Tay's phone, tucked into the satchel sitting at her feet, buzzed. She pulled it out and looked at it, surprised to see Richard's name flash across the screen.

Zoe leaned over to peer at the phone. "Who's calling you?"

Tay returned her phone to the satchel. "It's no one." But it wasn't no one. Richard would only call her if he wanted something, which made her stomach tighten. She'd gotten into this mess because she'd let him charm her into a half-assed relationship. What would keep her from doing that again?

That was what bothered her the most—that she hadn't said no to him even when she should have. She'd made that mistake over and over in their relationship. When she thought back, one of the things she hated the most was how often she'd avoided the word "no." *Of course he didn't respect me. Somehow, in this relationship, I forgot to respect myself.*

The thought was jarring, and her eyes grew damp before she could stop them. Trying to quell her emotions, she took a gulp of her iced tea.

"Hello, everyone!" Dressed in a red suit and looking ready for a date instead of lunch out with her girlfriends, Kat Carter slid into the seat beside Tay and placed her cup of coffee on the table. "Sorry I'm late. I hope you guys don't mind, but I ate with a client a half hour ago. I just came to say hi."

Zoe brightened. "What property did you sell?"

Kat smiled. "The old mill sitting at the head of Sweet Creek."

Sarah gave a happy hop. "Kat, that's huge!"

"The commission is insane. I'm going shopping when I leave here."

"Who bought it?" Zoe asked.

"An Atlanta company. They go to smaller towns that are growing and buy old, abandoned industrial buildings on the cheap and turn them into sleek, fancy condos." Kat looked around the table. "What were you all talking about? You looked serious when I got here."

"We're talking about Tay's mystery phone call," Sarah said promptly. "The one she didn't answer."

"It was spam," Tay said, hoping she sounded bored instead of bothered.

"Spam calls are the worst," Kat said. "Tay, how's the research into Sarafina going? I saw Ella at the post office yesterday, and she said you were thinking of writing a book about Sarafina and heading in 'new directions.'"

"I'll recap," Zoe offered. "The letters in that old tin found in the Dove house were love letters to Sarafina from William Day, the train robber."

Tay added, "Which raises more questions than answers, but it's a fresh direction for my research."

Kat sipped her coffee. "So Sarafina had an admirer. I'm not surprised. She did some darned cool things."

Zoe stabbed a slice of hard-boiled egg with her fork. "Tay, you'd better prepare for success. Sarah made me read that article you wrote about Shakespeare. The one where you said he didn't write all the sonnets, but only some. If you can make dry stuff like that interesting to those of us who suffered through high school lit, then you'll make a book about an exciting woman like Sarafina sell like crazy."

Sarah nodded. "You should have your book launch party here in town, too."

"Easy, people!" Tay said, trying not to laugh. "There is no book yet. I not only have to write it, but then I have to sell it to a publisher."

Kat rubbed her hands together. "I can't wait to read it. I'm going to put a copy into every thank-you basket I give to my clients."

"That's a great idea." Zoe took a sip of her iced tea. "So, Tay, tell us what you found out about the trial."

"Not much yet, as I haven't read all the transcripts. I know it was covered by most of the major newspapers and that the trial was held about two weeks after the robbery."

Sarah looked up from her sandwich. "Two weeks? I wouldn't think they would have been ready for a trial that fast."

"Things were different back then, plus all three of the defendants were seen at the scene of the crime, and one of them confessed and was a witness against the other two. It was considered an open-and-shut case." Tay pushed her half-eaten sandwich aside and pulled a thick folder out of her satchel and placed it on the table. "These are articles about the train robbery. The story made the front page in just about every major city."

Zoe, Sarah, and Kat eagerly took various articles. Tay watched as they skimmed. "There were dozens of stories in the national press, but these were the most detailed."

Sarah looked up from her article. "I wonder if this was the first time Dove Pond made the national news?"

"Probably," Tay said. "It was a sensational story for the time. You have small-town suspects who manage to pull off a bold train robbery in broad daylight, an exciting shoot-out between some Pinkerton agents and the robbers, a bunch of gold that went missing, and then a gripping trial—as far as news stories go, it was big."

"Pinkerton agents?" Kat asked.

"The Pinkerton Agency was a security company founded in the 1850s, before most towns had an established police force. The agents were hired both as investigators for certain crimes and as a protection service, especially by the railroads."

Kat put down her article. "It says here that close to fifty thousand dollars in gold was stolen. What would that be worth today?"

"Around forty million dollars." Tay pulled her plate closer and took a bite of her sandwich. She'd already taken a second one before she realized everyone at her table was frozen in paralyzed silence. "What?"

Sarah had pinched the bridge of her nose and closed her eyes as if silently counting to ten. She dropped her hand back to her lap. "Are you saying that somewhere around here, in our little town, there's a stash of gold worth forty million dollars?"

"No." Tay put down her sandwich. "Hundreds, maybe even thousands of people came looking for it. If it was ever here, it's gone now."

Kat put her elbows on the table, her fingers laced together. "Hold on. Why did people believe the gold was hidden here to begin with?"

"A large portion was never recovered. Since the robbers were all apprehended here in town the night after the robbery, the prevalent theory was that they didn't have time to stash their portions anyplace else."

Sarah's eyes couldn't have gotten any wider. "Wait until I tell Grace about this. She'll find a way to incorporate the story into one of our festivals."

"I doubt she'll want to draw attention to it," Tay said. "Although, in my opinion, there's no way that gold hasn't already been found." She'd had plenty of time to think this through yesterday while waiting for the transcript copies at the courthouse. She didn't yet know a lot about William Day, but the little glance she'd gotten of him through the letters he'd written to Sarafina had given Tay an idea of his character. "If I had to guess, then I'd say William Day gave his portion to someone he trusted."

"And they hid it?" Kat asked.

"Why bother? Think about it. If you'd been given the task of overseeing someone's stash of gold, and then they died in prison, what would you do?"

Kat looked disappointed. "I guess I'd spend it."

"Exactly," Tay said.

"Ohhh!" Sarah leaned forward, her eyes wide. "Maybe he gave it to Sarafina!"

"I doubt it," Tay said. "We have letters from William to Sarafina, but not the other way around. She moved away while he was in jail, too. It seems to me that if she cared about him, that wouldn't have happened. She'd have stayed nearby, where she could have at least visited him."

Everyone was silent a moment as they considered this. Finally, Zoe pointed out, "If Sarafina had that gold, she would have been able to live very comfortably in New York."

"But she didn't," Tay said. "Sarafina's life in New York is well-documented. I've got a copy of her landlord's ledger and she rented a very small room in a boardinghouse during her early years. I know what she was paid at the newspaper, too, and she never once lived outside that limit. Not until she got married to David Tau did she move uptown, and that was because he was wealthy in his own right."

Sarah propped her elbow on the table and rested her chin in her palm. "I guess she didn't take it, then. Whoever did would have suddenly been wealthy but would have had to hide it."

Tay nodded. "Which is why I want to get my hands on the *Registers*." She wanted to see Rose's family records, too, if possible. She thought of Rose's expression when she'd mentioned William Day and grimaced. *That's going to take some doing, though.*

Zoe leaned back in her seat and said in a blissful tone, "I have to say, this story would make a great movie."

Sarah nodded slowly. "I'd watch that."

Kat added, "Just think of the casting! The Days have that black-hair-and-blue-eyes thing going, which is devastating on a man."

"Zac Efron," Sarah said.

"He has brown hair, but good enough." Kat clasped her hands to her heart. "What about the love child of Cillian Murphy and Megan Fox?"

"Now, that would be the perfect man," Zoe said with a sigh. "I had a dream about Cillian just last night."

"Wait!" Kat said. "We should cast a local. Luke Day must look a lot like William—they share DNA, after all."

"He's cute," Zoe admitted.

"Cute?" Kat scoffed. "He's *gorgeous.*"

Tay tried to keep from rolling her eyes. These two. They were always on the hunt.

Sarah laughed. "Kat, do you have your eye on Luke Day?"

"Oh no. He has Lulu now, and I'm not ready for that. He's nice to look at, though. I—" She straightened, her gaze now glued to a spot over Tay's shoulder. "Look! He just came into the café."

Zoe and Sarah looked over their shoulders. Tay refused to join in the fray. *For the love of heaven, it's just a guy.* And yet her gaze dropped to where she'd stored her phone. She understood that excitement of waiting for a call, or a message, or even just a look. *Was I that bad?* She didn't have to think about it for long. Yes, she'd definitely been every bit that foolish.

Zoe sighed. "It should be a crime when a man like that wears flannel. He's nerd handsome *and* flannel handsome. It's a deadly mix."

Sarah nodded thoughtfully. "He's a long, tall drink of water." She leaned a bit more to her right so she could see around Zoe. "Or a particularly delicious piece of cake."

Zoe gave Sarah a cutting look. "You have a guy, so stop looking. I'm the only one at this table ready for this challenge. You're taken, Tay doesn't seem interested, and Kat's bailing because of the Lulu Factor."

"Yup." Kat held up her hands. "I've given up my claim."

"Thank goodness," Zoe said. "Otherwise, we'd have to fight for him. I would have been down with anything but Jell-O wrestling, as I have a certain style to think of."

Tay smiled, although she was already thinking about going through the *Register*s at Rose's. "I think I'll leave you guys to—"

"Mind if I join you?" Luke stood by their table, a cup of to-go coffee in one hand. He smiled at everyone, although his gaze went right to Tay.

She wasn't sure whether to nod at him or smile or what.

Zoe scooted over, pushing Tay more into the corner. "You can sit here!" She patted the now-empty seat beside her.

"I'll get a chair." Luke set his coffee on the table, grabbed a chair from nearby, flipped it around, and sat astride it. "So? What's going on? This must be an important meeting. There's too much talent at this table for it not to be something significant."

Zoe beamed as if she'd just been handed an extra scoop of ice cream, while Tay began collecting the scattered news articles. *Sheesh. How could anyone fall for a line like th—*

"You're so funny!" Zoe leaned closer to him. "We were talking about hidden treasures and one of your ancestors, William Day."

His gaze instantly returned to Tay, his sleepy blue eyes suddenly intent. "Were you, now?"

Sarah pushed her empty plate away. "Your grandma won't like knowing about this. She's pretty protective of the family name."

Kat nodded. "She threw a giant hissy fit when Grace wanted to do that timeline display of the town's history at the Apple Festival a while back."

Luke grimaced. "She didn't like that William Day was named as the mastermind of the robbery."

Sarah glanced at her watch and winced. "I hate to break this up, but I'd better get back to the library. My assistant is only part-time."

Kat's phone rang. She looked at it and frowned. "Oops. I have to take this. It's a client." She sent her friends a regretful look. "Sorry to dip, but it's important." She gathered her things and slid out of the booth. She was already talking on her phone as she went out the door.

Zoe sighed deeply. "I have to go, too." She pulled on her coat and joined Sarah, who had just picked up her purse. "We'll pay on our way out. Tay, let us know if you find out anything new." With a wave, they left.

Tay put away her folders and latched her satchel. "If you'll excuse me, I'm heading over to the bookshop. I need to speak to your grandmother."

"Right. About that . . ." He sent her a look that could only be described as "self-satisfied." "I spoke to Grandma Rose on your behalf. I've good news, too. She will not only allow you access to all the *Registers*, but she'll also let you see the Day family archives."

Oh wow. I didn't expect that. She couldn't help but grin. "Luke! That's— Thank you!"

"Sure. *And*, in addition, she'll bring back all the documents relating to William."

Tay's grin faded. "Bring back? From where?"

His eyes twinkled. "My grandmother is the family archivist for a reason. She doesn't hesitate to protect the family secrets when she deems it necessary."

"Wait. You're saying that she *removed* some of the documents? But . . . they're *archives*. You don't remove documents from archives. How could she just— I would never . . ." Oh dear. Where should she begin?

"I'm not fond of the practice myself." He sipped his coffee. "Don't worry. I'll make sure she brings it all back. But I should mention that she also asked that I be present whenever you're reviewing the archives."

Great. Just great. Tay supposed she shouldn't be surprised. She grabbed her things and stood. "If you want to be there, that's fine, but I should warn you that you'll be bored."

He took a last drink of his coffee, set it on the table, and then joined her. "Since I have to be present, then I'd like to offer my assistance."

"Assistance? Doing what?"

"Whatever you need done. Let me point out that I do know my way around a computer. That has to be helpful in some way."

Right. Her sisters always offered to "help" with her research, too, but they, like everyone else, quickly found it tedious. Plus, although they caught the obvious things, they tended to miss the more obscure references, the ones that were often the most important. Luke would likely be the same way. When the time came to actually do the work, he'd get bored and would then wander off to do his own thing, which was fine with her.

Still, there was no need to tell him that. "We'll see." There. That was neither a yes nor a no. I *should have been a diplomat*. She flashed a fake smile. "If you'll excuse me, I should visit your grandmother."

"I'll walk with you." He followed her to the door, taking a quick step past her so that he could open it for her.

As she walked past him, she murmured, "Thank you."

He fell into step beside her, and she tried to think of something to say, but nothing came to mind. Finally, she blurted out, "Do you work full-time at the bookshop?"

"I work a few hours a day there. I have another job, though."

"Oh?" She gestured to his flannel shirt. "Lumberjack? No, wait. Your grandmother said you do computer stuff."

He laughed, his eyes crinkling. "It's a bit simplistic to call what I do 'computer stuff.'"

That was vague. She glanced at his feet, noticing his rather frayed tennis shoes. Was there a Genius Bar at the mall in Asheville?

"Now I get to ask you a question," he said. "What are you hoping to find in the old *Dove Pond Registers*?"

She pulled her attention from his shoes. "Local newspapers are gold for a researcher. They often hold innumerable clues about personal relationships and events, details missing from larger, national newspapers—small things that might otherwise be overlooked. For example, they might mention how Farmer Brown's lost brown cow was found by Mr. Jones, or how Miss Palmer held a tea for the preacher's wife and their two daughters."

"That type of reporting can prove who knew who, and maybe even why."

"Exactly." She was slightly impressed he understood that much just from what she'd said. "You can learn a lot from a local newspaper, like the social standing of various citizens, how active certain members were in a society, what groups they might have been involved with—that sort of thing. Some articles can lead you to other sources as well."

"Other sources?"

She rubbed her hands together, warming to one of her favorite topics. "If you discover from a newspaper article that Subject X brought up an issue for the Masons at the town hall meeting, you'll know to search through the available Masonic records from that year. Or maybe Subject Y won a ribbon at the fair for the biggest calf. Now you know to look at town records that list the sale of livestock. See? One mention can open a whole new direction for your research."

They turned the corner and stepped onto the street, the breeze making the sign for Rose's Bookstore swing on its cast-iron bar. Luke said in a thoughtful tone, "From what you said to my grandma the other day about those letters, you are looking for confirmation of Sarafina Dove and William Day's relationship."

She'd have to give him credit. He was fast. "I want to—" Her phone buzzed, and she stopped and pulled it from her satchel. Richard's name lit up the screen yet again. *For the love of heaven, what does he want?* She frowned at her phone just as the answer came to her. *Ah. The book. Did I miss citing a source?* The phone stopped buzzing abruptly, and she could imagine Richard's mouth tightening as it did whenever he was irritated.

She fought a sigh and supposed she might as well get it over with. She turned to Luke. "I'm sorry, but why don't you go ahead? I'll meet you there when I'm done with this call."

His gaze flickered over her face, but he shrugged. "Sure. I'll see you at the bookstore."

Tay watched him head down the sidewalk and disappear into the bookshop before she turned away. Then, leaning again the brick wall, she called Richard.

"Finally!" he snapped. "I've been trying to reach you for days."

"I'm on leave. What's up?" There. That sounded brisk and uncaring, didn't it? And yet a knot had formed in her stomach and refused to let go.

"I have a form I need you to sign. I'm going to email it, but I thought I should explain it first."

"A form for what?"

"The book," he said impatiently. "The publisher would like to list just me as the author, rather than both of us."

"*What?*"

He gave a noisy sigh. "There you go, overreacting."

"Overreacting? Richard, I did all the new research and wrote most of that book!"

"Nonsense. I wrote some of it."

"Two chapters out of twenty!"

"Stop shouting."

"I'm not shouting, I'm—" She caught herself and took a deep breath. "Why do they suddenly want to change things? Did you—"

"It wasn't my idea. And it's not because anyone thinks you're unqualified or anything like that. It's just that John—our editor—thinks my name will mean more to our audience, as my vitae is much more focused on this type of research."

"Your vitae is better? I've had more papers published than you."

"And I've had more books published than you. Tay, it's about the marketing. That's all publishers think about. Don't worry that you won't get credit for your work, because you will. Your name will be listed inside as a contributor."

Her jaw tightened. She hadn't been able to get angry before, but now? Now it was all she could do to talk without her voice shaking. "I don't like this, Richard."

"Neither do I, but it's what they want, so sign the form. Okay?" When she didn't answer, he added, "I'm sure you don't want to put our publication deal at risk."

"I won't sign that form."

"Darn it, Tay! Will you stop being unreasonable! This is why we didn't work out. You were always so fricking unpredictable, and—"

She hung up the phone and stood there, staring at it. *How could he? How* could *he do such a thing?*

She pushed herself from the wall, stared into the sky, and said through gritted teeth, "Richard, you elf-skinned, dried meat's tongue, bull pizzle!"

A choked laugh made her spin around.

Luke stood there, the breeze ruffling his black hair. His coat was gone now, so he had his arms crossed over his chest, his shoulders hunched against the wind. "Sorry about that. It's not often a person gets to hear Shakespearian-level insults like that."

She frowned. "What do you want?"

"I came to see if you were okay. You looked pissed."

"Did I?" She tried to keep the hiss out of her voice but couldn't.

"You were death-glaring the world into flames, and I got worried you might turn that weapon on the bookstore. We have insurance, but I don't think it covers that."

Tay threw her phone into her satchel and then dropped the bag onto the ground. If she kicked it just right, the whole thing would fly into the sky and land on a rooftop somewhere. Or she could just stomp it until it broke into a million pieces and—

"Whatever that bull pizzle did, it's obvious you're worked up about it." Luke leaned one shoulder against the brick wall, his arms still crossed. "You want to talk about it?"

"I don't even want to think about it," she snapped.

He nodded as if he'd expected that response. "It's none of my business, but it can help to air things out when you're upset."

She leaned her head against the wall and stared at the clouds slowly moving past. She'd decided a while ago that there was no reason to keep anything a secret anymore, but that hadn't made it any easier to talk about it.

Still, practice made perfect—maybe Luke was right and it would help to talk things through. "It's a short but tragic story. My—" She caught herself just before she said "ex." There was no need to load up her story with unnecessary details. "About a year ago, the head of my department asked for help with a book he was contracted to write. Because of his recent promotion at work, he didn't have time to do the necessary research. He asked me to go to Oxford to validate some of his research and to even coauthor the book." She sent Luke a hard look. "'Coauthor'—that was his word, not mine. So I agreed. Now that the book is done, even though I ended up writing far more than just half, as he was so busy, he wants all the credit."

"He *is* a bull pizzle, then."

She pinned Luke with a flat stare. "How many times do you plan to use that phrase today?"

He tilted his head back and squinted into the air as if doing an invisible math problem. "Four more times. You might want to avoid me until then."

"I'm tempted to leave right now."

"You could. But first, I have a few things to say about that bull pizzle. It seems like you're facing a classic power grab. Do you have evidence of his promises? Emails or phone messages or anything like that?" At her nod, he said, "Call in some help before you get too upset. A lawyer, perhaps."

That was actually good advice. She sighed and rubbed the back of her neck where it ached. "I will. It just hurts because he and I—" She flushed and pressed her lips together. Heavens, she couldn't seem to stop blurting out her every thought to this man. "It doesn't matter."

But it did, and she was sure Luke knew it, too. She sighed and straightened up so she was no longer leaning against the wall. "Like I said, it's a short, tragic story."

He nodded slowly. "My eleventh-grade English teacher, Ms. Hughes, a known alcoholic with an acerbic wit made of the purest vinegar, always said tragic stories are the best."

"I'd rather have a happily-ever-after, thank you very much." Which she wouldn't get. Not this time, anyway. Sighing again, she picked up her satchel, dusted it off, and hung it over her shoulder. "We should go. Your grandmother will be waiting."

His gaze went from Tay to the bookstore. "She's supposed to be adding up yesterday's receipts, but it looks as if she's staring out the window at us instead."

Tay turned to look and, sure enough, there was Rose Day, her face framed by a windowpane. "That's some CCTV you've got there."

He chuckled. "It may not be high-tech, but it's effective."

"And disturbing." Tay straightened her shoulders. "I should go talk to her. I'm excited to see both the *Registers* and the family archives, especially the missing ones."

"Then let's go."

They were soon on their way across the street. As Tay walked, she made a decision. After she got things settled with Rose, she'd start looking for a way to deal with Richard's newest insult. It was time she stopped avoiding and started acting. Whether he knew it or not, he'd thrown down the gauntlet, and she was finally angry enough to pick it up.

CHAPTER 11

TAY

Tay gritted her teeth and hefted the heavy box from the back of the Jeep she'd borrowed from her next-door neighbor and swung it toward the waiting book cart. As she did so, her knee bumped the cart and sent it rolling away, out of reach of the box she was struggling to hold on to. "Stupid cart! Why don't you have a wheel lock like a real cart?"

The cart didn't answer, so she staggered forward, setting the box on the top shelf just before it slipped from her hands. "Whew!" She straightened and rubbed her lower back. That was the last one, thank goodness. Now all she had to do was maneuver this antiquated cart to her new office in the back of Rose's Bookstore.

Thank goodness for Rose Day. Despite Richard's little foray into stupidity, last week had still turned out to be a red-letter week for

Tay. Rose had been surprisingly helpful during their meeting, which Luke had arranged and mediated. Tay had been impressed at how gifted he was in dealing with his grumpy grandmother. By the time he'd finished cajoling, complimenting, explaining, and encouraging, Rose had agreed to allow Tay to look through her pristine copies of the *Register*s and had given her unfettered access to the Day family archives, including the now-no-longer-missing items related to William Day.

But even nicer, when Rose noticed Tay eyeing the huge, empty desk located in the old office that they used as a workroom to unpack stock, she'd suggested that Tay use it as her office for as long as she needed it.

It was almost too good to be true. Even Luke had seemed surprised by that.

Tay closed the back of the Jeep and pushed the creaking cart down the sidewalk. She was almost at the bookstore when her phone rang. She dug it out of her pocket and saw her sister Cara's name flashing across the screen. "Hello?"

"Hi!" Cara said in her usual no-nonsense voice. "Hadn't heard from you in a while and thought I'd check in."

"Sorry I haven't called. I've been busy working on a new project."

"I've heard all about it. Sarah's already dying to read it, and Ella believes it'll make a great movie. How does it feel to be home? Are our younger sisters driving you batty yet? Did Sarah make good on her promise to let you use the library conference room as an office?"

"She did, but it turns out it's a public space, so a lot of groups had reserved it for their meetings."

"That's no good."

"Right? Plus, all three of them kept coming by to see what was going on, which was annoying. But I found a solution. Rose Day offered to let me use the empty office in the back of her bookshop. It's super private, *and* she said I'm welcome to it for as long as I want it, too."

"Glad you found a place to plant some roots while you finish Sarafina's biography. I hope it goes well. I guess you'll be going back home to your apartment once you're done."

Back home. Back to her tiny apartment that wasn't big enough to hold all her things. Back to working for a boss she no longer respected or even liked. Back to a life that suddenly seemed so far away, she didn't recognize it.

Tay glanced down the quiet street. It was a cool, crisp morning, and the bright sun slanted its gold light across the redbrick buildings with their sandstone trim and distinct decorative patterns. The large windows glinted and sparkled, reflecting the glow. Better yet, as they were behind Ava's new Pink Magnolia Tearoom, the faint scent of coffee and cinnamon drifted through the air.

It was quiet here. And peaceful. For a moment, she wondered if she really wanted to go back home to a place that suddenly felt far away and lacking. But what else could she do? As nice as it was here, she couldn't see hersel—

"Tay?"

"Sorry. I'm in the middle of moving my things into my new office. Can I call you later?"

"Sure. I'll be here."

"Awesome. Catch you soon." Tay hung up and stuck her phone into her back pocket, then grabbed the cart and pushed it in the direction of the bookshop. *I need to get everything in place and organized. I don't have time to think about other things right now.*

It took her several tries to get the creaky old cart through the front door, but she finally managed, the bell announcing her arrival.

"Sweet baby Jesus, look at that!" Rose limped out from behind the counter to poke her cane at the boxes. "It's your third load, too. Is all of that research on Sarafina Dove?"

Tay patted the top box. "I've been collecting information on this subject for almost eight years now, so I have a lot of it."

"Didn't you fly here from England? How did you get all of that onto a plane?"

"I didn't bring it from Oxford. My apartment in Boston is too small to hold all my research, so I keep a lot of my things in a climate-controlled storage unit. Before I came here, I had my friend May ship the boxes marked 'SD' for Sarafina Dove to my sisters' house."

"It's a good thing that desk back there is so big. You're going to need it. When Luke gets back, I'll send him in to explain our filing system." Rose limped back to her place behind the counter, shooting a hooded glance at Tay as she went. "Luke says he asked to help with your research. You'll be glad to have him. He's good with paperwork and the like."

Tay smiled politely. "I bet he is. But I can't take him away from you like that."

"No. Take him." Rose slid back on her stool and pinned the scanner with a hard look. "Please take him and keep him from installing more computer crap."

Tay had to fight to keep her smile in place. "I'll see if there's something he can do."

"He can start by bringing back that cart once you're done with it." Rose propped her cane to one side and picked up a book that sat next to the register. "He's out on some errands now. Won't be back until eleven." She opened her book and removed her bookmark. "That reminds me: I want to introduce you to Lulu. She should be here around three."

"Oh. I should still be here then." Tay wasn't sure why Rose wanted her to meet Lulu, but she couldn't think of a reason not to.

Rose shot her a suspicious look. "You like children, right?"

Tay blinked. "Like them? I suppose I do."

"You *suppose*? What kind of an answer is that? It's an easy question. Yes or no."

It was an easy question but, to be honest, Tay hadn't really given it much thought. "They're okay. I mean, I don't like the screaming ones, but the rest are fine."

"You'll like Lulu, then. She's not a screamer, but she does sarcasm like a pro. I've been told that's a sign of intelligence, although Luke doesn't appreciate it."

Through the town gossip vine, Tay had heard about how Lulu had ended up living with her uncle in Dove Pond. Under those circumstances, Tay supposed a little sarcasm was warranted. "Sarcasm is an art form. I can relate, too. I have six sisters. Sarcasm is how I survived."

"Ah. You did grow up around a lot of girls, didn't you? That could help." Rose seemed pleased at the thought. "You and Lulu will get along just fine."

I don't know what that's about, but it seems like the perfect time to leave. "I'm sure we will. I guess I'll go unload these boxes now." She pushed the cart to her new office and parked it near the huge desk.

A few minutes later, she stacked the final box in the corner and took the time to look around. The larger office that Rose used—which was on the other side of the bookshop—was the old editor's office. Between them, Rose's grandfather and father had served as the newspaper's editors in chief for almost a hundred years.

The smaller office where Tay stood now had belonged to the clerk. She suspected that the clerk had also served as the chief typesetter, as the huge desk was covered with miscellaneous ink stains. Although the clerk's office didn't have the size or prominent placement of Rose's, it was blessed with an abundance of light due to the two large windows that overlooked the sidewalk, and the large glass window that opened into the bookstore. A row of bookshelves lined the back wall and framed the door that led to the climate-controlled storage room.

She stood at the desk and ran her hand over the worn wooden surface, happy at the thought of having so much room to organize her books, notes, and other research materials. It was a relief she wouldn't have to pack up and move them again, too. Every time that happened, she worried an important piece of information, especially her DON'T FORGET and FURTHER RESEARCH Post-its—a cornerstone of her organizational method—might get stuck to the back of another piece of paper or drift unnoticed to the floor.

But now that was a worry of the past. Eager to get her things organized, Tay returned the cart to its place near Rose, who was too immersed in her book to notice. Tay knew that feeling, so she just smiled and returned to her new office.

She was just starting to unpack the first box when the door flew open and Ella appeared, wearing a cute red dress and cowboy boots, a heavy blue sweater hanging over one arm. She grinned and placed a pastry box and a cup of coffee in front of Tay.

"What are you doing here?"

Ella's grin faded. "Why? Am I not allowed?"

"No, no. I'm just surprised to see you, that's all."

"I just delivered some muffins I made to Ava's new tearoom and thought I'd stop by and say hi."

"Ah. That was nice of you." Tay eyed her sister for a minute. "You didn't knock."

"Why would I? I saw you through the window, and you didn't look busy."

Tay pointed to the box she was unpacking. "I didn't look busy?"

"Well, not *very* busy," Ella corrected. "But hey, I brought you an office-warming gift. Coffee and chocolate crème éclairs. Surely that counts for something."

"Thank you." The coffee smelled heavenly. It wouldn't hurt to drink it. "Where's Gray?"

Ella pointed to the front of the store, where her boyfriend stood in the aisle, his dark head bent over a book. He flipped a page, read a little more, and then closed the book and tucked it under his arm before browsing his way farther down the row. "He's a huge reader. I think he spends more on books than he does at the feed store, and he has a whole herd of Highland cows."

"Impressive." Tay liked Gray. He was quiet and had a quick sense of humor, but more than that, Ella was obviously head over heels for him—a first for her.

Ella sat down in the old orange chair in front of Tay's desk. "This is a big office. I expected it to be smaller."

"It'll look even more spacious once I get my things organized." Which she'd do more quickly if she didn't have visitors. Tay placed the last files from the box on the desk and then opened another box. Ah, there were her binders. She pulled them out, one at a time, and stacked them two-deep. She really needed some shelf space. *A file cabinet would be nice, too.*

By the time Tay finished emptying the box, Ella had left her chair and was wandering around the room. She gestured to the windows that looked out over the side street. "There's a lot of light in here."

Tay nodded absently and cast a curious gaze over the bookcases that lined the back wall. Each one had six shelves, and the bottom four were filled with—of all things—old and faded shoeboxes. That left the top two rows of shelves empty. *My binders would fit that space perfectly. I wonder if Rose would mind me using it?*

Ella wandered back to the desk and began straightening the stapler and other office supplies Tay had just set out into a neat row. "This desk will work, but the chair is a bit sad."

"I kind of like it."

Ella gave her a flat stare. "You like anything that's too old to use."

Tay couldn't argue with that. She really did like the ancient chair, a relic of the same era as the desk. It was wooden, with wooden ball casters, the red leather seat worn and mashed flat. "I may need to buy a support cushion, but other than that, it's good as new."

Ella's eyebrows rose. "Really?" She sat in the chair, which creaked as if she weighed a million pounds. She glared down at it. "It sounds as if it's trying to take its last breath."

"The base just needs some oil."

"Oil is exactly what it needs. Pour oil on it, toss it on a pile of wood, and then burn it. It's anything but what a chair should be—comfortable and quiet." Ella got up, wincing as the chair protested again. "That thing must be two hundred years old."

"It's possible. Rose says that both this desk and chair were used back when her granddad was the editor of the *Register*."

"It looks as if it hasn't been oiled or cleaned since then." Ella twisted around, trying to see the back of her dress. "I hope I don't have to go home and change."

Tay eyed Ella's trendy outfit and then looked down at her Harvard sweatshirt and faded jeans, and wished she knew how to dress the way her sister did. Ella always wore bright colors and fitted clothing, while Tay was happier in loose, comfy clothes. *I should probably update my look.* And yet Tay knew she wouldn't. Her comfortable clothes were like a hug she gave herself. "There's nothing on your dress. You look ready for a fashion shoot, as usual."

Ella's gaze flickered over Tay. "And you dress as if you're still a grad student."

"I own some dresses. I wore one yesterday."

"You brought a total of two dresses with you. I know because I've looked in your closet."

Tay frowned. "Why did you do that?"

"I was bored and curious, so—" Ella shrugged.

"I didn't see the need to bring fancy clothes. I'm just here to work." To emphasize her point, Tay opened another box and started to unpack it.

"If you want to go shopping, let me know. Erma Tingle's little boutique here in town has some surprisingly stylish things in it." Ella pointed to the other, much smaller desk that sat in the corner of the room. "Who will work there?"

"Rose and Luke use that desk when they're unpacking the new stock."

"Ah. So Luke will be here sometimes."

Tay shrugged. "I suppose so."

Ella slanted her a side look. "He seems like a nice guy."

He did. And he'd done so much for Tay already, including use the term "bull pizzle" no fewer than six times during her meeting with Rose. Tay had to stifle a laugh when she remembered his grandmother's irritated expression every time he worked it into their conversation.

Ella cupped her hands around her eyes and peered through the picture window into the bookstore. "Where *is* Luke, by the way? I didn't see him when we came in."

"Rose said he had some errands."

"Ah." Ella dropped her hands back to her sides and wandered to where Tay was working. "I bet you'll see a lot of him."

"Hopefully I won't see him very often, as I really, really, really need my space." She looked at Ella expectantly, but her sister didn't take the hint.

In fact, Ella had already moved to the door beside the bookcases. "Where does this go? Do you have your own break room?"

"That's the climate-controlled room where the old copies of the *Register* and the Day family archives are kept." Tay had to fight the urge to rub her hands together in excited anticipation. "It used to be the subscription office for the newspaper."

"There's so much history in this place. I—" Ella's phone chimed, and she pulled it out of her pocket and looked at it. "I almost forgot. I've got a Zoom call in thirty minutes with my content team, so I need to head out. I'll have Gray drop me off at home." She picked up her sweater from where she'd left it on the back of the orange chair. "Don't forget the family dinner Ava's planned for tonight. Should I tell everyone you'll be eating with us?"

"Sure." Why not? It wasn't as if she had other plans.

"Great. I'll let them know." Ella headed out the door, waving as she went. "See you later."

Over the next hour, Tay emptied two more boxes and organized some files. As she worked, she was aware of Rose's curious gaze occasionally wandering in her direction, and she wished her office window had blinds like the one in Rose's office.

Still, the window was sort of fun, as Tay could see the comings and goings of all of Rose's customers. It was interesting how people shopped for books. They would wander around, seemingly aimlessly, picking up a book here and there. They'd read a page or two and then either put the book back or give it a little pat before taking it to the counter.

It was close to eleven when Luke finally arrived. By then, more than a half dozen customers were milling around the store. Everyone smiled at him, two calling out a greeting, while Rose immediately began asking him questions about an order. He handed Rose a small brown bag stamped MOONLIGHT CAFÉ as he patiently answered her.

Tay watched him as she separated a new batch of files into convenient stacks on one side of the desk. Luke seemed to find it easy to talk to everyone he met, his smile warm and contagious. She wondered what that was like.

Luke waved, and she suddenly realized she'd been absently staring at him, lost in her own thoughts.

Her face heated. "Way to go, Dove," she muttered to herself as she gave him an awkward, hurried nod and then turned away to dig into the open box sitting on her desk. "Yeah, that didn't look weird at all."

A scant few minutes passed before a quick knock announced Luke. He came in carrying a box, which he set on the other, smaller desk before casting a quick glance around. "Grandma Rose was right. You have a lot of stuff." His gaze found the coffee cup on her desk. "I was going to offer to make you some coffee, as there's a station in Grandma's office, but I see you already have one."

"Ella brought it, but it's probably cold now."

"Would you like me to make you a cup?"

"No, thank you. I'm good."

He eyed the stacks of binders and folders. "You need a file cabinet. I'll bring one from upstairs. We have a few old ones stored there."

Grateful, she flashed him a smile. "I could use one. Is that what you keep in the second story? Office furniture? I'm surprised you haven't expanded the bookshop up there."

"Stairs are difficult for Grandma Rose. Besides, she likes being able to see all her customers from her perch behind the counter." He cast a glance toward the front of the shop, shaking his head when he saw his grandmother stabbing the point-of-sale pad as if it had insulted her. "She doesn't like technology. What's worse is that it doesn't seem to like her, either."

Tay put the empty box in a corner with the others. "She mentioned you've been dragging her kicking and screaming into the modern era."

"More screaming than kicking. She has a bad hip, you know." He grinned. "When I first got here, Grandma Rose was still using carbon copies to record sales. It was archaic."

"You've managed to do a lot in just a short while, then. Rose mentioned that you did computer stuff before you moved here."

He raised his eyebrows. "Did you say 'computer *stuff*'? I was a programmer for a cutting-edge cybersecurity company. That's not 'stuff.' "

She had to laugh. "Sorry! To be honest, when I first arrived, I thought you worked at a Genius Bar or a phone repair shop or something like that."

His mouth dropped open, although his blue eyes twinkled. "I've never been so disrespected in my whole life. If we lived in other times, I'd be challenging you to a duel right now."

"I'm glad we live in a more genteel era."

"Speak for yourself. It was a great-paying job, but to be honest, I didn't love it. After I got Lulu, I cut back. Now I'm a consultant for a number of small companies. I make a fair penny doing it, too."

"Good for you. Are you happier now?"

"Yes." He sat down in his chair, the seat creaking as loudly as her own. "I set up my own servers in one of the guest rooms at the house, and I work there most evenings so I can match the time zones of my biggest clients."

His own servers? *Wow. His job is much more complex than I'd imagined.*

He opened the box he'd brought in and emptied it, piling new books on his desk.

She continued to organize her things, separating her files into neat stacks that defined different facets of Sarafina's life. There was the "letters and correspondence" stack, the "newspaper investigations" stack, the "information about Sarafina's New York/marriage years" stack, and now a growing "Sarafina in Dove Pond" stack. She eyed the new folders with a smile.

"You never answered my question the other day. Actually, it was more of a favor."

Surprised, she looked at Luke. He'd already unpacked his box and had just put down the iPad he'd used to log them in. "I'd like to officially become a member of your investigative team."

Here we go. He was going to be just like her sisters, which was a disappointment. "I don't have a team."

"If there were two of us, then it would be a team, wouldn't it? To be honest, I feel as if I've earned a place on it."

She frowned. "Earned?"

"I spent a good amount of time working Grandma Rose over to get you access to the real-deal William Day information, didn't I?"

"You did, but—"

"And that turned into something more, as she gave you this lovely office, too."

"You were as surprised about that as I was," Tay pointed out.

"True. But still, it wouldn't have happened without me. So . . . may I join your team?"

This was the last thing she needed. "I prefer to work alone."

"I understand. But you have a lot of research to go through. Surely you could use the help. Think of me as your grad assistant. I'm here to do the dirty work—make copies, find sources, get coffee. That sort of thing."

It would be nice to have an assistant, a real one. She couldn't deny it. But that wasn't Luke. "It's very nice of you to offer to help, but you don't know my system."

"I can learn it."

He spoke so firmly and calmly that she almost believed him. "I'm sort of picky, too. For example, I don't like it when people talk while I'm working."

"Noted. I prefer to work in silence myself."

"A lot of the work is slow and tedious."

"And you think programming isn't? Please."

She struggled to think of another reason to tell him no and couldn't find one.

He must have read her expression, because he crossed his arms and leaned back in his creaky chair, a complacent smile on his face. "Tell you what. I'll help for a week, and if at the end of that time you think I'm more of a hindrance than a help, I'll stop."

She eyed him cautiously. "You'll stop."

"Completely. I'll stay away and will only come in here to check stock into the system or to do the returns."

She wished she could just say no and be done with it, but she couldn't deny that he'd already been a big help. *It's only temporary. In a week, I'll let him know how much I appreciate his efforts, but that I'll be better off doing this alone. And that will be that.*

She nodded. "Fine. A week, then."

"Yes!" He fist-pumped the air and spun his chair in a circle.

She had to laugh. "I'm warning you. It's going to be boring."

"As if!" He settled back into his seat and grinned at her. "What do we do first?"

"I have to get unpacked, but once that's done, I have some things I need to search for in the old *Registers*. In fact, I have a list of things."

He got out of his chair and came to her desk. "Maybe I can help with—"

"No! I need to do this part myself."

"Sure." Luke selected a pen from the holder on her desk and clicked it a few times and then put it back. "By the way, what did you decide to do about that little problem you had? The one that called you the other day."

It was amusing to hear Richard described as "that little problem." She rather liked that. "I spent an hour on the phone this morning with a colleague who teaches intellectual property classes. He says I have a strong case and gave me the name of a lawyer to call, should I need one. He also suggested that, for now, I simply write Richard an email explaining my concerns and then wait and see what happens."

"He thinks Richard will back down?"

She nodded. "He said the fact that Richard wanted me to sign the form handing over all the rights shows he knows how weak his position is."

"Just one email and you're done?"

"I hope so. Although this whole thing has probably surprised Richard—he's not used to hearing me say no." Which was embarrassing to admit.

"Really?" Luke looked seriously shocked. "I don't see you as the 'can't say no' type."

That was gratifying to hear. "I'm not usually. I don't know what happened, but I wasn't myself when—" She stopped, realizing that she was about to sink into a convoluted explanation about something even she didn't understand. "It'll all work out. If Richard gives me any problems, I'll call in the lawyer my friend recommended."

There. That was simple and easy. She couldn't believe she'd almost admitted her flaws to the guy standing beside her desk. She'd been so pathetically *weak* where Richard was concerned, and on some level, she was terrified that the-woman-who-never-said-no might be who she really was. *I will never date again. I can't afford to. I should pack up all my things and find a desert island and—*

The sound of a page turning made her look up. Luke now sat on the corner of her desk, leafing through the contents of one of her folders.

She frowned. "What are you doing?"

"Reading these transcripts from the trial. Is this what you went to Asheville for last week?"

"I got them from the Western Regional Archives office."

He turned the page. "It's fascinating. It would make a great movie, wouldn't it?"

"That's what my sister Ella thinks." Tay watched as he finished reading the page and turned to a new one. "I hate to bother you, but don't you have a few things to do, like—I don't know—run a bookstore or something?"

He didn't look up but tilted his head toward the window overlooking the aisles. "See Grandma Rose at the counter? She's already settled in, reading a book, and is more than happy I'm not there."

Tay had to lean to one side to see, but he'd called it. Rose was right where Luke said she'd be, and she did look content, lost in one of her ever-present books.

Luke flipped to a new page. "She prefers to run the bookshop on her own. The second I get up out of her chair, she rushes out of her office to claim it."

"It's nice of you to give her a hand here."

"I like being useful." He finished reading the transcript and slid it back into the file before eyeing the growing stacks of binders and folders on her desk. "You've already gathered a lot of information. I'm impressed and a bit daunted."

"It's exciting, not daunting." She reached over and took the folder out of his hands, closed it, and replaced it on the pile. "But if it's too much for you—"

"Not at all." He reached past her and picked up another folder, this one green with a bright yellow Post-it that read "News Articles About the Train Robbery." He flipped it open and scanned the top article. "I'm not that busy these days."

She blinked. "But you've got Lulu, and you're helping your grandmother with the bookshop, *and* you said you work in the evenings—"

"It's a part-time job." He closed the file and handed it to her. "Why don't I start working on the *Register*s while you finish organizing your office? That way I can prove just how good I am at tedious things."

Or prove how bad he was at them. She thought about arguing, but he looked so hopeful that she didn't have the heart. "Sure. Why not?" She replaced the file he'd just handed her back on its stack and then dug her yellow notepad out from under a pile of books. "Here. Compile a list of every mention, meeting, or transaction made by Sarafina and her aunts, as well as William Day and his family. Oh, and those of Marcus McCleary and Ellis Johnson, too. Neither of them had families, so that'll be simpler."

"That sounds easy enough. Is that all you need?"

"For now, yes."

"Okay, boss. I'll get started as soon as I finish scanning in the new stock." Luke carried the notepad to his desk and settled back into his seat, his long frame making it seem smaller than it was. "By the way, I was surprised at how much speculation was going on in that article about the train robbery."

"That's the real problem with using the news as a source, even today. I have to cross-check their supposed facts."

He grimaced. "That's sad. Have you read the transcripts for the trial?"

"Most of them, yes. The folder you had earlier was just the pretrial hearing record. There are pages and pages of transcripts from the actual trials." She caught herself looking at her satchel, where a fat stack of photocopies rested, already sorted, tabbed, and waiting for a thorough reread. "It was interesting. It's common knowledge who committed the train robbery—William Day, Marcus McCleary, and Ellis Johnson. While I was in the courthouse, I looked up their criminal records. Prior to the theft, Day had never been arrested, not even once."

Luke looked surprised. "Our family lore swears he was a town troublemaker."

"He was labeled as such, but the lack of an arrest record makes me wonder if that's all it ever was—a label."

Luke nodded thoughtfully. "That happens. Still does."

"McCleary had several run-ins with the law for things like petty theft and public drunkenness. But Johnson had a long record that included far bigger and more violent crimes. In fact, about ten months before the robbery, he was arrested for manslaughter but was never convicted, as the sole witness disappeared."

Luke whistled. "A seriously bad guy, then."

"Apparently so. And get this." She leaned forward, unable to hide her excitement at the strides she'd made in the past few weeks. "Johnson testified in court that William Day was the mastermind behind the train robbery. That it was Day who came up with the idea and did all the planning. The only one of the three with no criminal record."

"That doesn't make any sense."

"Exactly! Johnson got some sort of special deal from the prosecution for testifying. Because of all the national attention, the prosecutor went after William the hardest, and then McCleary. To muddy William's reputation, McCleary's criminal record was emphasized over and over, and then the prosecutor hammered home the fact that Day and McCleary had been close since elementary school. He repeatedly called them 'as alike as two peas in a pod.'"

Luke rested his elbows on his knees, his gaze glued to her face. "Guilty by association."

"Right. The media pushed that narrative, too. By the time they got done, popular opinion condemned both Day and McCleary."

"Didn't they defend themselves in court?"

"They tried. Day testified that well before the robbery, he'd warned McCleary about Johnson and his schemes, but his friend wouldn't listen. On the day of the robbery, Day discovered their plans and raced after McCleary to try to stop him. McCleary's testimony backed up that testimony, too. According to him, by the time William Day arrived, the robbery and the shoot-out were already over."

Luke had straightened in his seat. "Day wasn't even there?"

"Not according to his and McCleary's testimony. McCleary said Johnson was the only one armed, too. Of course, Johnson denied all of it, saying it was Day who'd planned the whole thing, and that both

Day and McCleary were armed, while he wasn't. But I think he was lying."

"Yes!" Luke smacked his hand on the arm of his chair. "By gosh, *this* is the reason Grandma Rose should stop editing our archives. She's assuming the truth will be worse than reality when, in fact, the opposite is just as likely to be true."

Tay couldn't agree more. "When I read through the transcripts, I was hoping some of the train passengers had testified, but none of them saw anything, as the gold was stored in the final baggage car of the train, well out of their sight. That's where both the robbery and the shoot-out occurred."

"I daresay there was a lot of confusion that day, too."

She nodded. "Two of the Pinkerton agents didn't testify because they were still in the hospital at the time of the trial. The two who did testify couldn't agree on much of anything. One gave a blistering condemnation of all three men, saying he saw them stealing the gold *and* carrying weapons. But the other one testified that there were only two robbers—Johnson and McCleary. He said that while those two were trying to escape, William Day arrived by horse and pulled the wounded McCleary out of the line of fire."

"That's in the transcript?" At her nod he frowned. "None of that's in any of the articles I just read."

"It was the heyday of yellow journalism. There are errors in almost every news article that was printed. What's worse is that, at the time, smaller newspapers that couldn't afford to send someone to cover an event in another state would take the news articles from those larger papers and reprint them word for word. You can see how popular opinion quickly moved against William Day."

"Surely his lawyer saw what was happening and responded to the accusations during the trial?"

"When you read the transcripts, you'll realize how incompetent William's lawyer was. The prosecutor saw to it that William and McCleary were labeled 'troublemakers' and 'greedy thieves,' while Johnson was lauded for 'coming clean' to the prosecution. He was portrayed more as a reliable witness than a thief."

"What was he sentenced to?"

"Reduced sentence of five years. He was the star witness, after all. Day and McCleary were sentenced to twenty-five years apiece."

"First rat to the cheese wins."

"Every time." She leaned back in her chair, the old iron bearings creaking loudly. "What's ironic is that if Johnson hadn't been a drunkard, he and McCleary might have gotten away with it."

"You really think so?"

"It's possible. But the night after the robbery, Johnson went to a bar somewhere outside of town and proceeded to get drunk and bragged in front of a dozen witnesses about having a lot of gold. He was arrested shortly afterward."

"What a fool." He shook his head slowly. "It's funny, but my parents told me and my sister, Caitlyn, the story of the train robbery a dozen times at least, but they didn't know any of these details."

"There's a big debate among historians as to the reliability of unrecorded oral histories. At times they are remarkably accurate, but not always. Details can fade with each retelling, and there's no way to discern bias."

"Especially not when there's someone like my grandma Rose trying to clean up the family image." He cast an admiring glance at Tay. "You've figured out a lot of things already, and you haven't even dug through the family archives yet. I can't wait to see what you discover once we set you loose in there."

Her gaze immediately went to the door beside the bookshelves. "I don't suppose you'd mind showing me those now, would you? Your grandmother said you should be the one to do it."

His blue eyes twinkled with amusement. "I thought you wanted to get organized first."

"I can't wait," she admitted.

"Then let's have a look." He was already walking toward the door. He opened it, flipped on the light, and then stood to one side. "After you."

She walked into the room and took in a deep breath, loving the old-paper smell. The room was small compared to the office they'd just left, but it was packed with shelves filled with large, clearly marked boxes in which newspapers were stored flat and pristine. "These are the same type of storage boxes they use in most university archives."

"Acid-free, every one of them." He gestured to the back of the room, where smaller boxes lined the wall. "Those are the Day family archives. Grandma Rose brought back the records that mention William Day. They're in that blue box on the bottom shelf."

"Where was she hiding them?"

He grinned. "In a box under a bed in one of the guest bedrooms. She's usually super picky about keeping the archives in a climate-controlled room, but I guess she was okay with the William Day information getting a little faded and moldy."

"I'll never understand that. I'm glad you convinced her to bring them back." She ran her fingers over the closest boxes, eagerly reading the labels. "This is awesome. I should be able to dig in starting tomorrow morning." She gave a sad sigh at the thought of waiting. "Speaking of which, I should get back at it."

He followed her back into the office, and they went to their own desks.

He placed her yellow pad in front of his chair and sat down. But instead of reading her notes, he watched her sorting through her files. "Once we document all the mentions of Sarafina, William, the train robbers, and their families, what will we do next?"

She placed a stack of folders in front of her and sank into her creaky chair. "One of the biggest questions I have about Sarafina's past has to do with her career as a journalist." The thought had dawned on her in the middle of the night when she'd been awake and trying not to think about stupid stuff. Lately, instead of going through the endless what-ifs about her time with Richard, she'd instead thought about the what-ifs of Sarafina's and William's real lives. It had helped, as Tay had stumbled upon some new concepts.

"The accepted story is that Sarafina got her job as a reporter in New York by begging an editor to give her an assignment so she could prove herself. She supposedly annoyed the poor man until he gave in. But I'm not sure I believe that just annoying an editor would be enough to get a job back in those days, especially for a woman."

"How so?"

"If you were an editor at a major newspaper, would you give a very young woman—one with no experience whatsoever—an assignment, even an impossible one? Why would he bother?"

Luke tapped his fingers across his notepad, a thoughtful expression on his face. "You're right. He would expect a reference of some sort and a sample of her writing even— Oh!" He leaned forward. "You think she was a reporter *before* she went to New York."

Tay nodded. "This is where she lived, so I think it's possible she wrote for the *Register*. She'd have used a pseudonym, too, as being a female reporter would have been a scandal in a small town like this."

"That's an interesting theory. How do you plan to prove it, if she wrote under another name?"

"I took copies of all the articles Sarafina wrote during her time in New York and made a list of common phrases she used. I want to use those phrases to identify articles she may have written for the *Register* in the years right before she left town. Once I do that, I will run those articles through an AI application to confirm it."

Luke's eyes brightened. "Wow. This is going to be fun."

He seemed as excited as she felt. Smiling, he picked up the notepad she'd given him. "I'll start looking for these names, then."

"You have to read very, very carefully or you'll miss something. Your biggest enemy is boredom. Even I catch myself skimming after a while."

"Boredom is my friend. You should try watching *The Little Mermaid* two hundred and seventy-one times."

She had to smile. "Lulu's favorite?"

"She can quote every line." He leaned back in his chair and eyed her with a questioning gaze. "I know I haven't proven myself yet, but I have another favor to ask."

She felt her smile slipping away. "What's that?"

"I have free time some evenings. How about I try solving the secret code Sarafina wrote in that poem she sent to her daughter?"

Tay almost dropped the file she'd just picked up. "How do you know about that?"

"I'm friends with Nate Stevens, who owns Ace Hardware. One of your sisters mentioned it to him when she came in to buy shoe polish."

"That would be Ella. She has more boots than common sense." Sheesh. Her sisters were something else. "They talk too much."

"Can I see it, then?" He smiled, his eyes crinkling at the corners. "Unless you're afraid I might crack it, that is. I'm pretty good at puzzles."

"I'd love for someone to do just that." Heavens knew she'd tried. Still, he was asking for a lot, wasn't he? "Haven't I already given you enough to do?"

"During the day, sure. But I can't take the *Registers* home, can I? Grandma Rose would pluck out my eyeballs if I even suggested such a thing. Which leaves me with free evenings, especially since Lulu goes to bed at eight."

"Didn't you say you had computer stuff to do at night?"

"Some. But I always have time for a good puzzle."

Goodness. Give this man an inch and he takes a mile. Still, Tay supposed it couldn't hurt. "Fine." She leaned across the desk to pull a folder from a pile. She removed a copy of the poem, carried it to his desk, and handed it to him.

He began to read to himself, his lips moving as he went through it. Tay had read it so many times that she could quote it with the same accuracy Lulu could quote *The Little Mermaid.*

A truth, a name, a number.
Told to all yet soon mentioned by none.
So he carved it in stone where peace meets up in oaken silence.

Tay thought it an oddly beautiful poem. Almost haunting. *Ah! He needs to read the letter, too.* She went back to her desk and found the typewritten letter Sarafina had sent with the poem to Lucy. In it, Sarafina had explained to her daughter that the poem held a clue to the "family secret" but that Lucy should consider closely whether she really wanted to know it or not, as "secrets aren't always answers."

Tay had always liked that phrase. Research was similar—some answers merely raised more questions. She placed the letter on the edge of her desk and slid her fingers along the scrawled signature as she'd done a hundred times before. In a blinding second, Tay was with Sarafina once again. She was at home, wearing a loose robe as she signed the letter she'd just removed from her typewriter.

Tay could smell the oil lamp, feel the brush of the breeze that came through the nearby open window, and hear the noisy street below. She got only one quick glimpse of Sarafina's emotions as she wrote her name before the pen lifted and the vision ended. *She wondered if her daughter would follow the clues hidden in the poem or if she'd tuck it away and forget it.*

The whole thing fascinated Tay. She glanced over at Luke.

He was reading the poem over and over, his eyebrows knit. He was so sunk in his own thoughts, trying to see through the lines to the meaning beyond, that he seemed to have forgotten Tay was in the room.

She'd thought she was the only one who did that sort of thing. *He won't figure it out, but he seems serious about helping.* That was something.

She handed him the letter. "Sarafina sent this with the poem to her daughter. Context is everything, so you should read them together in order to—"

A sharp rap startled them both.

Through the picture window, Rose glared at Luke, lifted her hand, and shook the scanning wand in his direction. She then feigned throwing it away.

Luke muttered under his breath as he got up and headed for the door. "I've told her a hundred times not to shake that thing." He glanced over his shoulder and said in a grim tone, "I'll be right back."

Tay had to laugh as she watched him duck out of the office just in time to save the poor scanner and then gently lead Rose back to the counter.

Shaking her head, Tay returned to her desk. She could hardly wait to see what new things the *Register*s and the Day archives would reveal. Had Sarafina written for the *Register*? And if so, how had it come about?

So excited she could barely sit still, Tay forced herself to settle into her creaky chair and get back to work.

CHAPTER 12

SARAFINA

JUNE 6, 1895

I've time now—too much of it—to think about things, which has made me miss you deeply. Falling in love with a stranger is easy. But falling in love with a friend is far more complicated, as there's always the chance that, if things go awry, both your love and your friendship could be smashed on the rocks of resentment.

With you, because of your strength and generous heart, I never worried about those treacherous seas. I knew that, together, we'd sail them without mishap.

—letter to Sarafina Dove from William Day

Sarafina had her aunt Emily Anne to thank for her new career. A scant month ago, Miss LaFont—in a dramatic way reminiscent of a Shakespearean play—had ordered Sarafina to leave her school and never return. It had all happened after an especially disastrous morning when Preacher Caldicott from the First Baptist Church of the nearby town of Glory, North Carolina, came for tea.

Miss LaFont seemed inordinately excited about the coming visit, and Sarafina and her fellow students quickly realized why when the new preacher turned out to be both handsome and youngish, if a little round in the middle. It was obvious by the way Miss LaFont fluttered her lashes at his every word that she'd already grown fond of his company.

Things went fine until they ran out of sugar after the preacher poured four heaping spoonfuls into his tea. Miss LaFont immediately sent Sarafina to the kitchen to refill the bowl. Glad of the respite, Sarafina had obliged. The sugar was kept in the butler's pantry, and it was there, while Sarafina was on her tiptoes, reaching for the tin, that the preacher—who'd excused himself on the vague pretext of needing "a breath of fresh air" after a sudden cough—had taken it upon himself to try to steal a kiss.

Shocked, Sarafina had reacted without thought. She'd used the tin she'd just grasped to wallop her attacker right in his pursed mouth and had sent the portly man—bleeding from both lips and dizzy from the blow—plummeting to the ground, his flailing limbs hitting and dislodging every shelf as he went. Glass crashed and tins bounced all around them, flour puffing into the air like a cloud that rained white upon the preacher's face and black frock coat and dusting Sarafina's dark blue skirts.

Everyone came running. The girls had been shocked and breathless as the preacher, woozy and red-faced, climbed to his feet and, cupping his split lips, staggered away without a word. Miss LaFont, her hopes of at long last finding her own true love cruelly dashed, had subjected Sarafina to a screeching diatribe that ended in banning her from ever again darkening the door of her school.

Sarafina couldn't have been happier at this outcome. Thankfully, after hearing the details of the event, her aunts had applauded her actions, calling them "justified and brave."

Of course, her father had been far less understanding. Before they could send him a letter explaining the events of the day, he'd received a hand-delivered missive from Miss LaFont giving her own shaded version of Sarafina's expulsion. He'd been furious, but not furious enough to make an extra trip out to see her. Instead, he'd vented his anger in a long letter to his sisters, filled with thundering underlines and shouting exclamation marks. Sarafina was unsure exactly what he'd said in that letter, as, after reading it, Aunt Jane had consigned it to the fire and said simply, "He's angry. That's all you need to know. Write him and explain the situation and leave the rest to me and your aunt Emily Anne." What they said to Papa, Sarafina never knew, but he never mentioned the incident again.

Sarafina hoped things would go back to the way they had been before she'd begun attending that horrible comportment school—her time relatively free and her own—but alas, her aunts had other plans. Every morning at breakfast, they handed her a list of chores to do while they were busy with their daily errands and activities. Although she hated housework, she completed the tasks with only a small amount of complaining. It wouldn't do to garner more scrutiny, as she was determined to keep her aunts from realizing that every Tuesday, while they were at their weekly meetings, she met William at her fishing spot.

She enjoyed those Tuesday meetings more and more. When William missed a week because of a job he'd just taken, Sarafina missed him terribly. Even though they did the same thing every week—she fished or wrote while he read—each visit seemed fresh and new. He was always surprising her, too. After she'd complained for a few weeks about having to pay larger and larger sums of breadcrumbs to the greedy Blackwing, William had found a way to end the crow's greedy ways. For weeks, unbeknownst to Sarafina, he had practiced making a hawk's sharp call. When Blackwing appeared and started demanding far more breadcrumbs than Sarafina had brought, William had cupped his hands around his mouth and made the call, which was so real sounding that other hawks had answered. Soon, several were flying in circles over their fishing hole.

Sarafina was delighted with the outcome. Not only did the hawks scare away all the other birds, including Aunt Em's tattletale crow, but Sarafina didn't have to worry that the hawks might reveal her secret meetings to her aunt Em. Her aunt was not fond of birds who ate their brethren, saying in a cross tone whenever she happened to see one flying overhead, "They're traitors, those birds! Every one of them!"

And so, free from Aunt Em's spies and no longer forced to attend Miss LaFont's hated school, Sarafina's time at the fishing hole with William was now even more idyllic, and they were getting closer each time. She was just beginning to believe that things couldn't get any better when, for some reason she never fathomed, Aunt Emily Anne got a bee in her bonnet.

Sarafina thought that Aunt Em's most notable quality was the way she moved in and out of her special world and real life. There were days when she barely spoke to anyone at all, humming to herself, or murmuring exclusively to the birds that came to sit on her windowsill every morning. But then, out of the blue, usually over a biscuit or a cup of hot tea, she'd say something surprisingly sharp that let everyone know she hadn't completely abandoned this world. Not yet, anyway.

So it had been one morning when she and Sarafina were sitting at the breakfast table that Aunt Em had said in a calm tone, as if she were talking about the weather, "I don't mean to be rude, my dear, but you seem to have too much free time on your hands."

Sarafina, her fork halfway to her mouth, had paused. "I've been staying busy. I've been doing chores, working on the mending, writing my stories, fishing now and then, and—"

"About that fishing. According to my poor Blackwing, there is a hawk infestation at the lake."

Oh no! Did that stupid bird tell her about William? Sarafina refused to give up her one afternoon a week with William. She couldn't. Those hours had become the brightest, best parts of her life.

Pressing a hand to her uneasy stomach, Sarafina cast a careful look at Aunt Em, but could tell nothing from her serene, rather disengaged expression. Of her two aunts, Sarafina loved Aunt Em just a smidge more. She was a tiny woman with soft brown hair that curled around her face and round cheeks, her smile adorably dimpled. Where Aunt Jane, who was tall and angular, tended to be stern when she was displeased, Aunt Em used a more subtle and yet far more painful method of reproach. Over the years, she'd mastered the art of guilt and could send a person—namely Sarafina—sad, lamenting looks that cut with the precision of a surgeon's knife.

Aunt Em gently set her teacup back on its saucer. "When you're done with breakfast, change into your lavender dress."

Wait. What's this? Bewildered, Sarafina asked, "May I ask why?"

"The color suits you." Aunt Em smiled her usual cheerful, distant smile. "You need something more to do than mere chores and sitting at a lake while— Ah, there's your aunt Jane."

"I made more toast." Aunt Jane set the plate of toast in the center of the table and resumed her seat. She selected a piece and started to butter it. "You were telling Sarafina something just now. Did I interrupt you?"

"Not at all," Aunt Em replied calmly. "I've decided that Sarafina needs a job."

Aunt Jane dropped her toast butter side down on the tablecloth.

Sarafina's mouth fell open.

"Close your mouth, dear." Aunt Em picked up Aunt Jane's toast and set it on the edge of her plate. "Mr. Edward Day will be coming by later this morning to speak with her. I've already suggested she wear her lavender dress. It suits her, doesn't it?"

Aunt Jane put her butter knife down with a clink. "Edward Day, the editor of the *Dove Pond Register*, is coming by to speak with Sarafina about a *job*?"

Aunt Em blinked. "Is there another Edward Day?"

"No! But I—" Aunt Jane pushed her plate away and took a deep breath. "Emily Anne, I hate it when you do this. Please start at the beginning."

Aunt Em delicately wiped her fingers on her napkin. "It began when Mr. Day heard that our Sarafina is quite the writer."

Aunt Jane blinked. "From whom?"

"From me, of course." Aunt Em brushed a toast crumb into a napkin and placed it to one side to feed to the birds even now lining up on the windowsill. "While at church a few weeks ago, I told Miss Hamilton about Sarafina's short stories. You know them, Jane. She reads them to us by the fire most evenings and—"

"Of course I know her stories!" Aunt Jane burst out impatiently.

"No need to yell. I'm glad you remember them. It would have been so hard to explain that part if you hadn't. Anyway, I didn't realize that Mr. Day was in the pew behind me when I was talking to Miss Hamilton. But yesterday, when I was out and about, I ran into him, and he mentioned that conversation and asked if Sarafina might be interested in writing for his newspaper. Naturally, I said yes."

"*What?* You agreed to allow *our niece* to write for a *newspaper*?" Aunt Jane looked as if she might burst into outraged flames.

Aunt Em didn't seem to notice. She was too busy wiggling her fingers at the cardinal that was hopping up and down on the sill, staring at her as if she were eating its food.

Sarafina wisely stayed silent. She had a vague, admittedly glorified idea of what being a reporter might entail because they'd been featured in several of the dime novels she loved to read. In them, the intrepid reporters investigated dangerous crooks and morally corrupt individuals, every page filled with excitement and danger. The lives of those fictional reporters were so far removed from Sarafina's sheltered, humdrum one that she'd never thought about pursuing that particular vocation herself.

She knew that all Aunt Em wanted was to keep her busy—in fact, too busy to visit her fishing hole and William. But she found herself wondering if a job like this wouldn't give her even more freedom.

"No!" Aunt Jane slapped her hand on the table, stiff with outrage. "No niece of mine will write for a newspaper! It's undignified."

Aunt Em smiled at her toast and took another bite.

Sarafina cleared her throat. "Since Aunt Emily Anne invited Mr. Day over, we have to at least talk to him, don't we? It would be impolite not to. He's coming all the way here—"

"No." Every line in Aunt Jane's thin body was taut with disapproval.

Oh dear! This wouldn't do *at all.* Sarafina clasped her hands together under her chin. "*Please* let me talk to Mr. Day! Aunt Emily Anne is right. I'm no longer going to Miss LaFont's, so I might as well take a job and learn to write even better—"

"No," Aunt Jane repeated. Her tone could only be called "frigid."

Unperturbed, Aunt Em said, "Sarafina will make a wonderful reporter."

Aunt Jane's mouth thinned. "Our brother won't like it."

"All the more reason to do it," Aunt Em replied with her usual placid smile. "If we ask her father, you know what he'll say."

Aunt Jane's mouth thinned even more. "Marriage."

Sarafina's mouth went dry. "M-m-marriage? Why would he say that?"

"Because he's already said it, and more than once, too." Aunt Em cast her gaze toward the ceiling as if counting something only she could see. "Seven times, in fact. Eight, if you count the last time he *started* to say it, but your aunt Jane cut him short."

"I was tired of hearing it." Aunt Jane's face was so red that it looked as if she'd been slapped. "I'm sorry to say it, Sarafina, but your father is a fool."

Aunt Em sighed. "He's archaic in his thinking and believes that your ultimate destiny is to become the wife of what he calls a 'successful man.'"

"A successful *older* man." Aunt Jane almost snapped the word in half. "He thinks an older man might know how to control you."

"Control?" Sarafina realized she was now gripping her butter knife as if she were about to stab something. "I don't— That's—"

"Nonsense is what it is!" Aunt Jane said forcibly. "Not all women are 'destined' for marriage. In fact, some of the happiest women I know live quite comfortably on their own."

"Which is why I'm pleased Mr. Day is coming by today," Aunt Em said in her calm, detached tone. "Jane, our Sarafina is much too young to be thinking of marriage. A gilded cage would never suit her. She's far more magpie than canary."

Was it better to be a magpie than a canary? Sarafina wasn't sure, but she knew better than to ask such a thing of Aunt Em, who, if prompted, could talk for hours about the personalities of various birds. So instead, Sarafina said, "I love to write, so perhaps becoming a reporter will suit me. I won't know until I try."

Aunt Em took a sip of her tea. "Do you promise, as a reporter, to always tell the truth?"

Sarafina nodded.

"And to never ever slant the news toward the wealthy and privileged?"

Sarafina held her hand up. "I promise."

Aunt Jane sniffed, although she looked far less unhappy than she had a moment ago. "I haven't agreed to this yet."

"But you will," Aunt Em said as she reached for another piece of toast. This one she crumbled onto her plate, making more breakfast for her birds. "Sarafina, dear, do you also vow to cover *all* the musical events in town?"

Aunt Jane cut a gaze her way. "The newspaper should cover those now."

"They should," Aunt Em said sadly. "Yet there wasn't one mention of the coming special cantata choir performance in Sunday's paper."

Aunt Jane was the lead soprano in the cantata. She didn't have a particularly inspiring voice, but what she lacked in ability, she made up for in enthusiasm. "The *Register* never announces our cantata performances." She sniffed disdainfully. "That's why people don't come."

"It's sad." Aunt Em scraped the breadcrumbs on her plate into a waiting napkin. "So unfair. It's very kind of Mr. Day to come here to offer our Sarafina the opportunity to work ten hours a week reporting on things like your choir's amazing cantata. I suggested that she should attend your practices every Tuesday afternoon so she'd get a better understanding of music. Mr. Day thought that was a particularly good idea."

Sarafina's heart sank. *Ah. Now I see what Aunt Em's doing. But it won't work. I'll find a way around it.* She would, too. No matter the cost.

Aunt Jane settled her egg cup on her plate. "It's a part-time position, is it?"

"Just a few hours a week," Aunt Em answered as she folded her napkin so the breadcrumbs wouldn't spill. "She'd be doing it under the utmost secrecy as well. Mr. Day was very insistent that she should use a pseudonym. I'm certain, too, that once he realizes how well she writes, she'll be given some of the newspaper's choicest assignments." Aunt Em beamed as if what she'd just said had already come true. "For now, in addition to covering the smaller events in town, he wants her to write a weekly column featuring housekeeping tips."

"Ha!" Aunt Jane scoffed. "As if she knows any."

Sarafina wet her dry lips. "I would need your help with it, Aunt Jane. No one knows how to keep a thrifty, clean house better than you."

Aunt Em gave her an approving look. "Our Sarafina will learn so much from this."

Aunt Jane locked her gaze on Sarafina for a long moment. Then she put down her spoon and delicately wiped her mouth with her napkin. "Your aunt Emily Anne is right. The lavender gown is the perfect choice."

Sarafina couldn't stop from grinning. She couldn't wait to tell William about this. It might mean her Tuesday afternoons would be busier, but if she was going to be working in town, they might be able to meet up there. Of course, they'd have to be careful to avoid the town gossips.

She cast a quick look at her aunts, her heart sinking as she realized they were among that number. *I wish they knew him the way I do.*

Aunt Jane's spoon gently clinked against the side of her cup as she stirred milk into her tea. "Sarafina, after you change, bring that last short story you wrote, the one about the shoemaker. Mr. Day will want to see the quality of your writing as well."

Sarafina mumbled a quick "Yes, ma'am" and left. She was halfway up the stairs when she heard Aunt Jane say to Aunt Em, "I wish you'd tell me before you did things like this."

"Things like what, dear?" Aunt Em had replied in her usual distracted voice.

Sarafina hurried to her room to change. As she dressed, she wondered yet again what it would be like to be a reporter. Mr. Day was right in suggesting she write under another name. She kicked her morning dress out of the way and pulled her lavender gown from the wardrobe, an idea occurring to her. She'd write under the name V. E. Fine, which stood for Very Exceptionally Fine—that was exactly what she wanted people to think of her reporting.

The front bell rang announcing Mr. Day's arrival, and her heart skipped a wild beat as she checked her appearance in the mirror and then hurried downstairs. If she could get hired as a reporter, then she would no longer write just to amuse herself and her aunts. Now her writing would have a purpose.

She couldn't wait to tell William.

CHAPTER 13

ROSE

Rose positioned her tote bag more securely on her shoulder, leaned her cane against the wall, and unlocked the bookshop door. The old iron key made a satisfying *click* before she collected her cane and went inside, the bell welcoming her as she turned on the lights and let the door close behind her. For now, she ignored the sign in the window and left it flipped to CLOSED. She still had an hour before she opened. And while she loved her customers, there was something special about this time of the morning when she was here alone. It soothed her spirit, even on restless days.

Every independent bookshop had its own personality, one established by the carefully curated stock and the caring attitude of the staff. She'd worked hard to make sure that the readers who visited her store always found a welcome atmosphere, a book (or ten) that spoke to them, and if not a cheerful smile—she had her limits, after all—at least the knowledge that she was glad to see them and loved books just as much as they did.

She limped to the counter and dropped the keys into the small dish beside the register. She set the mail to one side, to be sorted through later, and then printed up the online orders. Every once in a while, she would pause, look around, and soak in the wonder of owning this amazing place. She was blessed. Truly and wonderfully blessed.

Her gaze moved from the orders she'd just slipped into large manila envelopes to the stack of mail. Reluctantly, she picked it up and started sorting it. Her heart sank the second she saw an envelope with the word LATE stamped in red.

She glanced at the still-locked door, glad Luke wasn't around. Muttering under her breath, she tucked the letter under her arm, picked up her cane, and headed for her office. She went to her desk, opened the bottom drawer, and tossed the letter onto the dozen or so others that sat there. Then she slammed the drawer shut and dropped into her seat.

She crossed her arms and leaned back, staring with unseeing eyes out the picture window that looked onto her beloved bookshop, searching her mind and imagination for an idea—any idea—about how to handle the predicament she'd gotten herself into. *I knew better, too. But at the time, I couldn't think of a way out of it.*

Five years ago, an unusually strong winter storm had blown through their town and had iced up every tree and power line, leaving broken limbs and downed cables in its wake. Most of the town had gone without electricity for a week. While her old house had enough fireplaces to keep the pipes from exploding, the bookstore hadn't. It also hadn't had a decent roof, either. When the storm finally abated, the entire store had been left in shambles.

Her savings had already been depleted by her expensive-to-maintain house, so when the roof *and* pipes failed during the same storm, she'd been faced with necessary repairs that were far more than she could afford.

Her first instinct had been to go to the First People's Bank and talk to Zoe Bell, who'd taken over the loan portion of the bank from her father, Arnold. Rose had a personal relationship with Zoe, but knew the bookstore's income wouldn't be enough to secure a loan. So Rose hadn't bothered to ask First People's Bank for help.

Instead, she'd gone to a lender in Asheville, one known for financing risky businesses with higher-rate balloon loans. She now realized that the term "balloon" was a joke. It just meant that the entire amount of the loan would be due one day down the road. "It should be called a lead balloon loan," she muttered to herself as she aimlessly kicked at the drawer holding the late notices. "They don't float at all. They just crash to the ground with a thud."

Scowling, she rubbed her forehead where it felt tight. It was her fault and no one else's. Of course, at the time she'd gotten the loan, she'd stupidly believed that her beloved bookstore with its new pipes and roof wouldn't need any additional repairs. And yet other things had gone wrong over the years, stealing the money she tried to tuck away for the coming due date. A field mouse had chewed into some wires in the attic, which had been super costly because the resulting inspection after the repair had turned up some "irregularities" that she'd been forced to have fixed. A few months after that, the main water line to the building that serviced their one and only bathroom had rusted through, and they'd had to dig up a concrete floor in the basement for that not-little repair. And then the floor under her office began to show signs of—

Sheesh! She didn't want to think about all the "and thens." Each one hurt like a punch in the stomach. *I have to find a way to pay off that loan. I have to.*

Which meant she should get to work, and right now. She sighed, collected her cane, and left her office, shoving aside all thoughts about that stupid due date. For the next half hour, she kept busy. She ran a duster along the bookshelves, straightened a few stacks that looked as if they might tumble, marked some books for sale, and swept the floors.

Once that was done, she put away the broom and made her way to the front windows. She peeked through them, carefully surveying the street outside, where the first hint of spring had given the almost barren trees a faintly green look. Not a car or person was in sight. *Good.* Reassured, she headed to Tay's office and let herself inside. She had a nice half hour before Tay would arrive, coffee in hand, her satchel tucked under one arm.

Every morning for the past week, Rose had added this little journey to her daily chores, in which she would sit at Tay's desk and go through the notes on the yellow legal pad always left there. To her surprise, reading the letters William had written to Sarafina had softened her opinion of the man. Whatever his faults, greed or otherwise, he'd loved that woman dearly. If Rose thought that Tay would focus on that one aspect of William Day's, she'd be a lot happier. Still, Rose had to admit that she admired the younger woman for a number of reasons. She'd watched Tay over the past week and had learned a few things. For one, she was a hard worker, showing up at nine sharp every morning and working until seven at night, and sometimes later. She always took a stack of folders with her when she went home, too. Rose liked that. Hard work was a sign of a responsible adult. Luke needed more of that in his life, with his don't-like-to-work-hard personality.

Tay had passed the preliminary Lulu test, too. The two weren't close yet, but Tay had been friendly at their first, brief meeting, and it was obvious that Lulu hadn't hated her. That was promising. Lulu was slow to warm up to new people, so it would take time.

So far, after a week's analysis, there was only one thing Rose didn't like about Tay. No one could argue that the professor wasn't a super-smart and cute sort of girl. She also looked much younger than her thirty-odd years of age, too. But sadly, she wasn't much of a flirt. That was disappointing. In the past week, Luke had spent hours every day in this office helping Tay go through the old newspapers looking for God knew what. From what Rose had observed from her perch at the counter, the two usually sat at their desks, not even looking or talking to each other, but just staring at old *Register*s.

Rose made a face. She was sure that was as much Luke's fault as Tay's. Heaven knew Rose had done her part in getting these two together—she'd been the one to suggest that Tay use the office as a permanent base to begin with. Had they been normal human beings, the two of them would have taken it from there. But instead, nothing exciting had happened. *Lord love you, Luke. There's a brass ring right in front of you. Grab it!*

Sighing, Rose leaned her cane against Tay's desk and pulled her reading glasses from her front pocket to start snooping through Tay's latest notes. After ten minutes, she sat back in the noisy chair, slightly satisfied with what she'd read. It didn't appear that Tay's research was overly focused on William Day yet. True, she was looking for mentions of him and the other robbers in the newspapers, but that was all. *She won't find much. I've already looked.*

What was odd, though, was that Tay and Luke were also searching the old *Register*s for a series of phrases. Rose closed the notebook and returned it to the correct spot, her gaze moving over the other items on the desk. Four *Register* articles written by a V. E. Fine had been photocopied and were neatly lined up side by side, some of the phrases from the list she'd just read highlighted in yellow.

Rose frowned at the articles. They had very little in common. The first was a rather short piece on the use of vinegar as a window cleaning agent. The second was about a fight that had broken out during a town hall meeting, while the third article covered a barn that had burned down behind a house on Dogwood Street. The final article was an interview with a local man who'd been wounded during the War of 1812. *I wonder who V. E. Fine was and why Tay's interested in him. I need to ask L—*

"Rose?" Tay stood in the doorway, her stuffed satchel hanging from her shoulder, her eyes wide with surprise. She wore a blue jean jacket over a blue and green flannel shirt, her thick blond hair tucked behind her ears. She set her coffee on the corner of the desk. "What are you doing in here?"

Rose briefly considered lying but couldn't think of a single excuse that made sense, so instead she shrugged. "I'm sitting in this creaky-ass chair, wondering who this V. E. Fine was."

A flicker of annoyance crossed Tay's face, but all she said was "You saw those articles."

"They were right there, staring at me." Rose grabbed her cane, stood, and moved out from behind the desk. "You're early this morning."

"I couldn't sleep so I decided to go ahead and come in." Tay passed Rose and placed her satchel in her chair. "Do you do this often? Come in here and see what's on my desk?"

Every morning. "Nope. Wouldn't think of it. I came in today to use the spare desk to prep the online orders, and I happened to see the articles you have out on display. So . . . who is that Fine person?"

Tay didn't look enthusiastic about sharing what she knew, but she shrugged and said, "We think that's Sarafina's pseudonym."

"Oh!" Rose eyed the articles with renewed interest. "You think she wrote for the *Register*?"

"Sarafina used certain phrases while writing later in her life. Luke and I marked the articles where we saw some of those phrases, and they all seemed to have been written by this V. E. Fine." Tay went to hang her jacket on the rack in the corner of the office. "Luke and I still need to find some primary corroborating sources, but it's promising."

"Interesting. You should check the *Register* ledgers."

Tay's eyebrows rose. "Ledgers?"

"The financial records. Luke didn't show those to you? I swear that boy never listens to me." She shook her head. "Check the ledgers for the months those articles were printed. You can't pay a pseudonym, so the real reporter's name should be listed there."

Tay's gray-green eyes gleamed. "Rose, that's so helpful! I'll look for those right now."

"Here. I'll show you where they are." Rose headed for the archive room and led the way through a maze of shelves to the back unit. She used her cane to indicate the bottom row, where a line of thin books filled the shelf. "The years are written on the first page of each ledger."

Tay bent down and selected a ledger, checked the date, and then returned it. She counted down four more ledgers and chose another. "Here it is. Rose, thank you." Tay carried the ledger back to her desk.

Rose followed. "Speaking of Luke, is he helping or getting in your way?"

"Helping. To be honest, it's been nice to have him here."

Rose could tell that Tay hated admitting that. "He's smart. Always has been. Both he and Caitlyn."

Tay sent her a curious look. "He doesn't talk much about his sister."

"It's painful for us all. She's different from her brother, always had a wild side. We got used to it over the years, I suppose, and we missed the signs that she was going off the rails." Rose sighed. "Her parents and Luke always say she got involved with some punk and lost her way, but he wasn't the cause of her problems. He was just a symptom."

"It's sometimes hard to accept that someone you love is having problems."

"It's harder to accept it when you can't understand it. Luke feels especially responsible for what happened. They used to be close, but he started having to travel for work and was gone a lot. He and Caitlyn drifted apart, so he wasn't around when she started having issues."

"Issues?"

"We thought it might be drugs, and there may have been some involved. We know she was gambling heavily, and spending money like it was water. One of the psychiatrists she saw used the term 'manic.' Whatever you call it, she lost her way and got wilder and wilder and embezzled a good bit from her employer. The way she carried out the theft was sloppy and as obvious as all get-out, too."

"You think she wanted to get caught?"

"Between you and me, I believe that's exactly what she wanted to happen. She's always struggled with taking care of both herself and Lulu. Every time life got difficult for her, someone in the family would rush in and fix things." Rose winced. "We shouldn't have done it, but we did. We all hoped that she'd suddenly mature and start being more responsible, but she never found her balance in life. Maybe going to jail and facing the consequences of her own actions will push her down the right road, but I don't know. We've been disappointed so many times now."

Tay's gaze had softened. "It sounds as if it's been tough on all of you."

"Luke especially. He's done more than his fair share to make things right by stepping in to raise Lulu."

"He's kind."

Rose leaned a little closer. "*And* single."

"Rose!" Tay's face had turned pink. "He's not—I'm not—"

"Whatever." Rose had said what needed to be said. *I hope I at least planted a seed.* She gestured to the stacks of files on the desk. "I'd better let you get back to work. But let me ask you something. It's neat to know that Sarafina might have written for the *Register*, but is it really important?"

"It's very important. It's always bothered me that everyone thought she just showed up in New York City and got a reporting gig without experience of some sort. Who does that? And if she did write for the *Register*, it could give us an idea of the personal connections she had in town. For instance, if she worked there, then she must have known your grandfather Edward Day. Those connections can help us understand who she was and why she took the path in life she did."

Rose nodded. "Fascinating stuff. I'm glad Luke's helping out."

"He's been working hard. Besides going through all those *Registers*, he's also attempting to solve the great secret-code mystery."

"Ah. The poem that tells a family secret."

"Luke told you about that. I gave him the poem last week."

"No. I heard it from the postman, Mr. Robinson, when I stopped to get the mail Wednesday." She caught Tay's shocked expression and shrugged. "You can't throw a rock in this town without hitting some gossip. Personally, I think the notion that the family secret is something big is poppycock. People don't deliver big news in poems. In fact, when I stopped by the Ace Hardware, I put ten bucks down that it'll be 'nothing more valuable than a set of china.'"

"Ten— Rose, people are *betting* on that? At the hardware store?"

"Nate Stevens has the chart behind the counter. I'm surprised you didn't know about that, as I saw two of your sisters when I was there. Ava put ten dollars on 'love affair,' while Sarah wagered twenty on 'secret baby.'"

"I can't believe this." Tay closed her eyes and pressed her fingertips to her temples. "And my own sisters, too."

Rose felt sorry for Tay. The whole town was watching—and wagering—on what that silly poem might reveal about the Doves. *At least there aren't any family secrets hovering over my family. That's a blessing, I suppose.*

Tay dropped her hands from her temples and managed a wan smile. "I should get to work. Thank you again for showing me the ledgers. In fact, thank you for everything you've done, especially for letting me use this office."

"Psht. It was no big deal. No one else was using it, anyway."

"It's been nice not having to pack up my things every time there was a meeting." Tay looked around the office, her gaze moving out to the bookshop. "I sometimes wonder what this place looked like back in your grandfather's day. I bet it was something."

Rose had always thought the same thing. "He tripled the subscription rate and went from a four-page edition to twelve, all by the end of his first year as editor." She nodded toward the main room of her bookstore. "My grandfather had two Franklin presses right out there on heavy tables in the middle of the room. Said they were something, those presses."

"I bet." Tay picked up one of the articles sitting on her desk. "The reporting was really good back then. It's accurate and sharp, and much better than the bigger papers."

"Grandfather did a good bit of the reporting in the early days. Later, he employed a whole slew of women from town to do it. Said they wrote cleaner copy than any man could."

"He was a pioneer in women's rights."

Rose pursed her lips. "You might call it more of a marketing move. He could pay women less, and by hiring them from different families around town, the *Register* got two and sometimes three new subscriptions per hire. Everyone and their mother likes to see their name in print, even a pseudonym."

"That was brilliant of him."

Rose couldn't have agreed more. According to family lore, her grandfather's investment in the newspaper had been an expense that he incurred because he considered it crucial to the health of their town. Fortunately, his other businesses generated enough to cover the cost of running the *Register*. Rose thought her grandfather also liked the prestige and gravitas the position of editor gave him.

She'd just started to say as much to Tay when the bell over the front door rang and Luke came in. Rose noticed that his gaze moved immediately to Tay's office. *You didn't look for me at all, did you?* She supposed she should feel a little scorned by that, but it was a good sign that maybe things between him and Tay were moving along better than she'd thought.

Children today were so complicated. Back in her day, when a man pursued a woman, everyone knew it. He'd bring her flowers, dress up to visit her, sit beside her in church, and then put a ring on her finger—all in public. Now it was secret text messages and Netflix and whatnot. *Yet another reason our society is doomed.*

Luke came into the office and cast a searching gaze in Tay's direction. "Good morning. Everything okay?"

Tay smiled. "It's all good. Rose has been helping out this morning. She showed me the ledgers."

Luke cast Tay an apologetic look before he took his jacket off and hung it over the back of his seat. "I'd forgotten about those."

"No problem." Tay was already bending back over the open ledger. "I know about them now."

Rose sniffed. "If you two are set, then I'll head out front and get ready to op—"

"Look!" Tay pointed to the ledger. "Sarafina *was* V. E. Fine!"

Luke jumped up and hurried to her desk to look. He rested a hand on the back of her chair as he bent over to see the ledger, his face even with hers.

"The ledgers are color coded." Tay ran her finger down the page. "There's blue ink for expenses and payroll for the *Register.* Black ink for a grist mill Mr. Day owned. And green ink for the photography studio—things like 'chair prop' and 'flowers.' See?"

Rose noticed how close Tay's and Luke's heads were. *If either of them turns just the littlest bit, they could kiss.*

"Tay!" Luke pointed to the bottom of the next page. "During the same month, William was paid as a photographer's assistant!"

Tay couldn't have looked happier. "Aunt Jo was right about the pictures in the tin—the man Sarafina was interested in wasn't standing in the photo with her. He was behind the camera. We need to document all of this. If we look in the other ledgers, we might find out how long they worked in the same building." She turned to smile at Luke just as he looked at her.

For one perilous second, their lips were a scant inch away.

Do it! Rose silently urged.

They both gave a start. Tay yanked her head back toward the ledgers so quickly that Rose was certain the younger woman must have pulled a muscle, while Luke straightened up as if on a spring and headed back to his own desk.

He sat down and started moving papers around, his face as red as Tay's. "I'll just, ah—" He picked up a notebook and a pen and began flipping the pages as if looking for something.

Rose stifled a frustrated groan. She scowled at both of them and then said shortly, "I'm going to open the shop." She didn't wait for a response but headed back into the bookstore, slamming the door behind her.

Something was definitely happening back there, even if neither Tay nor Luke seemed able to accept it. *Come on, Luke. Don't you let me down, too.* Rose went to the front door and flipped the CLOSED sign to OPEN. Then she settled behind the counter, found the box of new bookmarks, and added them to the display.

The bell rang as the first customer of the day entered. Rose smiled at Miss Tilghman and then looked back at Luke and Tay. He'd pulled his chair close to her desk, and they were bent over the ledger, talking excitedly.

Rose watched them for a while. Maybe she should follow Luke's advice and stop worrying so much about William Day's reputation and do as other people did: focus instead on the gold. She could use a fortune in gold right now. She cast an uneasy glance at her office, where the stack of notices seemed to be mocking her.

The truth was, no one needed to find a pot of gold more than she did.

CHAPTER 14

LUKE

It took Luke a lot longer than he'd expected to figure out the clue hidden in the mysterious poem Sarafina wrote for her daughter. Almost two weeks in fact, and he'd even cheated by running it through several AI apps. When that didn't help, he'd written a quick program to try to discern the meaning, but nothing seemed to work.

That is, nothing had worked until exactly two fifteen that afternoon. He'd been sitting at the counter at the Moonlight Café with a cup of coffee, doodling on the back of a napkin while on the phone with a fellow cybersecurity specialist who was complaining about a troublesome client, when his brain had landed on the answer with a definitive thud. He'd been so pleased with himself that even now, almost an hour later, he was still fighting the urge to do a happy dance.

"Nailed it," he murmured under his breath, unable to stop himself from giving the air a quick fist pump as he thought about how excited Tay would be.

"Are you punching the sky?"

He looked down to find Lulu eyeing him with suspicion. He was walking her to the bookshop from the bus stop, her small hand tucked in his. "This is called a fist pump." He demonstrated it for her. "It means you're winning at something."

Lulu made a fist and pumped it in the air, hopping a little as she did so.

"Well done," he said approvingly, as he did whenever she copied him. He loved those moments. Loved them more than he'd thought possible.

When he'd first gotten custody of Lulu, he hadn't realized how addicted he'd become to her antics. But addicted he was. Now she was such a huge part of his life that he had trouble remembering what it had been like before she'd arrived. It was as if everything had gotten bigger, brighter, and better.

He shifted her book bag to his other shoulder and opened the door to the bookshop, smiling as she ran in ahead of him. He followed, his gaze instantly turning toward Tay's office.

He expected to see her sitting at her desk, her head bent over old *Registers*, just as he'd left her not three hours ago to run some errands, but she was nowhere to be seen. *Where is she? I have to tell her—*

"She'll be back in a few minutes," Grandma Rose said from where she sat on her stool behind the counter. "She went to Ava's tearoom to pick up a snack for Lulu."

Lulu yelled "YAY!" at a decibel level that made him wince.

"That's enough of that," Grandma Rose said firmly.

"Look, Grandma Rose. I have pump fists." The little girl swung wildly at the ceiling with both fists and would have fallen had Luke not scooped her up under one arm like a sack of flour, which made her giggle.

Grandma Rose snorted. "You're a wild one today, aren't you?"

Luke carried Lulu to the children's corner and plonked her onto her chair. "You have homework to do." He stooped down, opened her backpack, and dug out her crayons. Then he found the assigned page and placed it on the little table. "It says to color the circles red and the squares purple."

Lulu leaned to one side so she could see around him to the door. "I'll wait until Miss Tay comes with my snack."

"You can have your snack once you finish your homework." He could see Lulu was about to argue, so he stood up. "You'd better hurry. If she brings cupcakes, it'll be hard for me to resist eating a second one, and then there won't be any for you. Just saying."

Lulu didn't like that one bit, but after burning him in place with an outraged glare, she picked up her purple crayon and started to color, although he noticed she wasn't even trying to stay within the lines.

He wandered over to where Grandma Rose sat watching him. She'd been doing that a lot lately, eyeing him as if she were trying to guess his weight. "What are you looking at?"

"That's exactly what I'm trying to figure out."

What did that even mean? But before he could get clarification, the door swung open and Tay came in. She looked like a college student today in her jeans, sweatshirt, and jean jacket, her glasses perched on her head. She waved at him and Grandma Rose and then stopped by Lulu's table, reached into the bag she carried marked PINK MAGNOLIA TEAROOM, and placed a pink cupcake in front of Lulu.

"Thank you!" Lulu greedily reached for the cupcake.

"What did I say?" Luke warned. "Homework first."

Lulu's smile melted into a frown. "I want a cupcake!"

Tay set the bag to one side and stooped beside Lulu. "Is your homework hard?"

"No," Lulu admitted with a pout. "I just don't want to do it."

Tay nodded as if that explained it all.

Luke was glad to see that Lulu was warming up to Tay. Even though Lulu had a personality bigger than her small body, ever since Caitlyn's trouble, she tended to be shy around those she didn't know.

"I have an idea." Tay cupped her hand around her mouth to whisper loudly to Lulu, "Strike a deal with your uncle. Offer to do half of the work for half of the cupcake. You get the other half when you finish."

Lulu immediately turned to Luke and announced, "I'll make you a deal."

"Oh, you will, will you?"

Her curls bounced with each nod. "I do half of my homework, then I eat half of my cupcake. I'll save the rest for when I get done."

Luke could hear Grandma Rose muttering from behind the counter, saying how she'd have never gotten away with striking a deal back in her day. He rubbed his chin as if considering Lulu's offer. "That seems pretty fair." He went to where she sat and held his hand up for her high five. "It's a deal."

Lulu slapped his hand hard and then picked up her cupcake.

Tay ruffled Lulu's hair and then got back to her feet, reclaimed her bag, and came to the counter. She set the bag in front of Grandma Rose. "There are cupcakes for both of you, too."

"You are sweeter than sweet tea." Grandma Rose came out from behind the counter and elbowed Luke in the ribs. "Isn't she?"

"*Ow!*" Luke rubbed his side and shot her an annoyed glance. "What was that for?"

"It was to remind you to thank Miss Tay for being so nice. How many women do you know who'd get you a cupcake without even asking?"

He frowned at his grandmother. *Good Lord. This woman.* Over the past week, it had become painfully obvious that she was matchmaking. Worse yet, she was doing it with the delicacy of a crazed bull in a glass shop.

Tay had noticed it, too, because she began backing away toward her office. "I should get back to work and— See you two later." She spun around and hurried off.

Great. Just great. Luke turned back to Grandma Rose. "What in the heck was that?"

"Nothing." With an air of satisfaction, Rose watched as Tay went into her office and closed the door before settling down at her desk. "I was just making small talk."

"You were making small talk and big problems." He wondered if he should find out when and why she'd decided to interfere in his love life, and then realized it would be a waste of time. "Mind watching Lulu? I need to tell Tay something."

"Sure." Grandma Rose eyed him with interest. "Tell her what?"

He shot her an impatient glance. "Something about work. Nothing else."

Grandma Rose couldn't have looked more disappointed. "You're not going to ask her what she's doing for dinner or invite her over for 'Netflix and chill' or—"

"Stop it! Whatever this is"—he waved in her general direction—"just quit."

Grandma Rose sniffed. "I was just trying to help. But I heard you, so get, then."

He started to reply, when some customers came in. *Hopefully that will keep Grandma Rose busy.* Without another word, he made his way to Tay's office, careful not to look as if he was hurrying.

Tay was seated at her desk, reading an old *Register* line by line, searching for the names on her "must find" list.

"How's it going?" he asked.

"Slowly." She didn't even look up, her glasses resting about halfway down on her nose. "I just discovered that, according to the paper, Sarafina's aunt Jane sang in the cantata and was pretty good at it too." Tay turned a page, her gaze still on her work.

He went to his desk and found the folder holding the original poem and letter from Sarafina. He tucked it under his arm, dropped into his chair, and slowly wheeled his way to her desk. He wasn't exactly sneaking up on her, as the thing creaked as if it were about to explode. It was more of *Hey, look! An announcement is about to be made!*

She looked up just as he rolled his chair up next to hers. "What is it?"

This was it. The moment he'd been waiting for. He leaned back in his chair and grinned. "I solved the riddle."

She just stared at him.

His smile slipped. "I solved it, Tay. I really did."

Her eyes widened and her mouth formed a perfect O.

She looked so cute that Luke grinned as he reached over, put one finger under her chin, and closed her mouth. "*This* is why we need a wine fridge. We could be having champagne right now."

Her gaze was now locked on him. "Before you tell me what you think the answer is, explain how you got it."

"Sure." He opened the folder and pulled out the original poem and letter and set them side by side. "I made the same error at first that others must have. Because Sarafina wrote this toward the end of her life, everyone—including me—assumed that the poem held clues that pertained to New York City, where Sarafina and David were married and Lucy was born. But then it dawned on me. What if the family secret has to do with Sarafina's earlier life when she lived here?"

Tay's brows knit as she considered this. "You think the clues in this poem are about Dove Pond. From the records we have, we know that after she left, she only returned to town one time, and that was with her husband, David. It was a very short and hurried visit, too, less than a week. That makes it seem that she'd decided that her time here wasn't all that important."

"Maybe she had a reason not to return. A disagreement with her aunts or—I don't know. All I do know is that I think the clues in this poem are about Dove Pond. Once I realized that, the whole thing made sense." He leaned forward. "It works, Tay. Every line works."

Tay absently rubbed her neck just below one ear, as if easing the tension there. "It's a stretch, but . . . you might be right." She tapped an insistent finger on the poem. "Now give me the details."

He pointed to the first line. "Where do you find all of these things: a truth, a name, a number?"

"I don't know. I've read this poem a million times and I couldn't come up with anything."

"They're on a tombstone, Tay. A truth, a name, and a number." He counted it out on his fingers. "The fact that they're dead, the name of the deceased, and the date they died."

She scooted forward, her chair complaining as she did. "Go on."

"Now look at the next lines. *Told to all yet soon mentioned by none. He carved it in stone where peace meets up in oaken silence.*"

"Now that you've determined the beginning line was about a tombstone, I would guess this portion is talking about a graveyard."

"Exactly." He didn't have to explain it, but he did anyway. "*Told to all yet soon mentioned by none.* When you die, it's announced in newspapers, in church bulletins, and on death certificates, and yet soon the names of the dead are rarely spoken."

She nodded slowly. "*So he carved it in stone where peace meets up in oaken silence.* For decades people have said that the term 'oaken' was important. When I thought of New York City, I couldn't find a connection. But if it's Dove Pond, then it's the Oak Hill Cemetery."

"Yes!" He leaned back and grinned. "Which is owned by my family, by the way."

"It's a private cemetery? I didn't realize that."

"Oh yes. And it's old, old, old." He was grinning from ear to ear and felt about two feet taller, and he was pretty tall to begin with. "What do you think? Do I deserve champagne or not?"

"It works." She still looked slightly stunned. "It really works."

"I guess that Dove Pond was in Sarafina's heart, even though she didn't visit but that one time." He cut a glance at Tay. "How much of a record is there for that visit, by the way?"

"We only know about it from something David wrote in a letter to his solicitor. He wrote that they'd come here and had met with the town council and 'had made their request.' Other than the fact they only came that once and they stayed for less than a week, we don't know anything else."

That was interesting. "What did they request of the town council?"

"No one knows, as the minutes for that particular meeting are missing." Tay pushed her chair away from her desk. "We need to visit Oak Hill Cemetery. The family secret could be right there."

"Or there could be another clue," he pointed out. It would be a little disappointing if all it took to find a treasure was one simple riddle, no matter how many weeks it had taken him to decipher it.

"How far away is the cemetery?" Tay asked. "I know what road it's on, but it's been ages since I've been by there."

"It's a twenty-minute drive, no more."

She jumped up and began collecting her things. "Since your family owns it, I assume there are only Days buried there."

Luke rolled his chair back to his own desk. "There's a Dove family section, too. Their property abutted the Days', and they shared the plot for a while before they sold it along with some farmland." At her surprised look, he added, "I looked up the property records last night, as they're all online and I couldn't sleep. When I was in high school, I mowed the cemetery every Friday afternoon, too."

She grabbed her jean jacket from the back of her chair and pulled it on. "I'll drive. My Jeep is just outside." Satchel and coffee in hand, she led the way out of the office.

Grandma Rose looked up as they neared the counter. "Going somewhere?"

He nodded. "We're off to check something out."

Lulu, halfway through eating the last half of her cupcake, stood. "Can I go?"

"Sit," Grandma Rose said firmly. "Your dad and Miss Tay have some work to do."

"Thank you." Luke gave Lulu a quick hug and a goodbye before he followed Tay out the door and to the parking lot, where a red Jeep Cherokee sat.

"Nice wheels," Luke said as he climbed into the passenger seat.

"I wish it was mine, but I'm borrowing it from Trav Parker."

"He and Grace live next door to you all. I'd forgotten that." Luke liked Trav, who owned the only repair shop in town and was a gifted mechanic.

Tay buckled her seat belt. "Grace was the one who suggested Trav lend this Jeep to me. He must own five or six vehicles, and Grace says she has to play car Tetris every morning before work, just to get out of her own driveway."

Luke laughed as he buckled his seat belt. "That would get old." He watched as Tay expertly backed out of the parking space, and they were soon on their way. As she drove, he shot her a quick glance. "The style of this vehicle suits you, but I never took you as the Jeep sort."

She flashed him a surprised look. "What's the 'Jeep sort'?"

"You know, outdoorsy."

She sniffed. "I can be outdoorsy."

"Really?" He turned in his seat so he could see her expression. "How many times have you been camping in your life?"

"Once, when I was ten."

"I see. Do you fish, then?"

She turned the Jeep off Main Street. "No."

"Sail?"

"No. Look, I'll save you some time. I don't camp or fish or sail. But I do walk."

He had to smile at her lofty tone. "You mean hike? Like in the woods?"

"No, just walk, and usually on sidewalks. That's still outside. I've always lived in cities near universities, and you can't do those other things there. But you can always walk."

He couldn't argue with that.

She stopped the Jeep at a stop sign, and then drove on before casting a curious glance his way. "Do *you* fish or hike or any of those things?"

"I camp, hike, and read at least one book a week. Some weekends, I ride my Kawasaki KX 450 around the old fire roads through the mountains. In between, I'm raising Lulu, which presents its own challenges." Mentioning Lulu almost always won the day. Women usually sent him admiring glances when he reminded them that he, a single male, was voluntarily raising his own niece.

He waited, but all Tay did was murmur, "Interesting," in such a bland tone that he was pretty sure she thought him anything but.

Luke had decided a while ago that Tay's prickliness was due to her ex. He'd taken the time over the past week to get the gossip on Tay Dove and had managed to catch Kat Carter at the Moonlight Café in a particularly talkative mood. Her version of Tay's betrayal had little to do with book rights, so in some ways, he knew more than she did. But she knew a few interesting facts Tay hadn't shared. Mainly that

Richard was her department head and her boss, and secondly that Tay hadn't dated much at all before this last relationship.

Those two facts explained why that jerk's behavior weighed so heavily on Tay. Getting over heartbreak was never easy, and from the sound of things, it had been a first for her. Luke stared out his window in the general direction of Boston. *Thanks for making life hard for those of us who might want a chance, jerk.*

Tay turned onto Hill Road, which was surrounded on each side by brown winter pastureland that was just turning green and would soon be dotted with gold and purple wildflowers. A brisk wind roiled the fields, making the grass wave as if it were an ocean. Behind the fields rose purple and green-gray mountains that touched the blue sky.

Tay must have noticed the vista just as Luke did, because she sighed. "Even in the winter, it's pretty out here."

He couldn't agree more. "Do you miss living here?"

Her gaze returned to the road ahead. "I miss belonging someplace."

He could understand that. "I was a little discombobulated when Lulu and I moved here. I'd visited once in a while, because of Grandma Rose, but living here is different. Now it feels like home. I like it."

"It's a nice town. Maybe one day I'll move back."

"Really? You've thought of doing that?"

She grinned. "Not really, no. But I should. I always end up in college towns that are charming and eclectic because they feel like home to me, like Dove Pond." She pursed her lips thoughtfully. "To be honest, it would be nice to be closer to my sisters. They're— Oh. There's the cemetery."

An old wooden sign hung from a post that had aged to a faded gray. She turned into a small gravel lot and parked. He didn't wait for her to turn off the engine before hopping out and going to open her door.

He was just being polite, but her stiff, murmured "Thank you" was anything but appreciative. *Sheesh, she has more boundaries than breaths.*

He closed the door and followed her to the gate.

"I wonder how many cemeteries are in town."

He knew the answer to that because he'd looked just last night. "Seven. Five of them are located on private property, like this one. I haven't seen them all, but they're probably just as small. Then there are the two main ones, which are owned by local churches in town."

Tay unlatched the gate and pushed it open, the hinges protesting loudly. Oak Hill Cemetery was so named for the lone oak tree that towered over it and predated the town by at least a hundred years, if not more. The huge branches shaded the cemetery below and hindered the grass in some spots, so brown patches of earth were visible here and there.

Luke followed Tay through the gate, watching as she headed for the closest tombstones. Overhead, the wind shook the huge oak, sending down what must have been the last clinging leaf to join the others already thick on the ground. The tombstones were unevenly spread out and set in rows that, over time, had become less than straight. They were of different sizes and cuts, the lettering on some so faded as to make it difficult to discern the names and dates.

She knelt at the first tombstone and grimaced at the sight of the lichen covering the surface. "It's a good thing Grace left some cleaning supplies in that Jeep. Would you mind getting those rags and spray bottles from the bucket in the back? We may need to clean these in order to read them."

"Sure." He went back to her Jeep and collected the items she'd requested. He returned and tossed them to her, admiring her deft catch.

She looked around. "Where's the Dove section?"

He nodded toward the back corner, and she rose and went to look.

She stooped in front of the first Dove tombstone and sprayed it down. "We should take photos of each one. That could be useful later."

He pulled out his phone and took a shot of the closest headstone, and then cast a critical eye over the picture. "We should take the photos in black and white. That should show the details better, and we can adjust the exposure when we need to."

She tried it on the next tombstone. "You're right! I'll do it that way from now on." She set to work then, her attention focused on her job. After moving methodically from headstone to headstone, she stopped at the end of the first row. "These must be some of the oldest tombstones in Dove Pond. This one says 1714."

"I think so." He rubbed clean some of the closer tombstones. "For a private plot, there are a surprising number of other families here. There are Doves, Carters, Parkers, and even some McClearys. I never noticed that when I was mowing the grass."

She shot him a curious look. "Who mows it now?"

"Grandma Rose hires it out. She takes her duties as family scion very seriously."

Tay went back to cleaning and photographing headstones, pausing when she reached the center row. "Ah! It's Marcus McCleary's grave."

Luke came to stand beside her. It was a rather plain headstone, flat and rectangular. Carved neatly into the greenish gray surface was MARCUS WINSTON MCCLEARY, APRIL 19, 1873 TO JULY 15, 1897. "Take a lot of pictures."

"I plan on it. According to the court records, he died in prison just two months after he went to jail. That was no surprise, though. Some of the newspapers reported that he never recovered from his injuries from the robbery, plus he was already suffering from tuberculosis, too." She took a picture of the headstone and then checked it to make sure the lettering was readable.

"William Day wasn't injured, and yet he didn't last long after that, did he? What was it? Six months later?"

"Not quite four."

"Wow. And he was healthy. I guess jails were pretty brutal back then."

"I suppose so." She moved to the next tombstone and sprayed it down. "I wonder if there are medical records from that jail. I should check that, although it would be rare. Still, it doesn't hurt to look." She continued to work, finally reaching the last tombstone in her row. "Here is William Day's grave." It was a simple gravestone, much like the others. It read RIP, WILLIAM HARRIS DAY, BORN 1-3-1876, DIED 11-1-1897. "The famous Dove Pond bank robbers, both in the same cemetery."

Luke shook out his rag and hung it over the fence at the edge of the graveyard and then slid his cold hands into his pockets. "I've seen these tombstones hundreds of times but never really paid attention to them. And now, here I am, hoping they'll let us decipher a supposed message from the past."

She reexamined the two headstones, peering at first one and then the other.

"See anything of interest?"

"No," she said in a regretful tone. She straightened and sighed. "Let's clean the rest of these. Maybe something will stand out."

He nodded. "Something has to."

They worked quietly after that, cleaning each and every tombstone. He had to admit, it would have been a little anticlimactic if the answer to Sarafina's coded message had been on the first marker they saw or emblazoned on William Day's tombstone. Puzzles were like that: if they were too easy to solve, a person could feel cheated.

He finished cleaning the final tombstone in his row and took a picture of it. As he did so, he glanced over at Tay and noticed how precisely she worked. She gently brushed the stones with the rag, as if they might crumble under her touch. Time and again, he'd witnessed how patient and careful she was. *I like that about her.*

They finally finished their task, and he waited as she took a photo of the final tombstone and then joined him. "Let's look at the pictures and see if we can spot anything special."

They traded phones, and he swiped through her photos as she looked through his. He paused now and then, wondering if the shape of the tombstones could mean anything, although they were all rather common. Then he went back and tried to see if the death dates might contain codes or a hidden meaning, but again he came up empty.

After looking at the final photo for what felt like the hundredth time, he handed her phone back. "I don't see anything."

"Me neither." She couldn't have looked more disappointed.

"Nothing seems unusual. There's some random scoring on the tops of some of these, but that's normal for stonework."

Her gray-green gaze flew to him. "Scoring?"

He pointed to the closest tombstone, and she went to look. He followed, more to hear what she had to say about it than to see it again.

There, on the top ridge of the stone, were two marks. They weren't anything to look at—just a line, followed by a chipped area. "Maybe they were in a vise of some sort while the carving was being done."

"Some have it and some don't. I don't know a lot about how they used to carve these things back in the day." She stood silently for a moment. "It's weird there's both a line and a chipped area, almost as if—" She froze and then stepped closer to the stone. "The poem."

"What about it?"

"That one line. *Where peace meets* up *in silence.*" Her gaze moved from the tombstone to somewhere far over his head.

"Up? You mean this tree?"

She clasped her hands together and gave an excited hop. "Can you climb it?"

"Are you serious?" He looked at the huge, rambling, heavy-limbed oak that spread over their heads. "*This* tree? Why?" He wasn't afraid of heights. They just made him uncomfortable.

"Because once you're high enough, you'll be able to take a picture of the tops of all the tombstones."

He tilted his head back and stared at the branches overhead, his shoulders tightening. "How far 'up' are we talking about?" When she didn't answer, he glanced back at her.

She was gazing at the tree and grinning with excitement. It wasn't a special grin, not for her, but it made her eyes shine.

All his concerns and worries disappeared at the sight of that grin, and, to his surprise, he heard himself say, "Sure. I'll do it."

She tore her gaze from the tree. "Are you sure? I don't want you to take any undue chances if—"

"Heck no. Why, I've climbed a tree twice this tall before," he lied as he approached the gnarled trunk. Tree climbing wasn't exactly in his repertoire, a fact he'd discovered last summer when he'd had to save one of Lulu's kites, but he wasn't about to admit that to Tay. "This is nothing."

"Thank you," she said in such a fervent tone that he forgot his growing worries.

So it was that, five minutes later, Luke found himself precariously draped over a swaying limb, holding his phone as he tried to balance himself while taking a photo.

"Did you get it?" Tay called up to him.

"Just about." He tried to sound confident, but the branch was bobbing under him, and he wondered if he should have chosen one with more girth. "I just need to—" He slipped a little to one side and grabbed the branch with both hands, his phone almost falling from his grasp.

Whew: His heart raced as he waited for the limb to cease bouncing. When it did, he managed to get the necessary photographs. "I took a bunch of pictures. I'm pretty sure we'll have plenty."

"Did you get the whole graveyard? Maybe you should climb out a little farther just to make sure you have at least one shot with every tombstone in it."

He stuffed his phone into his coat pocket and eyed the branch in front of him. The end tapered some, and he wondered if it would hold his weight.

Still, she was watching, and he'd already gone this far, so what the heck, right? "Right," he told himself. "What's a few more feet of death?"

"What? I'm sorry. I didn't hear you."

"Nothing!" he called, although it wasn't nothing. He took a steadying breath and slowly crept forward a little at a time, the branch bouncing with each movement.

He swallowed a lump in his throat and carefully balanced himself. *There. That's not so bad.* He took a moment to slow his breath. Then, hanging on with one hand, he reached into his pocket and pulled out his phone. Gravity was doing something weird and trying to make him swing upside down on the branch, and it took all his concentration and leg strength to remain upright as he tried to take the picture. It took a few moments, but he finally managed to do it. "Got it!"

She gave an excited hop and clapped. "Thank you, thank you, thank you!"

It felt good, seeing her happy like that. *I guess I did my part.* "I'm coming down now." He slid his phone back into his pocket and, moving very slowly, inched his way backward, trying to avoid the smaller twigs that tended to slap him as he crept past.

He slid back a little farther, some of the rough bark coming loose under his rigid grip. *Just a little more. A little more.*

He'd made it another foot when, to his horror, he heard a loud *CRACK!*

The branch dropped a sharp inch, bouncing crazily beneath him.

Then it gave way, and he was abruptly dropped onto the branches below, flailing wildly. For what seemed like an eternity, he bounced down the tree, hitting what felt like every branch, every limb, before a few seconds of welcome silence engulfed him. With a suddenness that he couldn't quite comprehend, a huge *WHOOMP* knocked the wind from his chest even as a stab of pain shot through his wrist and arm.

Everything faded to black.

CHAPTER 15

ROSE

Rose leaned on her cane. "You're a darned fool."

"Apparently so." Luke, sitting on her stool behind the counter where he'd been downloading the online orders, adjusted his arm brace. "Fortunately, I just sprained my wrist, that's all."

That wasn't all. He'd *badly* sprained his wrist, and it now looked like a black sausage stuck in a sling. "You also got bruised and scraped up and had a concussion. It's a wonder you're not dead. What were you thinking, climbing a tree like that? You're not ten, you know."

"I know, I know." He hit a button on the screen and the printer came to life. "It was stupid. Like I told you last night, I was just trying to help Tay."

"Help? By climbing a tree like a chimp? It's a good thing Tay didn't ask you to jump into hot lava, because you're the sort who'd do it." Rose narrowed her gaze on her grandson. "You were showing off, weren't you."

"Me? No! Of course not." As he spoke, he flushed and then gently touched his jaw where an angry red laceration ran from his chin to his ear. Beyond his sprained wrist, some serious bark rash on one of his arms, and a series of multicolored bruises on his chest and back, he had few other injuries—which was fortunate, indeed.

Rose had to fight the urge to fuss at him again. As far as she could tell, the only good thing that had come out of yesterday's hijinks at the cemetery, of all things, was that she no longer wondered if Luke was interested in Tay. That arm brace was hard proof, which would have been terrific news if he hadn't made such an idiot of himself in the process.

Rose clicked her tongue. "You scared poor Lulu nigh to death, coming home all bruised up and wearing a brace. And now the whole town is buzzing about how you got injured while looking for William Day's lost gold stash, thanks to Zoe Bell, who saw Tay practically carrying you into Doc Bolton's office." Which was icing on a very bitter cake, in Rose's opinion.

"We're not looking for gold. I mean, if we find it, then terrific. But Sarafina told her daughter these clues led to a family secret, nothing more."

"What better family secret could there be other than a nice, big pot of gold? Plus now the whole town thinks they know what you're doing. Just this morning, Erma Tingle stopped me while I was unlocking the store to ask what you two planned on doing with the lost gold once you find it." Rose scowled. "I warned you all about that at the beginning. But would you listen? No."

Irritated, she picked up a duster. "That's another thing. You looked like a fool in front of Tay. What sort of a man can't climb a tree?"

The words elicited an immediate reaction from Luke. If he was red before, he was now on fire. *Good. He should know how ridiculous he looked.* Lord love the man, but it was possible that he'd totally blown his chance with Tay yesterday. Which explained her weird reaction when she'd brought Luke home after their visit to Doc Bolton. Not once had Tay looked Luke directly in the eye. *She was as embarrassed for him as I was.*

Rose stifled a sigh. *I guess he's back to square one.* "This whole thing is a mess. Before you two are done, this town is going to have the worst case of gold fever anyone's ever seen." Unwilling to look at his scraped face another minute, she pointed the duster toward the front of the store. "I'm going to hit those shelves while things are quiet. It's been slow this morning, but that'll change soon enough, thanks to you two."

He stood. "I'll do it."

"Doc Bolton said you need to rest that wrist as much as possible. Once you're out of that sling, you can dust all you want." Cane in one hand, duster in the other, Rose made her way to the front shelves and set to work. *I can't believe he pulled such a stunt in front of Tay. What was he think—*

"Give me that." Luke had appeared at her side and claimed the duster. "I have two hands, you know."

She started to argue, but had to admit he was doing pretty well with his other hand. She sat down in one of the overstuffed reading chairs that were sitting about the bookstore. "Just what have you and Tay found out so far? And don't give me generalities. I want specifics. You hardly tell me a thing, and I eat two meals a day with you."

"It's not a secret. So far, we've found evidence that it's quite probable that Sarafina knew William well, which is no surprise, considering the letters the Doves found in that vault in their chimney. But now we have some context. The *Register* ledgers show that not only did Sarafina report for the newspaper but William was being paid as an assistant for the photographer's studio his uncle ran from the second floor."

"So they probably saw each other often."

"That's what Tay thinks." Luke straightened from where he'd been dusting a bottom shelf and fixed a calm and steady gaze on her. "You already knew all of this, though, as you read Tay's notes every morning."

She sniffed. "You know how I hate surprises." She got up and reached for the book cart. "I'll get the new stock unloaded."

"Grandma, no. I'll get it—"

"That wrist will not be picking up any boxes. I may have a bum hip, but after your impressively bad fall, the rest of me is in better shape than you."

"I can't let—"

"Shush. There's just one box and it's small, too. I'll be back in a minute." She hung her cane on the cart and pushed it to the back room, walking at a crisper pace than she normally would in order to keep him from following. It annoyed her to be treated like an invalid when she just had a touch of arthritis now and then and a hip that didn't like movement. She found the box and headed for the front desk where the scan wand sat.

The front bell rang and Tay came in. This morning she was dressed in a pair of jeans, a large, boxy sweater with cream and tan stripes, and a pair of tan boots. It was funny, but even though Tay always seemed swallowed by her shapeless clothes, the effect was still feminine.

Luke had already turned toward her, a welcoming smile at the ready. "There you are."

Tay joined him, her gaze instantly resting on his brace. "How are you feeling?"

"Me? I'm made of steel." He flexed his good arm as he spoke.

Tay moved away. It was a tiny movement, no more than half a step, but Luke saw it at the same time Rose did. He flushed and dropped his arm.

Rose rolled her eyes. What had the boy been thinking to do something as corny as an arm flex? That sort of tomfoolery might have worked on a flirtatious woman like Kat Carter, but not the serious type like Tay Dove. Rose sent her clueless grandson a sour look. *Lord, child, read the room.*

"I'm sorry you fell." Tay eyed the angry scrape on his jaw and made a face. "You got pretty scratched up."

"I was lucky the ground around that tree was thick with dead leaves. But I'm doing okay. I'm not even taking any pain medicine this morning. Not a single— Oh. That reminds me. I need your phone number."

Tay's gaze returned to his face, her suspicion evident. "Why?"

Rose frowned. Goodness, why was this woman so touchy?

To his credit, Luke seemed unfazed by Tay's reaction. "I need to send you the pictures I took yesterday, especially the ones of the tops of the headstones."

"Ah." Relief flickered across Tay's face, although her cheeks remained pink. "Let me see your phone."

He unlocked his phone and handed it to her.

She put in her number and then returned it. "I thought about those pictures last night, but I didn't want to bother you."

"I wouldn't have been bothered at all." He bent over his phone. A moment later, he said, "There. You should have them all."

"Thank you." She sent him a guilty look. "Again, I'm really sorry you got hurt yesterday. I never should have asked you to climb that tree."

Luke shrugged, and then winced. "Forget about it. I have to say, though, before my dive to the ground, it was a lot of fun. I felt like we were in an Indiana Jones movie."

"This job isn't usually so exciting."

"Really? I guess I'm just lucky, then. By the way, I have an idea about the tombstones. You were right about needing a photo from above."

She moved a little closer to him. "What did you see?"

"A lot." He swiped his phone to a certain photo. "This is the one I took right before I fell. See the markings on the tops of some of the tombstones?"

She nodded. "There are chipped places and those lines. So?"

"Think of them as dots and dashes."

She slapped a hand over her mouth, her eyes wide. "Morse code!"

Rose frowned. *Darn it, I asked him what he'd found out and he never mentioned that to me.*

Luke grinned, looking as pleased as a cat with cream. "It's an anagram. The letters are *a-n-t-n-f-u-n-i-o-w-t-o*." He pulled a folded piece of paper from his jeans pocket and handed it to her. "I wrote them down for you."

She took it eagerly. "Luke, this is fabulous! I wonder what it spells."

He put his good elbow on a nearby shelf and leaned on it, and Rose noticed how close his face was to Tay's as they looked at the notebook paper together.

Tay shook her head in wonder. "We should work on it now. Do you have time?"

Rose was surprised at the warmth in Tay's voice. *Well, well, well. Luke may be able to recover from his own silliness after all.*

Luke grinned. "Me? I have nothing but time."

Tay stared at the paper. "I had a thought last night. I've always assumed that the family secret had something to do with Sarafina and David Tau. But the fact that William Day was buried in that cemetery makes me wonder if that's true. What if the secret Sarafina was going to share with her daughter involved William in some way?"

"Wait. That's . . . You're not suggesting that William might be Lucy's father rather than David?"

"No! William died years before Lucy was born. It can't be that. I just . . . I don't know. It was just a thought."

"We'll keep it in mind," Luke said. "I'm getting more and more curious about this secret, though."

Rose wished they would quit talking about William Day.

Luke absently toyed with the strap on his wrist brace. "Do you think the secret had to do with the gold?"

"Maybe, but . . ." She bit her lip. "It's possible, although Sarafina and David left Lucy very well provided for."

Luke frowned. "So Lucy was already well-off."

"She was Sarafina and David Tau's only heir. On top of that, her French husband came from a wealthy wine family."

"Maybe that's why Sarafina wasn't more insistent about her daughter following the clues. Because Lucy didn't need more money."

"The wording in that letter, plus the fact that Sarafina hid the end result with what appears to be layers of riddles, makes me think she wanted Lucy to reflect really, really hard about whether she *really* wanted to know this particular family secret. Which leads me to believe that, whatever it was, it might have been upsetting to Lucy in some way."

All this talk about whether there was gold made Rose nervous just listening in. Determined to put an end to Tay and Luke's conjecturing, she grabbed the book cart and pushed it closer to them. "Sorry to break up your little meeting but, Tay, you should know that people in town are beginning to talk about you and Luke searching for the lost Day gold."

Tay grimaced. "I know. My sisters were buzzing about it last night after I got home. People are saying we're close to finding it, which is about as far from the truth as you can get."

"What are you going to do about that?"

"I don't know what I can do. I've told everyone that we have no way of knowing what the end result of this quest will be, but no one seems to be paying any attention."

"Why would they?" Rose said glumly. "It's more fun to think there's a pot of gold at the end of this search. If I was honest, I'd admit that I wish there was, too." She caught Luke's suddenly worried look and, to distract him, picked up the small stack of new books on her cart and shoved them into his hands. "Here. Shelve these."

"But Tay and I were just going to—"

"I'll wait for you," Tay said. "I'm going to email these photos to the drugstore and get prints for my records."

"I'll be there as soon as I'm done." Luke watched as she left. As soon as Tay's office door closed, he started shelving the books Rose had given him.

Rose watched him work. It seemed that Luke and Tay were getting along pretty well, despite his being chump enough to fall out of a tree right in front of her. It also appeared that, because of their little foray into the cemetery, their little town was about to wake up to the once-dead whispers of William Day's lost gold.

The bell rang as the door opened and some customers came in. Luke called out a welcome while Rose went to her spot behind the counter. The first thing tomorrow morning, she'd comb through Tay's research notes and see just what those two crazy kids were getting into. "I wish they'd tell me," she muttered to herself. "But that's what I do. I read and I know things."

Boy, if that didn't describe her life, she didn't know what else would.

CHAPTER 16

TAY

Tay stared at the paper Luke had given her this morning, every letter written in his strong, clean handwriting. *So, Sarafina, you made a puzzle out of another puzzle. Kudos.*

Smiling, Tay glanced over at Luke. He sat at his desk, his dark head bent over his notepad. Unaware she was watching, he dropped his pen and adjusted the sling's shoulder strap, wincing when he pulled it too tight.

A twinge of regret hit her. When he'd fallen from that tree yesterday, time had frozen. If she closed her eyes, she could still see him flailing wildly as he crashed through branches large and small, bark and twigs flying before he landed on the ground in a heap.

That was why she'd hardly gotten any sleep last night. He'd seemed so confident about his climbing abilities that she hadn't thought he was in the least danger. *I mean, if he'd felt unsafe, he would have said something. Wouldn't he?*

She forced herself to turn her attention back to the notepad in front of her. Luke was unlike any man she'd ever met. He was smart, had a great sense of humor, and—oddly enough—seemed to love research. In addition—bless his heart—he was certainly willing to go to extreme lengths to help with their current project.

That last one really caught her attention. *Why* is *he so enthusiastically helping?* She refocused on her notepad, where just this morning she'd scribbled a myriad of words while solving the anagram. At the bottom of the page, she'd written the answer and had it neatly circled. After the complexity of the original poem and the difficulty they'd had getting a view of the graveyard, the anagram hadn't been all that difficult.

She realized that Luke had swiveled his chair in her direction. "Solved it, didn't you?"

Tay had to smile at the satisfaction in his voice. "A while ago. I was waiting to see how long it would take you to figure it out."

He flashed his usual lazy grin. "I told you I'm good at puzzles. I do the weekly crossword and word scramble in every newspaper I find."

Ah. She should have known. "You figured it out last night, didn't you?" At his nod, she added, "I've never had the patience to do crosswords." She tapped her finger on the circled answer on her notepad. "The anagram spells out 'town fountain.' "

He tossed his pen onto his notepad and pushed his chair back from his desk. "Should we go look?"

She found his enthusiasm—mustered even when he was wearing a sling and sporting various bruises from his fall—appealing. "I'm surprised you haven't already visited the site."

"Without you? I'm not that type of partner." He tilted his head to one side and eyed her suspiciously. "Wouldn't you have done the same?"

"Me?" Her gaze dropped to her notebook. "To be honest, I hadn't thought of us as partners exactly."

His happy-go-lucky expression vanished. "You would have gone without me?"

She might have. "Sorry. I'm used to working alone."

Luke shook his head as if deeply disappointed. "Don't you think I deserve equal billing in this little enterprise? I've been here for every challenge. I figured out the poem, and then I got this." He pointed to his wrist brace. "Doesn't that count for something?"

"You've helped a lot." When he just continued to stare at her incredulously, she grinned and added in a generous tone, "You've helped me so, so, *so* much, and I'm deeply grateful. *But*, I feel I should point out that I could've climbed that tree by myself."

"Really?"

"Really. It was pretty tall, so I might have had some difficulty getting up on that first limb, but I'd have been good after that. I'm not afraid of heights either."

"So if I hadn't been here, you would have gone to the cemetery and climbed the tree alone?"

"And probably fallen alone, too," she admitted.

He chuckled. "You should be glad I see us as a team. I solved that anagram last night and could have gone to the fountain by myself, but I didn't because I'm loyal."

"I appreciate that. I do. It's just that I've never liked group projects. I've had some bad luck with that experience."

"Ah yes, that bull pizzle guy. Hey, don't let one bad guy define all the rest of us."

Tay grinned. *Bull pizzle guy. Ha!* It was odd, but the lost and dazed feeling she'd been fighting since she'd returned home had faded a little after the day she'd gotten so mad at Richard.

There was a brisk knock, and Grace Parker stuck her head around the door. The mayor was dressed as usual in a neat suit and heels and looked as if she belonged on Wall Street rather than Dove Pond's quaint Main Street. "Hello, you two!"

She came into the office and set her briefcase on the corner of the large desk. "Tay, I brought you the items you requested."

Luke's eyebrows rose. "What's this?"

"I texted Grace," Tay admitted. "Right after I solved the anagram."

Grace reached into her briefcase and removed a red folder. "Tay asked for copies of the town meeting minutes from Sarafina's day."

Tay eagerly took the folder. She really liked Grace. Businesslike to the max, the mayor was a huge improvement over the previous one.

Grace pulled out some more folders. "I also brought all the documentation we have about the town fountain as well."

"Wow." Luke sent Tay an appreciative look. "You're fast."

"So is Grace." Tay jerked her thumb toward the mayor. "She's efficient, isn't she?"

He nodded mutely.

Grace opened the top folder. "The fountain was built in 1920, the maintenance fund appearing in 1925. It was established by an anonymous gift."

"How anonymous?" Luke asked.

"Completely. Don't know to this day where that money came from. There's no mention of it in any of the town minutes, although"—she frowned at the folders she'd just placed on Tay's desk—"there's one set missing, so perhaps that information was mentioned there. According to some notes I read, the maintenance fund was established because the fountain construction was faulty from the beginning, which was a bit of a scandal. The fund allowed the town to redo the fountain's plumbing so that it worked effectively."

Tay absently tapped her fingers on her desk. "The missing meeting minutes wouldn't have been from April of 1925, would they? That's when Sarafina and her husband, David Tau, visited Dove Pond."

Grace's eyebrows rose. "You think the fountain fund was a gift to the town from the Taus?"

Tay nodded. "I do."

Grace made a face. "Personally, I hate that fund. It's unnecessarily complicated."

"How so?" Tay asked.

"According to town bylaws that were written a few months after the donation, only a thousand dollars a year can be spent from the fund, and it must be used to improve some aspect of the town, with an emphasis on the fountain upkeep."

Luke frowned. "A thousand dollars? Where did that amount come from?"

"I don't know. But I'd bet the answer is in that missing meeting record."

"Hmm." Tay tapped her fingers on the folder, her gaze unfocused. "A thousand dollars in the 1920s was a very generous annual allotment."

"True," Grace said. "Back in the day, the funds were used for a lot of things beyond the fountain upkeep. But because of the specific wording, we've never been able to spend more than that thousand a year, which isn't much in today's dollars."

"How much is in that account now?" Tay asked.

"A lot," Grace admitted. "I don't remember the exact total, but Zoe would know."

Tay sighed. "It must be frustrating that there's money just sitting there, but no one can touch it."

"Can't you change the town bylaws to free it up?" Luke asked.

"Oh, we've tried," Grace said with a wry grimace. "The process to alter the town bylaws underwent a drastic overhaul in the sixties, and now it takes a town-wide vote. Sadly, there's a large portion of our town that believes the word 'change' is synonymous with 'cultural rot.' Every time I've gotten it on the ballot, it's been voted down."

Tay shot a curious look at Grace. "How much was the original donation?"

"I'm not sure, but it's now in an investment account, so it's been growing quickly. If the original intent of the donor was simply to keep the fountain in good shape, then they'll be happy to know that their gift has been quite successful, although the last mayor let the maintenance lapse so that the fountain sat empty for years on end."

"The fountain runs now," Luke said.

"Of course it does," Grace said sharply. "As if I'd let the fountain or anything else in this town sit around broken."

Tay had to grin. She glanced over at Luke. "See what competent management can do?"

"Impressive!" he returned.

Tay turned back to Grace. "May we see all the financial documents surrounding that account? If the Taus made that original donation, then it may be of importance in some way."

"I'm always happy to share the town records with anyone who wants to see them. I'll have Zoe Bell bring those financials to you as soon as possible. I—" Grace's phone beeped, and she pulled it out of her pocket, glanced at it, and then returned it. "That's Zoe now. We're meeting about the next town festival, so I'd better go."

Grace closed her briefcase. "One last thing. It's exciting, what you two are doing. I'm always thrilled to learn more about the history of our town and all of that. But I worry how many people are talking about William Day's lost gold. It's just town gossip now, but if it goes viral for some reason, we could end up with a media nightmare on our hands."

Tay grimaced. "Rose is worried, too. But we're not looking for gold. It's obvious to me, at least, that Sarafina's family secret isn't going to be a treasure of some sort, but information."

"Are you sure?" Grace asked.

"Sarafina married a very wealthy man. So Lucy was very well-off because of her parents. She married well, too. A French nobleman who had extensive properties in southern France. Why would Sarafina go to such lengths just to deliver something to her daughter that she already had?"

"So you don't expect to find a pot of gold at the end of this little quest. That's good to know." Grace picked up her briefcase. "I'll start telling people that, but I have to warn you, there's a lot of talk already. I'm not sure I can staunch that flood."

Tay wished people would just leave it alone until she knew what was what. "Still, I appreciate your help."

"Sure." Grace headed for the door. "I'll speak to Zoe for you." With a final wave, the mayor left.

Tay picked up her sweater, which had been hanging on the back of her chair, and pulled it on. "Shall we go look at the fountain?"

Luke grabbed his coat and stuffed a notepad and pen into his pocket. "So . . . people are talking about the gold. It seems like everyone is warning us about that today. Maybe we should search the fountain at night? No one would see us then."

She had to laugh. ""If you think there are a lot of rumors now, imagine how many more there would be if we were seen digging around the town fountain at night. People would think that was proof positive that we're hunting gold *and* planning to keep it for ourselves." Tay pointed to his arm. "Because of that, I'm a hundred percent sure we've already had our tea spilled on every gossip chain in town."

He shook his head. "I guess it's best that we stick to doing things out in the open."

"I wish people could understand that there're bigger things to find in this world than gold. If we figure out Sarafina's mysterious family secret, it'll be like discovering a slice of history that no one even knew existed."

He sent her an amused look. "You really love your job, don't you?"

"It's a big part of my life. I suppose that's not true for you, though."

He shrugged. "I enjoyed my job at times, but not as much as I've enjoyed taking care of Lulu."

She couldn't fault him for that.

"Look, treasure or secret or whatever else we find, I'm in. I haven't had this much fun since I was in college."

That was oddly gratifying to hear. She eyed him curiously. "Can I ask you something? Why do you want to help?"

"It's fun, as I've said. I love puzzles, too, as you know. But to be honest, I also like the company." His blue gaze met hers. "That's okay, isn't it?"

What it was was awkward. Her face felt hot, as if she'd stayed in the sun too long. *Don't overreact. He said* like, *which doesn't mean that much.* Trying to rein in her self-protective instincts, she managed a casual shrug. "So long as that's all it is, you may officially join my crew." There. That hadn't cost her anything, had it? Not yet, anyway.

He didn't look all that thrilled with her answer, but he nodded. "Then let's go." He went to the door and opened it for her. "After you."

For the weirdest moment, she felt a flash of—was it disappointment?—at the ease with which he accepted the line she'd just drawn between them. Surprised at her own reaction, she collected herself and headed into the bookstore, buttoning up her cardigan as she went. She waved a quick goodbye to Rose before stepping out into the cool mid-March breeze, Luke following.

Honestly, between their success in solving some of Sarafina's more obscure puzzles, the amount of original materials Tay was finding, and the sweet office she was occupying in the most charming bookstore on God's green earth, Tay was living the researcher's dream. The thrill of her search was all she should be thinking about. And yet . . . and yet . . . *Sheesh. Stop it already!* She needed to focus on her work and nothing else.

Which was what she'd do from here on out. That decided, she turned down the street in the direction of the town fountain, her mind firmly locked on what they might find rather than the man who was walking beside her.

Oh, Sarafina, where are you taking us?

CHAPTER 17

SARAFINA

DECEMBER 9, 1897

Before the first time that we spoke, we were characters wandering through the same book, but on different pages, until suddenly, there we were, face-to-face. That's when we understood the story for the first time. . . .

—letter from William Day to Sarafina Dove

To her joy, Sarafina found that she didn't just like her life as Dove Pond's secret top reporter. Rather, she loved it. She'd expected Aunt Em and Aunt Jane would be her biggest fans, but she'd been wrong. From day one, William—insatiable reader that he was—had read every word she wrote and enthusiastically encouraged her to do even more.

It had been a fulfilling and rewarding year and a half since she'd started writing for the *Register*, and she'd enjoyed every minute, taking on more and more assignments until she was no longer a part-time reporter, but was working almost every day, covering events and writing articles on a wide swath of topics. Over this time, she'd gotten to know Mr. Day rather well, too, and found him to be a fair, if at times indifferent, boss who was so distracted by his many businesses that he always seemed slightly surprised to see her.

Sarafina's only real complaint regarding her new job was that, because of her bad handwriting, Mr. Day insisted she type every single article she turned in, something no other reporter was required to do. She supposed she couldn't blame him. Even Aunt Jane, whose own handwriting was only slightly less than horrible, described Sarafina's as "the scratching of a drunken chicken trying to catch an angry grasshopper."

Which was why she was here today, late one afternoon, sitting at a desk tucked away in the back office and typing up a story about the coming Harvest Festival. She was using Mr. Day's prized Remington typewriter, which she had mastered. She had to strike the keys hard to get the letters to print, which was strangely gratifying and made her feel as if she were shouting her stories to the world.

She turned the knob and cranked up the paper so she could reread the line she'd just typed. Relieved that every word was correct, she'd just reached for her notes to begin typing again when the front door opened and William entered. She'd been expecting him, but she had to fight the urge to give a happy hop in her seat.

She wasn't the only one thriving these days. In the past year, William had gotten so good at photography that he'd taken over the studio and was now making his uncle a pretty penny. She knew he was learning a lot about his craft, but he seemed to enjoy running a business even more than taking pictures.

Sarafina hid her hand on the farthest side of the typewriter so no one would see her wave to William. He gave her an amused look and then sent her a secret salute by swiping two fingers across his forehead as if he were brushing aside his dark hair. He then tilted his head toward the back door that opened onto the alleyway behind the building. Seconds later, he ambled in that direction and disappeared from sight.

Sarafina rushed to finish her article. The moment it was done, she placed it on Mr. Day's desk for his edits, and then, casting a cautious eye at Mr. Lews, the typesetter, who was working today as well, she slipped on her coat and pinned her hat back in place. With a quick "goodbye" over her shoulder, she left the same way William had.

Like him, she always came and went through the back door, as the alley provided a shortcut to the town stables, where her horse and buggy waited. The day after Sarafina's review of the church's cantata, in which she'd called the performance both "high-quality" and "as entertaining as any big-city performance," Aunt Jane had announced at the breakfast table that it was only right for Sarafina to use the buggy and Mrs. Milk, their old mare, for transportation as she "had a real job now." That left Aunt Jane and Aunt Emily Anne sharing the large carriage, which was pulled by the bays Papa had sent from town years ago.

Sarafina was grateful for her aunts' generosity. And to her relief, they seemed comfortable enough sharing the larger and nicer carriage.

Already feeling the December chill as it seeped into the back hallway, Sarafina stepped outside and onto the stoop, the small alleyway shaded and narrow. She found William sitting on the top step, an open book in his hand. As the door closed behind her, he got to his feet. "There you are."

She noticed the breeze sweeping down the alleyway, stirring dust here and there and ruffling her skirts. "Sorry you had to wait. It took longer than I expected."

The corners of his eyes crinkled as he smiled. "That's quite all right." He held up his book. "I stayed busy."

"So I see." She sat down on the stoop and patted the empty space beside her. "Come and join me." As William sat down, she leaned over and read the title of his book, *A Connecticut Yankee in King Arthur's Court*. "Do you like it?"

"I do. It's becoming a favorite and I'm only halfway through." He placed the book on the stoop at his side and turned to face her. "How long before you have to go home?"

She pulled out the small watch she kept on a chain around her neck. "A half hour. My aunts are expecting me to help with dinner."

"A half hour, hmm?" William slanted her a lazy grin. "Oddly enough, that's exactly how much time I have free, too."

Which was a lie, and they both knew it. He was always busy. If he wasn't taking photographs, he was unloading wagons at the stables, or helping Mr. Stewart stock merchandise for his dry goods store, or a dozen other things. That he was sitting here, with her, meant something, and she knew it.

Over the past year, their relationship had changed. The smiles had become more frequent, their conversations more personal, their feelings growing. But for the moment, they sat quietly, neither of them speaking. They knew each other well now, so silences like this were never empty. They both had things to say, but were comfortable sitting beside one another, just being together.

She knew how complicated his relationship had been with his abusive father, and William knew how much she loved her aunts but at times felt strangled by their views. He'd learned how difficult it had been for her being left behind, even by a father she had never been close to. And she'd learned how tragic it was to live in the shadow of a dissolute, selfish father who'd caused such harm to the people of their town that he'd left his child's reputation permanently stained.

She tugged her coat collar a little closer together. "I'm pretty sure everyone in town knows I write for the *Register*. Twice now, Mrs. Abbott has visited Aunt Jane to tell her in a very loud voice about how her son is going to run for town mayor and what a wonderful candidate he will be."

"Fishing for an endorsement, is he?"

She nodded. "And last week I overheard—supposedly by accident—how Mr. Carter is holding a sale on sewing notions at his haberdashery."

"You're in demand."

"Which is why no one complains. I just hope my father doesn't find out. He'd come roaring in and put a stop to it. Or try to, anyway." She cast a side look at William. "One day, I'd like to move out of this town."

"Me too. I would like to start over somewhere fresh, and see what I can do."

The idea wasn't new to either of them. Most of their deepest conversations had had to do with this very topic. *One day* . . . She smiled. Whatever they did, they'd do it together. "I hope we get to be fabulously wealthy."

"It would be nice." William idly picked up his book. "Can you imagine being able to buy as many books as you want?" He seemed to realize he'd sounded wistful, because he laughed softly. "I want a library filled with leather-bound books. Not an empty space in any of the shelves."

"Of course. A library stuffed with cozy settees and fat armchairs so you can sink into a number of perfect places to read."

"And bright electric lights so you can read at night."

She nodded her enthusiasm.

"We'll have to live in a city for that."

He'd said "we" as if it was the most natural thing in the world, and it made her heart skip a beat. She'd like that.

William put his book back on the stoop and stretched his legs out in front of him and crossed his ankles. "I'd like to make so much money that I can give it away to people who need it more than I do."

Her heart swelled. Almost every day, he said something that reminded her that he was far, far from the person she'd originally thought him to be. Lately, she'd been wondering what would happen if she invited him to her home to meet her aunts. *I should ask Mr. Day about that. He's gotten to be friends with my aunts.* Oddly enough, William's uncle hadn't discouraged her and William's relationship. In fact, he'd done what he could to advance it.

She cast William a side glance now and was surprised to see him looking down the alleyway toward the street, a frown on his face. She leaned forward to see what he was looking at and caught a glimpse of his friend Marcus McCleary standing beside a man she didn't recognize. "Who's that?"

William pulled his gaze from the street. "His name is Ellis Johnson. He runs a game out of the back of the stables."

She could see the worry in William's eyes. "You don't trust him."

"No one would. He's a known liar, thief, and worse. But Marcus . . ." William shook his head. "He won't listen to anything I or anyone else tell him. Not anymore."

"Anymore?"

William's eyes grew dark. "He's been sick. It's made him reckless."

Sarafina knew Marcus McCleary well enough now to find that statement less than surprising. Where William dreamed of having a library with all the books he wanted, McCleary's dreams were much, much bigger and far more rash. He wanted it all: land, money, houses, a wealthy bride. Worse, as time passed, he seemed to feel these things were owed to him.

His growing desire to enrich himself at all costs was leading him down a dark path. He gambled wildly, and—encouraged by his new acquaintances—even stole money. Sarafina knew most of this because she'd witnessed some of his and William's bigger arguments.

She wished William didn't feel the need to keep watch over

McCleary. Twice now in the past month alone, William had ended up in a fistfight trying to pull a drunk McCleary from a game in some back room. But whenever she suggested to William that he distance himself from his friend, he would just shake his head and say he wasn't that kind of a person. She respected him for that, even as it left her worried and uneasy.

A shout arose from the street, and Sarafina thought it might have been Marcus.

William must have thought so, too, because he was on his feet in a flash, hands fisted, his book forgotten on the stoop. He took two steps toward the street and then looked back at her, a torn expression on his face.

She knew he wanted to make sure his friend was okay, but also didn't want to leave. She felt that way every time they said goodbye now, too. She picked up his book and held it out. "Take this and go."

He came back to take the book, his hand closing over hers where she held it, his fingers warm against hers. "Tomorrow?"

She smiled. "Tomorrow."

He released her and, with a "thank you" smile, turned and headed toward the street.

She watched him until he disappeared, and then sighed and stood. She brushed the dust from her skirts and made her way to the stables. It was difficult to pinpoint the exact moment her and William's relationship had changed from friendship to what it was now, something more. It had happened slowly, the way the sun melted the frost on a cool spring day.

But right now, this very minute, Sarafina knew one thing, and one thing only: she and William were deeply, madly in love. She didn't know where the future would take them, but she already knew that, whatever happened, they'd face it together.

CHAPTER 18

LUKE

Luke sat beside Tay on a park bench, both of them staring at the town fountain, which they were now calling their "nemesis." They'd been here, examining the darned thing for hours now, and had nothing to show for it.

Tay leaned back, her feet straight out in front of her, her arms crossed as she scowled. "I can't figure it out."

"It's perplexing." Luke frowned, trying to tamp down his own impatience. "There's nothing there."

"We've missed something." She pulled out her phone and opened some photos. "I took pictures of every side. Do you see anything? I didn't."

"I've already looked at those. More than once, too."

She shook her phone impatiently.

He sighed and took it. After staring intently at every photo, he handed it back. "I don't see anything either."

"It has to be there!" Tay adjusted her glasses, the abruptness of her movements conveying her exasperation.

He eyed the fountain in frustrated silence. As structures went, it wasn't all that outstanding. It was of a good size, like most fountains of that era. The exterior was of red brick and capped with plates of smooth white marble that were common in these parts; there were a number of quarries dotting the nearby countryside. The interior of the fountain was concrete, just like that of every fountain he'd ever seen. And the spout and the piping seemed normal, too.

"I wonder . . ." Tay tilted her head to one side. "Is the concrete lining new? Could there have been tiles there at one point?"

"It would be nice if there had been tiles spelling out a new clue, wouldn't it?"

She nodded morosely. "But that would be too obvious."

"I'd think so. I can't say for certain if the lining is original, but concrete was pretty standard even in the 1900s."

"Really?"

"Yup. The Greeks had concrete over five thousand years ago. Heck, the earliest record of it being used was around . . ." He frowned, trying to remember. "I think it was 6500 BC."

She shot him a curious look. "How do you know that?"

He raised his hand. "Hi. My name is Luke and I'm a documentary addict."

She smiled. "Me too. How many do you think you've seen?"

"Hundreds, probably thousands. I know a lot of useless information. It's one of my—"

"Uncle Luke!" Lulu came running up, Grandma Rose not far behind. "Can I stay with you? I don't have any homework today."

Grandma Rose leaned against her cane. "She was driving me crazy, chattering like a mad monkey. I figured she could come here and play while you and Miss Tay do your thing." She looked around curiously. "What is your thing, by the way?"

"The fountain," Tay answered with an impatient sigh. "The clue we retrieved from the gravestones sent us here."

Luke eyed his grandmother curiously. "How did you know we were here?"

Tay elbowed him. "You know how."

He sighed. "Right. We're town celebrities. People talk."

Grandma Rose looked at the fountain. "I don't see anything remarkable about it."

"Neither do we," Luke admitted. From his seat on the bench, he leaned forward and zipped up Lulu's jacket, pulling the collar closer to her round face. "Lulu, you can play if you like. I'll be right here."

Lulu gave an excited hop. "I'm going to *swing*!" She yelled the last word as she hopped and skipped to the swing set on the other side of the fountain.

He watched her go and had to smile. It was beautiful today, the wind still chilly, but the smell of the grass warmed by the sun was enough to remind a person that spring wasn't far off.

He turned back to Grandma Rose. "Who's watching the bookshop?"

"I put up the 'Back in Fifteen Minutes' sign. It'll be fine, although I can't be gone long." Her gaze flickered past Luke and Tay to the town hall, which was located just across the parking lot. "You all have an audience."

He followed her gaze and realized that there were faces peering out at them from various windows. He recognized Grace and Zoe and— Hold on. Was that Ella and Gray watching from the town office? *Ugh. There is no privacy in a town like this.*

Grandma Rose nodded to the library across the street. "It looks as if Sarah and the new library part-timer are wondering what you two are doing, too."

Sure enough, Sarah and her new assistant librarian were now sitting on the top stoop of the library, watching Tay and Luke as if ready for a circus to begin. Now that he was aware of the onlookers, Luke noticed several other storefronts where people stood in their doorways. "The whole town is here. Well, part of it, anyway."

"There's not much going on in town today," Grandma Rose said. "They're hoping you'll find that gold, but it looks to me like they're bound to be disappointed. You seem to be at a dead end."

"For now, but we're not giving up," Tay said in a stubborn voice.

Luke liked how she snapped her words when she said things like that.

Grandma Rose didn't look impressed. "Yeah, well, good luck with that. If life has taught me anything, it's that what you want and what you get may be very different things. I— Lulu!" Scowling, Grandma Rose headed for the swings. "Who swings hanging upside down like that? It's dangerous!"

Luke watched her head to where Lulu was leaning so far back in her swing that she was indeed somewhat upside down. "I used to do that all the time." He noticed how badly his grandmother was limping today and wondered if he should speak to Doc Bolton about it.

Tay said, "She's a sweetheart."

Luke sent her a disbelieving glance, then realized she wasn't looking at Grandma Rose but at Lulu. "She *is* a sweetheart."

"It must be strange, becoming a parent all at once."

"It was a shock to both of us," he admitted. He matched his posture to Tay's, stretching out his legs and crossing his arms over his chest. "But it saved me, in a way."

She shot him a surprised look. "Saved?"

"I was drifting when Lulu first arrived. I was making money hand over fist, and it seemed as if I was super successful, but it didn't feel that way. I was deeply bored with work."

"So Lulu changed that."

He watched as Lulu, now sitting upright, kicked her legs so she could swing higher. She looked so little on that swing, her coat almost swallowing her, that his throat grew tight. "Having a child around can kick you out of the rat race and back into sanity faster than anything else on this planet."

"Did you hate your job so much?"

"I loved coding. Still do. It's what I did in the beginning. But then a friend of mine was working on a cybersecurity project and asked me to join him for a few months, so I took a little detour to help him. I made crazy money." Luke had to laugh when he remembered seeing his first paycheck. He'd been astounded and—although he hadn't known it at the time—seduced. "Before I knew it, I was working days, nights, and weekends, and taking on bigger and bigger projects until . . ." He gave a humorless laugh. "But I wasn't happy. It took Lulu to remind me of what's really important."

"How did she do that?"

"She loves simple things like coloring books and peanut butter and jelly sandwiches. Sometimes sharing a PB and J sandwich with your favorite kid can be one of the most joyous moments ever."

Tay's expression softened. "You really love her, don't you?"

He nodded, his chest unexpectedly heavy. He did. More and more. Which was both shocking and wonderful at the same time. He'd loved Lulu before, of course, but being responsible for her had changed things in ways he couldn't explain.

Lulu caught his gaze and waved, grinning wildly. The wind ruffled her hair, and she impatiently shook her head to get it out of her eyes.

He suddenly realized Tay was watching him, her gray-green gaze locked on his face as if she could read his expression, and he felt oddly vulnerable. What was it about this woman that made him tell her things he hadn't even yet told himself?

He shook off his thoughts and forced a smile. "So. What do we do about this fountain issue? We should give our audience something interesting to watch, at least."

"Truth. Let's go over what we know." She pulled her notepad from her pocket and flipped it open. "Let's do this chronologically. The fountain was built in 1920. I checked the Sanborn fire maps this morning, so the date is verified."

"The Sanborn what?"

"The Sanborn fire maps were made of most towns and cities for insurance purposes. They feature all homes, businesses, and points of interest in a town and were used whenever there was an insurance claim. The fountain first shows up on the 1920 map."

He sent her an admiring glance. "You know all the good sources, don't you?"

Her cheeks pinkened, and she looked pleased. "I know a few."

He'd bet everything she knew them all. She was such a sharp one, this bespectacled and quiet woman.

She cast a self-conscious glance his way. "You're staring."

"I was just admiring the view." Before she could respond, he slapped his knees. "All right, then. You've confirmed the earliest history of the fountain. What next?"

"The structure itself, which we examined this morning." She read off her notepad, "The exterior is a combination of brick and marble, the interior made of concrete with no tile or other markings that we could see."

He nodded, reluctantly returning his gaze to the fountain. "You checked to see if any of the bricks were loose, of course."

"More than once."

So had he. "Maybe it's a numbers game this time. How many bricks are in each row?"

"Ninety-five."

He liked that she didn't hesitate. She was as precise as a pin.

She added, "Then there are the capstones, which are standard. Two-inch-thick slabs of local marble." She handed him her notebook so he could see the figures.

He looked for a pattern in the numbers. "I don't see anything here."

"Me neither." Tay reclaimed her notebook and turned a page before handing it back to him. "These are my notes from the town records regarding the fountain. There's no record of the exterior ever needing repairs. However, the plumbing needed fixing a few times over its life, mainly for pipe corrosion. Under the last mayor, it completely stopped working, but as Grace mentioned earlier, the fountain somehow fixed itself. It sounds as if a clogged pipe released, but to hear people talk, it was a miracle of some sort. You'd have thought someone turned water into organic wine."

Luke read through her notes and then handed them back to her. "I wish that stupid fountain had been tiled. Those could have spelled out a clue."

"I know, right?" Tay slipped a glance back at town hall. "Grace and Zoe are gone, so we're not being stared at by quite as many people as before."

Luke scanned the rest of the area. "Everyone else is still watching, though. I feel like we're performance art of some sort."

"It's annoying," Tay said sullenly. "We should charge an admittance fee."

A voice behind them said sharply, "If you want to charge a fee, then you'd better do something more interesting than sitting around looking dejected."

Tay and Luke turned around to find Aunt Jo standing behind them on the sidewalk, cane in hand, her fat bulldog waddling behind her. In addition to bright white tennis shoes, she was wearing a red dress and a purple coat, which matched little Moon Pie's red coat and purple leash.

"Hi, Aunt Jo. Come and sit." Tay scooted over, making Luke do the same, and then patted the seat beside her. "Where are you going all dressed up?"

"I just got back from church. Everyone in a leadership position had to go through emergency ethics training." Aunt Jo settled on the bench, Moon Pie collapsing at her feet.

"Did you say 'emergency ethics training'?" Luke couldn't help but ask.

"Yes, and it was as boring as it sounds. We had to attend because Preacher Johnson, God bless him, named Wanda Cook as the leader of our Divorced Ladies Group."

"I like Wanda," Tay said. "She's a card."

"She's high-spirited and also recently rid of bad husband number three. Unbeknownst to Preacher Johnson, Wanda was still in the red-hot-rebound stage, and she took that attitude with her to the Divorced Ladies Group."

"Uh-oh," Tay said.

"It was like adding kindling to a forest fire. According to some complaints that were made, she encouraged the ladies in her group to engage in questionable activities."

"Define 'questionable,'" Luke ordered, leaning forward so he could see Aunt Jo better.

She looked over her shoulder and then tilted in his direction and said in a loud whisper, "Apparently Wanda used church funds to hire a party bus."

"A *party* bus?" Tay's eyes widened.

Aunt Jo nodded. "They went to see the Men of Means strip event at the luxury casino down toward Kings Mountain."

"Props to Ms. Wanda," Luke said. "That definitely qualifies as 'questionable.'"

"Is she in a lot of trouble?" Tay asked.

"It depends on who you ask," Aunt Jo said. "The ladies had a good time, so they weren't upset. In fact, Mary Ann Klaus said it was the best church trip she'd ever been on, and she'd pay double to go again. She said she'd never said, 'Thank you, Lord!' so many times in one day."

"I'd call that a win, then," Luke said.

Tay frowned. "If the ladies had a good time, then who made the complaint?"

"A jealous bag of wind." Aunt Jo snorted. "I suspect it was Kayla Breeze's soon-to-be-ex, Kyle. He's the small-minded sort and deserves to be divorced more than anyone I know. However thrilled the ladies were, the preacher was not happy to learn about the party bus. Now, because of tattletale Kyle, every deacon and group leader had to attend that ridiculous Ethics in the Name of the Lord Seminar this afternoon. I just got out."

"The question is," Luke asked Aunt Jo, "are you ethical now that you've had the training?"

"I was ethical before, thank you very much, but I doubt a little training will be enough to quell the demon lurking in Wanda's burning heart." Aunt Jo looked at Tay and Luke. "But that's not why I'm here. Any luck with this fountain?"

Luke couldn't help saying in a sullen tone, "I'm sure you've heard everything already."

"From more than one person," Aunt Jo replied calmly. "You two are doing the same thing you were doing when you fell out of that tree. You're out sleuthing for William Day's lost gold."

"No we aren't!" Tay said defiantly. "We're looking for the family secret Sarafina told her daughter about."

Aunt Jo didn't look convinced. "Tay, we've had this conversation before. Technically, a lost treasure could also be called a 'family secret,' couldn't it?"

"That's true," Luke murmured under his breath, wincing when Tay elbowed him.

Aunt Jo patted Tay's hand. "Sweetheart, there's no need to be such a pessimist. At least admit that it's possible—just *possible*, mind you—that some of that gold is still here in town."

"It's highly unlikely. For one, the sheriff confiscated Johnson's gold right away, which meant that only McCleary's gold was left. Then, during and after the trial, hundreds of people came to town looking for that gold. And they did so for months and months."

"I heard all about it from my great-uncle," Aunt Jo said. "Those people dug holes everywhere, drained wells, and broke into houses. Why, the old Day barn was torn apart by one enthusiastic group of treasure hunters. I heard tell they were Masons from Asheville, but that might have just been a rumor."

Tay frowned. "Everything you just said indicates that the gold was probably found and removed long ago."

Aunt Jo sighed. "I suppose that's true."

"When you think about it," Luke added, "the only thing we *really* know is that whoever found the gold had to be an out-of-towner."

"How do we know that?" Aunt Jo asked.

"Because if someone from town had suddenly shown up with wealth like that, it would have been noticed, even back then."

"Exactly," Tay said in a firm tone. "That gold is long gone. I'm sure of it."

"So you're just looking for a family secret instead of gold." Aunt Jo stared at the fountain. "You two are about as exciting as mud on a pig."

"It's not our job to be fun," Tay said.

Luke heard the defensive note in her voice and sent her a quick, reassuring smile.

"Since I'm here, I might as well help you out." Aunt Jo leaned over and tried to read Tay's notebook. "What do you have so far?"

"Nothing yet." Tay pulled off her glasses and rubbed the bridge of her nose. "We didn't find any markings on the fountain, and the whole thing is glued together with cement, although I did spend a considerable time examining the bricks to see if any were loose."

"And you looked inside the fountain, too."

"Of course," Luke answered. "The water's pretty clear, which isn't surprising, as they just refilled it now that it's warmer. So we got a good look at the bottom and the pipes."

"What else?" Aunt Jo asked.

"That's about it," Tay admitted.

They all sat staring at the fountain, the minutes ticking by.

Aunt Jo tilted her head to one side. "Did you look *under* everything?"

Tay sent her a frustrated look. "Under what?"

"Under the pipes, and under that little ledge, and under . . ." Aunt Jo waved her hand in the general direction of the fountain. "Just *under.*"

Luke frowned. "Under, huh?" He glanced over at Tay. "I hate to admit this, but she's right. We couldn't see under any of those things. To do so, we'll have to climb inside."

"Inside?" Tay eyed the water with mistrust. "It'll be cold."

"So what?" Aunt Jo grabbed her cane and got to her feet. "Luke, climb in there and see what you can find."

Sheesh. Was he the only one with a pair of legs in this place? Still, curious, he got up and went over to the fountain.

"No!" Tay was on her feet in a flash. She grabbed his good arm and pulled him back. "You're not going in that water. You're injured."

"I just need to walk around the edge and see if there's anything out of place or printed under the—"

"It's probably slick in there, and you could fall. We don't know how clean that water is, or—"

"That's not an issue," Aunt Jo said firmly from where she stood nearby, looking more and more like a manager rather than an onlooker. "This fountain has never been cleaner now that Grace is the mayor."

"See?" Luke smiled reassuringly at Tay. "It's clean. I'll be careful. I'm just—"

"Whatcha doing?"

They turned to find Zoe and Grace now standing by the far side of the fountain.

Luke had to fight to keep his smile. "You all know exactly what we're doing."

"Hi!" Kat Carter hurried up and slipped her arm through Zoe's. "Thanks for the text. I wouldn't miss this for the world."

Tay gave a frustrated sigh. "You guys need to chill. We aren't looking for gold. It's some sort of family secret."

Kat nudged Zoe. "Gold could be a family secret."

"That's what I said!" Aunt Jo said with obvious satisfaction.

"But it's not!" Tay said impatiently.

Luke sighed and favored their audience with a flat look. "Will you all just stop it with the gold?"

Zoe nodded. "Of course." She leaned closer to Kat and said out of the side of her mouth, "Not."

For the love of heaven! "Clues, people!" Luke said firmly. "We're looking for *clues* to a *family secret*!"

"Luke's going into the fountain," Aunt Jo announced. "To look for *clues*." She air quoted the word for emphasis.

"Ah." Zoe nodded sagely. "You mean *gold*."

Luke heard Tay muttering under her breath, about every other word a curse word. He could commiserate. He was feeling the same way.

He felt a poke on his calf and turned to find that Aunt Jo had placed her cane against his leg.

She gave him a little push. "Get in there, Day. You're the tallest and most mobile of this group."

Tay whirled to face Aunt Jo. "Luke can't go into the fountain. He's not supposed to get his arm wet."

Zoe scoffed, "That sling is Velcro'd on. He can take it off for a minute or two, can't he?"

Aunt Jo offered, "Luke, I'll hold your sling while you're in the water."

"That's classic Aunt Jo," Kat said in a low tone to Zoe. "Did you see how she didn't hesitate or anything? Just solved the problem without even breaking a sweat."

Zoe nodded enthusiastically. "Stronger than an angel, that one."

Tay put her hand on his arm. "Luke, don't listen to them."

He shouldn't, but . . . his gaze found the clear, icy water of the fountain. It had reached fifty degrees today, which was balmy for March, but he knew the water would be much, much colder. Still . . . the clue had to be in this fountain, and the only place they hadn't been able to look was under the pipes and under the edge of that ledge.

"Hi, guys!" came a cheery voice behind him. "What's going on?"

Oh my gosh. How big is this audience going to get? Luke pressed his good hand over his eyes before moving it to see Tay's sister Ella join them. She was holding hands with her boyfriend, Gray. He lifted his hand in greeting.

Zoe called out to Gray, "How's that herd of Highland cows doing?"

"Terrific. Adorbs is getting big. I think he might outgrow his dad once it's all said and done." Gray looked at Luke and grinned. "I hear you're taking up tree diving as a hobby. I've got a few tall ones out at the farm if you run out of them at the cemetery."

"Shut up." It was an inelegant answer, but it was all he had right now.

Tay sent them both a surprised glance. "You two know each other?"

Gray's grin widened. "When Luke first got to town, Blake told me how good he was with computers, so I hired him to update the system I had installed at my farm."

Aunt Jo sent him a questioning look. "You needed a computer system for a farm?"

Ella answered, "Gray keeps crazy meticulous records. It's a science, what he's got going on there." She looked from Tay to Luke. "What are you two doing here? I heard you were searching for the lost Day gold, but it appears to me that you're just hanging out."

"Lazy, both of them," Gray agreed.

"That's exactly what I was about to say," Aunt Jo said brightly.

Tay sent Aunt Jo a dark look. "We're thinking right now. We—"

"Luke should hop into that fountain before the temperature drops," Zoe called out.

Ella looked at the fountain, her eyebrows drawn in concern. "Into, like *into* the water?"

"Do it! Do it!" Kat and Zoe chanted.

Luke frowned. "They want me to jump in and look for clues."

"Which he isn't going to do," Tay said firmly.

Surprised at the emotion in her voice, he glanced at her.

Her mouth was tight, her eyes sparkling behind her glasses. "We just need to look under this ledge. I'll go get a mirror and we'll—"

"Nonsense," he said briskly. "I can do it." It was funny, but seeing her worry made him want to jump into that fountain all the more, cold or not. "I'm going to demand hazard pay from here on out, though."

Tay's mouth quirked at his joke, but her worried look remained. "Don't do it. Let me get that mirror and—"

"Let Luke do his thing." Aunt Jo beamed at them as if she were the deciding factor. "Get on with you, now."

He sat on the edge of the fountain and pulled off his boots and then tucked his socks into them. "I don't suppose any of you brought a towel?" He was greeted with a chorus of nos and nopes. "Terrific. I'll just—"

"What's going on here?"

Luke grimaced at the new voice, which he immediately recognized. *Not Blake.* The last person they needed to see was the town sheriff.

Blake crossed his arms and rocked back on his heels, his badge catching a glint of the late-afternoon sun as he eyed Luke's discarded boots and socks. "Getting ready to take a swim, are you? I don't suppose you noticed that 'No Swimming' sign over there?"

Tay stepped forward. "See? Luke can't go into the fountain. It's illegal."

Aunt Jo snorted. "All he's going to do is wade around. It's too shallow to swim in."

Blake eyed the sign. "Hmm. The posted rules don't say a word about wading, do they?"

"Hop in, Luke!" Aunt Jo said brightly. "You have things to do."

Kat raised her phone. "Tell me when you're going in, as I want a video."

"No!" Tay said. "He's not going."

It was rather adorable how worried she was about him.

"He won't be long." Aunt Jo squinted at the fountain as if she'd suddenly become a fountain-sizing expert. "Ten minutes, maybe twenty if he moves like a turtle."

"I'll get hypothermia if I stay in longer than that." Luke supposed he was lucky they didn't live in Alaska, or they'd have suggested he shove the inconvenient blocks of ice out of the way before he climbed in.

Blake's mouth twitched as if he was trying not to smile. He took a few steps to the side of the fountain and looked over the stone rim and into the water. "Be careful in there, Luke. It's probably slick. There. You've been warned." Then he reached over and slapped Luke on the back just a little too hard. "Good luck, buddy."

Luke rubbed his shoulder and glared at Blake.

The sheriff just grinned. "Tay, if he hits his head or looks as if he's drowning, call 911. I'd have you call me, but I'm clocking out to get a cup of joe. Kat, send me a copy of that video, will you?"

Luke fisted his hands. "If I still had my boots on, I'd fight you right now."

"You're bootless, so you'd lose. Have fun. I'll be thinking about you as I have a nice cup of hot coffee in yon warm tearoom. See you all later." With a blithe wave, Blake ambled away, leaving Luke surrounded by amused women and a chuckling Gray.

A small hand slipped into his, and Lulu looked up at him, her blue eyes wide. "Uncle Luke, are you going swimming?"

Grandma Rose stood behind her. "He deserves a good dunking."

He ignored her. "No, Lulu. I'm just going to walk through the water. Miss Tay thinks she lost something in the fountain, and I'm going to see if I can find it."

"What did she lose?"

His dignity, for one thing. "I'll let you know when I find it."

Grandma Rose took Lulu's hand in her own. "Lulu, how would you like a cupcake? I can't stay here for this nonsense."

That was all it took for Lulu to lose interest in her uncle. "I want a strawberry cupcake!"

"Let's go, then." Without another look, Grandma Rose and Lulu headed for Ava's tearoom.

Luke felt oddly abandoned.

Aunt Jo announced, "I can't stand around all day, so I'm going to sit with Moon Pie over there." She headed for the bench.

"Hey, Luke!" Grace called. "I hate to bother you, but Zoe and I have reservations to get our nails done in about thirty minutes. At this rate, we'll have to cancel, and there's a fifteen-dollar cancellation fee."

He refused to even admit he'd heard that, but he couldn't help but mutter, "It's a wonder people aren't selling tickets."

At his side, Tay gave a surprised, choked laugh that made him instantly feel a little better. She had a delicious laugh that began in her throat and bubbled over him, as warm as a blanket right from the dryer. He straightened his shoulders, wincing a little when the sling pulled at his wrist. He'd have to be careful not to get it wet, but he was sure he could do it.

He reached down, grabbed his boots and socks, and moved them next to the bench where Aunt Jo sat, well away from the fountain ledge so they wouldn't get splashed when he climbed in.

That done, he straightened and took the final steps toward the fountain. He was just getting ready to step over the ledge when something flashed by him.

A large splash sent a wave of startlingly cold water over him as he blinked.

There, standing in the fountain in front of him, her jeans now wet to her thighs, stood Tay.

CHAPTER 19

TAY

The iciness of the water stole Tay's breath while the heavy scent of chlorine made her cough, both of which she'd expected. But what she hadn't been prepared for was the depth. The fountain hadn't seemed that it was more than knee-deep for Luke. But for her the icy wetness was mid-thigh, and it was cold, cold, cold. *This is the price I pay for being so darn short.*

But the worst part was that she and Blake had been right about the bottom. It was as slick as glass, and her first step almost sent her face-first into the water. Gasping, she grabbed the side of the fountain and hung on for dear life as her tennis shoes became skates and slid in various directions. She should have shed them before getting in, but as she'd been trying to head off Luke, she hadn't had time. She glanced his way now and caught a glimpse of his scowl.

He muttered a curse. "I said I'd go!"

"Yeah, well, you're injured and I'm not." *Not yet, anyway.* She took a careful step forward, keeping a firm grip on the fountain's side. Although she walked very slowly, one of her feet slipped to one side. Once again, she was pitched forward and lost her grip on the ledge, catching it just in time to regain her balance.

Ella was now standing by the fountain near Luke, her smile long gone. "You should have let Luke do it!"

"Am I the only one who's noticed the poor guy has been injured?" Tay asked. "His arm is still in a brace!"

"He has a sling," Ella said. "I know he got hurt. But you're not the most coordina—"

"*What?*" Tay couldn't keep the irritation from her voice. "For your information, Ella, I'm *perfectly* capable of wading around this fountain by myself." To prove her point, she took another cautious step forward, still gripping the ledge. "See? I'm fine in here. I'll even—" Her feet shot out from underneath her and, with a huge splash, she fell right onto her backside.

The icy coldness slammed the air from her lungs and made her gasp, a whole mouthful of chlorine water filling her mouth and making her choke as she flailed wildly, unable to regain her footing.

She was just getting worried when an arm snaked around her waist and she was instantly placed onto her feet, where she stood, panting crazily. Her wet hair was plastered over her eyes as cold water ran over her.

She shoved her hair out of her eyes and blinked hazily, only to find Luke standing in front of her, his good arm still firmly around her waist while she hung on to him with both hands.

Through her water-clogged ears, she could hear a cacophony of voices calling out and asking if she was okay.

"I'm fine," she sputtered, releasing him but staying close. "Luke, you shouldn't be in here. It's slick and you'll—" Her feet started to slip again, and, without thinking, she grabbed him a second time.

For a horrifying moment, they both wobbled dangerously, but then Luke lifted her off her feet once again as he swung her toward the side of the fountain. "Hang on to that ledge!"

She grabbed it and, with a slight struggle, managed to balance herself. She pressed her thigh against the edge and clung to the marble top.

"Sit!" he ordered with an exasperated look.

Not trusting her own balance, she sat on the fountain ledge and scooted back until only her feet dangled in the water.

"Stay there." Luke carefully waded toward her, and she noticed that only his good arm was wet from the shoulder down.

"How are you not falling?" she asked, amazed.

"He's a natural athlete," Aunt Jo said from her bench, Moon Pie now nestled in her ample lap. "He looked pretty impressive, vaulting over the edge of that fountain when you started to fall."

"Like Spider-Man," Kat said.

Luke ran his hand down the side of his wet coat, a stream of water pouring from the pocket. "Feel free to use all the superhero references that come to mind. That's better than this morning at breakfast when Lulu told me that I looked like a muffin because I was getting round."

Aunt Jo chuckled. "The truth hurts, doesn't it?"

He cast her a sour look. "I'm not getting round."

Tay could attest to that. She'd just spent almost an entire minute plastered up against him, and even through his coat, she could tell he was sporting a pretty athletic build.

"Hey, Tay!" Zoe called out. "Since you're just sitting there, feel around with your feet. Maybe there are raised letters or symbols on the bottom."

It was a thought, Tay supposed. Holding on tightly, she slowly slid forward until her feet touched the bottom. Still sitting, she moved her feet in small circles. After a minute, she shook her head. "Other than a few nickels, there's no raised texture."

"Take off your shoes," Zoe ordered.

"No, no, and no!" Luke scowled. "We have too many generals out here and not enough privates. All of you except Tay, be quiet." He turned her way and flashed that lazy half smile that was uniquely his. "Climb on out. There's no need for both of us to be in here. I won't get any wetter than I am now."

Ella had moved closer to the fountain, Gray behind her as she leaned over the water and peered at the bottom. "What exactly did you all expect to find in there?"

"We don't know," Tay admitted, reluctantly scooting back and then swinging her feet out of the fountain and back to the sidewalk. "But our last clue led us here."

Luke, who was already trying to see under the water spout, added, "Sarafina's clues have been like that. They lead you somewhere, but the instructions beyond that are pretty vague or nonexistent."

Which made them all the more challenging, which Tay loved. She caught a knowing look from Luke and realized that he'd read her mind. She smiled, as she knew he felt the same way.

Although Tay hated to admit it, if there was anything this search for Sarafina's secret was teaching her, it was that one could find a certain joy in sharing a task with someone.

Aunt Jo called out, "Come sit with me. You're shivering."

She was. Her wet hair was stuck to her neck and cheeks, and she couldn't feel her feet very well. She went to sit beside Aunt Jo, and was gratified that at least one side of her was instantly warmer.

Crossing her arms, she watched as Luke slowly made his way around the circumference of the fountain, running his fingers under the small ledge. He took only five or so steps before he stopped and bent down, his gaze locked on the top layer of bricks directly under the ledge.

Tay slid forward on her seat, the cold forgotten. "What is it?"

"When you fell, water splashed over these bricks." He lifted his head, and his eyes met hers. "Tay, there are letters here."

Kat squealed. "Oh my gosh!"

"That is Indiana Jones–level cool!" Zoe added eagerly as she, Kat, and Grace crowded closer. "What do they say?"

Luke didn't answer, as he was too busy splashing water over the almost hidden top row of bricks, moving carefully around the fountain.

Tay left Aunt Jo's side and went to see the letters. They were faint, and far from professional in appearance, but letters they were. And these weren't scrambled, either, but spelled out something definitive and, best of all, had been carved by hand.

Bending down, Tay leaned across the marble-topped edge of the fountain and reached under the ledge to place her fingertips on the letter closest to her, an *e*. Instantly, the present day faded and she was there, at night, as the writer scratched the letter on the brick. The empty fountain looked new and he was stooped down, an awl in his hand as he worked.

It was a much warmer time of year, the scent of flowers heavy in the night air, and she could feel the expensive cotton of his shirt, see the white gloves he'd left on the fountain's marble edge.

Someone close—a woman—whispered, "David, hurry. We'll get caught!"

The writer looked up, and there, her face only partially revealed in the moonlight, stood Sarafina. She was older than in the photographs Tay had seen. She had laugh lines around her eyes, and her hair had streaks of gray, but she was as beautiful as ever. She was, perhaps . . . forty years old? Maybe older?

Tay wasn't sure. What she was sure about was that this man, the one writing the code in the moonlight, was deeply, wildly in love with his wife. Just that one look, exchanged briefly under the dimness of moonlight, had warmed his heart. "Almost done," he whispered to her before he went back to work, his face reflected in the fountain's water.

He was handsome, with dark hair, a neat beard, a piercing gaze, and a determined air. Tay recognized him from the few photos that were available of him. *That's definitely David Tau.*

"There," David said quietly into the darkness. "As soon as I finish this letter, we'll—"

He lifted the awl and she was no longer there, watching in the past.

"Tay?" came a voice at her side.

She blinked. The warmth had disappeared, and she was back, perched on the edge of the fountain on a chilly afternoon, wet through and through.

Luke's worried face came into view. "Are you okay?"

"I'm—I'm fine. I touched the letters and saw"—she waved her hand—"some things."

Aunt Jo clapped her hands. "Oh! What did you see?"

Tay shook her head. "I'll tell you later." Her teeth chattered so that she was barely understandable.

Luke scowled. "You need dry clothes. Your lips are turning blue."

She couldn't argue. Shivering wildly, she stood, wrapping her arms around herself as she tried to collect some warmth. Had a wind sprung up? It certainly felt like it.

Luke turned to where Kat and Zoe were. "Would one of you write this down as I read it off?"

"I'll do it!" Zoe pulled a pen and a piece of paper from her purse.

He read the words. "*Nine seven keyed in brass by the people.*"

"Heavens, but that's random." Still, Zoe wrote it down and then came to their side of the fountain. She waited for Luke to climb out and put his socks and boots back on before handing him the paper. "What does that mean?"

"We don't know yet," Tay said, her voice shivering along with her. "But we'll figure it out."

Luke stuffed the paper into his back pocket. "You're shaking like a leaf. I'll drive you home. Aunt Jo, can you stop by the tearoom and tell Grandma Rose I'll be back after I drop Tay off at her house?"

"Sure." Aunt Jo set Moon Pie back on the ground and picked up his leash. "I could use a good cup of tea, anyway."

"Come on." Luke slipped his hand under Tay's arm and guided her down the sidewalk to where his truck sat in the town parking lot. Soon they were on their way, the seat heater gradually calming her shivers.

She wiped her hands over her wet knees and felt water drip down her legs and into her shoes. "Sorry for getting your seat wet."

"That's nothing compared to the time Lulu spilled an entire carton of chocolate milk in here." He turned off Main Street, the truck bouncing a little as they went over a crosswalk. "I'll spare you the rancid details, but trust me, spoiled chocolate milk odor is not an easy thing to get rid of."

She smiled and wondered if Lulu had really spilled chocolate milk on the seat or if he was just saying that to make her feel less awkward. He was such a nice guy. The total opposite of Richard, too. *Why was I ever interested in that guy, anyway? I must have been crazy. Crazy, or maybe I was just crazy lonely.*

The thought caught her. Was that what had happened? Had the solitude she usually loved so much become burdensome in some way? It was entirely possible.

"Warm enough?" Luke asked as he turned the truck onto Elm Street.

"Getting there. That's an interesting clue. It seems more specific than the others."

He murmured, "*Nine seven keyed in brass by the people.* What could that mean?"

"I have no idea. But I'm surprised no one has noticed those letters before."

"The marks only show up when the brick gets wet, and it's protected from the rain by that little ledge. We're lucky you splashed that line of bricks with water." He pulled the truck up to her house and parked in the driveway at the end of the walk, but left the engine running so the cab stayed heated.

"I did find out something new, though."

Luke turned to face her. "Oh?"

"David Tau wrote the letters on the fountain. I saw his face reflected in the water—" Tay bit off the rest of her sentence and sent him a careful glance. They'd never talked about her Dove family ability, but to her surprise, he didn't appear the least disbelieving.

He seemed to understand the reason for her hesitation, because he shrugged. "If there's anything I've learned this past month, it's that if you say something happened, it happened. You're neither flighty nor a liar."

That was unexpected, and she couldn't help but feel relieved. She rarely talked about her special ability with anyone. People either didn't believe it or started acting weird and asking her to do things as if she were a circus performer. "A lot of people think it's nonsense, but it's not. The truth is, whenever I touch writing, I feel, hear, smell, and see everything the writer does. And this time, I saw David Tau etching the letters on the fountain bricks. Sarafina was with him, too."

"Interesting," Luke murmured. "Up until now, I've been thinking this was a Dove family secret and that David Tau was incidental to it. But apparently not." He leaned back in his seat and smiled at her.

"Whatever happened, I'm sure we'll figure it out. We've come this far, after all."

She nodded, and despite being cold and wet and somewhat exhausted from their adventures of the day, she was comforted by his words. He was right—they'd figure it out. When they worked together, it seemed that there was very little they couldn't do.

She tucked a wet strand of hair behind her ear. "I should get inside. Thank you for everything, both today and yesterday, too. I couldn't have asked for a better partner."

"It was my pleasure." He reached for his door handle. "I'll walk you to—"

"No, thank you!" He was wet, too, and still injured from his fall. The last thing he needed was a cold on top of that. So she hopped out of the truck before he could climb out. "I can take it from here. See you tomorrow!" With a wave, she closed the door and, huddled in her wet clothes, hurried inside.

She closed the front door behind her and was glad to find that she was alone in the house. Shivering, she headed to her room. Things were progressing well now, although this last clue seemed a bit tougher. *Nine seven keyed in brass by the people.* What could it mean?

Whatever it was, she and Luke would work it out. They had to. The answer was close. She could feel it.

CHAPTER 20

SARAFINA

MARCH 27, 1897

As we go through this life, we take memories of people we love with us. They sometimes appear in a phrase we might have heard them say, or in a certain thought they'd shared about an item or place. But you're more than that. With me or not, you're in every word I utter, every thought I have, every breath I take.

—letter from William Day to Sarafina Dove

Sarafina walked back and forth on the bank of the pond, her boots sinking into the damp ground, her skirts swirling around her rapidly moving legs, her hands jammed into the pockets of her short coat. She tried hard not to look at William as she paced, but she couldn't help glancing his way every few seconds.

He was sitting on the log near the bank, a scarf half hiding his face as he read through a sheaf of crinkled, tea-stained pages, the rough draft of an article on the new phone exchange in Asheville that she'd just written. Every once in a while, he'd nod—or frown—and write something with the stubby pencil he always carried in his pocket. His smiles were like gold, but the frowns cut like broken glass.

She grimaced at her own silliness and went to the fishing line she'd set after handing him the article, pretending to check that it was properly in place.

The paper crackled, and she whirled to face him. But all he was doing was smoothing it over his knee. He finished and started reading again.

She stuffed her hands back into her coat pockets and resumed her pacing in an effort to curb her impatience. She was thrilled that Mr. Day now trusted her to take on the most serious assignments. The readers liked her work, too. It was exciting to be at church or in town and hear people she knew discuss her articles, even debating the issues she'd worked so hard to define.

Just having a job had changed her. It had given her a purpose and a place, and she now knew who she was and what she wanted to do, which was a feeling she savored and one her aunt Jane said all women should know. Her aunts had grown even more enthusiastic in their support of her work. When she'd shared that she wanted to become a reporter for a big newspaper in a large city, they hadn't hesitated at all, but instead had applauded the idea.

She supposed she shouldn't be surprised by that. In his rare letters, Papa had written more than once that Sarafina was not to listen to her aunts' "radical ideas about women" and instead was to follow the words of their preacher on "the morality and correct behavior of women in general." According to Aunt Jane, his way of thinking was "feudal poppycock."

William turned the page, the paper noisy in the quiet, the scratch of his pencil following. She stared out at the blue water, which had dulled in the grayness of the day. William would finish soon enough. All she had to do was wait.

Sadly, her ability to wait was, according to Aunt Jane, poor on good days and dismal on bad.

She stole a glance at him. As if the sky above knew she'd be looking at that exact moment, a beam of sunshine broke through the clouds and shone on him, outlining his shoulders and making his silky dark hair look blue-black.

Unaware of Sarafina's admiration, he made yet another mark on the page.

So many marks! She tried not to show her impatience but couldn't stop a huge sigh from passing through her lips.

William's mouth quirked into a smile. "I heard that."

She sent him a sheepish look. "Sorry." She dug a hole in the ground with the toe of her boot and morosely eyed her fishing line, which was depressingly still.

"All right." He slipped his pencil back into his pocket.

He's done! She took an eager step toward him. "So?"

"It's good." He patted the log. "Come and see what I've written. I only had a few questions."

Relieved, she pulled her coat close and sat beside him. He returned her papers to her, and she anxiously scanned the comments he'd added to the margins. He was right; there weren't that many. She smiled, blissful. "Thank you for reading this. These are fair comments."

He flashed a smile at her. "I told you so."

She folded the papers in half, then in half again, following the creases from where she'd folded them before, and slipped them back into her coat pocket. "I was hoping you'd love it as much as I did."

His eyes darkened and he reached over and captured her hand, his fingers warm where they laced with hers. "The thing I love isn't the news article, good as it is. It's the author."

Her face heated and, with a pleased smile, she leaned against him, her head resting on his shoulder. They stayed that way for some time, luxuriating in the simple moment. The leaves rustled overhead, the sun slipping in and out of view, changing the vista from shadowy to bright and then back again. She smiled as she thought about how their relationship had changed over the past few years. They'd started as friends and then gradually, one smile at a time, had become something more.

She hadn't shared this information with her aunts yet, although their opinion of William had improved greatly over the past few months. She knew exactly who she had to thank for that, too—William's uncle, and her editor, Mr. Day.

To Sarafina's delight, Mr. Day had become a part of everyday life at the Dove household. Oddly enough, her aunt Emily Anne was the reason for that new development. At some point, Mr. Day's relationship with her aunt had moved from acquaintance to close friend. Then it had changed yet more, and now Mr. Day was Aunt Em's ardent suitor. Most days when Sarafina returned home she'd find him sitting in the parlor, dressed in his best, and smiling at Aunt Em as if she'd just said something brilliant.

Sarafina was delighted that her aunt seemed to welcome Mr. Day's visits, justifying it by saying that it "behooved them all" to hear directly from Sarafina's editor how she was doing in her career. It had taken Aunt Jane some time to warm up to Emily Anne's beau, but even she was no match for Mr. Day's broad warmth, charm, and seemingly endless admiration for her beloved sister.

His influence in their house was immense. Not only did he bring marvelous gifts, like baskets of flowers and books and chocolates, but he also brought his warm opinion of his nephew, William. And Sarafina couldn't have been more grateful. The timing had been just perfect.

Although she'd longed to do it, Sarafina had been at a loss to find a way to tell her aunts about William. She knew that if she attempted to speak highly of him, they would have instantly been suspicious of her motives. However, it seemed natural that Mr. Day would brag from dawn to dusk about his misunderstood nephew and commiserate about his unfortunate circumstances while also noting his superior work ethic and unbendable determination to do well. Soon, both of Sarafina's aunts were applauding Mr. Day for his kind thoughts regarding his ill-fated nephew, and growing more and more sympathetic to William and his circumstances.

Sarafina was extremely gratified as she watched her aunts' opinions of William improve. And she'd been beyond delighted when, just a few weeks ago, Aunt Jane had ordered Mr. Day to bring his "poor nephew" with him to Sunday dinner. William had arrived with his uncle, dressed in his best, which, although patched here and there, showed his dark, rugged handsomeness to its best advantage. She'd been ecstatic when, later that same evening, after their guests had left, her aunts had praised William's excellent manners and obvious intelligence.

But it wasn't until this morning that she'd begun to wonder if perhaps she'd been the one who'd been manipulated. While helping Sarafina set the breakfast table, Aunt Em had said to no one in particular, "If a woman who has decided to take on a career meets a man whom she hopes to wed, she should remember to be very clear that she expects to continue to work after the wedding. That sort of clarity will benefit both of their lives."

Sarafina had almost dropped the butter knife she was about to place on the table. "I— Pardon me?"

Aunt Em straightened a teacup to a more correct angle. "It's best to set such expectations early on, don't you think?"

Sarafina, not knowing what to say to that, had nodded, although her heart was racing like mad. Was Aunt Em letting Sarafina know that she was aware of her feelings toward William? Sadly, her aunt was so prone to making innocuous, out-of-the-blue statements that Sarafina couldn't be certain.

She would have been left in misery except for Aunt Jane and her blessedly direct way of saying things. Later on, after placing a platter of eggs on the table and taking her seat, Aunt Jane—her cheeks red even though she was doing nothing more exciting than buttering her toast with a bit more force than necessary—had blurted out, "No woman should be required to marry. You know how I feel about that. However, *if* she meets someone she cares for *and* he proves he's worthy of that care, then, naturally, one must not be closed-minded. Although marriage is, by law, an archaic institution, one should still be aware of its obvious benefits."

Sarafina had almost dropped her teacup into her lap. They knew. Better yet, they were each, in their own ways, giving her and William their blessings.

Her cheek now resting against William's shoulder, Sarafina gave a ridiculously happy smile. She should tell him. She raised her head, but before she could utter a word, the snapping of twigs announced the arrival of a visitor.

"I knew you two would be here," came a reed-thin voice from the path. Marcus McCleary appeared, a too-loose coat hanging over his narrow shoulders, his blond hair showing beneath the cap pulled low over his face.

Her face hot, Sarafina immediately sprang up from where she'd been leaning against William.

McCleary's amused yet irritated expression told her he'd seen everything.

William cut McCleary a dry look. "I thought you were working."

"Mr. Callahan let me off early." McCleary's mouth tightened, and he added in a sullen tone, "He always does that. I've yet to make a full day's pay there."

Although she'd tried, Sarafina had yet to grow fonder of Marcus. She had, however, come to appreciate him. He was rude, and abrupt, and possessed no discernible moral code, but he had a sharp wit and no one could deny that he admired and loved William like a brother.

Marcus leaned against a nearby tree and slipped his hands into his coat pockets. "We need to talk."

William pulled his book from his pocket and rested his elbows on his knees. "So talk."

Marcus removed a pack of cigarettes from his pocket. He slipped one into his mouth, tucked the rest away, and dug out a match. His gaze flicked to Sarafina and then back to William. "She should leave. It's private."

William's gaze narrowed. "She's not going anywhere. Either say what you came to say or leave."

Sarafina wandered over to her fishing pole and pretended to be engaged in seeing if the line was taut.

Marcus moved closer to William and spoke around his unlit cigarette. "We have an opportunity. A big one. One that—" He shot Sarafina a frustrated look.

William's eyebrows rose. "It must not be a good opportunity, or you wouldn't be worried about other people knowing about it."

"It's too good to pass up." Marcus lit his cigarette and flipped the still-smoking match into the woods.

Sarafina watched the arc of his match and wished for the hundredth time that he wouldn't do that. The forest floor was filled with old leaves and bits of broken twigs, perfect kindling for a wildfire.

William's gaze had followed the match, and he watched as it smoldered for a minute, then extinguished itself. He looked back at Marcus. "You can talk in front of Sarafina. You know I'll tell her whatever it is you have to say, anyway."

Sarafina had to turn away for a second to hide her smile.

Marcus swore under his breath before he took a drag on his cigarette. "Sarafina, whatever I say now is private. Got that?"

She shrugged, unwilling to promise more.

He muttered something and went to sit beside William. "We have an incredible opportunity. If things go well—and they should, because we have information from someone in the know—then we'll have made it, William. *Made.*"

"Who's this 'we'?"

Marcus leaned closer to William. "It'll be just the three of us. You, me, and Ellis Johnson."

William slanted a hard frown at his friend. "I don't trust that man and neither should you."

"He's not as bad as you think," McCleary said impatiently. "He's smart and has ideas on how to get ahead, ways to beat the system—" A cough suddenly burst from him, the sound harsh in the quiet. Still coughing, he dropped his cigarette to the earth and ground it under his heel even as he reached into his pocket for his handkerchief.

Marcus had never been well and had always had a cough, but it had gotten worse lately. Sarafina had noticed, too, that he was out of breath all the time, even when not coughing. She'd asked William about it, but he'd merely shrugged, although it was obvious from his closed expression that he knew something but wasn't free to share it.

Marcus finally stopped coughing, although he held his handkerchief over his mouth a moment longer.

William, his gaze dark with concern, asked quietly, "Do you need some water? I can—"

"No. I'm fine." Marcus wiped his mouth and stuffed his handkerchief back into his pocket. Still visibly panting, he returned his gaze to William. "For this to work, we need you. Johnson has great ideas, but he's not good at details. Not the way you are."

"Johnson has ideas on ways to get in trouble and that's it. Whatever stupidity you two are cooking up, I'm not getting involved."

Marcus pushed away from the tree he'd been leaning against, his jaw tight. "You're an idealist, William. And idealists lose in this life. You won't admit that the deck is stacked against poor people like us. If we want something, we have to take it or we'll never get it. The sooner you admit that, the better."

"However unfair life is, you can't go around breaking the law. Johnson is a criminal, and you know it. His version of getting ahead will only land you in jail."

"He may cross the line now and then, sure. But he's been forced to do that." Marcus must have forgotten Sarafina was close, because he was almost shouting now. "Damn it, William, I'm tired of always losing. Of always being broke and always wanting things I'll never have. Aren't you?"

"I'm not losing," William said shortly. "I have a plan. I've told you that. It'll just take time."

Sarafina knew his plan, as it was hers as well. They were both saving every penny they could, and when the time came, they'd leave Dove Pond for New York. There, armed with copies of her articles and a recommendation letter from Mr. Day, she'd get a job as a journalist, while William would open a photography studio using the old camera his uncle had given him in return for his help in the studio. Whenever William talked about their plan, he always included Marcus. He was to work as William's assistant until he found another, better-paying job. Or that was what William had proposed, anyway.

"Time," Marcus said bitterly. He pulled out another cigarette and lit it, flicking the match in the general direction of the first. "That's the one thing I don't have."

William closed his book. "You don't know that. Not for sure, anyway."

"Yeah, well, I know it better than most." He took several long drags on his cigarette and then dropped it by his feet and left it smoldering there. "I have to do this. It could be my last chance to—" He broke out into another fit of coughing, this one longer and more intense. He pulled his handkerchief out of his pocket again and covered his mouth, as if hoping that might stop it.

It didn't work. He coughed harder now, his pale face flushed.

Sarafina turned back toward the pond and bit her lip. As much as she disliked how often William ended up in harm's way because of Marcus, she couldn't help but worry about him. For some reason, much like William, she felt increasingly responsible for Marcus. He was a weak man, wildly impulsive, always outraged, and deeply desperate for a one-hit-solves-all answer to life. He lacked all the qualities that made her believe that William would eventually achieve everything he wanted—a willingness to make things work, calm acceptance of the things he couldn't change, and the patience to develop answers to the problems he faced.

Marcus's coughing spell finally eased and, panting heavily, he leaned against the tree and tucked his handkerchief away, but not before Sarafina caught a glimpse of blood on it.

It wasn't the first time she'd seen that. Sighing, Sarafina quietly pulled her fishing line from the water.

William's gaze was still on his friend. "Come and sit."

"No, I—" Panting slightly, Marcus pressed a hand to his chest as he struggled to breathe. "I'm fine. William, please reconsider. If this plan works—"

"Stop it. Whatever you two are planning, don't do it. It'll end up badly, and you know it."

"My life is going to end badly now, so what's the difference?" Marcus said bitterly. "At least Johnson is giving me a chance for things to get better while they can."

"There's also a chance things could get worse. A lot worse."

Marcus slumped against a tree and cursed. "You won't even listen, will you?"

Sarafina stashed her fishing rod back in its place and then went to rinse her hands in the pond. As she dried her hands on some moss, she cast a worried glance at William. There was an expression on his face that she'd never seen before—a cross between worry and, for the first time, fear. *He doesn't think he can stop Marcus from doing this, and he's afraid.*

A blue jay landed on the branch overhead and began scolding.

She glanced up at it and caught it staring at her. *Aunt Em wants me to go home.* Frowning, she looked at the sun and decided that, for once, her aunt might be right. There wasn't anything more for her to do here. Maybe, if she left, Marcus would be more willing to listen to William. They would be able to discuss the details of this "opportunity" more freely so that William could calmly point out its inconsistencies and put a stop to it.

She cleared her throat. "I should be going. It's getting late."

William stood. "I'll walk you to the creek."

Marcus, who was watching with red-rimmed eyes, said in a bitter tone, "She doesn't need anyone to walk her home. She knows the way better than you do."

William cut a hard look at his friend. "Wait here. I'll be back."

Sarafina smiled up at William. "Stay here. Marcus is right: I know the way. Besides, it sounds as if you two have a lot to talk about." She met William's gaze and gave him a meaningful look.

He understood, as he always did. A flash of irritation flickered through his eyes, but after a second, he nodded. "Be careful."

"Of course. See you tomorrow." As she passed Marcus, she gave him a polite goodbye nod.

He returned the nod, but as he did so, she caught a glimpse of his expression. He wore a look of such despair that she almost stopped to speak to him, to tell him that she understood his frustration with the world. That no matter how difficult life seemed, he needed to find a better answer, something safer.

But although she sympathized with his difficult situation, she also recognized the mulish set of his mouth. So instead, she kept going, leaving the two of them to continue their conversation.

It wouldn't be until the next week, when all three of their lives shattered into a thousand pieces, that she'd wish with all her heart that she'd followed her instincts and talked to him. She might not have been able to change Marcus's mind, but it might have relieved her of the deep, painful regret she would experience from that day on.

CHAPTER 21

LUKE

"Here's your classroom." Luke reached down and unfastened Lulu's backpack. He pulled it from her shoulders and handed it to her as a stream of students swirled past them in the hallway. "There you go. Have a good day."

"Wait." Lulu eyed him with a displeased look. "Did you get it?"

Not that again. "No."

She scowled. "I *told* you to get Tay a thank-you present. She deserves one."

He frowned and absently rubbed his neck where it was irritated by the strap of his sling. Since Tay's now-infamous fountain dunking last week, Lulu had decided that her uncle owed Tay something for "saving" him.

He stooped in front of his niece. "Look, I get what you're saying, and a thank-you present sounds nice and all. But I think it might be a bit much."

Lulu crossed her arms. "You don't have to spend much. Just get her some flowers."

"That's not what I meant. She's just not the type—" He caught himself. "Listen, I told her thank you. I said it very politely, and she smiled when I said it. That's enough."

Lulu's mouth turned mulish. "No, it's not."

Lord protect him from New Jersey divorcées with anger issues, which must have been Lulu's previous life. He raked an impatient hand through his hair and stood. Lulu didn't understand the situation. He'd worked too darn hard to get himself into Tay's good graces and wasn't about to risk that on a lame grand gesture. The timing wasn't right for it.

Not yet, anyway.

He opened the classroom door. "Go."

"Buy her some cupcakes, then. She likes those and—"

He leaned into the classroom. "Miss Fenton? Lulu's here!" He put his hand on his niece's shoulder, guided her into the room, and closed the door.

"Thank goodness for public education," he said fervently. He walked down the hallway, stopping to return his parent hall pass to the nice lady at the check-in counter before making his way to the parking lot. *That kid is killing my blood pressure.*

He wished he were at the point with Tay where he could get her a little something, and not just as a thank-you gift, but just because. Just because she'd allowed him to join her on this amazing adventure. Just because she tolerated his at-times-nerdy sense of humor without the usual eye rolls. Just because she was so smart, relaxed, funny, and everything else he'd never thought a woman could be.

He heard his own thoughts and grimaced. *I'm losing it. I really, really am.* Muttering to himself about having put his cart before his horse, he flexed his finally better wrist. It had taken a week, but he could now move it without squeaking like a mouse that had had its tail slammed in a door.

Luke started up his truck and drove to Ace Hardware, where he spent a good half hour picking up light bulbs for the varied and sundry light fixtures at the bookshop. That done, he stopped by the post office for a pack of mailers. Lately, Grandma had gotten into the habit of picking up the mail on her way home in the evenings, so he hadn't been here in a while. *I'll save her the trip today.*

He tucked the mail under his good arm and carried everything back to his truck. When he climbed in, he dropped the lot into the passenger seat. As he did so, a bright red stamped letter caught his attention. The stamp read PAST DUE THIRD NOTICE. The letter was from a finance company in Asheville that he'd never heard of.

That couldn't be good. Instantly uneasy, he did a search on his phone and winced at the huge number of negative reviews. Oh no. What had she done? Heart heavy, he turned on his truck and headed for the bookstore. He'd known Grandma Rose was having financial trouble. He'd overheard her muttering about it more than once, although she always denied it whenever he called her out.

But there'd been other signs, too. For one, unless a repair was absolutely necessary, it didn't happen. For another, whenever he mentioned an improvement or made a suggestion that would lighten her workload, she immediately rejected it based on cost, even before she knew the amount.

For the hundredth time, he wished she would let him help, but she refused to touch a penny. He'd given her large checks on numerous occasions, saying the money was for his and Lulu's rent. He'd hoped Grandma would use it for daily expenses or even upgrades, but every single time, she'd torn up the checks and then raised hell about how she didn't take charity.

He parked on the street, collected the mail and the bag of light bulbs, and headed inside. The Dove Pond Book Club had just had their Wednesday morning meeting, so the bookstore was busy, the numerous members wandering the aisles after putting in their orders for next month's selection. Grandma Rose was in her usual place behind the counter, taking those orders with the efficient, no-nonsense air of an admiral commanding a battleship.

He waved to let her know he was back before he went to the back room to store the light bulbs in the closet. That done, he put her mail on her desk with the exception of the red-stamped letter, which he carried back into the bookstore. There were still customers in the store, so he busied himself by reorganizing the best-selling rack.

As soon as the last customer left, he went to the counter and placed the letter in front of her. "This came in the mail."

Grandma Rose froze in place, her hand still hovering over the messy stack of bookmarks beside the register.

He pushed the letter across the counter. "What's going on?"

She opened the drawer under the counter, slid the letter into it, and then slammed the drawer closed. "It's junk mail. Nothing more."

"It's not junk mail, and we both know it. I looked up the company, and I know what they do. Grandma, if things are that bad, you have to let me—"

She slapped her hand on the counter. "I don't have to do anything! And stop offering me money. You know I won't take it."

"If you took out a loan and can't pay it, then—"

"I'm done talking about this. Did you finish with the new release rack? If you did, I have a whole list of items that could use your attention this morning." Scowling bitterly, she picked up a scrap of paper and jotted down a dozen or more tasks that didn't really need to be done, and handed it to him. "Do these." She picked up her cane and limped toward her office, saying over her shoulder, "When you're done with those, we'll talk."

But they wouldn't. Not about the loan or money or anything else important. Swallowing the urge to curse, he went to work on the items on her list. He had to figure out a way to get some money to her. But how? She had to be worried sick, and yet her pride wouldn't allow her to even admit how bad things were, let alone accept help.

As he worked, he looked back at Tay's office. She wasn't in yet, which was unusual, as lately she'd been arriving just as the store opened. Oddly enough, he found himself worrying about her, too.

That was concerning. He was getting way too wound up over Tay Dove and he knew it. But no matter how he tried, he hadn't been able to forget how, just last week, she'd leapt past him and into the cold water of the fountain like a modern-day Lara Croft. Since then, they'd been working together on the clue they'd found etched in the brick, which meant they'd spent most of every day together. He'd liked that. He'd liked that way, way too much.

If he had to name one reason why he found Tay so interesting, he'd have said it was her passion. He'd never met anyone who loved their job the way she loved hers, and he was jealous of that. To be honest, he'd never been passionate about anything, but watching the way she focused on every aspect of her research—how she beamed whenever they discovered even the tiniest bit of information from a dusty old record, and the enthusiasm she brought with her to every conversation—he wanted that. He wanted to feel that excited, that happy, that enamored of something.

What had made her like that? Was it because of her Dove gift? He couldn't stop thinking about how she'd touched the carved letters in the fountain. As she did so, her face had changed in a subtle way he couldn't describe. The effect had been astounding. It was as if, for a split second, she'd become someone else. Her face, her expression, her air, the way she held her mouth—everything had changed, but for such a short moment that he'd barely been able to register it before it disappeared.

If someone had asked him just a few short months ago whether he believed the rumors about the Dove sisters that flew around town as regularly as the seasons—about how, when there were seven sisters, as there were now, they were each blessed with a special power—he would have said no so firmly that it stuck. But now . . .

He mentally shook himself. He had more important things to think about. She was warming up to him, little by little, although not nearly as quickly as he'd have liked. Still, he could tell that his don't-rush-things methods were beginning to thaw this particular ice maiden. *Stay the course, Day. You can't afford to mess this up.*

He unboxed the new stock and registered it in the system. He'd just finished and was fixing himself a coffee when Tay finally arrived. She wore a long cardigan over a flowered dress today and looked adorable from head to foot.

Grandma Rose happily eyed the paper bag in Tay's hand that was stamped PINK MAGNOLIA TEAROOM.

Tay carried it to the counter. "Ella made Victoria sponge cake for Ava's tearoom, so I brought you some."

Grandma Rose peered inside the bag. "I was wondering what was keeping you."

Luke joined them at the counter. "I don't suppose you got me a Victoria whatever-it-is?"

Tay shot him an amused glance. "No, but you know where Ava's tearoom is, so feel free to get one for yourself."

He narrowed his gaze on her chin. "I see you already had one." Her hand flew to where he'd looked and he laughed. "There's nothing there. I was just giving you a hard time."

Tay grinned, but Grandma Rose fixed him with a hard look. "Hey!" she barked. "Stop teasing my best customer."

"*Best* customer?"

Tay raised her hand. "That's me. I've bought at least a half dozen books a week since your grandmother let me use the office, and probably more."

"It was more," Grandma Rose assured Tay. "I won't bother you with the exact number, as I know you already have trouble sleeping."

"Oh, I slept like a baby last night."

That caught Luke's attention, and he realized she appeared pretty darn happy for this early in the morning. Had she figured out the new puzzle? No, she wasn't that excited. It had to be something less exciting, but just as satisfying. "Did you get some news on your book woes?"

A slow smile curled her mouth. "I've been letting my lawyer do the talking, and, oh, how she must have talked."

"What did you get?"

"My name as the author, with an internal note stating that Richard contributed significantly to two chapters."

"I'm surprised he went for that."

"You know how narcissists are. I offered to put his name as a coauthor, but he had to be listed second since he did so little of the work. He flatly refused that, so . . ." She shrugged. "Here we are."

Luke got the impression that if Grandma Rose hadn't been nearby, Tay might have done a victory dance. He held his hand up for a high five. As she slapped it, he said, "I'm buying you lunch today."

"Done! Now, if you'll excuse me, I should get to work. I'll catch you all later." She was gone by the time she said the last word.

Luke watched her hurry to her office. Maybe Lulu was right and he should have gotten Tay a present.

He turned around and realized his grandmother was watching him. "What?"

"Nothing. Have you two figured out the fountain code yet?"

"No."

"I wish you all would get a move on and find that gold. I'd like to refresh the place a bit."

"Grandma, I've told you dozens of times that if you need money, I'll be happy to—"

"I'm not taking money from my own grandchild." She scowled at him. "I have my pride, you know."

Great. His grandmother wouldn't let him pay rent, but she'd happily accept stolen gold from a train robbery. *I can't even.*

"Stop looking at me like that. I'm just kidding about the gold." She settled on her stool and pulled a book from under the counter, a bright red bookmark peeping from between the pages. "You should know that this silly treasure hunt of yours is starting to get people riled up. Grace told me this morning that our one and only law enforcement officer had to chase numerous people out of the fountain after you and Tay took that swim last week."

"I'm sure Blake can handle it. He needs something to do, anyway."

"Nonsense. Your fake gold hunt is an embarrassment and it makes this town look cheap." She sent him a sour look. "Help Tay figure out what that family secret is and be done with it before the gossip train runs over the whole darn town."

"Right. I guess I should go help Tay, then." He started to leave, but then—on impulse—he stopped and gave his grandmother a quick hug.

"Idiot," she muttered, although he caught her faintly pleased smile. "While you're back there, make yourself useful and scan in the returns, too. They're in the box beside your desk."

"Will do." He collected his coffee and made Tay a cup, too. As he walked toward the office, he saw that Tay was already sitting at her desk, her head bent over an old *Register*. Her finger moved down the page as she read. In the past few weeks, while working next to her, he'd discovered a lot of random things. She read faster than he could, she had bifocals—she tilted her head up just the tiniest bit whenever she wanted to read something—and she drank more coffee than anyone he'd ever met.

He was halfway to her office when, idly glancing at the shelves as he walked past, he noticed a title he hadn't seen in a few years. He stopped and, placing the coffees he was carrying on the edge of a nearby shelf, picked up the book. He'd loved this one. *And I know right where it needs to go.*

He tucked the book under his arm, collected the two cups of coffee, and continued to the office. He walked in, and Tay looked up from where she sat, half-hidden behind a stack of folders.

"I brought you a little something. Two little somethings, in fact." He walked around her desk, set the coffee near her pencil holder, and then placed the book in front of her. "It's *Beartown* by Fredrik Backman, one of my favorites. There's adventure, quirky characters, humor, emotion—it's like the everything bagel of books. Read it if you ever have trouble sleeping. You'll be entertained, and you'll never feel alone."

Her gray-green gaze, framed by her glasses, lifted to meet his. "That's the problem with not sleeping while everyone else is, isn't it? You feel alone."

He nodded. There had been plenty of nights after he'd first been tasked with taking care of Lulu that he'd lain awake feeling that very thing—alone. "It's worse at three a.m. for some reason."

"Everything is worse at three a.m. Thank you for this." She put the book on the small stack that rested on the corner of her desk. She caught him eyeing her book stack and made a face. "Such is the cost of working in a bookshop. It's like working in a bakery. Weight gain is expected."

"Hey, I wasn't judging."

"Good." She took a sip of her coffee. "Ah. It's perfect. Thanks. By the way, I had a thought about the clue we've been working on."

"Excellent." He sat in his chair and wheeled it next to hers, stopping to pick up his notebook as he rolled past. There, on the front page, he'd written out the clue. *Nine seven keyed in brass by the people.* All around were notes and squiggles and the numerous disproved theories he and Tay had come up with over the last week while trying to solve it.

He parked his chair next to hers, rested the notepad on his knee, and poised his pen to write. "So . . . what was this thought you had about Sarafina's latest riddle?"

Excitement warmed Tay's gaze. "Sections."

He blinked. "Sections?"

"We keep looking at this as one long code, and we haven't been able to figure it out. So let's break it into sections and look at one word and phrase at a time. We can make a list under each section, and if we see some crossover . . . bingo!"

"That's a great idea." He looked at the clue and then drew a slash after *nine seven*, the word *brass*, and the final phrase *by the people*. He showed it to her. "Was this what you had in mind?"

"Exactly." She scooted closer, her head next to his. "Let's do the numbers first. We'll brainstorm a list of possible answers and then go from there."

The faint smell of her citrusy shampoo reached him, and he had to move away a little so he could think. "How about . . . a house number?"

She nodded, so he wrote that down.

She said, "Maybe letters of the alphabet? A *G* and an *I*."

He added that to the list.

They were quiet a moment, the clock on the wall ticking softly. "Ah!" he said. "A post office box number."

They added a few more random thoughts and then sat quietly for a while longer.

Tay leaned back in her chair. "Let's move on to 'brass.'" She bit her lip and stared at the wall. "I can only think of decorative things."

"That's where you see brass nowadays, but we have to think like it's the early 1900s. Brass was used for a lot of things back then."

"Right." She tapped her fingers on her desk. "Doorknobs."

He wrote it down. "And kitchen utensils."

"Also post office boxes. The old ones had brass doors and were very elaborate."

He looked up. "Post office boxes also had numbers. We have a crossover between the two lists. Should we check to see if there's a post office box number seventy-nine?"

"Absolutely, although . . ." She frowned. "Post office boxes have to be paid for annually, don't they? It might have been closed long ago."

"Maybe they paid in advance?"

She shook her head. "The rates for those boxes would have increased dozens of times between now and then, if not more. Besides, it would have gotten packed with junk mail, too, and rendered useless decades ago."

"We should call Mark Robinson at the post office. He'll know."

Tay was already reaching for her phone. She spoke to Mark for a few minutes and then hung up. "It can't be a post office box. He wouldn't tell me who was renting it, but he said they'd only had it for the past twenty years or so, and they have no connection to Sarafina or anyone else."

He sighed. "Back to brainstorming 'brass,' then."

They worked on for another twenty minutes, adding over a dozen more things to the "brass" line, and then moved on to "by the people."

"This phrase is intriguing." Tay frowned at the notebook in his hands. "Does it mean the brass work is 'by the people,' or that the thing made with brass is 'by the people,' or is 'by the people' written on the brass thing somewhere? I have no idea."

"Neither do I. We could be here all year if we wrote a list of things made 'by the people.'"

They stared in silence at the phrase until, out of the blue, a thought struck him. "Maybe it's a government thing. 'By the people' was in Lincoln's Gettysburg Address."

"That's possible, I suppose." Her gaze still locked on the notepad, she absently tapped her pen on the edge of the desk, the clicking sound loud as they sank into silence.

He realized he was chewing on the end of his own pen, and he slipped it back into his shirt pocket. "It's a very slogan-y phrase, isn't it?"

She nodded absently. After a long moment, she said slowly, "Slogan-y. You're right. It sounds familiar, too, as if—" She stopped, her eyes widening.

He leaned forward. "What?"

"It *is* a slogan," she said in a breathless tone. "For a bank. 'A bank for the people, by the people.'"

Luke had to fight the urge to jump to his feet. "The First People's Bank where Zoe works! The slogan is carved on the concrete plaque by the door."

"Seven nine! It wasn't a post office box but a safe-deposit box! I need to talk to Zoe. She'll know who it's registered to."

"But . . ." His excitement faded a bit. "*If* she can tell us. There might be both privacy *and* property rights involved if it's a safe-deposit box."

Tay didn't seem the least fazed. "Zoe will know the rules."

"And don't safe-deposit boxes open with a key? We haven't found a key, so—"

"But we have." Tay smiled. Opening her drawer, she pulled out an old tin box and fished out an ornate key threaded onto a chain. She placed the key on her desk.

"Is that the box your sisters found in the fireplace surround?"

She nodded. "This key was in there, too."

He couldn't have been more excited. "And there we have it: a safe-deposit box number *and* a key. Now to get permission to unlock it."

"I'll call Zoe."

Smiling, he wheeled his chair back to his desk. Even though he was no longer close to the phone, he could hear Zoe's excited voice as she and Tay talked.

It was a good twenty minutes or longer before Tay finally hung up. "Zoe was in the Moonlight Café with some friends, but she ran across the street to her office and looked in the old ledgers for the name of the owner of the box."

"And?"

"Safe-deposit box seventy-nine is in Sarafina Dove's name."

"We got it right!"

"Indeed we did. Zoe said it's an older box, one of the originals, and the doors are made of decorated brass." Tay gave an excited hop in her chair. "*And* . . . Sarafina paid for a fifty-year lease on that box, too."

His smile disappeared. "We're past that."

"Zoe says we might be fine. In the 1970s, the bank was required by their insurance company to install newer, more secure boxes. The bank made everyone come in and move their things over, but no one came for that one."

"Uh-oh."

Tay shook her head. "Her father was in charge of the bank back then, and he loved those old brass boxes. Said they were historical and beautiful, and he'd be darned if he'd remove them. Once the brass boxes were marked 'out of use,' he had one wall of the old vault replaced with a glass wall and a door, and it's now a conference room. Those old brass boxes are still there and are undisturbed."

"Whew. That's good news. Will she open the box for us?"

"Yes. We can't remove the contents without the proper paperwork, which will take time, but we can look. Since I'm a direct descendant of the family, Zoe thinks I might be able to claim the contents, as Lucy never had children of her own. Well, providing no one in my family files a counterclaim, that is."

"Your sisters would never fight you on that."

"I know, right? It'll probably take me a while to get full ownership, but Zoe said she needed to take an inventory of what's inside, anyway. For today, we can at least take a peek."

He rubbed his hands together. "I can't wait to see what's in there."

"Me neither. I—" Her phone rang and she glanced at it, then frowned.

Instantly, his euphoria over their find dissipated a little. "That's Richard, I take it."

"He's probably calling to tell me how to edit the book so he can take credit for that, at least. That's how narcissists are."

Luke shot her a curious look and then said in a carefully neutral tone, "When you used to talk about Richard, you always seemed . . . bruised, I guess. But today you're just annoyed. That's progress."

She made a face. "I used to think I was heartbroken, but now I've realized that the only thing that got hurt in that relationship was my pride. I just got lost in—" She caught herself and wrinkled her nose. "I don't know why I'm telling you this."

"Why not? We're partners, aren't we?" He closed his notebook. "When do we meet Zoe?"

"In half an hour. She's going to have papers for me to sign, and she'll have the box out and ready for us to open."

"You're lucky she knows you so well, or you might have had to go through even more legal mumbo jumbo to get to it."

"It helps that she's even more excited than we are." Tay pursed her lips, her brow furrowed. "I hate to say this out loud, as I don't want to tempt fate, but it feels as if we're getting close to the end here."

It did. He wondered what, exactly, he would do with his time once they finished this adventure. The thought instantly depressed him. He'd had more fun sitting back here, in this old office, looking through dry documents and teasing Tay than he'd had at any other point of his life for the past thirty years. His gaze moved to Tay. He thought he knew why, too.

She caught his look and smiled. "It's been fun."

Her admission surprised him, but he found himself nodding. Yes, it had been. "What will you do when you finally solve Sarafina's mystery?"

"I'll finish writing her book."

That was what he'd expected her to say. She could do that here in Dove Pond if she wanted to. "I can't wait to read it."

She quirked her eyebrow at him. "And you?"

"That's a good question. Sadly, I don't have an answer for you. All I know is that it won't be as much fun." *Not without you sitting next to me.*

"We should go." Tay got up and was pulling her cardigan back on, her face slightly red. "Ready?"

Luke stood and pushed his chair back under his desk and joined her. Five minutes later, he and Tay walked into the First People's Bank. The building had been constructed during the 1850s, and while the interior had been redone numerous times over the years, the exterior had been left untouched. Luke loved this bank. He loved the redbrick façade, with its light tan brick accents around each arched window, and the wrought-iron front door and bank windows.

Zoe met them in the lobby, looking chic as usual. Her hair was pulled into a slick bun, and she was wearing a very dashing retro cherry-red pantsuit, which fit her like a glove. "This way, please." She tucked a sheaf of papers under her arm and led them to a conference room, her gold hoops swinging from her ears like bells.

Luke followed Tay inside, stopping when he saw Grace already sitting at the big table, which was empty except for an ornate brass safe-deposit box.

"Ah, there you are!" Grace refolded the spreadsheet she'd been reading and tucked it into the pocket on the outside of her briefcase. "Hello, Tay. Luke. I hear you've discovered yet another clue."

Tay sent Zoe a questioning look.

"Sorry," Zoe said brightly, although she didn't seem the least bit sorry. She placed the papers on the table and gestured for Tay and Luke to take a seat. "I was having breakfast with Grace at the Moonlight when you called. She heard everything, so, since we'll need an extra witness to sign the form for the box, I thought she'd come in handy."

Grace clasped her hands together. "Besides, as the mayor, I'm keeping an eye on this search of yours. Our poor sheriff spent the past week chasing people out of the fountain, and he had to answer two calls caused by people getting stuck in that tree at the Day family cemetery, too."

"People can be crazy," Luke said as he and Tay took their seats.

Zoe snorted. "Crazy about gold." She sat down beside Tay and began organizing her papers. She pulled one from the stack and handed it to Grace along with a pen. "You and Luke will need to sign this to verify that all contents of this box were returned to it. I can't sign, since I work here, and neither can Tay, as she's already stated that she'll soon be filing a claim."

Grace signed the form and slid it across the table to Luke, who scrawled his name on the line marked with a tab.

Zoe set the paper to one side and handed Tay the rest of the pages. "You'll need to fill these out to make your claim. Bring them back when you're done and I'll start the process." When Tay nodded, Zoe scooted a little closer to the table. "You said you had the key?"

While Tay looked in her purse for the key, Luke leaned forward to get a closer look at the box. It was about a foot long and four inches by four inches in width and height. Luke turned it this way and then that, admiring the beautifully scrolled brass work on the small door. "It's a work of art."

Zoe gave a satisfied smile. "The original boxes are all like this. Just beautiful. We could have used the space for another vault, but Dad couldn't stand the thought of throwing them out, so he made them into a 'decorative wall' instead."

Tay found the key, her gaze meeting Luke's. "Ready?" she asked softly.

A trill of excitement lit him up. Darn, but he loved it when she lowered her voice like that. "Let's do this." He slid the box to Tay.

She inserted the key into the lock and turned it, a satisfying click sounding in the quiet.

"It worked!" said Grace.

"Open it," Zoe added eagerly. "Pour everything out on the table so we can all see what you've found."

Tay opened the door and then gently tilted the box so the contents would come out.

Nothing happened.

Luke frowned.

"Shake it harder," Zoe ordered.

Tay shook it, but still nothing happened.

"Let me see that!" Zoe grabbed the box and peered inside. "There's nothing in here but a piece of paper, and it's stuck under the edge of a corner weld." She reached in, pulled out a yellowed piece of paper, and handed it to Tay.

Grace's smile had disappeared. "That's it? That's a bit disappointing."

Luke leaned closer to Tay so he could read the paper with her. There, etched in pen, was a map. It was a strange map, though, and consisted of a large rectangle broken by random angles, a dark squiggle of broken lines, and one large X.

Tay laid it out on the table so everyone could see it.

Zoe leaned forward, her eyes widening. "Lord help us all, it's a genuine treasure map! There's even an 'X' on it."

"I feel like a pirate," Grace said in a breathless voice.

But Tay's eyebrows were drawn together as she stared at the map. "There are no words on this. I don't even know what it represents."

She was right. Luke touched the thick middle line. "Could this be Main Street?"

"Maybe. Or maybe not. I can't tell." She dropped back into her seat, her gaze locked on the paper. "There are no identifying marks anywhere. Not one street or building is labeled."

Grace frowned. "You're right. As treasure maps go, this one sucks."

"It's pretty sparse on information," Zoe agreed. "How are you all going to figure this out? I wouldn't even know where to begin."

"I don't know that we can," Tay admitted, her shoulders slumped.

"Maybe there's more to it." Luke picked up the paper and held it up so the light from the window shone through it. After a moment, he grimaced and returned the paper to the table. "Nope. Nothing."

Zoe suddenly gasped. "Hold on! I once saw a movie where a detective had to pee on a piece of paper to get the secret information."

Everyone looked at her.

"Hey, I'm not saying that has to happen here."

Tay sighed. "This is going to take some thinking."

"I hate to say this," Zoe said, "but you can't take that map with you. However, you can copy it if you'd like."

Luke immediately ripped a page from his notebook. "Hand it here."

"Go ahead," Zoe said. "Just don't damage it in any way."

He placed his paper over the map and traced it. Once he was done, he slid the original to Tay. "Find out what your Dove gift says about this."

Surprise flickered over her face, and then she smiled. "Sure."

He watched her with interest as she pulled the map closer, making sure she touched only the edges of the page.

Grace asked, "Have you ever done this with a map before?"

"Yes. Only hand-drawn ones, of course, although they were all far more elaborate than this."

Zoe scooted closer. "Touch it, Tay. Tell us what you see."

Tay took a steadying breath and then rested her fingers on the closest drawn line.

Luke leaned forward in his seat, fascinated. For a second, Tay didn't move at all, but sat as if entranced. Suddenly, her eyebrows drew together and there it was, that moment when—just for a second—an expression washed over her face that made her look as if she were someone else.

She let out a breath and blinked her eyes and then looked around the room as if surprised to find herself there.

Zoe's gaze moved over Tay's face. "What did you see?"

"The map was drawn by Sarafina."

Yes! "And?" Luke asked, unable to look away from Tay.

"David Tau was with her. She was sitting here at the bank, too. This safe-deposit box was right in front of her. She drew the map very quickly, so I didn't get to see much, but judging from the style of David Tau's clothes, I'd say it was sometime in the 1920s."

This was big. So big. But still . . . Luke frowned and drummed his fingers on the table. "This is really starting to bother me. We've both been thinking it's a secret about Sarafina, since the clues are all here in her hometown. But her husband, David, who, as far as we know, had no ties to Dove Pond at all, was here with her, planting these clues for Lucy to follow. The family secret had to have involved him as well."

Tay nodded. "I was wondering the same thing."

They were all silent for a moment until Grace said, "If you want to find out why David was involved, then I suppose you two will have to follow these clues to the desired end."

"That's what I was thinking," Zoe said.

"Don't worry." Tay tucked her copy of the map into her satchel and then handed Zoe the original. "Luke and I are committed to figuring this out. We won't stop until we do." She collected her things and stood. Luke did as well.

Zoe returned the map to the box and locked the ornate door before handing the key back to Tay. "Before yesterday, I'd have told you all that if you did find gold under that X, to bring it here and put the money into a nice investment account, but now I know that won't happen."

"Why not?" Tay asked.

"If you find the gold, you won't be able to keep it. I did some research. After the robbery, an insurance company paid the claims. During the financial crisis in the 1930s, the company became insolvent and was dissolved."

Grace leaned forward. "So there's no one to stake a claim, then."

"No, because when that company dissolved, it owed what would now be millions of dollars to various banks in New York."

Tay winced. "And those banks are still around and would have a claim?"

"A very valid claim, according to my source," Zoe said. "Once they find out about that gold, they'll all come running."

Grace looked disappointed. "I was hoping someone in town might get rich off that."

"Won't happen. It'll be tied up in court for years and years, and when it's all said and done, the person with the most aggressive lawyer will walk away with it."

Grace shook her head. "That's sad. I guess, for us here in Dove Pond, the real riches would be in unlocking that discretionary fund that is limited now to the fountain upkeep. If I could figure out a way to convince people to reallocate portions of that, it would be of great help to the small businesses around here."

Luke's confusion must have been evident, because Zoe explained, "Grace wants to use that fund for grants to deserving small businesses. A lot of them are still reeling from supply chain and staffing issues and—well, you two know how things are."

Hmm. Would Grandma accept a grant from the town? Or would she consider that charity, too?

Grace collected her briefcase and stood. "I should get back to the office. Call me if there's anything you all need." She waved and then, with a smile, left.

Zoe got up from her chair. "I'll put the box back after you two are gone. Should I see you out?"

"No, thank you," Tay said. "I know you're busy, too."

"Okay. See you two later." Zoe left, and Tay and Luke gathered their things and were soon walking back to the bookshop.

Luke cut her a side glance and could see that she was deep in thought, her head bent, the spring breeze teasing the hair that had escaped her ponytail. He stayed quiet and let her think.

The map was an intriguing item. He wondered what the lines might represent. He tried to imagine their little town from the vantage point of a drone and realized that no streets matched the layout. *What could it be?*

They turned the corner and the bookstore sign came into view at the end of the street. Tay suddenly seemed to realize how quiet she'd been and shot Luke an embarrassed look. "Sorry. I was just thinking."

"Me too. Figure anything out?"

"No." She bit her lip. "Sort of."

"Sort of?" He grinned. "That sounds like a yes."

"Maybe. I don't know how to read this map yet, but I think this is the last and final clue."

"Why?"

"Because X marks the spot, right?"

Ah. That made sense. "I wonder why Lucy didn't even try to follow the clues her parents placed for her. I don't think I could have just walked away."

"Me neither. But . . . maybe she knew just enough about this particular secret to avoid it."

That had to be it. *She either knew or at least suspected what this family secret was and decided it was safer or less hurtful not to know.*

They neared the bookshop and Tay hurried the final few steps so that she reached the door first. She swung it open. "I'll go make some copies of the map. Would you find the town surveys I pulled a few weeks ago? They might be of help."

He followed her inside. "Sure. I'll do it now."

She flashed him a smile and then headed for the copier, the wood floor creaking in her wake.

Luke went into the office to find the survey maps. They were so close to finding an answer that he could taste it. Which made him wonder what he was going to do when it all ended. Would that be the moment that Tay, after crossing her last *t* and dotting her last *i*, would pack up her things and leave?

As much as he hated to admit it, it was possible that when this search ended, so would their friendship. For reasons he wasn't yet sure about, the thought depressed him.

Luke sighed and started looking through the stacks of folders on Tay's desk for the one holding the survey maps. *One thing at a time, Day. One thing at a time.*

CHAPTER 22

TAY

"X marks the spot," Tay whispered to herself as she stared at the map yet again. "Oh, Sarafina. What were you thinking?"

Tay rubbed her tired eyes and pulled the survey maps forward. She tried to find the same pattern that was featured on Sarafina's map, but nothing matched. Muttering to herself about "impossible tasks," she dropped the maps on her desk and leaned back in her seat. Her gaze wandered across her desk, out the picture window, and into the bookshop until she found Luke. He stood at the counter, ringing up two women who were buying a ridiculously large stack of books, both talking excitedly. She had to laugh at the faintly exasperated expression on his face as he tried to navigate the conversation.

He was such a nice guy. She turned her attention to the three books stacked on the far corner of her desk. Every day, she found another book left there by either Rose or Luke. She'd noticed that

Rose tended to like sentimental books, while Luke's were more character oriented. It was nice, because it gave Tay a multiflavored reading experience.

She reached over and picked up the top book, the faint vanilla book scent wafting up to meet her. She wished she could just disappear into it right now and leave this frustrating puzzle behind for a while.

Tay placed her hand flat on the book. During the ups and downs of her life, books had greeted her, held her, warmed her, and made her both laugh and cry. They'd been with her in her loneliness and in her darkest hours. And in the past few months, they'd kept her company when she couldn't sleep. Better yet, she'd found that disappearing into a book while she faced a problem would sometimes reveal an answer she hadn't yet thought of. *Maybe I should just read for a while and let my brain rest until—*

The door opened and Rose limped in. "Figured out that weird map yet? It's been two days now."

"Not yet," Tay admitted, putting the book down. "Luke and I are going to have another brainstorming session this afternoon."

Rose made her way to the chair next to the desk, her cane thumping on the wood floor. "Luke's been telling me how important this research on Sarafina is to you." Rose sat down and leaned her cane against the wall. "I know she was one of the first women journalists and all that, but who tortures their own child with cryptic codes and poorly drawn maps and—"

Tay laughed. "Easy, now! Lucy was super close to her parents, so I'm sure there was no torture involved. Maybe Sarafina did all of this to make it more fun. We don't know."

"Fun? Pah!" Rose frowned. "You want to write about a real hero, then write about Elizabeth Friedman. She was a cryptographer through Prohibition and both world wars. Now, that was an interesting woman, and I'd bet my bottom dollar she didn't draw stupid maps like that."

"Elizabeth Friedman knew Sarafina, and they corresponded on occasion." Tay stood and leaned across the big desk to a stack of purple folders. She dug through them, pulled one out, and placed it in front of Rose. "Some of their letters are in here."

Rose opened the folder and looked at the top letter. "This doesn't even make sense."

"That's because it's written in code."

"Good Lord!" Rose slapped the folder closed and tossed it back on the desk. "I suppose all of these letters have been decoded by now, right?"

"The decoded version was on the back of that same page."

"Oh." Rose reclaimed the folder and looked at the letter once again. She read the translation, pausing once to guffaw here and there. "Your ancestor had a nice sense of humor, didn't she?"

"At times."

Rose put the letter back into the folder and returned it to Tay's desk. "When you're done here, what are you going to do?"

"Tonight? If we don't figure out how to interpret the map, I'll probably go home and have some of Ella's cheeseburger casserole and—"

"Not tonight!" Rose sent her an exasperated look. "I meant, what are you going to do once you've solved this little mystery? Are you going to stay here and work, or are you going to pack up and go back to Boston and teach at that college with your ex looking over your shoulder all the time, or—"

"I don't—" Tay bit back her irritation. "I don't know what I'm going to do then. I haven't thought that far ahead."

"You should. Luke, Lulu, and I have gotten used to having you here. It would be nice if you'd tell us what you plan on doing next. If you're going to leave, then we should know."

Will they miss me? Tay hadn't thought about it, but . . . she would miss them, too. "To be honest, I haven't really given it a lot of thought. It's been nice to be here, though." She glanced past Rose to the bookshop and saw Luke helping some customers carry their new books to their waiting car. *It's unusual to see a store offer that kind of service. Only here, in Dove Pond, would that happen.*

She liked that far more than she'd realized. "I don't want to return to Boston." The words tumbled from her lips, surprising her.

She pressed her fingers to her mouth. "I didn't mean to say that."

"But you did," Rose pointed out. "So stay here."

"It's not that easy. I'd have to find a new job and a place to live."

"You can stay with your sisters until you get that sorted out, can't you? There are a lot of colleges around here. Appalachian State is very close, in fact. That's a good college."

Tay couldn't argue with that. But still, she wasn't yet ready to make a decision. "It's a very good college. I'll think about it."

"Do that." Rose looked up as the bell rung, but it was just Luke returning. "We've had a difficult year, my family. I'd be lying if I said we were all okay now. To be honest, Caitlyn took a bit of my pride with her to prison."

"Your pride?"

Rose sighed. "I saw her the month before things went south. I knew something was wrong, but I didn't say anything. I told myself she'd tell me if she needed help."

Tay thought of all the lies Richard had told her and how she'd foolishly believed them all. "Sometimes it's easier not to notice the bad things. I think we've all been guilty of that at some time or another."

Rose shook her head. "And maybe, if I'd paid more attention, I could have helped Caitlyn. I'll never know."

"It's not your fault. Caitlyn made those decisions. And she's the one who has to pay for them."

"But now I wonder if I can trust myself to—" Rose swiped at her eyes. "Goodness, look at me. I don't usually ignore bad news, but I did then and look what happened. Worse—" She glanced back out into the bookstore. As if reassured that Luke was far away, she added, "To be honest, I've caught myself doing it since, too. I hate that."

"It's tough once you lose your confidence. You have to earn your own trust back. And you can only do that when you admit the truth to yourself, whatever it is."

"I suppose so." Rose absently ran her hand over the folder in her lap. She was silent as she sat there, a thoughtful expression on her wrinkled face. "I have a bit of a problem right now. It's nothing—Well, that's not true. But I can't keep avoiding it the way I have been."

"If there's anything I can do, let me kn—"

"Lord, child, there's nothing you nor anyone else can do about this. I'll have to work my way through it on my own." Rose seemed to realize her tone of voice had been a bit harsh, because she forced a smile. "But thank you for that. It was sweet of you. We're all glad you're here, especially Lulu."

"She's an amazing child." Tay looked out to where Luke stood at the counter, his gaze occasionally moving to the clock over the door. Tay knew he was already thinking about picking up his niece. "I wouldn't worry about Lulu. She's lucky to have such a great uncle."

"He's a good boy." Rose shot Tay a questioning look. "You know that, don't you?"

Tay's face grew warm. "I do."

"He's handsome, too. Don't you think?"

Tay nodded. She knew he was cute and charming and kind. She just wasn't sure what to do with those realizations, none of which were new, but all of which made her feel awkward.

"Well, handsome as he is," Rose continued, "he's clearly lacking as a cartographer. Let me see this map Sarafina drew."

"It's not the original." Tay handed it to her. "Luke traced a copy of it. As you can see, the lines don't match any roads here in town or any of the county maps, either. We've looked."

Rose squinted at the map and then handed it back. "What a horrible rendering. All I saw are boxes and lines and an X. It could be roads or property lines or fences or— Good Lord, it could be anything."

"We're narrowing it down. So far, we've figured out what it isn't, so that's something."

"You'll figure it out." Rose got to her feet and reclaimed her cane. "You're smart and you've come this far. I know you won't quit."

Of course she wouldn't quit. How could she?

"I guess I'd better head back to work. Luke has to go get Lulu soon." Rose waved and then left, closing the door behind her.

Tay leaned back in her creaky chair, her gaze following Rose as she made her way to where Luke stood at the counter. He said something to his grandmother and then grabbed his coat and headed for the door.

Tay watched him leave, listening to the little bell ring as the door swung closed. He wouldn't be gone long, but she noticed how small the bookstore seemed when he was gone. It was as if the walls had all moved closer together and—

Walls. She stood so abruptly that her empty chair went rolling backward into the bookshelf behind her. If she drew a box around the crisscrossing lines on the map, it would no longer look like intersecting streets, but would instead look like the blueprint of a building. *Oh my gosh. It's a floor plan, not a map!*

She held up the floor plan. The gaps could be either windows or doors, the long lines were walls, while the small rectangles were most likely furniture of some sort. *What buildings were associated with Sarafina?* There was Dove House, of course, but it was so distinct with its huge foyer, large porch, and round turret that she couldn't see a match. *What other building was associated with her? She went to the Baptist church, and she worked—*

Tay's eyes widened. *She worked here, at the* Register.

She held the map up, her gaze moving from it to the bookshop and back. The offices lined up, and so did the front door and the bow window beside it. Some time ago, Rose had said that the two presses had sat on tables in the middle of the room that was now the bookstore.

It fit. Every aspect was represented, which put the X in one spot.

She was still standing there, too shocked to move, when Luke came back with Lulu. He settled her into her seat at her table and had just started to take off his coat when he saw Tay.

Her expression must have still looked stunned, because he immediately joined her. "Hey, is everything okay?"

"I figured it out," she managed to say, her heart pounding wildly. Her hand shaking, she held the paper up. "It's here."

"What?"

"The X is right there, in this building." She pointed to where Lulu's little table and chair sat. "Sarafina hid her family secret under the floor of the *Dove Pond Register*."

CHAPTER 23

ROSE

"I can't believe you two," Rose said from where she sat at the counter, her gaze moving from Luke to Tay and then back.

The two of them stood where Lulu's chair and table used to sit, the wood floor now exposed. Lulu had protested mightily when Luke had told her they'd have to move her things and had been appeased only when Tay had promised to read a book to her a little later.

Rose shook her head. "Who on earth would hide a secret under the floor of a newspaper office? Reporters tell secrets. They don't keep them."

"Reporters keep plenty of secrets," Luke retorted. "They have to, in order to protect their sources."

"This isn't about sources," Rose said, trying not to sound old and testy and realizing she'd failed. "You really think the gold is hidden here?"

"Gold?" Lulu inched closer. "Are we looking for *treasure*?"

Luke and Tay both shook their heads. Tay said, "This is something else."

"Like what?" Rose asked impatiently.

"We won't know until we look."

Luke rubbed his hands together. "I'll fetch a crowbar."

He turned to go to the storage room, but Rose snapped, "Oh, no you don't! No one is getting a crowbar. I refuse to sacrifice one floorboard of this place just to find out some best-forgotten family secret."

"Grandma Rose!" Lulu hopped up and down in a circle. "Find the treasure! Find the treasure! Uncle Luke, find the treasure!"

Rose scowled. When Tay and Luke had rushed out to tell her about their belief that they knew where Sarafina's—heck, Rose didn't know what to call it—*stuff* was hidden, she'd been properly flummoxed. But that was just the beginning, as she quickly realized they were hell-bent on ripping up a portion of her beloved bookshop's antique floor.

She'd made them wait until their regular closing time, hoping their rampant enthusiasm would cool off.

It hadn't worked. So now, here they were. She was sitting in her usual place, feeling a little attacked, while Lulu happy-danced circles around Luke and Tay. Rose asked sourly, "Can't you get some sort of X-ray machine in here to see what's under that floor so you don't ruin these original floorboards?"

"That would take days to arrange," Luke said. "And I don't know who has that sort of equipment."

Neither did she. She crossed her arms over her chest. "I can't allow this."

Tay came to the counter. "Rose, *please.* I promise I'll pay for the repairs. And Luke will be super careful not to hurt the flooring any more than necessary. Won't you, Luke?"

He made a Boy Scout pledge sign. "I promise."

Lulu was still hopping in circles. Rose supposed she shouldn't have gotten her great-granddaughter that huge bear claw from Ava's new tearoom. *Sugar, thy name is hyper.*

"I just don't understand why you think it's here," Rose muttered for the umpteenth time in the past hour.

Luke cut her a frustrated gaze. "Look at the map. It's obviously this building. The windows and doors and walls match everything on the page."

Rose stared at the map yet again, turning it this way and that. "I suppose it does. But why would Sarafina hide her family secret here? This place has been a Day family business since the beginning."

Tay's smile slipped a bit, and Rose could see she'd given the younger woman something to think about. *Good. Someone needs to be thinking.*

Luke rubbed his chin. "That's a good question. All we know is that Sarafina and David Tau came back to town for just that one week. During that time, they did all the work it took to set these clues in place. Maybe this was the only building they could readily access? Sarafina would have been familiar with it, too. She once worked here, after all."

Tay nodded. "That makes sense."

"It does, doesn't it? I'll get the crowbar."

He was gone before Rose could open her mouth. *Darned fools, both of them.* She muttered under her breath, "I've never seen two people more excited to demolish something."

Luke returned with the crowbar and grinned at Tay. "Should we?"

"No," Rose repeated. "I don't like you all tearing things up!"

Tay said quickly, "Come on, Rose! We're so close to figuring this out!"

"That's a 'you' problem, not a 'me' problem."

Luke frowned, while Tay placed her fingertips to her temples and started rubbing.

After a moment, Tay dropped her hands to her sides. "How about this? What if I don't just fix this part of the floor, but I pay to fix *all* of it."

Rose eyed Tay suspiciously. "What do you mean, 'all of it'?"

"I'll pay to have the entire bookshop floor sanded and refinished."

Well, that put things in a new light. "Even the offices?"

"Grandma!" Luke protested, cutting her a disappointed look.

"What? She offered."

Tay grinned. "Those too."

"That's too much," Luke said.

Tay waved her hand. "I'm almost related to a contractor."

"Ah. Dylan. He'd probably give us the friends-and-family discount if we asked nicely."

"We?" Tay asked.

Luke smiled. "We're partners, remember?"

Rose cut them a curious glance, some of her outrage subdued by the little smile they were sharing. *Well, well, well. That's nice to see.* A tug on her sleeve made her look down.

Lulu stood at her side. "Grandma Rose, pretty please with sugar on top, let Uncle Luke look for treasure."

They were all ganging up on her. She grimaced. "No one is listening to me, are they? Fine. Do it, then. It's stupid, but if you want to, I won't stop y—"

"Great." Luke carried the crowbar to where Lulu's table used to be and tapped the floor at his feet. "Here, right?"

"Yay!" Lulu yelled.

Tay held up the map and did the calculations again. "Right there."

There was no X in the floor, which would have been far more exciting, Rose decided. She watched as Luke found a space between two boards and went to work.

It took him about ten minutes to pry the old, tight boards from their spots, but after just four floorboards had been removed, Luke paused. "I see something."

"What?" Lulu asked, rushing forward.

Tay caught the little girl by the waist and hoisted her up, out of danger.

Rose had to send Tay an approving nod. The woman did very well with Lulu. She did well with Luke, too. "Thank you."

Tay smiled, pulled out a nearby chair, and set Lulu on it. "Stay here until your uncle is done. You'll be able to see everything then."

"I'm going to stand," Lulu announced. She stood in the chair and leaned against the high, padded back, staring at the hole Luke had just made.

Rose grabbed her cane and went to perch on the arm of Lulu's chair so she could help keep the child in check. It was the perfect place from which to view Luke's handiwork. There, at the edge of the fourth board, was the rusty corner of an old tin box.

Luke hurried to pry up the next two boards and free the box. He bent and picked it up, swiping decades of dust off before handing it to Tay.

She pressed her hand flat on the rough cover, and Rose could see the excitement in Tay's eyes.

"If it's gold, it's not much," Rose said, fighting to keep the disappointment from her voice. Tay had said there wouldn't be any, but Rose hadn't been able to banish every bit of hope she'd been holding on to.

"Maybe there are diamonds in there!" Lulu's eyes couldn't have been any wider. "Or cake!"

Luke came to stand with Tay, peering over her shoulder as she set the box on the counter. Rose got up and came closer as Tay pried the cover off the old box. It took some work, but it finally popped open and revealed a small, leather-bound book.

Rose leaned in closer. "That's it? Just a book?" She gave a disgusted sigh. "All of that searching and all you got was that?"

Tay set the tin aside and ran her hand over the leather cover. She took a calming breath and opened it, her eyes widening.

"What is it?" Luke asked before Rose could say the words.

Tay looked up, tears in her eyes. "It's William Day's diary."

Oh my gosh. Rose couldn't tear her gaze from the book. "If it's William Day's, then it belongs to our family."

"Of course it does," Tay said. "But I need to look at it first."

"No. Not until I've read it." It was silly, and she knew it, but she'd worked hard for so many years to keep their family's dirty laundry from being aired.

"Why?" Luke asked. "Grandma Rose, let Tay see it for a few minutes and then it's yours."

"If that diary proves that William wasn't involved in the robbery, then I'll let all of you take a look. Heck, you can have it printed in the *Register* if you want. But if not—" Rose scowled. "I'm not saying what should happen then, but I won't want it printed anywhere."

"Where are the diamonds?" Lulu hopped off the chair before anyone could stop her. She went to the counter and, standing on her tiptoes, picked up the box. She turned it upside down and shook it. "It's empty."

"Lulu, don't—" Rose began, but Lulu had already dropped the box and was now on her hands and knees, peering into the hole Luke had made in the floor.

"What's that?" Lulu pointed.

Luke went to look. "What's what? I don't see— Oh." He bent

down and reached back under one of the boards. When he straightened back up, he held a large, empty-looking canvas bag.

"Whose is that?" Rose asked, eyeing the bag.

"I'm not sure," Luke said. "But judging by its proximity to the box, I'd say they were boarded up together."

Rose noticed how large the bag was. "Maybe that once held the gold."

Luke turned it here and there, examining it. "Perhaps." He untied the bag and looked inside. "There's something here."

Tay, the diary still in her hands, came to look. "What is it?"

He reached in and pulled out a dirty, faded, striped shirt, the numbers 4-5-1 sewn where a breast pocket should have been. "It's . . . a prison shirt."

Rose's heart sank.

Luke showed it to Tay. "Did prisoners really wear things like this?"

Tay nodded. "It made them easy to spot if they escaped." She reached out and touched the numbers. "This was Marcus McCleary's."

Rose pressed a hand to her heart and realized she'd been holding her breath. "How do you know?"

Tay said, "They were recorded in the prison records. William's number was 9-0-1. Is there anything else in that bag?"

"No." Luke returned the shirt to the bag and set it aside. "I guess the diary is the real treasure."

Rose held out her hand. "Let me have it."

Tay hugged the book. "Rose, please let me—"

"No! Hand it over!"

"Grandma," Luke said, frowning. "She can't let you have it. We all know that if you don't like what you read, you'll hide it."

Rose huffed. It stung to hear the rebuke in Luke's voice. "It might be wrong, but it's the way I do things. Besides, this has nothing to do with Sarafina. Why would William Day's diary be of interest to her and David Tau's daughter— *Oh!*" Rose blinked. "Is it possible that Lucy was William's illegitimate daughter?"

Tay shook her head. "Lucy was born years after William died in jail. But, Rose, that's exactly why the diary should be public. You keep wanting to hide the fact that William Day was involved with the robbery, but you can't erase him. He existed and who he was, and why, are important even if you don't like the things he did. The answer to everything is in this diary. We just have to be brave enough to face it."

Blast it, why did Tay have to go and say something like that? It wasn't fair. And yet . . . Rose's gaze dropped to the stack of floorboards Luke had pried out of place. Maybe . . . maybe it was time she faced all the truths in her life, those of her current family as well as those who'd gone before them.

A tug on her sweater made her look down. Lulu looked up at her. "Let Tay read that book. She really wants to. I can tell."

Oh Lord, who had given this child such beautiful, thickly lashed blue eyes? Rose couldn't say no to those.

She bent down and gave Lulu a hug before straightening back up. "Okay, Tay. Go ahead and read it. But just promise you'll go easy on William in that book you're writing, no matter what's in there."

"I promise I'll be fair." Tay sat down at the counter beside Rose and opened the diary.

Rose pointed at Luke. "You! While she's reading, put those boards back in. I'd better not be able to tell they were ripped up to begin with, either."

"Will do. Lulu, do you want to be my helper?" Lulu ran to Luke and he set to work.

Rose pulled a chair close by so she could see everyone, and sat.

At the counter, Tay opened the book and took a deep breath, but instead of reading it, she rested her fingers on the inky pages. Her face tightened and then changed, and for an eerie second, Rose had the impression she wasn't looking at Tay at all, but at someone else. . . .

CHAPTER 24

SARAFINA

MAY 19, 1897
THE NIGHT OF THE TRAIN ROBBERY

It's dark here, and dreary, but Marcus keeps telling me to hang on to the light, to cling to the hope that things will get better. I don't see how they could, but at times he seems almost giddy with certainty, so sure our situation will improve, that even I am starting to think that maybe, just maybe, things might turn around and I'll find myself back with you. When that happens, heart of my heart, no matter the cost, I will never again let you go. . . .

—letter from William Day to Sarafina Dove

Sarafina awoke with a start, clutching her blankets to her chest. She blinked in the darkness, wondering if she'd dreamed the rattling noise that had yanked her from her sleep. Everything was silent except for the faint hoot of an owl.

The bright moonlight spilled through the window and cast shadows onto the floor from the tree outside.

I must have dreamed it. She rubbed her eyes sleepily and was just getting ready to settle back down when the rattle of a pebble against her window made her turn in that direction. *Goodness! What was that?*

She stared at the window, her heart pounding. *Could that be William?* She couldn't think of anyone else it might be, but he'd never done such a thing before. Had something happened?

She threw back the covers, tiptoed to the window, and peered down into the backyard. A familiar figure stood just below, dressed in a coat she'd never seen, a hat pulled low over his brow. He was half-hidden in the shadow of the tree and she was surprised she recognized him at all.

She slid her window open and leaned out. "William?" she whispered.

He stepped forward, the moonlight falling across his face, marking his tight mouth and creased brow.

She'd never seen him look so serious. "What's—"

"Please come down," he whispered back, his tone ragged. "I have to speak with you."

She glanced over her shoulder. Her aunts had rooms at the front of the house, so she didn't think they could hear her. Still . . . She nodded to let him know she'd be right there.

She softly closed her window and quickly got dressed. Minutes later, she hurried through the house and stepped into the backyard, where he waited. The scent of damp grass met her as the moonlight showed his strained expression and bright, worried eyes, his dark hair sticking to his damp forehead.

"What happened?"

"Marcus—" William's voice broke. He swiped his eyes with a hand that shook.

Oh no. Her own heart racing, she took a step forward, her hand out.

But he backed away, shaking his head. "I just have a few minutes, but I had to see you. You're going to hear things soon that aren't true. I wanted to tell you what happened before they—" He caught himself and paused. When he spoke again, his voice was steadier, but lost somehow. "Marcus and Johnson robbed a train."

"*What?*"

"It went badly, as you'd expect. Johnson is a fool. I warned Marcus about that man months ago, but—" William took off his hat and shoved it into his pocket before he raked a shaky hand through his hair. "The train was carrying a gold shipment. The company must have gotten wind of the robbery, because there were Pinkerton agents on board and there was a gunfight and Marcus got shot and—" William's voice broke, and he pressed his hands over his eyes. "It doesn't matter. It's bad, though. So bad."

"Is Marcus—" She couldn't say the word.

William dropped his hands, but she could see that his eyes were wet. "Not yet." His mouth thinned. "Johnson ran away and left Marcus to take the fall. He was trapped there, hidden behind a rock, and the agents were closing in, so I . . ." He rubbed his throat as if the words had caught there.

She grabbed his arm. "Tell me."

"I helped him." William tried to pull free, but she hung on. He wet his dry lips. "I rode in and got him."

"You did what?"

"I had to save him, but I think it might have looked . . ." William turned and took two paces, every step jerky and uneven, and then came back. "After I got him home, I realized that it might have looked as if I was involved."

"With the robbery?"

He gave a miserable nod. "I just went there to stop him, and I heard the gunfire when I got close, and I—I didn't even think. When I reached him, there was so much blood, I thought—" William swallowed noisily. "My only thought was to get him out of there."

"How did you know he'd be there?"

William leaned against the trunk of the oak tree as if too weak to stand. "He'd been acting strange all day, and then he up and disappeared without a word. I knew something wasn't right. He stays with me sometimes, and when I went to put another log on the fire, I found the train schedule there, partially burned. I knew as soon as I saw it what they were going to do."

"That fool!"

"I should have figured it out sooner; then I could have stopped him." William pushed himself away from the tree and began pacing, talking faster and faster. "I arrived just in time to save him, but nothing more. We're finished, Sarafina. People are out looking for the robbers and they're saying— Oh God, how did this happen?"

She tried to wrap her mind around what he was telling her. "How badly was Marcus hurt?"

"He was shot in the leg. He's lost a lot of blood, but I think he'll be all right if he stays still. I bandaged it as best I could, and Uncle Edward—" William clamped his mouth closed and winced. "I shouldn't have said that."

"Your uncle knows?" A wave of relief washed over her. "He'll know what to do."

"He shouldn't get involved," William said harshly, still pacing back and forth. "He stopped by the house to bring me some dinner and saw me carrying Marcus inside. I told my uncle to leave, but he refused. I didn't want him to get involved, but Marcus had lost so much blood. I—" His voice broke once more.

She wanted to hug him, but he was pacing far too quickly for her to do more than watch.

"Marcus, the fool, has a bag full of gold but not enough blood. I think he'd trade all of that gold for his health now, if he could." William stopped in front of her. "But that's not all."

"Not all?" What more could there be?

"I have to get back before—" He caught himself and reached for her hands, holding them in his own cold ones. "It's worse than you think. Johnson was arrested a few hours ago. He was drunk and had bragged to anyone who would listen about how he'd robbed the train."

"He admitted that? In public?"

William nodded, anger in his eyes. "When Johnson left the bar, the sheriff was waiting outside. He was arrested. I don't know if he was hoping he'd be let off the hook or—I don't know, but Uncle Edward heard that Johnson is trying to strike a deal."

Her heart, which had been beating sickly, sank even more. "What did he tell them?"

"Lies. So many lies. I—" William released her hands and whirled away, only to turn back to face her. "Uncle Edward says Marcus needs to get a lawyer fast and confess everything. He wasn't the one who planned it or—or took a gun, or anything like that. That was all Johnson, but—"

She waited, but William just stood there, his mouth pressed into a thin line as he glared into the dark. "But?" she asked impatiently.

William's gaze returned to her. "Uncle Edward spoke to someone who was there when Johnson was arrested, and he was yelling as they dragged him away. He said he hadn't planned the robbery."

"He blamed Marcus."

"No." William took a deep breath. "Johnson said it was me. He said I was the one who'd planned the whole thing."

Her lips mouthed the word *What?* but no sound came, her voice silenced by her shock.

He nodded grimly. "Johnson's always hated me. He knows I've been warning Marcus about him. We got into a fight once, too. I don't think Johnson ever got over that. The sheriff is out looking for me and Marcus right now. Sarafina, they're going to arrest us."

A faint sense of nausea rose through her, and she realized she'd fisted both of her hands at her sides. She forced them open, giving them a gentle shake so the blood would flow back into her fingers. "William, what are you going to do?"

"Uncle Edward wants me to run, but I won't. If I do, everyone will think I'm guilty. Besides, Marcus can't move right now and I can't just leave him to face this alone. I'll tell them the truth and if that doesn't work, then I'll have no choice. I'll have to go to trial. So long as the judge is fair, I'll be acquitted."

She didn't know if she believed that. She'd covered only two trials for the newspaper so far, and she hadn't been impressed with the outcome of either. It seemed to her untrained eyes that popular opinion held an unfair sway over the results, and she was very afraid of how that would affect William's chances.

"As soon as it's light, I'll go downtown and talk to the sheriff. Uncle Edward says he'll support me as best he can, but he's done too much already."

Sarafina didn't know what to say. William's distress was obvious, and her own heart was thudding in an uneven, fearful manner. "Are you sure that's the best thing to do?"

His jaw hardened. "What choice do I have?"

Run. Don't go to the sheriff. She wanted to yell the words, but they stuck in her throat.

William must have seen her distress, because he caught her hands in his once again. "Don't look like that. I didn't do anything. I really didn't."

She squeezed his hands. "I know."

The look of relief on William's face surprised her. He managed to smile. "Don't worry. Marcus will testify for me. They won't be able to keep me after that, if it even goes that far."

Her heart ached for him. The people in their small town believed the worst of William already, even without evidence. How would a jury, which would be subjected to that very talk, be any different?

She suddenly realized that William didn't believe it would be. *He's not warning me. He's come to tell me goodbye.*

Her heart burned as if it were being ripped in two. "No," she said desperately. "Don't do this! Listen to your uncle. You don't know what might happen, and—"

He pulled her into his arms, his chin warm against her forehead. "Just trust me. Everything will be all right."

No, it wouldn't. She leaned against him, tears running down her cheeks. *How could this happen?*

William's warm breath fanned against her temple. "Don't let anyone know I came here tonight. For the next few weeks, act as if you don't even know me. You have to stay out of it. Let Marcus and me deal with the events of this night."

"But—"

He placed his hands on her arms and pushed her back just enough that he could look into her eyes. "Whatever happens, promise you'll wait for me. I will see you again. And when I do, we'll have the life we deserve. We'll go to a big city and start anew, and we'll be happier there. I promise."

"William, I—"

He kissed her once, firmly yet gently, and then stepped away, his hands dropping to his sides. "I have to go. Uncle Edward is with Marcus and I can't let them be found together. Wait for me, Sarafina. I'll find a way out of this." With that, he left, the moonlight following him as he disappeared into the thick woods beside her house.

She stood where she was for the longest time, the night wind tugging her coat and making her shiver as the tears slid down her face. But the cold wind that teased her coat hem was nothing compared to the fear that froze her heart.

CHAPTER 25

TAY

Tay blinked once, twice, three times. She was back in Rose's Bookstore, staring down at William Day's diary. She turned the page, but there were no more lines of his neat writing.

William's story had come to an end.

Exhausted and still haunted by the emotions she'd experienced, she closed the book.

Rose, who was handing Lulu some crayons, got up from her seat and came back to the counter. "What did you see? We've been waiting forever."

Luke looked up from where he'd just finished wedging the wood slats back into place to cover the hole in the floor and sent his grandmother a sharp look. "It's been five minutes."

"It felt like more," Rose said sullenly.

"It felt longer to me, too." Tay handed the diary to Rose. "William really did write this. He tells what happened the night of the robbery."

"And?"

"He wasn't involved in it."

Rose's startled gaze flew to Tay. "It says that? Really?"

Lulu, busy coloring, started singing a song Tay had never heard, although it had the word "really" in it about every fourth word.

Tay returned her attention to Rose. "Johnson had a grudge against William and pinned the whole thing on him. William knew the night of the robbery that he was going to be arrested and he could have run, but he decided to stay with McCleary, who was shot. He trusted the judicial process would prove his innocence."

Luke winced. "He must have been disappointed when he was convicted."

Tay had to agree. "He was shocked. The truth of what happened that night is exactly as William and McCleary testified. William didn't even arrive on the scene of the robbery until it was over. Johnson was the only one with a gun, but he fled and left McCleary wounded. William rode in and got his friend out, which, unfortunately, meant he was seen at the crime scene."

"He was innocent." Rose hugged the book and gave a triumphant smile. "Ha! Take that, history! You were wrong again!"

Tay had never seen such a blissful smile on the old woman's face. "Aren't you glad we found out the truth?"

Rose's smile widened. "Heck yes. All this time, I thought he was a scoundrel and worse."

"He wasn't just innocent. He was a hero, Rose. He risked his life to help a friend."

"I love this." As she spoke, Rose flipped through the diary. She stopped at the last page Tay had read and ran her gnarled fingers over the flowing words that covered the yellowed pages. "I'll make you a copy of this for your book on Sarafina. You'll have a lot to say about William now, won't you?"

"A whole lot." She would write about what a good person he was, and what a true friend he'd been to Marcus, even though the cost was high. And then she'd tell how he'd fallen in love with an intrepid soon-to-be-famous reporter.

A loud noise made Tay look over just in time to see Luke move a chair across the loose floor slats.

"I can't fix this," he announced. "I don't have the right nails nor the type of hammer to—" He caught his grandmother's expression and threw his hands up. "Don't worry. I already texted Dylan, and he said he'd stop by tomorrow with some tools and fix it right up."

"Tomorrow?" Tay raised her eyebrows. "That's fast."

"Yeah, well, I gave him my pitching arm in exchange, so it's not going to be cheap."

Pitching arm? Before she could ask, Rose exclaimed, "Well, I'll be!"

Tay looked back at the older woman and saw that Rose was still looking at the diary.

"Tay, look at this! There were two pages stuck together. Someone wrote something here. I don't think it was William, though, because the handwriting is different." She made a face. "*If* you can call that handwriting."

How did I miss that? Tay came to see. "What's it say?"

"I don't know. I can only read about every fifth word if that." Rose held the book at arm's length and squinted at it. After a moment, she lowered the diary. "Nope. Can't read it."

Luke came to stand beside his grandmother. "Bad handwriting. Sounds like Sarafina Dove to me."

Rose scowled. "Why would she have written in William Day's diary?"

Why indeed. "Rose, may I see that? I'll give it right back, I promise."

"Sure." Rose put the open diary on the counter and turned it so that the writing faced Tay. "Take a look and see if you can read that mess. I thought *my* handwriting was bad, but sheesh."

Tay slid the book closer, careful not to touch the spidery, blotted words.

Luke peered over her shoulder. "Yeah, it's just a few lines, but I can't read any of it." He shook his head. "No wonder the woman typed most of her letters."

Lulu's bright blue eyes suddenly appeared over the counter, her fingers curling around the edges as she stood on her tiptoes. "Can I see?"

Tay smiled fondly at the little girl. "Why not? This is a family project, after all."

"Would you like to sit up here?" At Lulu's nod, Luke scooped her up and perched her on the counter beside the diary.

Lulu bent to one side to look at it. "What letter is that?" She pointed to the page.

"That's not a letter," Luke said. "It's an inkblot."

"Oh." Lulu pointed to another place on the page. "What's this letter?"

Tay had to stifle a laugh. The squiggle looked more like a tornado than a letter. "I think it's supposed to be an 's,' but I'm not sure."

Luke pushed the diary to Tay. "There's more than one way to skin a cat."

That was one way to put it.

"Go ahead," Rose said impatiently. "See what she said."

Tay pulled the book to her, took a deep breath, and then rested her fingers on the first line.

Blackness fell, and then she was seeing what Sarafina saw. She was here, in this very room, although it looked vastly different. Two large printing presses filled the center of the room, racks of block letters and printing plates lining an entire wall. The smell of fresh paper and ink filled the air.

Sarafina was sitting in a chair, her pen flying over the page. In front of her, pulling up floorboards, was the man Sarafina had seen reflected in the fountain, David Tau.

Sarafina's pen scratched the smooth paper of the diary, and now, because Tay could see through Sarafina's eyes and could hear what she thought, despite the horrible handwriting, Tay could read every word. *Lucy*, the note began, *we struggled for years whether to tell you the truth. We finally decided that the decision had to be yours. This book was written by your father. This is who he was and, to me, always will be. . . .*

The words continued, sinking through her, shocking Tay even as she also felt the uncertainty with which Sarafina wrote. As the final word slid out of sight, Tay found herself back at the counter, Luke at her side.

Rose leaned forward. "Well?"

"I—I just . . ." She struggled to wrap her mind around what she'd just seen. Finally, she took a shuddering breath and said, "David Tau and William Day were the same person."

Silence met her.

Rose sank back onto her stool, looking shocked.

Luke pressed a hand to his forehead. "They—how did—" He shook his head.

"I know," Tay said. "I didn't see that coming. But maybe I should have. I saw David Tau's reflection. He had the right hair color, but I just didn't think about it."

"I can't believe this," Rose said. "I thought William died in prison."

"So did everyone else. Marcus McCleary was ill when he went to jail. He had tuberculosis. According to what Sarafina wrote, everyone knew it and he was expected to die soon, as the conditions weren't good. He used that to fake his own death, and then he traded places with William. It was a rather elaborate scheme. McCleary handled everything inside the prison while William's uncle made all the other arrangements."

"My grandfather helped?" Rose couldn't have looked more surprised.

Tay nodded. "William wasn't told about any of it. They knew he would balk at leaving his friend. When the time came, McCleary slipped some sleeping powder into William's evening meal and exchanged clothes with him. William's uncle bribed the prison doctor to say William was McCleary and to declare him dead."

Luke frowned. "Wouldn't the guards have noticed?"

"I'm sure they did, but by then their pockets were filled with gold."

"Ah. The gold. That'll blind a man."

"Won't it, though. When William woke up, he was on his way to New York with his uncle. Sarafina was waiting for them when they got there."

Rose took a deep breath. "I guess that's how McCleary repaid William after getting him in such trouble."

Tay nodded. "McCleary knew no one would suggest doing an autopsy on a body riddled with tuberculosis, too. He couldn't save himself, but he could save William. And he did."

Rose couldn't have looked happier. "So William Day was never a thief, *and* he didn't die in jail."

"This is incredible," Luke said. "This is why Sarafina never returned to Dove Pond except for that one week. She couldn't bring David with her, as the people here would have recognized him."

"It was far easier to live under a fake name back in those days. They didn't have many photographs, and the ones they did have weren't searchable or— Oh!" Tay gave an excited hop. "I just realized this. *Tau* means 'new' in Gaelic."

Rose sent her a flat look. "You know Gaelic?"

"A little. I wrote my thesis in college on William Wallace."

"Nice topic," Luke said, a silly grin on his face. "I still can't believe that David Tau was William Day."

"And married the woman he loved." Tay returned his smile. "William put McCleary's gold to good use and started a new life with her."

Rose looked a little disappointed. "So there's no gold."

"No. William took it to New York and invested it. According to Sarafina's entry, he sent the original amount back to the insurance company that had paid it out. So, in a way, the gold wasn't stolen so much as borrowed."

"Is there evidence of that?" Luke asked.

"Probably not. The company went broke later on, so—" She shrugged.

Luke shook his head, his blue eyes sparkling. "Now that's a family secret."

"Wait a minute." Rose crossed her arms over her chest. "William and Sarafina returned to Dove Pond when they put these clues in place. Didn't people recognize him then?"

"I think they did. It's significant that the only town meeting minutes that are missing are from that one day. I wish I could have been there for that."

Luke blinked. "You think those minutes are missing on purpose."

"I doubt they were even written. Remember, David Tau and Sarafina came bearing gifts."

"The Fountain Fund. It was an investment in this town."

She nodded. "There he was, with Sarafina, who was the town's hero, and he was handing out money. Plus, he had the support not only of his uncle, who was still running the newspaper, but by then Sarafina's aunts had accepted him. They visited Sarafina and David in New York so often, they had their own rooms at their house."

"No wonder the town welcomed him back. Who would turn their

backs on cash money *and* incur the wrath of both the Day and the Dove families?"

Rose snorted. "Only a fool would do something like that."

Tay patted the diary. "By the way, according to Sarafina's note, the fund wasn't supposed to be used solely for the fountain's upkeep. According to her, the money was supposed to be invested, and the returns used however the town council saw fit."

Luke picked up the diary and turned it over in his hands. "Our ancestors were pretty cool, weren't they?"

"They were. For the rest of their lives, he and Sarafina donated the returns of their investments back into their communities, both in New York and in Dove Pond."

"That's . . . that's . . ." Rose couldn't seem to get past that word. Her face creased with emotion, a mixture of relief and disbelief. "William wasn't what people thought he was."

Lulu, a sticker tangled in her hair and another on her cheek, tugged on Luke's shirt. She looked from her grandmother to Luke and then back. "Are we happy?"

Luke laughed and scooped up his niece in a hug. "We are."

Tay couldn't have been happier, either. What a terrific ending to their little adventure. *Oh, the books I'll be able to write about this.*

Rose ran her wrinkled hand over the diary, a look of wonder on her face. "Thank you, Tay. I guess I was afraid of the truth without even knowing what it was."

Tay smiled. She supposed that at some point in their lives, everyone did that exact thing—feared a truth they didn't know or understand, only to discover it wasn't as horrible as they'd expected.

Luke set Lulu back down and leaned against the counter on crossed arms. "I'm just awed by William's story. I can see why he and Sarafina wanted to give Lucy some time to decide if she even wanted to know the truth. No matter what, 'David' was the father she'd always known and loved."

"I think Lucy suspected the truth. At least she knew enough to decide she didn't need to know more." Tay smiled at Luke. "We should take copies of this to Grace."

He nodded. "Immediately."

"Why?" Rose asked.

"Grace wants to use the Fountain Fund to finance some annual small business grants to help the town out, but her constituents wouldn't allow her to access the money, saying it would be going against the wishes of the fund's originator. With this diary and the note from Sarafina, Grace can convince them to allow the money to be used for other purposes."

"Small business grants, eh? I'd like that." Rose patted the diary once more time. "Well, well, well. I suppose it's true that for every wish, there's an answer."

Tay wondered what Rose meant by that.

Rose pointed at her. "Tay Dove, I'm glad you came back to town."

Tay had to return the grin. "I'm glad I came, too."

"Things are going better since you arrived. Why, just having your office here has already increased our foot traffic."

"Really?"

Luke flashed her a smile. "We broke a record last month, and Grandma Rose thinks it's because people came to peek at you while you were working on the clues."

That was nice to hear. "I hope it lasts now that we've found the family secret."

Luke eyed the hole he'd made in the floor. "We'll break more sales records once people realize we found this family treasure under the floorboards here. Everyone will want to see the spot. While they're here, Grandma Rose and I will guilt them into making a purchase."

Rose snorted. "I like that."

Tay had to agree. "Maybe you should have Dylan replace those boards in the shape of an X."

Rose perked up. "That's a thought! Or we could have a table made in the shape of an X and circle chairs around it so people can curl up and read there."

Luke couldn't have looked more pleased. "I like the ambience of that."

Lulu plopped her fists on her hips. "I want a beanbag chair. I'll need something to sit on if you take my table and chair."

"We aren't taking your table and chair. We're just going to move them. But if you want a beanbag chair, I'll get you one." Luke bent down and took Lulu's hand. "But for now, you need to do your homework."

"Not now," Lulu protested. "We're still finding treasure."

"I think we've found all there is to find," Luke said. He led her to where he'd put her table and chair next to the window. "Do your homework while I tape down these loose boards until Dylan gets here to fix them."

Tay smiled. She liked that Sarafina and William had returned to Dove Pond and had brought both hope and happiness with them. As she watched Luke bend down to Lulu's level to help her pull her homework out of her book bag, an odd wave of yearning hit Tay squarely in the heart.

What was that? She had her research, her job, and her family. What more did she need?

But then again, she'd just finished her research, so most of what was left was writing. And she wasn't looking forward to returning to her job in Boston. In fact, looking for a job near here, as Rose had suggested, was a tempting thought.

She watched Luke as he settled Lulu in the children's reading section to do her homework, Rose beaming at them from behind the counter, the diary still resting under her hand.

Tay found herself smiling, too. This place, this moment, it all felt so familiar. So comfortable. So *precious.* Maybe . . . just maybe, coming home had also allowed her to find a treasure of her own.

EPILOGUE

TAY

Three months later, sitting in a lawn chair in the backyard of the Dove house, Aunt Jo used the rubber tip of her cane to poke Tay's foot. "I heard you might get that book of yours published."

"I might." She'd had some offers. Two now, to be exact, both from small university presses. But the agent she'd obtained just a month ago seemed certain they'd get some interest from a major publisher, too. She smiled and rested her head on top of Lulu's silken curls. Up until ten minutes ago, the little girl had been running in circles, chasing bubbles from the bubble machine Luke had plugged in on the back porch. But she'd finally tuckered herself out, and had come to settle in Tay's lap and was fast asleep.

"Good for you," Aunt Jo declared. "I'd tell you I'd buy a copy once it's printed, but I think I might wait for the movie." As she spoke, she used the cane to gently rub Moon Pie's back as he lay sleeping at her feet. "He sleeps a lot nowadays. Just like me."

"I don't blame him. It's nice today." It was a beautiful, sunny summer day. Just the kind she liked. The trees overhead rustled happily, while the babble of Sweet Creek complemented the hum of voices coming from the guests who were even now wandering around the assorted lawn chairs, waiting to eat some of Ella's barbecue. Here and there were small groups of chairs like the little circle Tay and Aunt Jo were sitting in. A pair of drink coolers sat near the back patio, while a bubble machine, badminton net, and small inflatable swimming pool had been set out for the children. People were wandering around, laughing and talking. *Trust Ella to know how to throw a party.*

There were so many people here whom Tay knew and loved. Ava, wearing a bright yellow pair of cutoff overalls, her blond hair in a braid over one shoulder, was sitting by the purple hydrangea bush and explaining to Kat the best ways to encourage the plant to flower. Nearby, Sarah sat by the firepit, her feet stretched out in front of her, her head buried in her ever-present book, while Ava's boyfriend, Dylan, reclined in the chair across from her, trying to figure out the game his daughter, Kristen, had just installed on his phone. Meanwhile, Ella and Gray were manning the grill area, wearing matching aprons.

"There you are, Tay!" Grace grinned as she sat down. She wore a red T-shirt that read DOVE POND SPRING FLING, which was neatly tucked into her jeans. "I was looking for you."

"Hi," Tay said with a smile. "I thought I saw you arrive."

Settling into a lawn chair, Grace balanced her plate of potato chips on her knee as she took a sip of her iced tea. "Sorry we were late getting here. I got a call from Zoe just as we were leaving. A city commissioner from Asheville has been asking for the criteria we used for the Dove Pond Small Business Grant we set up in May. They want to do something similar."

Aunt Jo snorted. "They wish they were as good of a town as Dove Pond."

"We are pretty awesome," Grace admitted. "Tay, thank goodness you found that note from Sarafina about the Fountain Fund. Because of that, I was able to get the necessary vote to use it for grants."

"There was a lot of money in that fund." Millions, in fact. Tay supposed that made sense, as the town had been allowed to spend only a thousand dollars of it each year.

Grace nodded. "I'm glad Rose was the first recipient. It seems fitting."

Tay didn't think she'd ever seen Rose so excited—except, perhaps, on the day she'd discovered that William Day hadn't been a low-life train robber, after all. "It was a generous grant."

Aunt Jo nodded her approval. "You all weren't stingy. Thirty thousand dollars is nothing to sneeze at."

Rose had needed that money. About a week after they'd found William's diary, Rose and Luke had a huge fight. Apparently Rose had taken out a loan with a shady company to make repairs on the bookstore and couldn't make the necessary payments. Worse still, she wouldn't let Luke help, which had apparently hurt his feelings.

The argument had ended abruptly when Luke opened his banking app on his phone and showed his grandmother the amount of money he had in his accounts. Whatever the amount was, it had a profound effect on Rose. She'd stopped shouting and had let her grandson write her a check right there on the spot. After that, their relationship had changed in a subtle but significant way. Rose no longer seemed worried about Luke. In fact, she'd started asking his opinion about her business much more frequently, and Tay could tell that he loved that.

"Mom!"

Grace turned to where her niece Daisy was throwing a softball with her husband, Trav. She smiled when Trav threw the ball super high and made Daisy run to catch it.

Tay tightened her arms around Lulu, wondering what she'd look like when she was that age. "Daisy's getting tall."

"And pretty, although she doesn't know it yet." Grace's smile held a hint of pride. "Right now, we're navigating our way through teenage snark years, which came hard on the heels of the pre-preteen snark years."

"Fun!" Aunt Jo claimed. "Grace, are you going to eat all of those chips? They can't be good for you."

Grace put the plate of chips on the small table at Aunt Jo's elbow. "Help yourself."

"That's my girl!" Aunt Jo beamed and took a handful of chips from the plate. "You came just in time. I was getting ready to ask Tay what she was going to do once she's finished her book."

Grace took a drink of her tea, her gaze returning to where Tay held the sleeping Lulu. "I don't think Lulu will let her leave."

Aunt Jo ate a potato chip. "Or her uncle."

Tay's face heated and her gaze found Luke, where he stood near the swing with Sarah's boyfriend, Blake. They were having some sort of earnest conversation, both of them animated and waving their hands as they made their points. A breeze ruffled Luke's dark hair, and she could tell from the way he spoke that he was enjoying the debate. Over the past few months, her relationship with Luke had slowly shifted from friends to Something More, and she was enjoying it immensely. It was the first time she'd ever dated someone who made life seem so . . . easy. *Easy but interesting.*

It was funny, but she rarely thought about Richard at all now. In fact, the few times she did, she thought of him only as a lesson. That mistake had taught her that her pride was too important to ignore. She would never accept such a sorry excuse for a relationship again. Not that she had to worry about that with Luke. He was an all-or-nothing sort of guy, and she'd found that she liked that.

Grace reached over and patted Aunt Jo's potato chip–free hand. "I can tell you're worried about poor Tay."

Tay blinked. "Me? Why?"

"Oh, I am," Aunt Jo told Grace. "I'm afraid she might pack up and leave. She needs this town, but she doesn't know it."

"Don't worry," Grace said. "She's putting down roots here in Dove Pond. I've seen the signs."

"Do tell!" Aunt Jo declared. "What signs?"

Grace gave Tay a considering look. "One is sleeping in her lap right now."

Tay snuggled Lulu a little farther into her arms, noticing that the little girl's hair smelled like vanilla cake and soap, her breath warm as it brushed her shoulder.

Grace continued, "And she bought the Jeep she borrowed from Trav. Everyone knows that Jeeps are for country living, not city living."

"That's the truth," Aunt Jo declared. "There are some nice drives around here."

Grace nodded. "And then there's the fact that although she solved the mystery about Sarafina's early life, she's still here. I've heard her say she's not scheduled to teach until the fall, but here she sits, looking happy and relaxed."

"She's not as pale as she was."

"I think she's sleeping better," Grace said. "The biggest sign that she might be staying is that she didn't leave when she could have. She's still here."

Aunt Jo's warm brown gaze rested on Tay. "So? Are you staying?"

That was the question she'd been asking herself since she arrived, and it was only a few weeks ago that she'd found her answer.

Lulu stirred a moment, but then snuggled against Tay and went back to sleep. "I've been thinking about it," she admitted. "I might have applied for a teaching position at Appy State."

Aunt Jo smacked her knee. "Yes!"

Grace grinned. "Need a reference? I know people."

"I'll let you know if I need another."

Aunt Jo beamed. "I'm glad you came home, Tay. We need you here."

Grace couldn't have looked happier. "So Dove Pond now has its own researcher. I'm already thinking of several projects I may need your help with."

Tay smiled and shifted in her chair so that Lulu's head was a bit more securely settled on her shoulder. Life was funny. She'd arrived back in town feeling wounded and alone, and had instead found joy and love in places she'd never thought to look. Maybe that was the magic of coming home. It wasn't just about healing; it was about growing, about finding one's self and realizing one's own potential.

And here, at home, with the help of her family and friends, old and new, she'd accomplished all that and more.

THE BOOKSHOP OF HIDDEN DREAMS

BY KAREN HAWKINS

A BOOK CLUB GUIDE

1. Tay Dove always goes to a bookstore whenever life gets difficult. Her favorite one is Rose's Bookstore, which is in her hometown of Dove Pond. Is there a place you like to go to when you're stressed-out or feeling hurt? What sort of an atmosphere cheers you up on difficult days?

2. In the beginning of *The Bookshop of Hidden Dreams*, Tay's reeling from a failed relationship. As the book continues, it becomes apparent that it's not the betrayal that hurt her so much as it was her loss of trust in her own judgment. Have you ever been betrayed by someone? Did you experience a similar loss of trust in yourself? If so, how did you overcome it?

3. Sarafina Dove grew up in the restrictive Victorian era but found herself longing for a life of adventure. She finds the life she craves when she leaves Dove Pond and gets a job as a reporter in New York City in the 1890s. Historically, there were several famous female reporters in the 1800s—Margaret Fuller, Nellie Bly, Winifred Bonfils, and Jennie June, to name a few. At the time, being a reporter was a daring, bold career for a woman to follow. Was there ever a career you wanted to pursue because you thought it would be exciting? Did you indeed pursue it? Why or why not?

4. Tay's life as a researcher has led her to being alone for long stretches of time, something she's gotten more and more comfortable with. Maybe even too comfortable with. Have you ever had a job or experienced a life circumstance that left you spending hours and even days alone? Did you enjoy that time? How did it affect you?

5. It seems to Luke Day's grandmother, Rose, that Luke, due to his intelligence and laid-back approach to life, has always had it easy, a fact that's consistently worried her. She thinks that, because he's had so little practice dealing with life's failures, he'll find it very difficult to face bad times. Do you think that people who've found life easy find it more difficult to face bad times than those who've had practice? Do you think a person can get good—or at least better—at dealing with sorrows and stress with experience? Or do you think it depends on a person's personality and how he or she approaches those difficulties?